Praise for LOVERS MEETING

'It's tough, it's gutsy, brimming with emotion and a cracking yarn – all that a good North East saga should be'

Sunderland Echo

Praise for CHRISSIE'S CHILDREN

'Catherine Cookson-readalike . . . a delight'
Colchester Evening Gazette

'This novel has the clear ring of authenticity . . . the depth of the setting gives it its richness'
Northern Echo

Praise for MARY'S CHILD

'Cookson fans will lap up this enthralling turn-of-the-century saga'

Hartlepool Mail

'Colourful . . . authentic . . . in the bestselling tradition of Catherine Cookson'
Middlesbrough Evening Gazette

About the author

IRENE CARR was born and brought up on the river in Monkwearmouth, Sunderland, in the 1930s. Her father and brother worked in shipyards in County Durham and her mother was a Sunderland barmaid. Her previous novels, *Mary's Child*, and its stand-alone sequel, *Chrissie's Children*, are both available as Coronet paperbacks.

Lovers Meeting

Irene Carr

CORONET BOOKS
Hodder and Stoughton

First published in Great Britain in 1998 by
Hodder and Stoughton
a division of Hodder Headline PLC

Coronet edition 1998

British Library Cataloguing in Publication Data
Carr, Irene
Lovers Meeting
I. Title
823.914 [F]

ISBN 0 340 68950 1

Printed and bound in Great Britain by
Clays Ltd, St Ives plc

Hodder and Stoughton
A division of Hodder Headline PLC
338 Euston Road
London NW1 3BH

1

Monkwearmouth in Sunderland, January 1888

Josie's memory of the giant came back to haunt her all through her childhood and on into her adult years. On that awful night when he came raging through the big old house down by the river, four-year-old Josie trembled in the huge kitchen with its broad black stove and its smell of baking bread. Her mother, Peggy Langley, blonde, gentle and pretty in her long, dark blue dress with its high collar, had insisted they enter by the kitchen door. Josie's father, David, dark and handsome in his best suit with its high lapels and narrow trousers, had bristled. 'What! Go into the house I grew up in by the back door?' But he had given in to his wife's fears that old William Langley would slam the front door in her face.

Peggy had pleaded, 'I just want you to make your peace with him before we go.'

Josie did not understand any of that. Her father had gone on into the house to seek his own father, William. Josie, her thin face framed by the bonnet that let a few strands of shining, coppery hair escape, watched him go out of wide grey eyes. She waited in the kitchen with her mother and she heard the bellowing, at first distant but rapidly approaching.

That first memory was burned into her brain by the threatened violence and her terror. The snow that had turned to hail drummed on the windows as the wind drove it. Darkness had come early on this winter day, so the windows were black glass that reflected the picture of her small face. The kitchen was lit yellow by the hissing gas lamp. A door in one corner stood open and showed the head of a flight of stairs leading down into a dark cavern of a cellar. Josie saw it as just a black hole that could hide monsters. But the monster came in through the other door that led into the house.

Her father came first, tight-lipped with anger. Behind him came the giant. Josie stood at her mother's knee and clutched Peggy's skirts, her eyes big with fright as she peered up at the black-bearded figure filling the doorway. He went on bellowing, 'Make it up? Be damned to that! Because you're going to America? You can go where the hell you like – but you won't stay in this house.' He glared at Peggy. 'I thought you would be behind this.'

David Langley, a slighter, shorter, clean-shaven copy of his father, stepped in front of William. Josie could see his fists clenched at his sides. He said, 'Father, I just wanted to—'

William did not let him finish: 'I thought you'd be wanting something, but don't call me Father! You lost the right to do that, along with a lot more, when you defied me five years ago. You married that woman and I turned you out. Or have you got her with a bairn again? Is that the reason you've come crawling back?'

'I'm not crawling! I want nothing from you!' Now David was shouting. Josie pressed one small fist against her mouth, her lips quivering. David went on, 'Aye! It was Peggy's idea to come here. She said, "Don't go across the sea without making it up with your father. And he'll want to see Josie."'

The giant's glare shifted to rest briefly on the small girl and she stepped back behind her mother to hide from those black eyes that bored into her. But then the glare shifted again, back to rest on her father, and William growled, 'You'll not get around me by using the bairn. I told you five years ago, that woman got you into her bed and with that child to wangle your ring on to her finger and her hands on to your money.'

'*That's enough!*' David Langley stepped forward and now he raised his clenched fists.

But Peggy seized his arm and held him back. 'No, David, please! Now come away. I want no more trouble.'

David retreated a pace at her urging, but reluctantly, and he said, 'I haven't seen James.'

His father said, 'Your brother's working at the yard. I sacked Elisha Garbutt a year back—'

David broke in, 'So I heard. After him being your manager for all of ten years, you walked into the yard one morning and told him he was finished. That's no way to treat a man who served you—'

But now his father cut short the reproach: 'Aye! And he was swindling me for most of those ten years!'

David protested, 'He had a wife and children. How are they living?'

William was unbending: 'Damned if I know because they left the town, but he had a lot of my money. They'll not starve and I'll not lose any sleep. I have proof of how he robbed me and he's lucky I didn't have him sent to jail. He knows it. I gave his job to Alfred Bagley and your brother is helping him.'

David was concerned. 'Don't push him too hard. James isn't fourteen yet.'

'He will be in a couple of months and I'm keeping my eye on the pair of them. He'll be ready to do the manager's job himself when he's a grown man and Bagley retires. James is a good boy.' And he warned, 'You stay away from him.'

David brushed that warning aside with a contemptuous wave of one hand. 'You don't frighten me. I'll not make trouble for James. I wish him all the best in life.'

He turned his back on his father and ushered his wife and child out of the house. Little Josie hurriedly led the way. The hail had turned to snow again, flying in their faces on the wind driving in from the sea. Josie felt the cold nipping at her nose and ears. Holding the hand of her mother, she walked away from the big house, separated from the terraced streets that surrounded it only by a high wall. But first they crossed the yard to the back gate. The surrounding walls, and the washhouse in one corner of the yard, stood black in the night, but the snow outlined the tops of the walls and painted the roofs white.

Josie looked back once as she came to the back gate and caught one last glimpse of her grandfather. The giant stood in the doorway, etched black against the light of the kitchen, menacing. Then Josie passed through the gate into the lane beyond and he was lost to sight. But he still loomed in her mind, terrifying.

'He frightened me, Mam.' Josie, eager to talk now, looked up at her mother.

But Peggy Langley whispered, 'Ssh!' Her eyes were on her husband. David Langley strode with face set and brows in a thick, dark line. His mouth was drawn down at the corners, bitter.

They came to the road that ran up from the river and James turned to walk down it. Peggy asked, 'Aren't we going to the station?'

David answered, 'No. I'm going to look in at the yard and have a word with James.'

'Your father said—'

'He can say what he likes. I'm not leaving without seeing James.' Then he added, 'I'm sorry you had to listen to him back there. He's a good man really but this time he's wrong and I can't get him to see it.'

Peggy squeezed his hand. 'I don't care. I want nothing from him. It's just – I know it hurts you.'

David smiled wryly. 'I'll get over it.'

Josie did not understand any of this but was simply glad to be free of the giant and his baleful glare.

They came to the gates of the shipyard, the name painted in bold letters: William Langley and Sons. David nodded at it grimly. 'He'll soon be changing that. I'm surprised he didn't do it long ago.' They passed the timekeeper's office and then they were walking down the yard. Ahead of them the hull of the ship being built rose like a steel cliff. Tall cranes towered above it and workmen swarmed over it. The din of the riveting hammers set Josie's hands to her ears. More workmen, grimy and with their faces sweat-streaked, hurried back and forth across their path. Then one turned towards them as David called, 'Sammy!'

The man he hailed was in his forties, broad, stocky, and he walked with a sailor's roll. His shirt-sleeves were rolled to the elbows showing tattooed forearms. He grinned at Josie but addressed David. 'Now then, Mr Langley.'

David introduced him: 'This is my wife, Peggy. Sammy Allnutt taught me a lot when I was a boy just new in the yard.' Then to Sammy: 'I'm looking for our James. I hear he works with Bagley, the manager here now.'

'Aye, and he's coming on fine.' Sammy nodded approvingly. 'He's just down the yard.' He gave a jerk of his thumb as indication.

David asked, 'How do you like Bagley?'

'All reet. He only has to do what your father tells him, but he's a canny feller. Not like that Garbutt. He was a wrong 'un. It was a good day's work when your father sacked him. And his boy, Reuben, was just fifteen years old when I last saw him and he looked set to be a sight worse. He used to walk round this yard wi' his father and looking down his nose at the rest of us like we were dirt. And he had an evil look to him.'

Peggy said disbelievingly, 'At only fifteen?'

'Aye, Mrs Langley,' Sammy insisted. 'I've seen a few bad 'uns in my time and fifteen or fifty, that's the word for him: evil.' Then he pointed. 'There's James coming up now.'

Sammy stepped aside and went on his way, with a nod to David and a muttered 'All the best to you.'

A youth came running up the slope from the river and the ship on the stocks. The frown cleared from David's face and he was smiling when his brother came panting up to them. Josie liked the look of this boy and did not hide this time.

'Thank God you came!' James Langley was tall for his near-fourteen years, not so dark as his brother and having the soft brown hair and eyes of his dead mother. He wore grimy overalls and there was a smudge of oil on his forehead. He gripped the hand David held out to him and smiled with pleasure. Then the smile faded. 'A chap came into the yard a day or so back and said he'd heard you were going to America.'

David nodded. 'That's right.'

James asked, 'Did you try to make it up with Dad?'

David nodded again, but said, 'No luck.'

'I thought so.' James sighed. 'I know his mind is set. I've tried to take your side, tried to put in a word for you, but he won't listen.' Young James loved his father and respected him so now he said unhappily, 'And I know he is wrong.' With that he reached out a hand to touch Peggy's sleeve. Then he turned on David and said wistfully, 'I wish I was going with you.'

'No!' David set his hands on the boy's shoulders. 'Someone has to stay here with Father and as he doesn't want me then it must be you. Bagley is a good enough man but he can't manage the yard without Father telling him what to do. And Father will be fifty this year. You'll have to take over Bagley's job in another ten years – and one day the Langley shipyard will be yours. You mustn't – can't – throw that away.' David let his hands fall then. 'We've got to catch a train. You get back to work.'

'Aye. I will.' James's voice was husky now; he was close to tears. He turned and started back down the slope, then paused to turn his head on his shoulder and shout above the din of the hammers, 'Write to me with your address when you get there and I'll come and see you in America one day.'

'I'll write to you, never fear.' David watched until his brother disappeared from sight beyond the hull on the stocks, then he cleared his throat and said gruffly, 'Come on, then.' He turned and walked back up the yard. Josie found that instead of being frightened she was sad and crying. When she looked she saw tears on her mother's cheeks.

Josie asked, 'Are you sad as well, Mam?'

Her mother managed to smile and shook her head. 'I think it's just this cold wind making my eyes water.'

Josie agreed. 'I suppose that's what it is.'

They came out of the yard, climbed the steep road up from the river then crossed North Bridge Street, hurrying between horse-drawn trams. So they came to Monkwearmouth station, its frontage like a Greek temple with its tall columns. Inside the station they collected the luggage they had left there earlier. All they had was in one big portmanteau. The platform was crowded and so was the train but they found seats crammed into a nearly full compartment with Josie wedged between her parents. As her damp clothes began to steam in the heat she felt her feet come alive again inside her buttoned boots swinging above the floor. When the train hissed, shuddered, clanked and then began to move, Josie peered past her father and out through a cleared patch in the mist on the glass. She saw only darkness and pinpoints of light. Her eyes closed.

Her mother said softly, 'She's worn out with all that's been going on.'

Her father agreed in a murmur, 'Aye.'

Josie was too tired to argue, but not asleep. She heard her mother say above her head, low-voiced so only her husband would hear, but harshly bitter, 'I suppose we should have expected your father would think I set out to trap you for your money.'

David Langley laughed grimly. 'If you had you'd have made a mistake, because I won't get it now.'

Peggy sighed. 'But you know what I mean: I was a servant lass wi' no family or money. He owns a shipyard and it would ha' gone to you in time. I don't blame him for not accepting me, but I didn't want him to turn against you.'

David said softly, 'I wouldn't change anything.'

Josie felt the warmth of that love, like the physical warmth that wrapped around her now. She sighed and relaxed.

Only a few hours ago they had left the house in which Josie had been born and raised. It was south of the River Wear which ran through the town. Josie had crossed to the north side often before this day, with her parents, to visit the Langley house – but that was when her grandfather was away on business. She had come to know it and love it. Now she hoped she would never cross its threshold again.

But she would – and regret it.

Tom Collingwood's journey through life had begun four years before, when his grandfather had saved him from the institution. Tom was eight years old now, in ragged jacket and trousers, barefoot save for a pair of old boots with more holes to them than leather. He stood on the station at Newcastle, long-legged and grubby, his thick, black hair hand-combed, and watched the Sunderland train come in. He saw the man and the woman, her carrying a child, but just as faces in the long blur of faces. He held out his hand and asked, 'Give us a ha'penny, mister. I'm hungry. Give us a ha'penny, missus. Give us . . .' He got a halfpenny from the man as he passed; the woman had her hands full with the sleeping child. Tom went on reciting the plea monotonously. He had stopped crying over an hour ago.

His grandfather had spoken his last words an hour before that: 'Christ! I could do wi' a drink.' He had mumbled them sitting on the pavement with his back against the wall outside the station. Before that he had called hoarsely through chattering teeth: 'Wounded in the Crimea! Spare a copper for an old soljer!' He was wounded in the Crimean War, that was true. But the crutch lying across his knees supported him only in the towns. He had carried it over his shoulder the length and breadth of Scotland and down into the north of England. He was bearded and brown, ragged and gaunt now. During his long life he had been a soldier and a fisherman, a seaman and a poacher – and something of a rogue all the time.

He was the only family Tom had ever known. His first memory was of his grandfather coming to the house where Tom's parents waited for burial. The tall old man, burly and strong then, had scooped him up into the fold of one arm and told him, 'I'll not let them put you in the orphanage.' Tom had been with him ever since.

But that was all over now, though Tom did not realise this for some time. He was uneasy and fearful when his grandfather, after a long silence, let out a deep sigh and then ceased his laboured breathing. The worried small boy could not wake the old man. Tom suspected the worst when the two policemen came slow-striding and one said, 'I don't like the look o' this one.' Tom did not like the look of them, either, had always been taught to steer clear of the 'pollis'. So he sidled away – but he heard: 'Th'ould feller's deid.'

He had been taught to seek shelter in crowds so he slunk into the station. He had begged there out of habit and there his loss came home to him and he shed tears for the rough, hard-bitten old man who had cared for him after his fashion. Now he realised that there was no one to tell him where to go, what to do. No one to find him a bed – of some sort – for the night. He was alone.

When the police came into the station he guessed they were looking for him. His grandfather had told him how he had been saved from the orphanage and Tom was determined not to go there now. The train was filling up again to return to Sunderland. He sneaked aboard it by hiding among a little group of passengers, workmen smelling of drink and shouldering through the gate. He found a seat beside them and as the train rattled along from station to station he learned that they were all getting off at a place called Monkwearmouth.

He got out of that station as he had entered the train at Newcastle. The ticket collector at the gate spotted him worming through among the workmen, all of them singing now, but Tom ducked under his clutching hand and ran away into the night. He walked around some of the streets of Monkwearmouth, row upon row of soot-stained houses with windows lit yellow. A fine, cold drizzle came in from the sea. He begged as he went but got nothing from the few people hurrying home.

When the streets emptied, and the lights in the windows went out one by one, he found a tenement where the front door had not been bolted. In the passage was a dark corner where he could not see his dirty hand before his dirty face. He had a few halfpennies in his pocket with a hunk of bread and a piece of cheese. He ate the food and slept on some old sacking with the mice skittering around him. All this was done as if his grandfather was still with him; he was clutching at normality. This was the only life he had known and he had been happy enough.

But now he was miserable – and lonely.

2

Liverpool, January 1888

Josie had no sense of foreboding when she and her family boarded
the emigrant ship, lying in the Albert Dock, in the late afternoon. The
wind whipping in off the Mersey was cold but excitement kept her
warm. The side of the SS *Blackhill* stood above the landing stage,
black-painted and massive to Josie's eyes. Smoke trailed from the
ship's two funnels as her sweating stokers laboured below, hurling
shovelfuls of coal into the furnaces to raise steam for her to sail.
Josie held her mother's hand, following her father as he carried their
portmanteau on his shoulder. They climbed the gangway to the deck
of the ship along with other passengers sailing to a new life in America.
Some had portmanteaux but most made do with a cheap suitcase or an
old kitbag. A few carried all their belongings tied up in an old shawl or
blanket.

David Langley set the portmanteau down and straightened his back,
worked his shoulders after ridding himself of the weight. He set an
arm about his wife's shoulders and smiled at her. 'We'll be sailing in
a few hours.'

Josie asked, 'Will we get to America tomorrow?'

Her father laughed. 'Not as soon as that! But not too long. It will
give you time to enjoy the cruise.' That was said to reassure his wife as
much as his daughter. Privately he doubted if a winter passage of the
North Atlantic would be pleasant. But he told himself they would all
survive a little bad weather and seasickness and be none the worse.

He lifted the portmanteau again. 'Time to go below.' He led the way
to the poop and a door opening on to steep stairs leading down into
the steerage where the emigrants would live during the crossing.

Josie stood at the head of the ladder, looking down into the dark
bowels of the ship. It reminded her of the stairs down into the cellar in

her grandfather's house. And it was then she felt the first queasiness, the first shiver shaking her, She wailed, 'I don't want to go down there!'

Her father joked with her, 'Well, you can't sleep on deck. What if it rains?'

Josie's mother picked her up, held her close and soothed her: 'It's warm and dry down below. It will be just like going downstairs in our old house.'

Josie clung tightly to her and so they went below.

Later that evening, Peggy Langley looked up into her husband's face and said anxiously, 'She's burning up! Oh, David, I'm frightened!' She held Josie in her arms – the little girl was flushed, her hair damp with perspiration.

David laid his hand on her brow, felt the heat of it and bit his lip. He looked around him. The steerage accommodation for the emigrants was down below the waterline and crowded, bunks stacked one above the other like huge chests of drawers. David had been to sea more than once. He knew what it would be like to be battened down in this dark hold for hours or days in bad weather, and he had learned from one of the ship's officers that the barometer showed they would get it. And in the North Atlantic? How would this child of his fare during such a crossing, three thousand-odd miles and lasting two weeks or more? And what lay at the end of it?

He ran his hand through his dark hair worriedly and looked down again at Josie's flushed face, saw the way she twisted restlessly in her mother's arms. And she cried out in fear, 'The giant!'

Peggy whispered, 'She keeps on about some giant, a bad dream she's having. She's not in her right mind, David.'

He nodded. 'She's delirious.' He made his decision. 'Come on, we're going ashore.' He hurried the partially relieved Peggy up the succession of ladders to the deck. She would not be fully relieved so long as Josie was ill, but she was glad to be able to deal with that illness on dry land where there were doctors.

They were only just in time; the gangway was about to be swung up and inboard by a team of seamen working a derrick. David and Peggy trotted precariously down the gangway's tilted length, and they had scarcely set foot on shore when it was lifted into the air by the derrick and a clattering winch. When they reached the gateway to the dock, David looked back and saw the *Blackhill* already clear of the landing stage and easing out into the stream, pushed by a fussing tug. The *Blackhill*'s siren blared farewell and emigrants lined her rails, waving handkerchiefs and hats. David bade his own farewell to her in silence and turned away. He told himself his dream of a new life was postponed, that was all. And he had no regrets. His daughter came first, and he smiled down at her. He told Peggy, 'We'll have to find a room for the night and then I'll fetch a doctor to her.'

They found the room in a boarding house run by a Mrs Entwistle. David brought a doctor to see to Josie and he diagnosed a fever and administered some medicine. He smelt of whisky and oozed confidence: 'She'll be right as rain in a day or two.' But he was right. When Josie awoke the next morning the fever was gone and she was full of life and questions: 'Aren't we going to America? When are we going? Will we go on a big ship like the other one?' And: 'Can I go out to play?' Because she could see through the window the children playing hopscotch in the street.

Her delighted parents answered all her questions laughingly but refused the request in that last. Peggy said, 'I think she ought to stay in today. If she is still all right tomorrow we can take her for a walk.'

David agreed and picked up his cap. 'I'll take a walk myself. I want to see about booking another passage.' He would also try to regain the money paid for the passage on the *Blackhill* but doubted if he would get it. And the longer they stayed in the boarding house the more the rent of their room would eat into his small savings, so he wanted a passage sooner rather than later. As he left the house he met Herbert Entwistle, husband of the proprietress, a skinny, obsequious man. He occasionally worked as a clerk but usually lived off his wife whom he beat regularly. Now he smirked and stood aside deferentially. David, who had disliked him on sight, nodded stiffly and went on his way. Entwistle sneered at his back.

Reuben Garbutt might easily have seen the Langleys when they entered the Albert Dock or left it because he plied his trade hanging around the dock gates, but he had missed them. Reuben was the only son of Elisha Garbutt, who had been sacked by William Langley for theft. When David and Peggy carried Josie off the *Blackhill*, Reuben and his gang were following a sailor.

The young Garbutt was sixteen years old while most of his gang were a year or two older, but he led by strength of personality, example – and fear. They wore ragged jackets and trousers, greasy caps or battered bowler hats. Some smoked stubby clay pipes. The sailor was dressed in an old blue reefer jacket and canvas trousers. He had been paid and he was drunk.

Reuben was tall for his age, broad and muscular with dark, piercing eyes. In the past year the precocious boy had grown into a young adult. He had learned that he was attractive to some women and was learning how to use that charm. But not today. He strolled close behind the sailor as he staggered through the streets, the six members of the gang spaced out over a score of yards following their leader. He waited with the confidence of experience for his opportunity and seized it when it came. The sailor turned into a street narrower than the rest – and empty. Reuben took two long strides to bring him up on the heels of his prey and with a flick of one booted foot he tapped the sailor's ankles so that he tripped and fell. Reuben was on the man's back before he sprawled his length, shoving his face down into the dirt of the street. The rest of the gang came running up as the sailor tried to fight and yell. Reuben cut off the cry with a hand around the man's throat and the others helped to pin him down. They went through his pockets, found his money and a watch, and one of them tied his ankles with a length of rope. Then they were up and running as a woman appeared at her door and shouted, ''Ere! What are you lot doin'?'

'A'right! This'll do!' Reuben snarled the command and halted his band after running for a minute and rounding half a dozen corners. They stood in a dark alley and Reuben took off his cap, held it out and demanded, 'Cough up!' They all tossed into the cap what they had stolen from the hapless sailor. Reuben counted the coins in the cap and remained with his head bent, staring down into it for some seconds. Then he looked up and said softly, 'I saw him change a sovereign in the pub. I could tell you to a penny what he had in his pocket. Somebody's holding back.' His gaze, dark eyes staring, travelled around the circle of faces, looking into the eyes of each of them in turn. He stopped at one, a skinny youth with a spotted face. Reuben said, 'You're a cheating rat, Sepp.' He did not raise his voice but its tone and his glare were sufficient. Sepp hurriedly dug into his pocket, pulled out more coins and threw them into the cap.

Reuben dismissed him with a jerk of the head towards the mouth of the alley. Sepp whined, 'What about my cut?'

'You'll get your cut if you try that again – right across your throat!'

Reuben held him with the terrible glare and Sepp backed off, turned and ran. Reuben showed his teeth in a grin. That was another skill he had learned in the past year: how to terrify.

He shared out the money in the cap, though his share was bigger than the others and he pocketed the watch. No one objected. His partners in crime then headed for a favourite pub, but Reuben set out for what passed for his home.

This was a single crowded room in a tenement. He climbed several flights of stairs in darkness to reach it, his boots clumping hollowly on the wooden treads. He found his mother and his four sisters, all younger than he, sitting on stools around the small fire that burned in the grate. There was a table, bare save for a crust of bread and a knife. On the floor lay two mattresses. Reuben slept on one of them, the four girls on the other. His father lay in a corner on the only bed. He alternately mumbled, coughed, raved and gasped for breath.

Reuben shoved through the half-circle formed by his mother and the girls to stand in front of the fire. He asked, 'How is he?'

His mother, sallow and dark-haired, shrugged. 'Still hanging on.' Her dress, like those of the girls, was old and greasy. She and her daughters stared listlessly into the fire. But then she looked up and asked, 'D'ye get any money?'

Reuben reached into his pocket, pulled out some coins and dropped them in his mother's lap. She fingered them eagerly, counting. Reuben knew how much there was and how much remained in his pocket. He warned, 'Don't spend it all on gin.' Then he shoved out of the ring around the fire and went to stand by his father's bedside.

The old man was skeletal, the skin drawn tight over his skull, his wispy beard tangled. His eyes were glazed and shifted wildly. When Elisha Garbutt was dismissed by William Langley he had already spent the money he had stolen and had saved nothing. The sale of the furniture in the house he rented in Sunderland had paid for him and his family to travel to Liverpool where he hoped to find work. Those hopes were soon dashed; without a reference he could get only badly paid menial work and little of that. Now he was at the end of a long year of starvation, illness and despair.

Reuben listened to the old man's mumblings but for most of the time they were incomprehensible. Only now and again did a few words come through clearly enough to be understood: '. . . Langley . . . damned Langleys . . . beggared me . . . Langley . . . damn them to hell!' Finally Reuben could stand no more, turned and almost ran from the room. He strode the streets, not mourning but raging. He was sure who was to blame for the downfall of his father and hence his family.

When Elisha Garbutt had managed the Langley shipyard he and his family had lived comfortably, members of a middle-class élite, and looked down on the people who served them. None more so than Reuben, who had strutted at his father's side, disdainful of the common workmen. He had furtively mauled the young girls who worked in the Garbutt house and counted them lucky to have the experience. He had looked forward confidently to a lifetime of full pockets come easily. At the same time he envied the Langleys as owners of the yard and believed his father really did all the work. Then William Langley had sacked Elisha and Reuben found himself a penniless outcast, humiliated, jeered at by the girls he had lorded it over. During the past year his hatred of William Langley had built upon itself and now it had crystallised into a determination to be avenged.

He returned to the tenement as the dawn was breaking and he heard the wailing as he climbed the stairs. He knew what it meant and did not need his mother to tell him as he pushed in through the door, 'He's dead!' The dirty blanket was pulled up over Elisha Garbutt's face. Reuben stood over the body, silent, his head bowed, but not in prayer. Inside he was cursing the Langleys, man, woman and child, and swearing to make an end of all of them – one day. He flung himself out of the room again, shoving his mother and sisters out of the way.

Garbutt's gang was not the only one following his villainous trade. Another pack of four, dirty and shifty eyed, saw David Langley on his way to the shipping agents. His route took him through a maze of streets where all the houses seemed to be tenements. They teemed with grubby children and harassed women. He wound his way through them and the four skulked after him. But then, thinking he saw a short cut, he turned into an alley that led to a court that was dark even in the light of day. Here there was not a soul to be seen and here the gang struck. They spread out and one overtook David and swung round in front of him. He demanded hoarsely, black and stained teeth showing through his straggly beard, 'Cough up!' He held out one hand open, palm up, while the other pulled a short iron bar from his pocket.

David checked for a second, startled, but then his reaction was automatic and he lashed out. His fist struck the other full in the face and he staggered back, but then his partners closed in from each side and behind. One locked his hands round David's neck and the other two seized his arms. He struggled desperately and the panting, cursing group staggered about in the gloom of the court. The bearded one wielding the iron bar stepped in again but took David's boot on his shin and yelped with pain and rage. 'You bastard!' And he struck out with his weapon.

David's jaw dropped as the club came down on his head. He slumped among his captors. For a second they held him up, then they let him go and he crumpled and fell in the dirt.

One of them cursed, 'You mad bugger! You've killed him!'

No one argued; the result of that fearful blow was obvious. Another muttered, 'You could swing for this.'

But the bearded killer whined, 'We're all in it together!' Then he shoved the iron bar in his pocket and ran, the others racing after him.

When Reuben passed that way an hour later there was a policeman beside the blanket-covered corpse. An ambulance with its team of two sweating horses stood nearby. A crowd surrounded them, all talking about the young man who had been killed. Reuben stood back and listened.

'Bloody murder! . . . Smashed his head open! . . . He was dead when they found him so they could ha' walked them poor horses 'stead o' whipping 'em along here at a gallop . . . could ha' been you or me . . .'

He shrugged – the man meant nothing to him – and went up to the room. He joined his mother and sisters, all of them drunk now, and took a bottle from one of them. He drank and coughed as the raw spirit caught at his throat, but slowly his temper improved. He consoled himself that he would not have to put up with them for much longer. He was making far more money than he could have done by working. He took the lion's share of everything the gang stole and he saw to it that they worked hard at it. He knew he had the power to charm or terrify and that those gifts would make him rich.

He told himself that must come first. He would wreak his revenge on William and all the Langleys but in his own good time. He knew where to find them.

* * *

'You are Mrs Langley, wife of Mr David Langley?' A policeman brought the news. He stood blue and burly in the dim hallway of the boarding house with its aspidistra on a table and its smell of boiled cabbage. Peggy Langley was nervous, standing in his shadow with little Josie holding to her skirt, then distraught with grief and shock when he told her awkwardly that David was dead. She knew she had to control herself for the sake of the child at her side and at first there was disbelief. Hadn't she kissed David, and seen him saunter off, only an hour or so ago? But then the policeman produced David's wallet and notebook, in which he had written the address of the boarding house. So she knew it was true.

Josie asked in a whisper, afraid of the big policeman, 'What's the matter, Mam?' The tears rolled down Peggy's cheeks, and now Mrs Entwistle came waddling to comfort her, with Herbert Entwistle tutting and shaking his head mournfully in the background. Peggy lifted Josie and held the child to her breast, let the older woman lead her to the parlour while Herbert fetched a nip of brandy. She was glad of any sympathy and comfort at that time. She could give little to Josie who could not understand why her father would never come back to her, and cried.

Herbert Entwistle handed Peggy the brandy and assured her, smirking, 'We'll help all we can, m'dear. You can depend on us.' He arranged for an undertaker, who slipped Herbert a commission. And the evening before the funeral Peggy, deathly pale in her black 'widow's weeds' and with hands shaking still, asked Herbert, 'May I speak to you in private, Mr Entwistle?'

He bobbed his head, expansively granting a favour now. He knew there was little money to be had out of Peggy Langley. 'O' course. Come into the office.'

The office, where Mrs Entwistle kept her records, was little bigger than a cupboard. There was a small table and two straight-backed chairs. They sat and Herbert waited while Peggy twisted her wisp of a handkerchief into knots, until he prompted impatiently, 'What is it, then?'

Peggy admitted, 'Will you write a letter for me, please?' Like many more, she was illiterate. Unlike many, she felt it keenly.

Herbert's sense of superiority made him confident. 'O' course I will.' He coughed, then went on apologetically, 'Trouble is, I have to charge.' He ended vaguely, 'Professional rules, y'know.'

Peggy, still embarrassed, said quickly, 'Oh, aye.'

Herbert looked in the drawer under the table and found some sheets of writing paper, a pen and a bottle of ink. The nib was rusted but he scraped it clean with a thumbnail and wiped it on the leg of his trousers. Then he dipped the pen in the ink and poised it over the paper with a flourish. 'Who is the letter to?'

'Mr William Langley . . .'

The letter Peggy dictated hesitantly was simple and short. It informed William of the death of his son, David, expressed Peggy's sympathy and her own grief and concluded, 'Yours sincerely, Peggy Langley.'

Herbert addressed the envelope and said, 'There y'are, ma'am.' He ventured, 'That'll be sixpence.' And added quickly as Peggy hesitated, 'That's for postage as well.' So Peggy paid him and he ushered her out, assuring her, 'You can leave it to me, ma'am, don't you worry.' Then he burnt the letter in the kitchen fire and pocketed the money.

The funeral was in the morning. There was a cold wind numbing their faces and a spit of rain as the few mourners gathered around the coffin with the clergyman officiating. The widow was in black with a veil, and the child stood by her. Josie was very straight in the back and her white face was turned up to look at her mother. That showed because everyone else looked down at the grass and clay of the churchyard. The only other mourners were the Entwistles, Herbert carefully long-faced and his wife dabbing at tears caused by grief – or the wind.

They all rode back to the boarding house in the solitary cab. Josie still could not comprehend the disappearance of her father, was bewildered and unhappy. She hated the Entwistles, the boarding house, the cemetery and the cab. She whispered to her mother, who sat clutching a handkerchief, 'Are we going to America now, Mam?'

Peggy shook her head. 'No. We're getting on a train to London.'

'Is that like America?'

'Better. You'll see.' But Peggy had no such confidence.

The cab waited outside the boarding house and the Entwistles got down, but the cabman went in and emerged within minutes carrying a portmanteau on his shoulder. He heaved this up on to the roof then climbed up on to the box and picked up the reins.

Mrs Entwistle wailed, 'I hope everything turns out all right for you, dear.' Herbert smirked and nodded agreement. He knew Peggy had paid her bill, had seen the money change hands. He would have most of that from his wife in a few minutes if he had to belt it out of her. He herded her into the house as the cab pulled away.

At the station a porter took the portmanteau and followed Peggy as she bought her tickets and went on to the platform. It was lined with passengers waiting for the train to London. The porter put down the portmanteau and touched his cap, but refused a tip from the young widow. 'Naw! You've had some bad luck lately, 'aven't yer?' And when Peggy nodded he told her, 'Put that back in your purse and save it for the little lass.' He patted Josie's cheek then hurried away.

Josie asked, 'Will we live in a nice house in London, Mam?'

'Oh, aye,' Peggy replied, knowing she probably lied. But she knew Josie was unsettled by events, frightened and needing assurance. Peggy was going to London because she would not stay here where her heart had been broken. And in London she might find work. She believed she could hope for nothing from William Langley. She would take nothing and thought, To hell with him and his stiff neck!

Peggy had no one to turn to but she had to think of Josie, and as long as she had Josie she had something of David. She knew no one in London but she remembered, when she had been in service with the Langleys, hearing of a Monkwearmouth boy who had gone to London and found a job there working for a Mr Urquhart. He might be able to help her. If not, well, she would have to find something, and soon, because her purse was almost empty. She held Josie more tightly and the child clung to her mother as the platform reverberated with the approach of the train.

It came rumbling in at speed, the brakes grinding, looming monstrous, belching smoke and steam and giving off a smell of hot metal and coal smoke. Then the friendly porter came back and lifted the portmanteau, settled Peggy and Josie aboard the train. 'There y'are, missus.' Another pat for Josie then he was gone with a farewell wave of his hand. With a jerk and a clanking of couplings the train pulled away. So Peggy did not hear the boys selling newspapers outside the station as they called shrilly, 'Dreadful disaster! *Blackhill* sinks with all aboard!'

That was not strictly true. While the *Blackhill* had been in collision in foul weather there had been a few survivors. But most of her crew and passengers had perished. And David Langley and his family had left her at the moment of sailing. Their departure had not been noted and their names were still on the passenger list.

3

February 1888

''Ere y'are, missus!' The hoarse voice caused little Josie Langley to look up with solemn, wide grey eyes. Peggy started out of her worried abstraction as the conductor of the horse-drawn bus bellowed to her over the heads of the other passengers. As she rose hurriedly to her feet he went on, 'Up that street there and then foller your nose like I told you afore.' He helped Peggy and her daughter down from the bus. This was a street of big, stylish houses, but Peggy and Josie had to pick their way between the heaps of horse manure that littered its surface. The street smelt of it, sharply ammoniac.

Left to herself, Peggy would have walked and saved the fare, but the day was chill with a spit of rain and she was worried still about Josie's health. The little girl seemed to have recovered fully from the fever, but Peggy was always conscious that David had left his daughter in her care. The bus had carried them from close to the lodgings Peggy had taken when they had arrived in London the night before. She had gone there warily on the advice of the cabman she had hired at the station, but had found the house comfortable, clean and reasonable in price. It needed to be.

Josie was dressed in her best, as was her mother. The little girl wore her blue woollen coat with its flounced skirt that ended just above her buttoned boots. These Peggy had polished until they shone. So did Josie's morning face, framed by her bonnet trimmed with fur. Peggy had not bought black for her child, despite Mrs Entwistle's obvious disapproval, because she had felt David would not have wanted it. But she wore the black coat and dress she had bought for the funeral because she grieved and because it was her best.

They followed the directions given them by the bus conductor and at the end Peggy asked the driver of a provision merchant's delivery van, perched on his box of a seat behind his horse's rump and smart in striped apron: 'Excuse me, sir, but is this New Cavendish Street?'

He guessed at her illiteracy but touched his whip to his cap. 'It is, missus. Which one did you want? Mr Urquhart?' Now he was impressed. 'Ah! Fine gentleman.' And he pointed out the house then clicked his tongue at the horse and rolled away on iron-shod wheels.

The Urquhart house was tall and high-windowed with three storeys standing above the street. Peggy paused on the pavement opposite, hesitating nervously. Josie, holding her mother's hand, pulled on it impatiently. 'What's the matter, Mam? What have you stopped for?' But Peggy could not explain how much hung on the next hour or so, knew the child would not understand if her mother told her they would have to go to the workhouse if she could not find work. That institution would put a roof over their heads but its spartan cleanliness and pitiless regime were as bad as any prison. Peggy prayed silently, 'Not for Josie, please, oh Lord.' Then she took a deep breath and walked across the street.

A flight of wide steps flanked by handrails rose up to the big front door with its shining brass knocker, but Peggy turned instead to the narrow steps that led down to the cellar kitchen under the house. She tapped at the door there and it was opened by a girl of sixteen or so, a kitchen-maid with a mob-cap on her curls and a white apron tied around her waist. Peggy asked, 'Can I speak to Mr Harvey, please?'

The girl's eyes widened. 'Ooh! I dunno. Arf a mo' an' I'll arsk. Who shall I say it is?'

Peggy shook her head. 'He won't know me. Just say I'm from Monkwearmouth.'

The wide eyes blinked. 'Where?' The girl had never heard of it.

Peggy repeated, 'Monkwearmouth.'

'Ah!' The girl mouthed the syllables silently, rehearsing, then said, 'Awright, I'll see if he's in.'

Peggy knew what that meant. As the girl disappeared and she was left to wait at the door she wondered if Harvey would see her. And thought with weary pessimism: Why should he?

''Scuse me, Mr Harvey, but there's a woman at the kitchen door arskin' to see you.' The girl, Elsie, stood respectfully at the door to the butler's pantry, a small, neat room that was his office. Albert Harvey, at thirty-one, was a young man for his job but he had already held it for five years. He was tall and lean with dark hair and shrewd dark eyes. He sat at the little table that served as his desk, in shirt-sleeves and black waistcoat, but his tailcoat hung ready on a hook. He had risen a long way in the world but was determined to go a lot further.

He knew what it meant when a strange woman came to the kitchen door asking to see him. They often did and they always wanted work. He never took them on. Instead he looked for the staff he wanted and then set about getting them. At that time he knew there would soon be a vacancy in the household – today if he allowed the assistant cook to leave without working her notice; she wanted to join her husband in service in a house in the shires. But Harvey already had his eye on the potential replacement, working in a large house only a few hundred yards away. Still . . .

The girl's mention of 'Monk-wear-mouth she says she's from.' That was something different. And Elsie went on, 'She's got this girl with her I think must be hers; little thing, all eyes.' That was different, too. The women seeking work never brought their children with them, to spoil their chances by whimpering or wailing.

Albert Harvey hesitated. He was a man of intelligence who reasoned things out, did not make hasty, emotional decisions. But now those two oddities of Monkwearmouth and the child made him curious. He said, 'Very well. Show her up.'

Josie did not like the pantry, windowless and lamplit, but she liked Albert Harvey and smiled at him as her mother led her in. Albert found himself returning that smile and it was still in place when he faced Peggy Langley. Probably the matter was settled then. He asked, 'What can I do for you, Mrs . . .?'

Peggy supplied: 'Langley, sir. Peggy Langley.' She started, 'I'm looking for a place, sir.' That meant she was wanting to work as a servant in a house. She went on to tell of her experience in the Langley house: 'I think I'm a good, plain cook and before that I was housemaid . . .' She told him of her marriage to the son of the Langley house but said nothing of William's reaction. That did not matter because Harvey could read between the lines. Peggy explained how she and David were on their way to America when he was killed.

Harvey thought, That's why the child is here. He guessed that, being alone and newly come to this city, the young woman would be reluctant to leave the little girl with strangers.

Peggy finished, 'So now I'm looking for a place.'

Harvey did not mention Monkwearmouth; he had never made

favourites for any reason and would not start. He had not been back there for over five years because his work kept him busy and he had no relatives living there now. But he remembered the Langley family, and old William in particular. He could guess why Peggy had not sought help from the old man, and while she had not pleaded he also guessed that she was in desperate need of the 'place' she was asking for. She was pale and her lips were pressed tight to stop them trembling; her hands in their black cotton gloves were clasped. And at her knee there was that small face smiling up at him.

He said, 'As it happens . . .' Peggy listened in a daze of relief, catching the phrases that meant so much: 'A month's trial . . . live in . . . wage of twenty-six pounds a year . . .' He finished, 'When will you be able to start?'

He was not surprised when she answered, 'As soon as possible.'

He suggested, 'Would the day after tomorrow be convenient?'

It would. Peggy had enough money to pay for her lodging for another two nights, but no more.

In Monkwearmouth, old William Langley was uneasy in his mind. He had settled down to work in his office in the Langley house but his thoughts kept turning to his elder son, his wife and his child. William was now uncertain. Had he acted justly? He glanced at the clock on the mantelpiece, saw it was mid-morning and decided it was time he walked down to the shipyard. He rose from his desk and strode out into the hall. At that moment the knocker banged on the front door. He knew that the maid had gone out on some errand so he opened the door himself.

The boy standing on the step held out an envelope. 'Telegram for Mr William Langley, sir.'

'I'm William Langley.' He took the envelope from the boy and gave him a halfpenny.

'Thank you, sir.'

William closed the door, frowning, and tore open the envelope. He wondered who the devil was sending telegrams to him at his private residence. They came to his office at the shipyard but never to the house. Some clerk had made a mistake . . .

He read the flimsy through the first time without taking it in – or maybe his mind rebelled against the news, refusing to accept it. He read it again and this time the reading was more difficult because his hands shook so that the paper shivered and the words danced. But the message was dreadfully clear: the shipping company regretted to inform him that David Langley, his wife and daughter had perished, lost with the SS *Blackhill*.

He said, 'No. *No!*' But he knew it was true. It all fitted. He had seen newspaper reports of the loss of the *Blackhill*, bound for America with emigrants, and David had said he was going to emigrate to America. He had said it in this house only a week ago.

William turned and walked through the hall and the long passage to the kitchen at the back of the house. The woman he employed as a cook, and the scullery maid who helped her, were working there but he told them, 'Get out.'

The cook looked up from the dish she was preparing, startled. 'I'm just getting the dinner ready—'

But William shouted, face twisted in pain, '*Get out!*' And the women backed away from him, snatched up their coats from the hooks behind the door and ran. They left the back door open and William shut it with a kick then sank down in a chair at the big scrubbed table.

He remembered: it was in this house that David had been born and grown up; it had been his home. It was in this room that he, William, had denied that home to his son and sent him away. He had stood in the doorway to the passage, David just in front of him. His woman – his son's wife – had stood by the table here with the little lass beside her and frightened out of her wits. William had seen that but hardened his heart.

He had been wrong.

And now he knew but it was too late, would always be too late.

He sat there for some time with his head in his hands, but finally he got up, walked back to his office and found paper and pen. He wrote a letter, without hesitation, just setting down what was in his heart. Then he put on his top hat and walked into the town to his solicitors in High Street East. There he asked Arkenstall for his will and attached the letter to it. The letter was to be opened after his death and was addressed to his son, James. It spelt out William's remorse and asked, 'Pray to God to forgive me.'

On his way home he went into the yard and sat in his office. There was work he could have done but he left it. Instead he sat looking out of the window. He could see nearly all the yard from that viewpoint and in particular he could see young James at work. He still had his younger son. He swore not to make the same mistake with James. Next time he would listen and give.

That was some consolation but David had been his first-born and he had virtually driven him out to die. He got up from the desk restlessly and set out for his house. The day was bitterly cold with an icy wind sweeping up the River Wear from the sea. He jammed his top hat tightly on his greying head and buttoned his overcoat. As he left the gates of the yard behind him a voice that he first ignored finally caught his attention: 'Got a ha'penny, mister? Got any grub?'

Little Tom Collingwood had found enough to eat – just – each day of the past week, but had only had hard lying. He was afraid to go to a dosshouse because of what might happen to him there – theft and worse – now that he did not have his grandfather as protector. Besides, he could not afford it. What money he had begged he had spent on food – and little of that. He would not go to any official or the workhouse because that would only end with him going to the orphanage. So last night he had slept with his back against the wall of a bakery where the baker had his oven and there was still some warmth. He had shared it with a half-dozen stray cats that had draped themselves over his body so they all lay in a huddle.

That had kept him from freezing and let him doze fitfully, but the cold in his legs and feet woke him at first light. He was glad to move to get warmth into his limbs. He knocked at back doors and was finally given milk and bread by an old woman. From there he begged his way down to the shipyards that lined the bank of the river. He knew that many of the men would leave the yard at midday to go home for their dinners. Some might have a few scraps left of the breakfast they had taken to work that morning. So he was waiting at the gate marked 'William Langley and Sons' – William painted over Hector; Hector had founded the firm – when the old man came out.

William stopped and they looked at each other. Tom saw another tall, bearded old man with a hard eye, a man like his grandfather. William saw a boy in tattered trousers and jacket over a ragged shirt and jersey. His toes stuck out of his boots and he had a watchful and hungry stare. And he looked a little like David Langley as a boy.

The boy said again, tentatively, 'Got a ha'penny, mister?' He did not ask for grub again. He could see this was a nob who would have money but would not be carrying food. But the 'nob' was not forthcoming and glowered down with those hard, black eyes. Tom tensed, ready to run if the old feller lashed out with the walking-cane he carried. But he did not. They stood for some long seconds while the wind whipped around them and Tom shivered.

Then the old man asked, 'Have you no home?'

Tom hesitated a moment but saw no trap in the question. He answered, 'No, mister.'

'Any family?'

That was different. Tom retreated a pace but did not run. There was something about the old man; he was not like his grandfather really, but . . . Tom said, 'I'm not going in the orphanage.'

William nodded, thinking, No family. A boy without family and living on the streets was not usual, but it was not unknown, either. William asked, 'Are you prepared to work for your keep?'

'Work? Where?' Tom's eyes slid round to the shipyard gate.

But William said, 'No, not in there. In my house.'

Ah. Now Tom understood. 'You mean in service.'

'That's right. You would be paid and get bed and board.'

Tom was tempted. Bed and board! And paid! But he said, 'I want to be a sailor, like my grandda was.'

'Is he at sea now?'

'No. He died a few days back.'

William saw the corners of the boy's mouth droop. There was sorrow there and he knew about that. He said, 'You're not big enough yet, but you can go to sea when you're older.'

The wind howled in again with a spit of rain that lashed cold in their faces. Tom was hungry. He said, 'All right, mister.'

So they went home together.

Josie asked, 'Mam, what's a bastard?'

A week had passed since Peggy had settled in as an assistant cook with a small attic room for herself and Josie. While Harvey had recruited Peggy, her employer, who owned the house and all in it, was Geoffrey Urquhart, a millionaire industrialist. She rarely saw him. Her work was in the kitchen and she spent long hours there. But her boss, and the man who ran the house with the assistance of the housekeeper, was Albert Harvey. He ran it efficiently and the staff were happy.

But this morning Peggy froze in the act of helping her daughter to dress. Josie asked again as she tugged the frock over her head. 'Mam, what's a bas—?'

Peggy cut her short: 'Where did you hear that?' She automatically went on smoothing down the frock. It was Josie's only other dress apart from her best, a rose pink that had washed nearly white; Peggy knew she would soon have to let it down.

Josie looked up at her, curious. Peggy was used to her constant questions, but this one . . . Josie said, 'One of the ladies in the kitchen said she thought I was a bastard. What does it mean?'

Peggy dismissed it lightly. 'It doesn't matter because the lady was wrong.' But when she entered the kitchen that morning she propped two sheets of stiff paper on top of the sideboard.

Albert Harvey saw them as he passed through. One was Peggy's 'marriage lines' and the other was Josie's birth certificate. He glanced at Peggy, working at the big table, and asked, 'Why are these here?'

Without looking up, heart pounding because she was afraid this might cost her the 'place' she needed so badly, Peggy answered, 'Some people thought Josie was born out of wedlock. Those papers show she wasn't.'

Harvey snapped, 'Put them away.' Then he said to no one in particular, for all the staff appeared to be working busily and unheeding, 'If I catch anyone talking like that they will be looking for another position.' He stalked out and Peggy sighed silently with relief. She collected the certificates – and many friendly smiles.

Some weeks later, Peggy asked shyly, 'Can I tell you something, Mr Harvey? I mean, just between you and me?' The request was made respectfully because, while a friendship had soon grown up between her and the butler, she took care not to presume on it. Harvey, for his part, was at pains not to favour her – or at any rate, be seen to do so.

Now he replied, 'I'll listen and hold my tongue, if that's what you mean, Mrs Langley.' They sat in his pantry with the door wide open, but nobody could linger and listen without Harvey seeing them.

'Thank you. It's just that, you being from Monkwearmouth, you'll have known the Langleys. So you must have wondered why I'm working here.' Peggy was pink-cheeked with embarrassment now, but went on to explain how William Langley had thought she had married his son for his money and turned them away. 'It wasn't so. I didn't want his money, not then, not now. I sent a letter to him only once, to tell him that David had been killed, but I didn't ask him for anything and I didn't tell him I was coming to London.' Peggy smiled, relieved to be done. 'I just wanted you to know that I didn't do anything wrong.'

Albert Harvey had suspected Peggy's background would be something like that, a family row leaving her estranged, so he was not surprised. He said, 'I'm sure you would not have done any wrong and I thank you for your confidence in me.' Then, to change the subject and relieve Peggy from further embarrassment, he asked, 'How is Josie settling down here?'

Peggy said doubtfully, 'Well . . .'

Josie was a problem. She was still too young for school and sometimes Peggy had to leave her in their small room, but most of the day the little girl spent in the kitchen, playing in some out-of-the-way corner. Inevitably she occasionally strayed and got under the feet of busy cooks and maids, was chided and there were tears. But one afternoon she got hold of a pencil and a scrap of paper and Albert Harvey found her on hands and knees, trying to draw. He had an hour or so to spare that normally he filled by reading, but now he took the little girl to his pantry and started to teach her to write her letters.

Josie picked it up quickly and Albert Harvey marvelled at the speed with which she learned to read and write. So he came to spend most of his spare time instructing the girl. Josie in turn revelled in her studies. She looked forward longingly to those few minutes, snatched here and there in the day, when he had time for her. She came to be fond of his neat and tidy but drab little pantry.

That could not last, of course. The lady of the house, Elizabeth Urquhart, slender, graceful and gentle, was that rarity at the time, an educated woman. She usually called the cook to attend her in the drawing room to receive instructions on the meals for the day, but occasionally wandered 'below stairs' to speak to her. One morning she did so and when passing the butler's pantry saw the lessons in progress and heard Josie reading aloud. Elizabeth halted and enquired, 'What have we here, Harvey?'

'Little Josie Langley learning to read, ma'am.' The butler stood up hastily and explained: 'Her mother is the assistant cook.'

His mistress looked down at his pupil and saw the small girl smiling up at her. She smiled in return and prompted the child, 'Will you let me hear you?' Josie was ready to oblige and did so, reading clearly and confidently. Elizabeth tested her by taking the book from her and pointing out some words at random, to see that she had not just memorised the whole passage parrot fashion. But Josie made no mistake.

Elizabeth handed back the book and asked, 'How old is the child?'

'Not yet five, ma'am,' answered Harvey.

His mistress tapped the tip of her tongue with one slim finger, thinking. Then she said, her mind made up, 'Well, I think she could do with more time than you can give her.'

Harvey agreed. 'Yes, ma'am, but she's too young for school.'

Elizabeth nodded. 'So she'd do better to attend in the schoolroom with the children. Take her up in the morning after breakfast.' She stooped to ask Josie, 'Would you like that? To be taught in a proper schoolroom in this house with my little girls?'

Josie was not sure. 'What about my dinner, please?'

Elizabeth's lips twitched. 'You will get your dinner with the girls, never fear. Now, will you come?'

Josie agreed happily. 'Aye, missus.'

Peggy Langley had her doubts when Harvey broke the news to her. She protested worriedly, 'She'll be up there with strangers and all on her own. She'll be out of her place with them.'

But Harvey knew the three young daughters – aged four, six and eight – and the governess, chosen by Elizabeth Urquhart, who taught them. 'They'll treat her fair and she'll learn a lot that'll stand her in good stead.'

Josie learned a great deal. Besides the lessons taught by the governess, she also learned of life on both sides of the green baize door. She absorbed the manners and speech of the Urquhart girls and those of the kitchen.

And more . . .

'Is that you again?' Harvey would greet her as she sidled into his pantry when school was over for the day. Josie loved to sit with him while he talked of his work and the running of the house. So that she learned not only what was done but why it was done.

Then in that summer of 1888 there was her first experience of Hallburgh Hall. 'We're going to the country,' Peggy told her daughter. 'All through the summer.' This was an annual event. It was the custom for the landed gentry to come to London in May for the summer 'season' then go to the country in the autumn for shooting, hunting and fishing.

However, Geoffrey Urquhart was not landed gentry but a businessman. So he would send his family to his country house for the summer while he stayed in London to attend to his business affairs. He would travel down into Surrey at the weekends.

So Peggy packed the clothes for her and Josie and they took a cab to Waterloo station, then a train into Surrey with the rest of the staff who were going to Hallburgh Hall. Geoffrey retained a skeleton staff in London to serve him.

'Mam!' breathed Josie, as a big horse-drawn brake carried all of them up the long drive to the house. 'Isn't it lovely! Isn't it big!'

The Hall was built of old red brick with tall chimneys and log fires in huge hearths. There were several huge rooms and a myriad of smaller ones, all connected by a maze of passages. Acres of lawns and pasture merged into woodland with a gurgling stream running through it. Josie had this for an enormous playground she shared with the Urquhart girls.

'Do we have to go back to London?' she asked at the end of that summer.

''Course we do,' replied her mother, 'but we'll be back every year.'

Josie had to be content with that.

And they did go back every year . . .

'Hey, missy!' The voice came out of the air. Josie's head turned as she searched for its owner. She was eight years old now and walking in the woods around Hallburgh Hall on a hot afternoon, alone and bored because the Urquhart girls had gone to Switzerland. She looked in vain but then it came again: 'Hey, missy!' And scornfully: 'Up *here*!'

Josie lifted her eyes. The tree standing only feet away from her was massive, its trunk a yard in diameter and without a branch for the first ten feet of its height. The boy sat on the lowest bough, his legs dangling. His feet were bare and in the summer heat he wore only shorts and shirt. He had a shock of yellow hair above blue eyes in a brown face and he grinned at Josie. 'I'm Bob Miller, after "Bobs", see?' Josie did; everybody knew 'Bobs', General Roberts, the soldier, who had made his name in India. The boy asked, 'Who are you?'

'Josie Langley.'

'You're up at the Hall.'

'Yes.'

Bob said, 'My dad's a gardener there.'

Josie knew there were three or four gardeners at the Hall. 'My mum is a cook.'

They were silent a moment, weighing each other up. Then Bob said, 'You didn't see me, did you?'

Josie asked, 'How did you get up there?'

'Can't you climb trees, then?' Bob taunted.

'I can.' Josie refused to be nettled. 'But you didn't climb that. Nobody could because you can't get your hands round it and there aren't any branches to hold on to. Did you have a ladder?' She peered about, looking for it.

'Naw!' Bob laughed, but was impressed by her reasoning. He admitted, 'I came up on a rope, see?' He lifted a loose coil of it and Josie saw that it was knotted around the branch on which he sat. 'I threw one end over then climbed up it double. Want to come up?' he invited.

But Josie suspected he was still goading her. She turned away and copied him: 'Naw.' She started to walk away.

'Hang on!' Bob called. And when she looked over her shoulder, he coaxed, 'I've got a house up here.' Josie could see something like a box in the branches behind him, was eaten by curiosity but still only shrugged. 'Here you are!' Bob was encouraging her and now he cast the coils from the branch so they unravelled and the rope dangled to touch the ground. 'Come on up.'

Josie wanted to but did not know how. She replied with dignity, 'Girls don't climb ropes.'

Bob urged, 'Nobody will know. Tell you what: I'll show you.' He grabbed the rope and came down hand over hand. He stood beside Josie but was half a head taller. 'You're not very big. How old are you?'

'Eight,' answered Josie. Was he talking down to her again?

But Bob said, 'I'm ten.' Then he softened it by: 'I expect you'll be big as me when you're ten. Now, what you do, you catch hold o' the rope up here wi' both hands, let the end of it lie over your left foot like that, and trap it there with your right foot. See? Then you straighten your legs and stretch up wi' your hands, pull up your legs, tighten them and straighten them. See?' He climbed some eight feet then slid back to earth and offered the rope to Josie. 'It helps if you spit on your hands first.'

Josie spat delicately and seized the rope.

After an hour and a great deal of spitting, Josie sat on the branch with Bob. The house was a rough lattice-work of small dead branches, making a box with one side open and just big enough to hold the pair of them. It served through that day as their ship, carriage, or home, as their imaginations took them.

Peggy worried for a while when Josie did not return to the house for tea. Then one of the gardeners, standing at the kitchen door while he drank a mug of tea Peggy had given him, said, 'Your little lass is down in the wood, playing wi' Jem Miller's lad. Don't ye worry about her.' So Peggy worked on, relieved.

Josie finally returned to the house as dusk was falling. 'I've been playing with Bob Miller.'

Peggy, busy with the preparations for dinner, said absently, 'That's nice.'

Josie went on, 'We've got a little house.' She wisely did not mention that it was perched in a tree. 'Bob's mam gives him some bread and cheese for his tea so he doesn't have to go home till it's dark. He shared it with me, but can I have some tomorrow, please?'

Peggy, hurrying from table to oven and red-faced in the heat of the kitchen, agreed readily. ''Course you can. Now move out of my way, there's a love.'

So Josie spent her days with little Bob Miller. She had to return to the house for lunch but after that she would run off to join him again, her bag of sandwiches in her hand. They were long summer days of blue skies and shimmering heat.

'Let's go swimming,' said Bob.

'You mean paddling.' Josie had waded in the stream with the Urquhart girls, searching for tiddlers.

'Naw!' Bob was scornful. 'I mean swimming – in the pool.'

Josie said doubtfully, 'You can't swim.'

'O' course I can!' Bob was indignant. 'Me dad showed me, said I had to learn because I'm going to be a sailor.'

'Are you?' Josie was still unsure.

'As soon as I'm old enough.' And Bob offered, 'Tell you what: I'll teach you.'

The pool lay in a hollow, downhill from the house and hidden in trees. The stream ran into it at one end and out at the other, leaving eddies on the surface and keeping it cool. Bob threw off his clothes and jumped in. Josie hesitated, but then he challenged, 'You're scared!'

'I'm not,' replied Josie, refusing to be beaten.

Bob taught Josie to swim, in between their making harbours and dams out of mud and a pier built of rocks. At the end of that first day, when Josie dragged her clothes on to her damp body to dry, she could dog-paddle. Inside a week she was breaststroking across the pool.

Until one day Peggy had to go hunting for her daughter and found her by following the sound of the yells. Josie and Bob were leaping into the pool so that it exploded in spray, two racing, shrieking, naked urchins.

'You won't see him any more,' Peggy declared, furious and shocked as she marched Josie back to the house. 'Disgraceful! I came looking for you because we're going back to London tomorrow. And *he*'s goin' for good. His father's leaving to work with his brother. So that little terror won't be here next year.'

But nor was Josie.

At the end of that summer the youngest of the Urquhart children went on to boarding school, the last to go, and the governess left. Josie moved to the local board school where she mixed with the children of servants, small shopkeepers and publicans. Her North Country accent had faded from lack of use by that time. She automatically fell back on the accent and language of the kitchen and fitted in. But she was always top of her class.

It was then that she bade a tearful farewell to Albert Harvey. The butler had come into a small inheritance and used this and his savings to take over a private hotel. He told Peggy and the tear-stained little girl, 'I reckon it's a business where you're always sure of a living. Everybody has to sleep somewhere, whether he's a tinker, tailor, soldier or sailor.'

When Josie had gone to bed he proposed to Peggy Langley but she told him, 'I'm sorry. You're a good man and I'm sure you'll get on and I'm honoured that you've asked me. But there was only ever the one man for me and that was David. God bless you for all you've done for me and Josie.'

Josie continued to have nightmares in which the giant came tramping and roaring to loom over her and she would wake shrieking. As she grew these became rarer – but she never forgot the giant.

And in Liverpool, Reuben Garbutt had moved off the street by the time he reached his twentieth birthday. Now he owned a pawnshop and lived in a comfortable flat above it. The shop, run by a fawning, frightened manager twice his age, made a good living for him, but not as good as he made from receiving stolen goods and selling them on. And then there were other enterprises – like funding a big robbery and taking a thick cut from the proceeds – where a reputation for ruthless violence stood him in good stead.

His mother and sisters still lived in the slum tenement. He rarely saw them. He had no photograph of them or his father in the flat. Nor did he have anything to remind him of the Langleys. He did not need any such aid to his memory. He would never forget the Langleys and his oath to avenge himself on them. When he was ready . . .

They did not meet there again, though Josie often went to see the ships and Tom, at that time serving aboard a collier bringing coal down from Sunderland to London, sailed into the Pool every week. Nor did either remember the incident later.

Now Peggy moved on and Josie went with her. After a while Josie harked back to the subject that worried her. 'I think all that trouble was Grandfather's fault.'

Peggy told her, 'Don't worry your head over what's done. Just forget about it.'

But Josie could not. 'When I'm big I'll give him a piece of my mind.'

Peggy's lips twitched as she recognised one of the cook's expressions, but she said severely, 'You'll do nothing o' the sort, miss. You behave yourself like the lady your father wanted you to be.'

That weighed with Josie, who had loved her father, and she was silent. But she was still vaguely determined that she would make William Langley pay for the hurt he had caused her parents, although she had no idea how she would do this.

It was a decision that would bring her close to death one day.

Olive Garbutt was facing her death that day. She lay in the bed in which her husband Elisha had died and waited for her son, Reuben. Her four daughters sat around the small fire, muttering among themselves and casting occasional worried glances in her direction. For the past few hours she had asked only for: 'Reuben. I want to see Reuben.' They had sent for him, reluctantly because they hated him for the way he had left them in poverty while he lived in comfort. But they knew it was their mother's dying wish. Still, they wondered at it, because she hated him even more than they did.

Now, in her mind, she was rehearsing her speech for when he arrived. She would be ready for him. She had exacted a promise from him to look after the girls and when she told him the truth he would want to renege on it. But he would honour it because he knew her curse would lie on him if he did not.

She would tell him: 'You're not Garbutt's son. You were born on the wrong side o' the blanket, you were. But your real father was a fine figure of a man, big and strong – hard, like you. He was a bad lot, *bad*, and you're going the same way. He frightened me sometimes but he had a way with him; all the lasses fancied him – but I had him.

He bedded me a dozen times and I laughed behind Garbutt's back. Garbutt was a snivelling, tight-fisted—' But she would not tell him that the man who had fathered him had been hanged for a knifing, and not his first.

She did not tell him anything. Olive Garbutt heard Reuben's heavy tread on the bare wood of the stairs but when he entered the room she was dead, staring wide-eyed and loose-jawed at the cracked and stained ceiling.

One of her daughters said, 'I think she's gone.' She bent over her mother, listening for a breath, feeling for a heartbeat, and found neither. She straightened and said, sure now, 'She's gone, all right.' Then she staggered aside as Reuben shoved her out of his way. He took her place, leaning over the bed. He hung there for a second or two, confirming his sister's verdict, then turned away.

He looked at the four girls and they returned his gaze with one of a mixture of hope and confidence. He knew the reason for that confidence and now he said, 'When she was took bad' – and he jerked his head towards the still body in the bed – 'she got me to promise to provide for you lot. Those were her words: "You've got to provide for the girls." And so I will.' He grinned at them.

But they exchanged glances among themselves, still uneasy.

He went on, 'There's a ship sailing for Australia the day after tomorrow and I'll pay for passages for all of you. On top of that I'll give each of you twenty pounds to give you a start out there. That should be enough; I hear there's plenty o' work out there for young lasses.'

They stared back at him, shocked. One began to cry and the eldest said, 'What if we don't go?'

Reuben eyed her, not smiling now. 'You'll wish you had.' That cowed her and she shrank back among the others. Reuben turned away but paused at the door to say, 'I'll get a doctor to come and certify the death and I'll see to the funeral. You be ready the day after tomorrow.' Then he left them weeping. He had his own evil course to follow.

While Josie Langley was living out the last of her childhood years.

5

August 1902

'You've as much right to a seat at somebody's window as some o' them people upstairs,' Peggy Langley complained as she struggled into her coat. 'You remember, you're as good as they are.'

'Yes, Mam,' Josie agreed, knowing it was no good to argue. She was eighteen now and an attractive young woman. She gave her mother's coat a final yank on to her shoulders and handed her the big cartwheel of a hat with its ostrich feather. 'Roger's trying to keep us a place but we'll never get to him if we don't leave here soon.' Besides, she had heard this kind of talk from Peggy Langley increasingly over the last two years and didn't want to hear it at all, let alone now.

Edward VII was to be crowned this day, belatedly because of an attack of appendicitis, but he was now recovered. Roger, a footman in the Urquhart house, had promised to save a place on the pavement for Josie and her mother to watch the procession pass by, but there were certain to be crowds. London had filled up with visitors and many families, like the Urquharts, had invited friends and relatives to stay with them and see the show. The Urquharts and their guests had in turn been invited to watch from the windows of a private house, owned by a business friend of Geoffrey Urquhart's, which overlooked the processional route. That was the reason for Peggy's mention of a seat at a window. But servants would see what they could from the level of the street.

'Come on, Mam.' Josie shot one swift glance around the room they had always shared. Her mother stooped before the chest of drawers to look in the mirror on top of it as she skewered a pin through the hat. Josie saw that all was tidy, the double bed neatly made with its little strip of carpet on either side, the small grate empty but clean.

In winter they were allowed a fire; Geoffrey Urquhart was one of the best of employers.

'Right, I'm ready.' Peggy straightened and moved towards the door. 'Though to tell you the truth I'd sooner stay home and let you tell me all about it afterwards.'

Josie coaxed her out through the door cheerfully. 'You'll feel better when you get out. And it's not every day you see a coronation. Why, there hasn't been one for more than sixty years. Lord knows when we'll see another!'

They descended the back stairs and left the house by the servants' entrance at the rear. Josie set off briskly but then had to slow for her mother to keep up. Peggy had become very short of breath in recent months and had difficulty in managing the steep and narrow service stairs at the back of the house. Josie wore her only good dress in a pale blue cotton; her working garb of black dress and white apron were hanging in her room. She was flushed with excitement and looked very pretty. Young men frequently told her so but she was still heart-whole.

Roger was one of Josie's admirers, a thin young man with his hair neatly parted in the middle. They found him, finally and with difficulty. Despite his early start he was still a yard back from the kerb with two rows of people between him and the road. He saw them and waved his cap. ''Ere y'are, girls!'

Josie wormed her way through the crowd with her mother in tow. 'Excuse me, please, our friend is waiting for us.' The people were good-natured and the men willingly made room for her so the women had to follow suit. Josie and Peggy wound up standing in front of Roger and were able to peer between the swivelling heads in front and the rigid ones of the red-coated soldiers lining the route. They saw Edward and his queen pass by with their escort of the Household Cavalry, and all the rest of the glittering procession. Josie danced and cheered excitedly all the while, until she was hoarse. It was almost done when Peggy Langley sagged against her.

'Mam? What's the matter? Mam?' Josie put an arm around her mother to hold her up and Roger came to her aid. Peggy's face was screwed up in pain, her eyes closed.

'Here, let's get her out o' this.' Roger forced a way through the crowd for them and then found a seat for Peggy on a low wall.

Josie crouched to look into her mother's eyes, open now but still squinted in agony. 'What is it, Mam?'

'A pain. Awful. Must be indigestion. Here.' Peggy laid a hand between her breasts.

Josie asked anxiously, 'Can you walk?'

'O' course I can walk. It's only indigestion. I want to go home.'

Roger urged, 'I reckon that's the best thing. I'll give you a hand.' So Peggy tottered home between Josie and the young footman and Josie put her mother to bed, with Peggy still murmuring, 'Just indigestion, I tell you.' But an hour later she had another, more savage heart attack. Geoffrey Urquhart was told by Merridew, the butler now, and sent for a doctor.

Josie knelt by the bedside, holding her mother's hand and frightened as she had never been. Peggy was grey-faced and drawn and no longer talked of indigestion. Now she said weakly, 'You've got to go up North and see Billy Langley. I never wanted owt off him but his son, my David, and the good Lord saw fit to take him from me. I never wanted the yard or the money. But you're David's lass. You should have his inheritance. So get yourself up there and tell him who you are.'

'Just rest, Mam. The doctor's coming. Just rest.'

But Peggy Langley died only minutes later and before the doctor could arrive.

Josie passed through the next few days, culminating in the funeral, in a blur of grief and tears. One of those who tried to console her, though he grieved himself, was Albert Harvey. He had been hugely successful since leaving the Urquhart household and now admitted to owning four hotels and that he was shortly to cross the Atlantic to open another in America. He blinked in astonishment and admiration at Josie and told her, 'You've grown into a lovely young lady. Your mother must have been proud.' Josie managed a tremulous smile.

The day after Josie returned from the cemetery Merridew told her, 'Mrs Carrington wants to see you.' And seeing her down-in-the-mouth look change to one of apprehension, the butler reassured her: 'Don't worry, she hasn't got any complaint about you.' But Josie wasn't so sure. Mrs Carrington was the housekeeper, a woman in her early forties, dressed smartly but severely in a dress of dark grey, her rich brown hair drawn back severely in a bun. She was a strict disciplinarian and insisted on everything being done just so. Along with the butler she saw that the household ran as regular as a clock – and the accounts balanced to a halfpenny.

'Sit down, my dear.' She pointed to a chair when Josie entered her room and the girl perched on the edge of it. Mrs Carrington went on briskly, 'Now, when you were taken on here you spent your first two years helping in the nursery, then when you were stronger you moved to kitchen-maid and for the past year you've been housemaid. Mrs Urquhart spoke to me this morning and said she thought a bit of a change would do you good.' Elizabeth Urquhart had said, 'The girl needs something to keep her busy, to take her mind off this sad business and help her get over it.'

'Yes, ma'am?' Josie was both attentive and wary now. She was ready to take on anything – but what was it?

Mrs Carrington did not beat about the bush. 'You spend an hour or two every day doing Letty Barker's work because she's too idle to do it herself.' Josie blinked. She hadn't thought that had been noticed. And Letty *was* lazy; Josie helped her because she could not bear to see a job badly done. The housekeeper went on, 'And I want you to help me instead.' She waited, not for Josie's agreement, because Mrs Carrington was confident that 'gels' of that age did not know what was good for them anyway. But she expected an acknowledgment.

Josie knew the rules too: 'Thank you, ma'am.' But she liked the idea.

'Very well, off you go.' Mrs Carrington closed the interview. 'And tell Letty I want to see her. *Now!*'

So Josie found herself learning a host of new skills, those of managing a household and a budget. She was eager and quick to learn and soon was as happy as she had ever been. She had not forgotten her mother's last wish but Sunderland and the Langleys were nearly three hundred miles away. And the scene in the kitchen of the Langley house, her memory of the giant, huge and raging, was still only too clear. Sunderland and the Langleys could wait.

6

June 1904

Josie sang as she worked, running a smoothing iron over the pages of *The Times* to remove the creases put in it by the paper-boy. Merridew would then lay it on Geoffrey Urquhart's breakfast table. Betty Baynes, the children's nurse, came hurrying into the kitchen. The two children she cared for were those of the eldest Urquhart girl, now married to an army officer serving in India, where they were living. They had left their son and daughter in the care of Geoffrey and Elizabeth Urquhart.

Betty peered over Josie's shoulder. 'Is the announcement in? Their engagement, I mean?' Josie flipped over the pages good-naturedly, though she was just as interested as she had grown up with the youngest Urquhart daughter, now to be engaged, and was the same age, twenty. Betty squeaked, 'There it is!'

They read the announcement together and then Josie said, 'Not long for you, now.'

Betty laughed and blushed. 'Just two weeks.' That was when she would be married. 'And it can't come too soon.' She blushed again as Josie cocked a teasing eye at her. 'I didn't mean that! I was talking about getting away from Mrs Stritch.'

Mrs Carrington had left the Urquhart service a month ago to join a bigger, ducal household where there was more scope for her considerable talents. Mrs Stritch had replaced her as housekeeper. Now Betty muttered, 'Should be Witch, not Stritch.' And went on her way. She would have to leave service when she married and so would escape the attentions of the new housekeeper. Mrs Stritch was a bad-tempered bully who blamed her staff for her own incompetence.

There would be no such escape for Josie and she had already incurred the hatred of Mrs Stritch. She resented the position of trust the girl had enjoyed under Mrs Carrington and had swiftly engineered

Josie's return to being just a housemaid. More than that, she had a strong suspicion that Josie could measure her inefficiency, comparing her performance with that of her predecessor. That was intolerable and Josie would have to go.

Josie had sensed this already and now bit her lip in worry at Betty's reminder. Then a name in the columns of *The Times* caught her eye: Langley. *Langley*! She read: 'To James and Mrs Maria Langley of Monkwearmouth in Sunderland, a daughter, Charlotte . . .'

'Come on, my girl. Finished that paper yet?' Merridew appeared at her side.

'Yes, Mr Merridew. Just now.' Josie handed it to him and he bustled away. She was left, startled by the news she had read, but at least it took the place of her worry about her future for a while.

That afternoon was Josie's half-day and she went strolling in the summer sunshine. She cut a trim figure in her black skirt that nearly brushed the ground and her high-necked blouse, topped by a straw hat with a black ribbon. All were cast-offs, given to her by the Urquhart daughters and she had learned a lot about dress sense and fashion from Gabrielle, Mrs Urquhart's French maid. Several young men took a second look but Josie was lost in her thoughts.

So James Langley had married and had a child. James was her uncle and his daughter was Josie's cousin. It was strange to realise that she had a family so far away in the north. Now Josie noticed Betty Baynes was ahead of her, pushing a perambulator with the two Urquhart grandchildren in it. Josie absently quickened her pace as her thoughts ran on: A family, yes, but she had never seen the wife or the daughter and had only the vaguest recollection of the boy James had been when she last saw him in the Langley yard. While her grandfather – she remembered him only too well.

Betty Baynes was swinging the perambulator around to cross the road, taking advantage of a break in the traffic. Beyond her was a coster's barrow piled high with fruit and parked by the kerb. The coster was bawling his wares: 'Luvverly apples an' pears!' A motor car had passed and was rumbling away up the road while a cart loaded with sacks of coal was approaching, drawn by a trotting horse, its driver seated precariously on the shaft. But there was plenty of time for Betty to cross – until the car back-fired with a *crack*! like a gunshot. It was passing the cart and the trotting horse took fright, reared and threw its driver into the road. Then it broke into a gallop.

Josie halted, hands to her mouth, then hitched up her skirts and started to run, shrieking, 'Go on, Betty! Get out of the way!' Because the nurse had frozen in the middle of the road, clutching the handle of the perambulator and staring at the oncoming cart as if mesmerised. It hit the coster's barrow and hurled it onto its side, fruit scattering and bursting across road and pavement, and came on without checking. Josie saw the terrified horse would run through Betty and the perambulator, spilling her and the children as it had spilt the fruit.

Josie raced on, her little straw hat blowing away unnoticed, as the horse bore down on all of them. She reached Betty just in time to seize the handle of the perambulator in one hand and plant the other on Betty's back. Her impetus, and strength born of desperation, enabled her to thrust the girl and the perambulator clear. But then something, horse or shaft, struck her shoulder like a club and the world exploded.

Josie woke minutes later with a circle of faces above her. One face was nearer and belonged to a heavily built, tweed-suited man who was kneeling beside her. He held her wrist in one hand, his pocket-watch on its chain in the other. When he saw that her eyes were open he said, 'Ah! You're with us again.' He slid his watch into a waistcoat pocket. 'Your pulse is all right. I'm Dr Featherstone and I saw the whole affair. Don't move, but tell me how you feel.'

Josie felt dirty and embarrassed. And: 'My shoulder feels numb.'

Featherstone said drily, 'I'm sure it does. That was quite a clout you got from that horse. Can you move your shoulder?'

Josie tried and winced but succeeded.

Featherstone nodded. 'I'm sure it hurts but that's a good sign.'

'D'ye reckon she'll be all right, Doctor?' The question was put by the driver of the coal cart, anxiously twisting his cap in his hands.

Featherstone said grimly, 'I think so, but you're damned lucky not to be answering charges over this.' He turned back to Josie: 'I've sent someone to fetch a cab. I want to take you home and have a proper look at you. Where d'you live?'

When they arrived at the Urquharts' house they found one version of the story had preceded them. Betty Baynes, almost hysterical, had run home with the perambulator and told her tale through a flood of tears. 'If it hadn't been for Josie, me and those little lambs would ha' been killed!'

Featherstone examined Josie and found nothing worse than heavy bruising of her shoulder. The blow had been enough to hurl her to the ground and the fall had rendered her unconscious. 'She was very brave. No doubt about it, she saved your nursemaid and the children.'

He recommended that Josie should keep to her bed for a day and Geoffrey Urquhart, shaken by his beloved grandchildren's narrow escape from death, insisted on it. Josie had time to reflect, with a shudder, that she had almost died.

When Josie resumed her duties next day, Geoffrey Urquhart summoned her to his study and gave her a chair. Elizabeth, his wife, sat in another while he stood before the fireplace. He said, 'I owe you a debt I can never repay. But is there anything I can do for you?'

Josie was at a loss for a moment, but then she remembered her worry and answered, 'I'd be grateful if you'd keep me on, sir.'

Urquhart knew nothing of Mrs Stritch's tyrannical rule and machinations. Startled, he said, 'Of course we're keeping you on. What made you think we were not?'

Josie stumbled over her words. 'I thought – Mrs Stritch thinks I'm not giving satisfaction, sir.'

Urquhart glanced at his wife. 'You'd better have a word with Mrs Stritch.' Then to Josie, 'You don't need to worry about that. Now, if you haven't any other request—?' He paused.

Josie shook her head. 'No, sir.' And she was about to rise, thinking that was the end of it.

But Urquhart went on, 'Well, Mrs Urquhart and I have talked it over and we propose appointing you to take over the care of the children when Betty leaves to be married in two weeks' time. How do you feel about that?'

Josie smiled with relief and delight. 'That would be lovely, sir.'

That night before she slept Josie marvelled at her luck. She did not realise that she was favoured not by fortune but because of her own efforts. The Urquharts knew her too well and would never have agreed to her dismissal, and they had already determined to offer her the post of nursemaid; Josie's saving the lives of the children had only brought forward the interview by a day or two.

Josie was happy – and less inclined than ever to venture into the North Country, to the house of the fearsome William Langley to demand an inheritance that did not attract her. She had not forgotten

7

London, April 1907

'Hey! Hello – Josie?' The tall young sailor was in bell-bottom trousers and the linen collar outside his jumper had been washed until it was a pale blue. He was not sure as he confronted her. And Josie was uncertain of him. She blinked in the sunlight of a warm spring day. There was something about his eyes, his grin – but she was used to tentative approaches by young men as she took the Urquhart grandchildren for their walk. She held their hands, ready to edge around this sailor, but hesitated. The river of other strollers in Hyde Park washed around the little island they made. He went on, 'It is, isn't it, miss? Josie – I forget your second name now, but it was at Hallburgh Hall.'

She supplied, 'Josie Langley.' And now at the mention of the Hall she recalled the boy who had grown into the young man before her. 'And you're Bob Miller.'

He grinned delightedly. 'That's right. I thought I knew your face. O' course, it's been – how long? Over ten years?'

'More like fifteen.' Josie smiled in response to his grin. 'I was about eight then.' And she was twenty-three now, slender and long-legged, with hair glinting coppery in the sunlight.

'That's right,' Bob agreed. 'I was ten when my old man moved up to Yorkshire to work with his brother, my uncle.'

'And you said you were going to be a sailor.' She thought he looked fine in his uniform. The cap hid most of the shock of yellow hair but there was no concealing the bright, blue eyes.

'Joined when I was seventeen,' Bob replied absently, still amazed at how his childhood friend had grown into this pretty girl, neat and attractive in her nursemaid's grey dress and white apron. 'What about you?'

'I work in the Urquhart house. My mam wanted me with her when I left school – and I wanted to be with her. So I started working for the Urquharts and I've been there ever since.'

'How is your mother?' asked Bob, and commiserated when Josie told him of Peggy's death. He said, 'My father died three years back and his brother went the year before. My mum didn't have any relatives left but me so she moved down here and found a little house in Lambeth.'

They examined each other shyly as they talked. They made a handsome couple, the tall, tanned, good-looking young man and the slender, smiling girl. But the children, Hugh in his sailor suit and Louise in her cotton dress, had become restless. So they all walked, Bob and Josie talking until they paused to listen to the *oompah-oompah* of a little German band, then went on. When it was time for Josie to go home Bob lifted a finger to his cap in salute – and they agreed to meet again.

Over the next weeks they met whenever Josie had a half-day, or a few hours off – and Bob could get shore leave from his cruiser, which was being refitted in Chatham dockyard. They visited the zoo, and the museums when it rained, but mostly they walked, talked and laughed. Until one Sunday he took Josie home to meet his mother and to have tea. Dorothy Miller was obviously delighted with the girl. Then a week or so later Josie chanced to mention that she had given up her half-day one week, to cover for a girl who was not well, and so would have a full day off the following week.

Bob said, 'Here, tell you what, how about a run down to the Hall? It would be a day out and we could see how the old place looks now.'

Josie knew how it looked because she went there every year when the Urquhart family visited. But she could see how eager Bob was and so she only laughed and protested, 'All that way?'

'It will only take an hour on the train – or less.' And Bob pressed her, 'My treat.'

'Have you come into a fortune, then?' Josie teased him, but wondering, because sailors were only paid a few shillings a week.

Bob shrugged that off: 'I've done some long cruises and I've got some money saved. Don't you worry. Well?'

Josie would never have considered going unchaperoned into the country with a young man but this was Bob, the friend of her childhood, and she gave no thought to propriety.

So they left Waterloo on a blazing June day. After a fast journey by train, and a slow one on a country bus, they walked the last miles to the Hall. They did not enter by the main gates where the keeper lived in his lodge. Instead they passed into the grounds through a farmer's field, where black-and-white cows followed them, curious. They also took care to keep out of sight of the house and they did not see another soul.

It was noon when they arrived at the pool. Bob had removed his woollen jumper after leaving the bus to walk in his 'flannel', the short-sleeved sailor's shirt. Josie, in a crisp, white blouse and wide straw hat, was still too hot. She had brought a light lunch of sandwiches for both of them, with a bottle of beer for Bob and ginger beer for herself. She laid the bottles in the pool to cool.

'It's just like that last summer.' She took off her hat and set it aside.

'It's all o' that.' Bob wiped the sweat from his brow with the back of his hand and gazed yearningly at the pool, its surface moving slowly, eddying as the stream ran through it. 'I could do with a swim now but I haven't got a costume.'

'That didn't stop you before,' Josie challenged. 'You're scared.'

'So are you,' countered Bob.

They laughed as they remembered that time when as children they had bathed naked. Then they were suddenly shy and Josie remembered that this was not just her childhood friend but a virile young man. She looked away and said, 'Yes, I am.'

They laughed again then, and settled for paddling.

Lunch was eaten in the shade by the pool and both dozed for a while in the heat of the day. When Josie woke she found Bob watching her. She smiled at him and he came to her and kissed her. He whispered, 'My ship's bound for the Med in October. Will you marry me, Josie? Please?'

'Oh, Bob.' Josie clung to him. 'Yes.' She knew how she was going to miss him. 'Yes.' And she responded to his caresses on that warm summer evening, because she loved him and they were as good as married, riding with him on a tide of passion.

Bob bought Josie a ring that took most of his small savings. They planned a wedding in September but he came to the back door of the Urquhart house one evening in early August. Josie hurried him away into another doorway, out of sight of the house or prying eyes.

'I told you not to come here, Bob. We're not allowed "followers" hanging about.'

'I'm not hanging about. I just had to see you. The ship's sailing early. Not for the Med, this is just a shake-down cruise after coming out of the dockyard. I'll only be away a few weeks, but I don't know exactly when I'll be back for the wedding.'

Josie peered at his gloomy face. 'Well, we'll just have to postpone it.' She was miserable but saw he needed cheering, and he was the one going to sea. So she tucked her arm through his and told him, 'I've got a half-hour or so. I'll see you on your way.' She saw him on to his train to Chatham, where his ship was lying, kissed him and told him, 'I love you.'

It was two weeks later when his mother came to tell her that Bob had been lost at sea. They learnt later that he had been employed on boat-work in bad weather, had dived in to rescue a mate in difficulties and both had drowned. Josie recalled the boy who was Bob saying proudly when he was ten years old, ''Course I can swim! I'm going to be a sailor!' Now she took Dorothy Miller to her room and they wept together. And Josie told her, 'I'm expecting.'

Bob's mother held Josie in her arms and said, 'You call yourself Mrs Miller now. That's what he wanted. You've got your mother's ring what she left you. Put that on. And you come and live wi' me. We'll manage, the pair of us.' And then hopefully, 'And maybe later on you'll be able to get some work to help out.' Because her small pension would not keep both of them, let alone a baby, and their savings would not last long.

Josie would have to leave the Urquharts' service but she had known that when she accepted Bob's proposal. She had intended to leave on her marriage, not this way, but the result was the same. The Urquharts were sympathetic but there was no question of an unmarried, pregnant girl caring for their children. However, they gave her a good reference: 'Mrs Josie Miller has given excellent service as kitchen- and housemaid, children's nurse and governess and assisting the housekeeper.'

So Josie went to live in the little house in Lambeth, with its kitchen and scullery on the ground floor and two small bedrooms above, reached by a steep, narrow staircase. It was damp and cold because they had to be sparing with the coal they put on the fire, but Josie began to look forward and to sing again as she went about the house, awkwardly now with the child she was carrying. She knew the grim future that lay ahead of her as an unmarried mother but she faced it with courage. Then one day the singing was cut short.

Dorothy Miller heard the scream and then the bumping fall as Josie toppled down the narrow stairs. She called on the neighbours to help her and got Josie into bed, cared for her and cried with her when she told her, 'You've lost the baby, love.' She comforted her through those dark days: 'Never mind, you're young. It'll soon be Christmas and a New Year, a new start.'

Josie managed to smile.

There was no bright beginning to 1908. Josie had recovered but early in January she found Dorothy Miller lying face down across her bed and unconscious. Josie ran for a doctor and he came in his puttering little motor car and told her, 'Your mother-in-law has had a stroke.' Dorothy was unable to walk, would be bedridden for the rest of her life. He wound up the polished brass starting handle of his car then drove away, and Josie was left to face up to her future. It was bleak. Dorothy would need a lot of attention and there was not much money, scarcely enough to feed the pair of them. But Dorothy had cared for Josie, now it was Josie's turn.

She heard the old woman calling for her, her voice quavering now, and answered, 'Coming, Mother!'

8

February 1908

'Now then, gal! What can I get yer?' Jerry Phelan eyed Josie where she stood on the other side of the counter. This was in the snug, a little room in his pub, the Red Lion, where his elderly women customers could sip their glasses of port, though younger women were not unknown there. If any girl entered the Red Lion alone he automatically suspected she might be a prostitute trying to ply her trade and would turn her away. But he thought this one was too quietly dressed for that, and she didn't look the sort, so he suspended judgment for the moment and wiped his hands on his long, white apron.

'Are you the manager, please, sir?' Josie asked. She was breathless and flushed.

'I'm the licensed vittler what owns the place. This is a free house, but you won't get nothin' for nothin' here.' Jerry cracked the hoary old joke. He thought that the girl had spoken well and began to wonder what she was doing in his pub.

Josie said, 'I heard you wanted a barmaid to work evenings.' She had heard this from a neighbour and had run the quarter-mile to the Red Lion.

Jerry nodded. 'Yus.' He eyed her still, but doubtfully now. 'Have you ever done this sort o' work before?'

'No. I was a maid. And a nursemaid. I have a reference—' Josie fumbled it out of her bag.

But Jerry waved it aside. 'That don't count for nothing. Can you pull a pint? Keep a barful o' thirsty men supplied and be cheerful while you're at it?' He started to turn away as someone in the bar shouted, 'Hey, Jerry!'

Josie said, 'I can learn. And I'm used to working hard.' She called after him desperately, 'And I'm prepared to give you a try; why can't you let me have a chance? I need the job and it sounds as though you need *somebody*!'

That stopped Jerry. And then the voice shouted again, 'Let's have a pint here, Jerry, for the love o' God!'

He hesitated still for a second or two, then nodded. 'Right you are. I'll see what you're made of. But I warn yer, I only lost me last girl yesterday when she walked out without notice 'cos she'd got another job up West. I haven't even advertised for anybody yet and when word gets round there'll be a dozen or more gals asking. So you cope or you're out.'

'I'll cope.' This was said with a determination that made Jerry blink. He was not to know how badly this slim young woman needed the few shillings he would pay her.

He asked, 'When can you start?'

'Now?' Josie offered. So Jerry lifted the flap of the counter and let her in.

Josie had left Dorothy Miller in the care of a neighbour for a few hours. The old woman had been fed her supper and settled down by Josie and the neighbour only had to look in on her occasionally. That was the only way Josie could get out to earn and earning was vital. Dorothy's small pension could not keep the two of them and their little savings were being eroded daily. And now the landlord had put up the rent. Dorothy knew nothing of these problems.

'That's right, love, you get a breath o' fresh air,' she would murmur vaguely when Josie told her she had to go out for a while. 'A young gal like you shouldn't have to be cooped up wi' an old woman like me all day long.' Then Josie would go to collect or deliver the washing she did to help make ends meet, or hurry down to the Red Lion to work through till eleven at night, finishing by scrubbing out the bar. She could not take a full-time job or one that was any distance away from the little house because Dorothy had to be cared for.

Then when Josie returned home and settled the old woman down to sleep, Dorothy would ask, 'Did you enjoy yourself, love?'

And Josie would reply, 'I had a lovely time.'

Sleepily: 'That's good. You're like a daughter to me.'

Josie kept the job. She learned to run a bar, spot the troublemakers and deal with drunks. She learned so well that Jerry asked her to work full time, but she had to tell him that was out of the question, and why: 'I have to look after my mother-in-law.'

He rumbled, 'You're a good gal.' And from then on there was an extra shilling in her pay.

Josie worked unceasingly all through that spring and into the summer. It was in June that she went into Dorothy Miller's room in the morning to find her still and cold. She had died peacefully and quietly in the night.

The funeral swallowed the small insurance money that was paid out – Josie found the insurance book in a box of papers and old photographs. There was one photograph of Bob but she put it in the hands of the old woman where she lay in her coffin. That was a part of her life that was behind her now.

Josie was determined to quit the house as soon as she could because it held no happy memories for her. She wanted to go back into service, where she would live in, and it was a life she had been raised in, that she knew. She spent some of her small savings on two new dresses. She would need new shoes soon, too, but she decided they would have to wait.

'I'm sorry. We don't require anyone at this time.' The Urquharts were travelling on the Continent and their new butler – Merridew had retired – did not know Josie. But Mrs Stritch did and she was still housekeeper, sitting at his side as he interviewed her. He sent her away with the suggestion, 'You might try the Coveneys.' But the Coveneys did not need staff either.

Josie remembered Albert Harvey and went to one of his hotels to try to get in touch with him, only to be told that he was in America on business and would not be returning for some months. She went on searching for a 'place', walking from one large town house to another, while her little savings shrank. They had almost disappeared when the Smurthwaites took her on.

Mrs Smurthwaite, overweight and overbearing, warned Josie, 'You won't be able to laze about here like in those big houses, Mrs Miller.' Josie was using the name she had taken at Dorothy Miller's behest. It was the name the Urquharts used on the reference they gave her which she had produced for Mrs Smurthwaite. That lady now went on, 'You'll have to pull your weight here. My late husband always insisted on that: "Servants have to pull their weight," he said.' Josie learned that Mrs Smurthwaite often quoted her husband, deceased for almost twenty years.

It was a much smaller household than that of the Urquharts. There was just one maid besides Josie. Daisy was a woman in her fifties who looked still older, worn out by years of service. Josie soon found that Daisy was lethargic so most of the work was left to her. Pilling, the butler, did little except care for the wine and was generally only half sober. He told Josie, 'That husband of hers was nothing. He inherited all his money from an uncle up North. There's a son, Hubert, but he's out in Monte Carlo at the moment and I've never seen him. Daisy's been here donkey's years and she knows him. She says he spends most of his time in France and talks the lingo like a native. A French chef told her that. He came here one night to cook for a special do and him and this Hubert rattled away at each other.' He squinted blearily at Josie. 'And Daisy says they can't keep a young girl here long on account of Hubert, so you be warned. He won't worry me. I've only had this job a month and I'm on the lookout for another.' But he couldn't look Josie in the eye when he said this and she suspected he knew he would have trouble finding another post.

But Josie told herself she had a roof over her head, the food was reasonably good and she was being paid £24 a year. It was better than walking the streets looking for work. She tried to settle in but after a month there came news that made her uneasy. Pilling said, 'We're moving up north for a few months. She wants to live in the country place the old feller left. All the toffs go off to the country in August but they go to shoot or hunt. She's going just to imitate them. But if she's hoping to go to the hunt ball she'll be disappointed.' He laughed raucously.

Josie did not want to go. When she learned that the house was only a mile or two outside Sunderland she almost gave in her notice. But then she told herself to be sensible. She need not go to the town. On the rare occasions she could be spared from her duties she could probably visit Newcastle or Durham. And she did not want to look for a job again so soon. She had saved little and needed a deal more behind her before she left Mrs Smurthwaite. So in August she travelled north.

She was not alone. Hubert Smurthwaite was returning from Monte Carlo after squandering the money his mother had given him. And Reuben Garbutt was about to exact his revenge on the Langleys.

9

August 1908

Reuben Garbutt sat in a pub in Whitechapel and told the villainous man beside him, 'Get rid of them.' Then he handed over a fistful of sovereigns and walked out. He had paid for murder. Garbutt was thirty-six years old now, tall, thick-set and powerful, with a square, thin-lipped face and a wide moustache. His dark eyes stared magnetically and he was attractive to women. He knew this and used them.

He was now an apparently legitimate businessman with interests in jewellery shops, property and a transport company, one of the first to use a large number of the new motor lorries. He had an office in the City and a London home in St John's Wood. He looked the part in a check morning-coat suit that fitted him perfectly, over a single-breasted waistcoat, a shirt with a high collar and a silk tie. His bowler hat had a curly brim, his gloves were a soft kid and his valet had polished his shoes until they glittered.

In truth he could have succeeded honestly because he had a flair for spotting a business opportunity. But crime was in his nature so he prospered from his activities in theft, receiving, extortion, blackmail and fraud. He had murdered in his time but now he used paid assassins.

He took a cab to King's Cross station and then boarded a train to Sunderland. There he hired another cab to take him to Owen Packer's office. There were a number of brass plates outside the door because Packer dabbled in various agencies, one being insurance and another, shipping coal. The plate for the latter read: 'Coal Carriers Ltd.' But the one above stated: 'Owen Packer. Solicitor.' That was his profession. He was skinny and cadaverous with a drooping moustache and yellow teeth shown in a perpetual smirk. Some years before he had successfully defended a criminal working for Garbutt. The villain, charged with robbery with violence, got off when Packer bribed a prosecution witness to change his testimony. Garbutt had then recruited Packer as his agent in the North-East – and particularly to report on the Langley family.

Garbutt sat in Packer's office and demanded, 'What's the position with the Langley yard now?'

Five years before, Packer had told him that orders for ships were few because of the depression, and added: 'The old man is trying to keep his men on when there's nothing for them to do. He needs money.'

Garbutt had responded, 'We'll lend him the money at a cheaper rate than the banks will.' Old William Langley had jumped at the chance. The loan came from a finance company, 'Shipbuilders Finance Ltd', and the only unusual condition was that James, William's son, should be manager of the yard. As this was already the case there seemed no problem. William did not know that the finance company was owned by Reuben Garbutt.

There had been other loans and Garbutt had come to Sunderland now to arrange one more. He sat in Packer's office, examined the document the solicitor had prepared, nodded his satisfaction and tossed it on to the desk. 'Good.' He was close to springing the trap now. He said, 'I need more information from inside the house. What staff is there?'

Packer shifted his long, skinny body in his chair, always uneasy under the piercing stare from Garbutt's cold eyes. 'Very few. There's a cook goes in daily and a girl to help her. Only the one maid lives in.'

'What about her? Who is she? What's she like? Any young feller seeing her?' Garbutt fired the questions at the solicitor.

Packer pulled at his drooping moustache, remembering. 'Rhoda Wilks is her name. Not much on looks. Getting on, over thirty. No young chap so far as I know – shouldn't think it likely now, at her age. She's quiet. I've never seen her smile. That's about all.'

Garbutt thought it might be enough, and early the next morning he went to look over the Langley house. It was built of red brick and formed the back wall of a square, the front of which was a main road leading down to the shipyards. The two sides of the square were terraces of houses that were once occupied by the professional classes, but they had moved out long ago and now the houses were tenements, with four or more families living in each of them.

Garbutt walked in a semicircle through side streets to arrive behind the house and began to watch the back of it. He was dressed now like a well-paid clerk in a plain, but good, dark blue suit. He soon knew the routine of the place. First the old cook and her assistant, a girl barely fourteen years old, arrived. Not long afterwards he saw the maid, in her black dress and white apron, empty ashes into a bin outside the back door after cleaning out the fires. She was dark and sallow, plain as Packer had said, and unsmiling.

All this he saw through the back gate of the house, always left open during the day. When he returned to the front of the house he watched it from the window of a public house, the Collier Lad, as he sipped rum and coffee and men hurried in and out on their way to work. Twice he witnessed James Langley leaving for work with his dark-haired wife and daughter, walking down the road towards the Langley shipyard. He also saw a lorry loaded with sacks of coal pull up outside the pub. Its driver and his mate tramped into the bar to be welcomed by the publican. They bought pints of beer and ate breakfast, the sandwiches they had brought with them. This, too, was obviously a routine.

Garbutt's next step was not so easy. He could not stay in the pub indefinitely because that would arouse curiosity. Instead, after a half-hour, he left the Collier Lad and walked through the streets surrounding the house, not strolling but striding as if on some business. He still contrived to pass the front and the back of the house every five minutes or so. He did this daily, morning till night, until on the fourth day he saw Rhoda Wilks leave the back door of the Langley house at mid-morning, a coat over her black dress and the white cap discarded for a hat. She carried a basket and was plainly on some errand. Five minutes later, her shopping done and on her way back to the house, she collided with a young man and knocked from his hands the papers he was carrying.

'Oh! I'm sorry!' she apologised, sure it was her fault, and crouched to pick them up.

Garbutt, who had engineered the mishap, went down on one knee beside her. 'No harm done.' He smiled at her, took the papers from her and helped her to her feet with a hand under her arm. 'But I'm looking for Thompson's yard – I've got some business there – can you tell me the way?'

'Oh! Aye, it's down here.' The road to Thompson's ran past the Langley house, as Garbutt knew. A minute later they were walking side by side and he was carrying her basket and chatting cheerfully, telling her all about himself. 'I'm Reuben Graham and I've been sent up here to work. I'm living in lodgings where they're all old people. It's nice to meet somebody young like yourself I can talk to.'

He had no trouble meeting her again. The discipline in the Langley house was easy and Rhoda could usually get out for an hour or two in the evening. Garbutt courted her assiduously. At those meetings and on her half-days he learnt that she had married sisters in Yorkshire and Cumberland and she envied them. He told her his 'business' was 'Gathering bits o' news for my boss in London. Same as them fellers that watch racehorses training, businessmen watch what the other fellers are up to so they can get one ahead o' them.' And when he saw a shadow of doubt cross her face he said softly, 'All's fair in love and war.' And he stroked her cheek.

He plied her with gifts, affection, tenderness and promises. When he eventually asked her to go away with him for a weekend she agreed, knowing it was wrong but by then not caring because one of the promises was of marriage. She was desperately afraid of growing old as a spinster. Rhoda faked a letter from her 'poorly' sister in Yorkshire, pleading with her to visit. Maria Langley, James's wife and the woman of the house, gave her permission – and money for her fare. Rhoda went only as far as Newcastle. Garbutt bought her fine dresses and underwear but warned her, 'Don't wear any of them back in Monkwearmouth. They're for your bottom drawer.' Wearing a gold ring bought by Garbutt, she passed as his wife in the hotel. He made passionate love to her for two nights and when she went back to the Langley house she was his.

He promised her a good life when they married but insisted that she played her part now and kept their romance secret: '. . . If you love me. All you have to do is to write to me once a week and tell me what's going on in the house, what the old man and his son are up to, what they're talking about.' So she returned to her duties outwardly the same young woman, though she often smiled dreamily, but now she was a spy in the house. Slowly, imperceptibly but surely, she began to change.

It was a month later when Reuben Garbutt sat in his office in London and read the letter from Owen Packer. Then he smiled and burned it, because he kept nothing, either in his house or his office, that could connect him with any criminal activities.

He took a train from King's Cross and headed north again. The solicitor had said depression in the shipbuilding industry on the north-east coast was appalling and the Langley yard was without an order for a ship or any work at all. Rhoda Wilks had reported an overheard conversation between William and James Langley that had confirmed this. She had also sent some interesting details of the family routine. Her letters were written in a childlike hand, misspelt and rambling, but they held nuggets of information. Garbutt decided his time had come. Now he would exact revenge for the death of his father and his family's humiliation.

'I wondered if you were ever going to come back again! It's been so long!' Rhoda Wilks cried out, and ran into his arms when he met her in Monkwearmouth that evening. He had not travelled to the North Country for months – during which she had yearned for him. He could read it in her face, knew it from the way she pressed her body against him. Rhoda was expecting a life of dignity and pleasure as Garbutt's wife, but more than that, she was a slave to his animal attraction.

They stood hidden in the shadows of an alley in the dusk and he kissed her hungrily and asked, though he knew the answer, 'When is your next half-day off?' He did not want to advertise how well he knew the details of her life.

'Tomorrow.'

So the next day he took her to Newcastle, to shop expensively and dine luxuriously, then to a hotel room and its bed. He questioned her gently in the languorous aftermath of their lovemaking. She complained to him, talking of James Langley, 'His wife keeps on at me. There's no satisfying her. The only peace I get is when she goes out. First thing every day she walks down the road with him as far as the yard; takes the little lass with her an' all.'

'Their daughter?'

'Aye, Charlotte.' Rhoda's whining softened. 'She's a bonny little bairn.'

Garbutt had learned all he needed to know.

When he took Rhoda back to the Langley house, stopping the cab two or three streets away, she complained before she got down: 'How much longer do I have to work here?'

He kissed her. 'Not long now.'

The next morning Garbutt was in the bar of the Collier Lad, watching the front of the Langley house. James and his wife Maria, with their four-year-old daughter Charlotte, left the house as usual. But this morning and the next the coal lorry arrived late, so that Garbutt did not have time to act. He waited in the pub on the third morning with increasing impatience.

In the house Maria, James Langley's olive-skinned, dark and attractive young wife, stood in the hall. They had met in Argentina when James was seeking an order for the yard to build a ship. Her parents had opposed the marriage because James was an Englishman, and turned their backs on Maria. But she had clung to her devoted husband. Now she was dressed for outdoors in a long tweed ulster, a wide-brimmed hat on her piled hair. She stooped and wiped the damp nose of her daughter Charlotte. Then she straightened to say to William Langley in her fluent but stilted English, 'I think she should stay at home today. She has a cold and there is a chill wind. I will ask Rhoda to look after her.'

'No, she can stay in my office with me.' William took Charlotte's hand. He added bitterly, 'There isn't much to do.' He had not long returned from a trip abroad spent in a fruitless search for orders for the yard.

Maria hesitated, still amazed at the way the old man was prepared to give up his time for this child. But then she pulled on her gloves and said, 'I do not like saying this again, but that girl Rhoda is more and more slipshod and insolent. I have warned her many times but she only gets worse. She cares for Charlotte well enough but the rest of the time—' She shook her head despairingly. 'I think I will advertise in the newspaper for a children's nurse. Charlotte needs someone now who can give her lessons.'

'It's true enough there's little to do,' said James as he came into the hall. He wore the old suit he kept for working in the yard, though the only toil there was in maintenance. He had heard his father's remark and now he added quietly, 'We can't keep the men on much longer, Father, with no work for them.'

William said heavily, 'Aye, we'll have to lay some more of them off, but not yet.'

Maria intervened then, having heard too many of these conversations. 'We must hope things will improve. Come now, James, or you will be late.'

They were late. The big lorry, loaded with sacks of coal, had been drawn up outside the Collier Lad for a minute or more. Its driver and his mate had got down and gone into the pub where they sat in a corner with their sandwiches and beer.

Reuben Garbutt, standing at the window of the pub, saw James and Maria emerge from the house. He sucked in his breath. *At last*! He left his post by the window and wound through the few idlers still in the bar – the blare of the shipyard sirens had summoned the workers ten minutes ago – and strode across the pavement outside.

The lorry was a big Commer with a chain drive, and Garbutt knew the type. One of his 'straight' ventures was a haulage business that used a number of lorries. Some of these were Commers and Garbutt had learned to drive them because he thought the skill might one day prove useful in his criminal activities. Now he swung the starting handle, hearing the beat of the engine, smelling its fumes.

In the bar of the Collier Lad the driver froze with a sandwich halfway to his mouth, then looked at his mate and asked, 'What was that?'

'Sounded like the Commer!' his mate replied. Then they were both running for the door to the street.

Garbutt drove the lumbering lorry down the road that ran to the river and the shipyards which lined its banks. On the left-hand side were the gable ends of the terraced streets which all ran down to the shipyards. On the right were the ranked, blank walls of the yards. The road was almost empty now, just a woman here and there, with her shawl around her shoulders, hurrying up the road towards the little shops in Dundas Street. And a tall, suited figure that was James Langley, his wife on his arm.

In the house William Langley said, 'Damn!' He had gone into the room he used as his office and found James's notebook lying on his desk. He had left it there the previous evening when he had been discussing the yard's affairs with his father. William took it to the door and looked out into the hall. He was just in time to see Rhoda Wilks come out of the kitchen. William called, 'Rhoda!' Then he went on, 'I've just found this and Mr James will be needing it. Take it down to the yard and see that he gets it, please.'

'Aye, Mr Langley.' Rhoda took the notebook from him, snatched her shawl from its hook in the kitchen and set off, calling to the cook, 'I'm away down to the yard on an errand for Mr Langley.' That was in case Maria returned before she did and started asking for her, the nit-picking cow.

Garbutt began to accelerate, slowly because the Commer was heavy and slow, but steadily it increased in speed. His eyes were fixed on his quarry. He could have paid any of a dozen assassins to carry out this deed – as he had hired them for the purpose before – but this he wanted to execute by his own hand. He had sworn an oath and waited for so long, now he would savour this as his reward.

James and his wife had been only two hundred yards ahead when he started after them. Now he was almost on them; he saw their white faces turn towards him and he swung the wheel to run the lorry into them. They stood between the hammer of the lorry and the anvil of the shipyard wall.

The noise of the approaching engine caused James and Maria to turn together, their heads jerking around as if at the tug of a string. For a moment they saw no danger as the lorry trundled down the road as if to pass them by. But then Maria glimpsed the face of the driver up in the cab, glaring down at her. The malevolence in his expression filled her with an instinctive fear and she screamed and clung to James. He acted as he saw the nose of the lorry swing towards them, leaping to one side and taking Maria with him. But Garbutt was just as quick to twist the wheel.

Rhoda Wilks, coming out into the road, saw it happen, saw the lorry swerve and mount the pavement, swerve again. Then there was the crash and the screams, the grinding of crumpling metal and the rumbling of broken, falling brickwork as the wall gave way. There was the hideous sight that went with the sounds. And then the silence. She stood, petrified with horror, her hands gripping the shawl pressed to her mouth.

Garbutt had been thrown forward on to the steering wheel by the impact and his face barely escaped breaking through the screen. He sat in that silence for some seconds, winded and hugging painful ribs. Then he remembered his situation. The door of the cab had sprung open and he half fell out on to the pavement. He looked at his handiwork and only then realised that the child was not with her parents. He swore, then turned his back on the scene and broke into a run.

At the end of the road a woman stood with her face obscured by a shawl held to her mouth. He almost ran past her, then realised it was

Rhoda Wilks. He stopped, panting, and demanded, 'What the hell are you doing here?'

Rhoda was shaking. She stared at him, her eyes wide with shock, and whined, 'You killed them.'

'It was an *accident*!' He turned quickly and stood beside her, looking back the way he had come, as the driver of the lorry and his mate came running up from the Collier Lad.

They paused beside Garbutt for a moment, staring down the road, and asked, 'What happened?'

Garbutt answered, 'It just ran into the wall. I thought I saw some people there—' But the two men were already running again, towards the wreckage.

Garbutt spun Rhoda around. He had to talk to her and he had to get away. He saw that she would serve as cover for him and linked her arm through his. 'You're coming with me as far as the station.' His tone and his grip on her arm, allied to her state of shock, quelled any thought of protest. But his thoughts were for later, when she had recovered from the shock. He had to keep her quiet. So as he hustled her up Charles Street he repeated, 'It was an accident! I was down this way and thought I might get to see you for a few minutes. Then I spotted the lorry. I just wanted to try my hand at driving one o' those things, for a bit of a lark. But when I tried to steer clear of them, he jumped in my way! You saw me swerve then?' It was an instruction as much as a question.

Rhoda had seen the lorry swerve. She sobbed, the tears coming now. 'I saw that, aye, but—'

'Never mind "but"! I'll have no buts!'

'You're hurting me!' Rhoda's face twisted in pain.

Garbutt did not relax his savage grip on her arm. 'Just remember that! It was an accident! And keep your trap shut! You hear me?'

Rhoda whispered, 'Aye.'

Now he loosened his hold on her. As they approached Monk-wearmouth station he changed his tone, became softer, cajoling. 'You don't want to get me into trouble for something that wasn't my fault, just a joke that went wrong. And we're going up in the world, I promise you. It won't be long till you can hand in your notice there and I'll come and fetch you away. Just be patient and keep quiet a bit longer. You'll be glad you waited.' He stopped outside the station, took her in his arms and lied, 'You know I love you.'

Rhoda wiped at her tears. 'Aye.' She had to believe him now.

In the train racing south, Reuben Garbutt stretched luxuriously in a first-class compartment. 'You've almost finished them,' he told himself. 'There's only the old man left now. When he's gone the yard will go with him, I'll see to that.'

When Rhoda Wilks returned to the Langley house she found it in shock and mourning. The old cook and her young assistant were wailing in the kitchen. The cook pulled her head out of her apron to tell Rhoda, 'Mr James and his missus are deid! It's awful. Mr Langley's in his office. He's been asking for you.'

So Rhoda went to him, apprehensive because of her knowledge, rehearsing the story Garbutt had repeated to her before he boarded his train. When she tapped at the door and entered she found William sitting at his desk with the young Charlotte in his arms. His face was drawn with grief as he looked over the child's head. 'There you are, Rhoda. You've heard?'

'I was there just after it happened, Mr Langley. I saw it, then everything went black. I think I must have been wandering the streets until I found myself in Nelson Square.' She felt tears coming again.

William Langley said, 'I understand. I want you to care for Charlotte. Will you do that for me, please?'

'Oh, aye, Mr Langley.' Rhoda took Charlotte from him and held the orphaned child to her breast. 'I'll look after the bairn.' And she left him to his grief.

In Lisbon, Tom Collingwood seized the two seamen who were grappling on the fo'c'sle and parted them. He threw one to his left and the other to his right. Both of them sprawled on the deck, bloodstained, panting and cursing. Tom rasped, 'I'll not have this on any ship of mine! We've got steam up and we're on the point of sailing! Any more trouble and I'll put that man ashore and leave him here to rot!'

They knew him, as did many another seamen now, to be a fair man but one who meant every word he said. They silently went back to work. Then, as Tom strode aft to the bridge of his ship, the second mate came hurrying. 'Cable for you, Captain.' Tom read it and the mate saw shock in his face and asked, 'Bad news?'

'Aye.' The cable was from William, informing Tom that James and

Maria had been killed by a lorry. Tom could guess at the old man's grief. 'The sooner we get home, the better.'

There was an inquest in Monkwearmouth but the few bystanders who had witnessed the incident had done so from a distance. They did not recognise the man who had stolen the lorry and their description – tall, dark and with a moustache – could have applied to hundreds of men in the area. The verdict was manslaughter by person or persons unknown.

After the funeral William told himself through his heartbreak that his grandchild Charlotte was his responsibility now. Her mother's people in Argentina had not wanted her to marry an Englishman and had never communicated with her after her marriage. William resolved to do his best for Charlotte, to bring her up as her parents would have wished. First of all, Maria had said she wanted a nurse for the child and that she would advertise in the *Sunderland Daily Echo*. He needed a housekeeper now, too. Someone to take the place of Maria? No one could do that. But he would advertise.

10

'And who the hell are you?' Hubert Smurthwaite was close on forty years old, bulky and with oiled hair plastered to his skull. His mother had gleefully announced that he would be arriving. The cabman who brought him the two miles from Sunderland station carried Hubert's case into the hall, collected his fare and sniffed at a small tip. As the cab rolled away behind its tired horse, Hubert tossed his light overcoat at Josie. 'New, aren't yer?'

'Josie Miller, sir. Yes, sir,' she answered.

Smurthwaite's little eyes roamed over her, looking through the neat grey dress and seeing the body beneath – and the gold band on her finger. 'You're married, then.'

'Widowed, sir.'

'You'll know all about it, then,' Smurthwaite leered. But at that point he saw his mother emerge from the drawing room and he shoved past Josie to go to her. 'Mummy! I'm so pleased to see you! Let's have some tea.' And he called over his shoulder, 'You fetch it!'

'Yes, sir,' answered Josie. She shook out the balled overcoat and as she did so a leather card-case fell from its folds. It lay open, and as Josie stooped to pick it up she saw that one of the cards, the little rectangles of printed pasteboard a gentleman used to introduce himself, had slipped out. The name on the card was 'Commander H. Sackville, RN'. Josie assumed the card had come from an acquaintance of Hubert's and replaced card and case in the inside pocket of the overcoat.

She was not to know that, in Nice, a middle-aged Frenchwoman was searching for Commander Hubert Sackville, who spoke French like a native and had promised to marry her. On the strength of that she had lent him the dowry she had saved, to buy a house for them, as he would not come into his inheritance for a month or so. Hubert had invested the money in the casino at Monte Carlo.

Josie hung up the coat and saw that her hands were shaking – with anger. But she told herself that Hubert was a bag of wind and all talk and she must not allow herself to be upset. Her hands were steady when she took the tea into the drawing room.

'—so if you could let me have a few quid—' Hubert broke off as Josie entered with the tray. He snapped at her, 'Put it down there,' and nodded at the small table near the chesterfield where he and his mother sat. Josie set down the tray, conscious that he was watching her. He ordered, 'And get out.' Josie obeyed.

She could sum up Hubert now. He was begging money from his mother and when he got it he would go. That would be good riddance. Josie went on with her duties, encouraged. She was still doing most of Daisy's work but coping with it. Her only recreation was to walk in the lanes around the house. Sunderland was two miles away and neither omnibus nor train connected the house to it. That did not matter because Josie had no desire to visit Sunderland, let alone Monkwearmouth where lived the giant. By the time the Smurthwaite household moved back to London in May for the summer 'season', she would have saved more money and be ready to seek another position. She had precious little saved now.

Hubert got some money from his mother but he did not leave. She gave him too little for him to do so because she wanted him at home for a while to keep her company. Hubert grumbled but stayed. For the next three days he drank through the morning, slept through the afternoon and started on the brandy before dinner. When Josie passed him during his waking moments, he watched her.

On the fourth morning Josie was making his mother's bed and thought she was alone on the upper floor when he stole up behind her and put his arms around her. Josie gasped with shock and flailed her arms as she tried to break free. Her elbow connected with Hubert's nose and she felt the jar painfully. A vase went flying from the bedside table and smashed. Hubert yelped, released her and clapped his hand to his nose as it began to bleed. Josie ran out and down to the kitchen.

She expected the summons, which came within minutes. Mrs Smurthwaite was judge while Hubert, a bloodstained handkerchief still held in one hand, was prosecutor. 'I told her she'd not made your bed properly and she told me to go to hell. Then she threw the vase into my face and ran off.' He pointed to the chunks of pottery that were all that was left of the vase.

Mrs Smurthwaite sucked in a hissing breath of disapproval and eyed Josie. 'Well, what have you to say?'

'It's not true, ma'am. I was making your bed and Mr Hubert came up behind me and—'

'How dare you!' Mrs Smurthwaite cut in. 'How dare you accuse my son!'

'She's a liar as well as a lunatic,' Hubert put in. 'Or maybe she's drunk. We seem to be getting through a lot of whisky.'

'I've a mind to call the police.' Mrs Smurthwaite glared at Josie.

'Oh, I wouldn't do that,' Hubert advised. 'After all, she's a widow. We don't want to be too hard on her. And we haven't got a witness so it would be my word against hers.' His eyes, gleaming and cunning, were fixed on Josie.

'They would believe a gentleman, of course,' said his mother indignantly.

'Of course,' Hubert agreed, 'but it's the laws of evidence, Mother.'

'I see,' she said vaguely, but not seeing at all. Josie saw only too well. If she complained to the police it would be her word against Hubert's. She did not have a witness, either.

Mrs Smurthwaite said, 'Then she'll just have to go. Today – now. I won't have her under my roof a moment longer.' And to Josie: 'You realise you are very lucky my son has decided not to press charges. I'll give you a week's pay and you can pack your things and go. Off with you.' She waved her hand in dismissal.

Josie was ready to weep, but not in front of Hubert. She wanted to fight her case but knew that if she tried she would be forcibly ejected. Hubert would like the chance to do it. So she kept her head high, with the proud lift to it she had always had. She looked down and through Hubert and his mother, turned her back on them and walked away. She told herself she would have had to have left anyway, knew she could not have gone on living under the same roof as Hubert.

A carter come from Sunderland called at the house every day to sell fresh vegetables. An hour later he lifted Josie's portmanteau on to his cart and climbed up on to his seat. Josie was about to join him when Hubert came out of the house and gloated: 'I hope this has taught you a lesson, my girl.'

'I am not your girl,' replied Josie. 'And you are not a gentleman. You are a bully and weak. You live off your mother and when she dies the money will run through your fingers and you will die in poverty and alone. Or you will steal and go to jail and die there.'

Hubert stared at her as if struck as she climbed up to join the carter on his seat. Josie's words planted in him an awful fear. He tried to laugh and said, 'Rubbish!'

Josie said only, calmly and with certitude, 'We will see.'

Hubert's laughter died. The carter cracked his whip and the cart rolled away down the drive. Hubert shouted after them shrilly, 'Witch!'

The carter glanced sidewise at Josie uneasily. 'How do you know what you told him?'

Josie grinned at him, feeling better for a while. 'I'm not a witch! I just told him what he is and what may well happen because of what he is.'

Now the carter grinned with her, relieved. 'You certainly put the wind up him.' And they laughed together.

Josie kept on a cheerful face during the long drive into the town, despite her worries. And despite her approaching Monkwearmouth, the home of the Langleys – and William in particular. She saw the smoke hanging over the river where the ships were built and the tall cranes rising stilt-like above the houses. That stirred memories. Then, as the sun dipped towards the inland horizon, a fog swept in from the cold grey sea. Josie shivered at the chill of it as it lay damply on her.

They entered the town by the Newcastle road and as they passed a public house called the Wheatsheaf the carter said, 'My stable is just at the back o' here, but I'll take you on to Monkwearmouth station. You can get a train there and change at the central station for Durham and London.' A minute or two later he set her down outside the station with its Grecian columns, but he shook his grey head over her. 'You've a lang way to gan, bonny lass.' Then he drove away.

Josie was left alone in the mist and the gathering dusk and the railway smell of smoke and steam.

'D'you have the foreclosure papers?' Reuben Garbutt barked the question as he strode into Packer's office in Sunderland and slammed the door shut behind him. He would wait no longer. He had struck the Langleys a terrible blow, now he would deliver another that would destroy them. He spent some time with the solicitor and finally arrived at the Langley house in the evening, walking up the carriage drive.

William had taken to dining early because the old cook had given in her notice, saying she 'couldn't cope no more', and the girl had left to take a job in a shop. There was still neither housekeeper nor nurse. William had put an advertisement in the *Sunderland Daily Echo* a dozen times and seen a dozen or more applicants but he had turned them all away. None of them met his exacting standards, particularly for the care of his granddaughter. So Rhoda Wilks was producing makeshift meals with much grumbling. She had told all of this to Garbutt in the frequent letters she wrote to him.

'Lord! What are you doing here?' Rhoda, in grubby white apron and cap, opened the front door to Garbutt and gaped when she saw him standing at the head of the steps. The thick fog that had drifted in from the sea in the late afternoon hung around the house, deepening the darkness, grey, damp and smelling of coal smoke. Behind Garbutt lay the garden inside its ornamental iron railings in the middle of the square. Rhoda could only see it was there by the fuzzy yellow bowls of the gas lamps set at its corners. The square was deserted but it could have held a hundred strollers and they would not have been seen.

'I told you I'd come for you.' Garbutt saw her surprise and grinned at her. 'Aren't you going to let me in?'

Rhoda glanced nervously back along the hall, then took a pace out on to the steps, pulling the door to behind her. She said, voice lowered, 'He'll hear you! He's just finished his dinner and he's having a glass o' whisky.'

'It's him I want to see.' Garbutt reached past her to set his hand on the door, but he, too, spoke in a hoarse whisper. 'You don't need to show me in. I'll introduce myself.' He shoved the door open and herded Rhoda into the hall ahead of him. 'You pack your duds. You're coming away with me.'

Rhoda whispered, incredulous but happy, '*Now?*'

'In about ten minutes. That's all it will take me to finish him.'

Rhoda paused at that, one foot on the stairs. 'What d'you mean? What are you going to do?'

'None o' your business. I'm settling a score. I've waited and schemed for twenty years to finish off the Langleys and now I'm going to do it.

Get on with you!' And he gave her a shove to start her up the stairs. 'Don't keep me waiting.' Their whispers scurried around the hall and then ceased, were replaced by the swift, repeated creaking as Rhoda climbed the stairs.

Garbutt crossed the hall to the dining room, opened its door and walked in. It was a long room with pictures of ships built in the Langley yard on the walls. The curtains were drawn and light came from a gas chandelier in the middle of the ceiling. The long polished table was bare, its cloth drawn, and at its head sat William Langley. Garbutt saw that his face was thin and haggard now, his hair grey. He peered at Garbutt and asked, puzzled, 'Who are you?' He started to rise.

'Please! Don't get up.' Garbutt advanced into the room, smiling. 'I am from the Shipbuilders' Finance Company – in fact, I *am* the Shipbuilders' Finance Company. We've lent you quite a lot of money in the past.'

William still stood. 'Yes, of course. I wonder why Rhoda didn't announce you? Never mind. What can I do for you, Mr . . . ?' He held out his hand and waited.

Garbutt did not take it, but answered, 'You don't remember me but that's not surprising because I was only a boy of fifteen when you sacked my father.' He paused, waiting, and when William stared at him, a confused old man now, Garbutt shouted at him, 'You don't even *remember*! My father, my family, me – you turned us all away to starve and you've forgotten us like we were so many bloody rats! My name is Garbutt! *Reuben Garbutt*! And you sacked my father, *Elisha*! Does *that* mean anything to you?'

It did. William withdrew his hand and slowly sat down. He replied wearily, 'Yes, I turned him out because he was stealing from me. I'm sorry it happened, sorry for you and your family, but I do not regret what I did. I think I acted correctly, even generously, because if the case had been taken to court he would have been jailed.'

Garbutt glared at him. 'I knew you wouldn't have any regrets but I think you'll have some now. The money Shipbuilders' Finance lent you, that *I* lent you – I want it back.'

William blinked, puzzled. 'You mean repayment of some of it? Now?'

'I mean repayment of *all* of it! Now!' And Garbutt pulled from his pocket the sheaf of documents drawn up by Packer and threw them on the table. They slid along its polished surface, spreading like a fan to stop in front of William. Garbutt sucked in a deep breath, showing his teeth in a smile. He went on softly as William stared down at the papers, 'Those are notices of foreclosure. Under the terms of the loans, they were liable to be called in if James ever ceased to be manager of the yard. And now he's dead.' He leaned forward to thrust his face close to William's. 'I reckon there's enough there to bankrupt you and finish Langley's altogether.' Then he straightened and laughed.

The harsh laughter went on for some seconds as he stood over the old man. But then he shut his mouth and recoiled as William suddenly set hands on the table and shoved himself to his feet. For a moment he was again the William Langley he had been, tall and broad. Deep-voiced, he roared, 'Get out! You're a damned villain like your father! But you'll get your money! The Langley yard will stay for Charlotte! You won't get it! I'll see you in hell—' He broke off, his face contorting in agony as he clutched at his chest. His knees gave way and he collapsed in the chair.

Garbutt stooped to peer into the twisted face, the staring eyes, then he backed away, felt his hand on the door and yanked it open. He passed through into the hall and saw Rhoda descending the stairs. She was dressed for the street in dark coat and skirt and wide-brimmed hat, and labouring under the weight of a wooden box that held all her belongings.

Garbutt took the box from her and started towards the front door. Rhoda asked, 'What's been going on? I heard shouting.'

'Never mind.' Garbutt beckoned her with a jerk of his head.

But Rhoda turned aside and peered into the dining room. In the gaslight from the chandelier she saw the gleaming length of the table and William seated at its head. She took a pace towards him but then halted and put a hand to her mouth. She turned a horrified face to Garbutt and whispered, 'He's dead!'

Garbutt answered exultantly, 'Aye. He ruined my father and I swore I'd see the end of him and I have. Now come on.' He seized her arm and hurried her towards the front door.

A child wailed somewhere high in the house and Rhoda stopped in her tracks. 'That's the bairn! That's little Charlotte! I can't leave the bairn on her own in this place – with him.'

'The brat's nothing to do wi' you!' Garbutt tugged at her arm, eager to be away now, but she resisted stubbornly.

'She'll be expecting me to go to her.' Rhoda turned to go back to the stairs but Garbutt swung her about to face him. As she opened her mouth to protest he slapped her across the face with a heavy hand, rocking her head on her shoulders.

'You bloody little fool! For years you've been wanting to get out of here and now you've got your chance. Now don't argue with me and come *on*.' He swung Rhoda's box up on to his shoulder and dragged the stunned woman out of the house and down the steps. He looked back once and gloated, 'That's the finish of the Langleys! I've done for them!' He laughed harshly as he hustled Rhoda away into the fog.

Josie had learned she had a half-hour to wait in Monkwearmouth station for a train that would take her to Durham to connect with the London express. She found a seat in the waiting room, which soon filled up with women carrying shopping and men returning home from work in Monkwearmouth. She dozed, wearied by the events of the day and the journey with the carter – and dreamt of Hubert Smurthwaite leering at her and reaching out for her with groping fingers. Then the dream changed to the old one of the giant hanging over her, threatening. She woke, whimpering, to see the other passengers staring at her.

Josie apologised: 'I must have dropped off.' But they still exchanged disapproving glances that said as plain as day: 'The woman's been drinking.' Josie peered out of the window at the fog swirling outside. Her feet were damp inside her shoes, the soles of them worn through and the heels run down, but she dared not change them for the pair in her portmanteau as they were the only good ones she had left. She was hungry but reluctant to eat. She was not destitute, had her small savings and the ten shillings Mrs Smurthwaite had given her in lieu of a week's notice. But there was a chill fear inside her because she had heard stories of servants who had lost their 'place', failed to find another and had no other home to go to. They had been forced into the workhouse, spartan and soulless, or had to sleep in the streets and beg their bread from the back doors of the big houses. Or sell their bodies.

Josie tried to push those thoughts from her mind. She had to find her fare to go south. But the fears returning, she asked herself, 'Can you *afford* to go south?' Then she wondered, 'Suppose I got some work here for a month or two, just long enough to save something, enough to pay my fare and a bit in hand?' She shrank from the thought of the journey through the night – and what awaited her in London? She had nowhere to live, no job. She would have to walk the streets looking for both. She hesitated and heard the rumble of the approaching train. The people around her stood up and streamed out on to the platform. She knew she had to get her ticket now but still sat on. She stayed there, undecided, until the train pulled out, clanking on across the bridge over the River Wear in a hissing of steam and puffing smoke, heading for Sunderland central station. And now she accepted the inevitable – she would have to look for work and lodgings here.

Josie handed in her portmanteau at the left luggage office and walked out of the station. She hesitated for a moment longer in the shelter of the huge arch with its Grecian columns, then plunged out into the fog. She knew where to start, ideally wanted a job where she could live in, and a public house could be the answer. She had passed one with the carter: the Wheatsheaf.

The fog seemed thicker now she was out in the streets, the gas lamps lighting little except a few feet around them and that with only an amber glow. She guessed this was because she was near the River Wear and the sea. There were few people about and those she met materialised suddenly out of the mist and disappeared as quickly into it.

The manager of the Wheatsheaf did not want a barmaid but suggested she try the Frigate, nearer the river in Church Street. There Josie went into the snug and asked the barmaid, 'Are you wanting another pair of hands here?'

The girl bustled along behind the bar to whisper to a man pulling pints of beer from a pump, and Josie saw him shake his head. She knew the answer before the girl returned, smiling apologetically, to say, 'Sorry, pet.' And then, because she had noted Josie's accent, 'You're not from around here. Have you just moved in?'

Josie replied drily, 'Not really. I came up from London to work in a house out towards Newcastle and I got the sack today. So I'm looking for a job and lodgings.' Then she amended quickly, 'Cheap lodgings.'

The barmaid said obliquely, 'Some o' these places want a sight more work out of you than they pay for.'

Josie supplied the information she was fishing for: 'I could manage the work but the young master tried to . . . interfere with me.'

'Ah! One o' them!' The girl scowled. 'I hope you gave him what for.'

'I did.' They grinned at each other. Then Josie finished, 'But that got me the sack.'

She turned away but then the girl said, 'Wait a minute. Would you like a bite to eat afore you go? I brought some sandwiches for me tea and didn't eat them all.' And she brought out a little newspaper-wrapped parcel from under the bar. 'It's a nice bit o' bread and cheese.'

'Thank you. That's very good of you.' Josie took the parcel and sat down on the little bench by the counter.

The girl smiled, went away but returned a minute later and set a glass on the counter. 'There's a drop o' something to wash it down.'

Josie fumbled in her bag for her purse but the girl said, 'Never mind. That's on the house. From the boss.'

Josie looked past her and saw the man still working the pump, beer frothing into the glass he held, but looking her way. She called, 'Thank you!' And he nodded and went on with his work.

Josie could have wept at their kindness but she was hungry. She munched on the thick slices of bread and cheese and sipped at the sherry, feeling it warm her. As she picked up the last crumbs she saw the newspaper that held them was the *Sunderland Daily Echo* of the previous day. It was filled with advertisements and Josie mechanically scanned the 'Situations Vacant' column. An agency in Frederick Street wanted housemaids and parlour-maids – but it would be closed at this time of night . . . Her eye ran on down the page and then one name stood out: *Langley*! 'Housekeeper . . . and children's nurse . . . Apply Mr William Langley.'

Josie's heart thumped. She could picture him, tall, bearded and raging, as she had seen him twenty years before, her grandfather, William Langley. The children's nurse would be for Charlotte; Josie remembered the announcement of Charlotte's birth, which she had read while ironing *The Times*. She wondered briefly why James or his wife – what was her name? Maria – why they had not placed the advertisement.

But then a voice said above her, 'There's a pub down by the ferry that might be wanting a lass to live in, leastways he did last week.' The publican looked down at her. 'If you go down Church Street . . .'

Josie listened carefully to his directions, thanked him and his barmaid for their kindness, then went on her way. The crumpled newspaper she smoothed out, folded and put in her bag. If she did not find work this night she would go to the agency in Frederick Street.

The fog was thicker now as she walked down Church Street towards the river, following the directions she had been given. She had yet to find a bed for the night. If she did not find one, and work, at this pub, then she would look for lodgings. She saw hardly a soul after she had passed St Peter's church. Now she was beginning to remember this place. She stopped in her tracks for a minute, breathing shallowly, as it came back to her, where she was and where she was headed. She went on. It was just about here that . . . She rounded a bend in the road and there was the square.

Josie halted. A carriage drive ran off from the road to the left. She remembered it made a half-circle to pass the Langley house and emerge again on the road further on. A terrace of houses rose to the left of the drive and on the right was a garden. There was another terrace, hidden in the fog now, on the other side of the garden. And at the back of the square, also hidden in the fog, was the Langley house. She could picture it: wide steps leading up to a front door, two floors with tall windows, a third with square, smaller ones where the servants slept. Josie had slept in rooms like that most of her life.

Was William Langley there, lurking behind that grey curtain?

Josie thought that he would be an old man of seventy or so now. And she was a grown woman. He would not recognise her. And then the idea came: she could face him, say she was Mrs Miller come to apply for the post, hold out the newspaper – and then walk away. She could lay this ghost for ever. If she dared.

She would.

Josie screwed up her courage and turned into the carriage drive. She would say, 'I'm Mrs Miller. I've come about the "place" advertised in the *Echo*.' She rehearsed it as she walked up the drive: 'I'm Mrs Miller . . .'

There were many gaps in the ornamental railings that ringed the garden in the centre of the square. The garden was a wild, neglected jungle of trees and shrubs, long grass and thistles. All of it was insubstantial in the fog, dripping moisture that glistened in the pale reflected light from a gas lamp on the corner behind her.

Then she heard harsh, mocking laughter and the crunch of footfalls on the drive. They were approaching her and there was something about the laughter that sent her sidling through a gap in the railings. She moved behind the bushes, hiding, and stared out as the tramp of feet came nearer. Josie blinked and shrank down as a giant with a huge head took shape, striding out of the darkness. Then she realised it was not a monstrous head but a box he carried on his shoulder. He dragged a woman along at the end of his arm. Her face was covered by her shawl but her voice wailed, 'You've killed him!'

The giant answered hoarsely, 'Shut your mouth! You're finished with him and that's what you wanted.' He yanked viciously at the woman's arm so that she cried out. She stumbled on at his heels, then together they blended into the dank grey darkness of the night. Their footfalls receded then were gone, and Josie was left alone.

She rose and took a breath, steadying herself, letting her thumping heart slow down. She realised the man had not been a giant, had only seemed so because she was crouching low on the ground and looking up at him. But she knew that, giant or no, he was dangerous.

Josie walked on, repeating her little speech again: 'I'm Mrs Miller. I've come . . .' Until the Langley house loomed out of the mist. It filled the back of the square and she found its front door standing open, the gas lamp in the hall casting a rectangle of light down the steps. She climbed them, yanked at the bell-pull by the front door and heard the distant jangle deep in the house, but no one came hurrying. Josie entered the house, paused in the hall and peered cautiously around her. She called, 'Is anyone there?' On a floor above, a child cried mournfully. A tall clock with a slow swinging pendulum ticked against one wall. But there was no reply to Josie's call.

She tried again: 'Hello! Is anyone there?' But still no reply broke the silence of the house. There were wide stairs at the end of the hall, closed doors to her right and one on her left that stood ajar, showing light within. Josie went to it and peeped through the crack. She took in the long, polished table and the pictures hanging on the walls, but only in passing. Her gaze was drawn straight to the man seated at the head of the table and she sucked in a sharp breath of shock, held it then let it out in a shuddering sigh. She clapped her hands to her face in horror as she realised this was a dead man.

The door creaked, a long drawn-out groan, as she eased it open. Josie caught her breath, then went to him, heart thumping and hands shaking. She edged slowly down the side of the table until she stood close enough to touch one of his hands. It had slipped down on to the arm of the chair in which he sat and was already cold, lifeless. His other hand still clutched his breast. His face was twisted with pain – of body or mind?

His eyes stared. Josie recognised her grandfather, now shrunken and dead.

She felt no sorrow. This was not as when her mother or Dorothy Miller died. Then she had lost those she loved dearly, but this was different. Her only recollection of this old man had instilled terror.

And yet . . . She had been drawn to this place against her will, until at the last, when she had thought to rid herself of a memory. That memory of her grandfather had haunted her all her life and she had wanted to be rid of him. Well, now she was, and she felt tears pricking her eyes.

11

'*Mam-mee!*'

Josie's thoughts were recalled to the living as she realized the child was still wailing overhead. She returned to the hall, wondering, Where are James and his wife, and the servants in this house? But no one came, and she climbed the stairs. Four doors opened from a long landing; the crying came from behind one of them. Josie opened it and found a nursery. A fire, its embers banked up with coal dust for the night, gave out only a red glow. It was sufficient to show a table and chairs, a rocking horse, shelves on one wall with books – and a cot. The child, a dark-haired, dark-eyed little girl in a nightie, stood in the cot. She held on to its rail and wailed, eyes wide.

'All right, now.' Josie ran across to the cot and lifted the child out, held the weeping girl to her breast. 'Whisht now, whisht.' She soothed and rocked the child, whispering and crooning. There was a rag doll, the worse for wear through loving, lying in the cot. Josie pressed it into the plump arms and they closed around it. After a time the crying ceased and the little body relaxed. Josie gently replaced her in the cot and covered her over. She stood by for a minute or two, watching the sleeping child. Then, sure that she was sound asleep, Josie left the room.

She started back to the head of the stairs but then froze as she heard a heavy tread in the hall below. She wondered if the owner of the harsh laughter had returned.

A voice called deeply, 'Who's up there? Is that you, Rhoda?'

Josie did not think this was the same voice she had heard earlier in the square, but she was still cautious. She walked to the head of the stairs and halted there, looking down. A man stood in the hall. He wore a sea officer's uniform of dark blue double-breasted reefer jacket and a peaked cap, but both were salt-stained, the cap broken-peaked. He carried a canvas kitbag on his shoulder and now took off the cap with his free hand as he saw Josie, revealing black hair that lay thick and unruly on his skull. He was unshaven, his face shadowed by the stubble, and his dark eyes and his voice were hostile as he demanded, 'Who are you?'

Josie slowly descended the stairs and stopped when she was eye to eye with him. She realized she was still two steps from the floor. This man had not seemed tall when she looked down at him from the head of the stairs, probably because of the breadth of his shoulders, but now—

Tom Collingwood saw a slender, auburn-haired girl, pale and wide-eyed. Her coat was well worn and her shoes down-at-heel but there was a proud lift to her chin as she faced him. Pretty? He decided: more than that. But there was a rasp in his voice as he repeated, 'Who are you and what are you doing here?' He eyed her suspiciously.

Josie was still shaken, nervous in this strange place, and this man was rough in his appearance. She blurted out her prepared speech. 'I'm Mrs Miller. I've come about the "place" advertised in the *Echo*.' She held out the crumpled newspaper and pointed with one slim finger. She was also suspicious. She had photographs of James Langley, admittedly when he was fourteen years old, but she was sure this was not he. And this tall, hard-eyed stranger obviously thought she might be a thief. That angered her and she demanded, 'May I ask the same question of you, sir?'

He blinked at that, taken aback by her challenge, but he answered, 'I'm Tom Collingwood.' He gave a stiff nod of the head which Josie acknowledged with a nod of her own. He went on, 'I live here when I'm not at sea. I'm a ship's captain.' He reached out a big, callused hand, took the paper from her and read it, then looked up at her, still suspicious. 'You were upstairs.'

'I've been seeing to the little girl. She was crying.'

'Charlotte?'

Josie remembered the name in *The Times* four years ago but realised she wasn't supposed to know because she was Mrs Miller, not Josie Langley. She answered, 'If that is her name.'

'Where's Rhoda?'

Josie shook her head. 'I don't know anyone called Rhoda.'

Tom muttered, 'The last I knew she worked here and was looking after Charlotte.' Then he concluded, 'So Mr Langley has engaged you.'

'No.' And as he stared at her again, 'I've been in this house less than an hour.' Josie took back the paper, put it in her bag and snapped it shut. 'When I arrived I found the front door open and—' She stopped there.

Tom echoed, prompting her: 'And . . . what?'

Her head had turned to face the dining-room and his gaze followed hers. Josie said, 'In there.'

Tom crossed the hall with long strides and Josie came quickly down the last two stairs and followed him. He stopped for an instant in the doorway, staring at the body of William seated at the head of the table, then paced slowly to stand beside him and finally sank down on his knees to look into William's face, gently touch his cheek.

Josie stood behind him and said softly, 'He's dead.'

He said hoarsely, 'Aye, you're right enough.' Then he bowed his head and his wide shoulders slumped. He gripped the old man's cold hands as if to try to drag him back from death. Josie heard him sob. His voice came to her, muffled. 'He brought me up from a boy. He was father and mother to me. Anything I am or have, I owe to him.' After a time he let go of the body and rose to his feet, rubbing the back of his hand across his eyes. Josie wondered at his love for a man who had turned her parents away.

Tom absently picked up the spread sheaf of papers from the table. 'He had a sad ending. He sent me a cable – I got it at Lisbon a week back – to tell me his son James and his wife had been killed by some madman driving a lorry.'

Josie had heard nothing of this. She whispered, 'Oh, my God! The little girl's parents?'

Tom nodded absently. 'Charlotte's, yes. Her mother was Argentinian and her parents disapproved of her marrying James. They've not spoken to her since. But I must write to them, if William did not.'

Tom did not notice Josie's shock, might have considered it excessive on learning of the death of two strangers, but he was frowning over the papers. Now he looked up, angry and puzzled. 'These are notices of foreclosure, debts being called in. William must have mortgaged the yard. But to foreclose like this!' He threw the notices on to the table as if they soiled his hands. 'Who could have done it?' Then he remembered he was talking to a stranger, and added stiffly, 'This is family business. I'd be grateful if you would not repeat anything of what you've heard or seen this night.'

Josie looked up at him, angered by the request, the implication that she might gossip. But then she saw the reason for it, and his pain. She said, 'I have something to tell you, Captain Collingwood.'

But not in the presence of the dead man. Josie led the way out into the hall and closed the dining-room door. She began, 'When I got here, I was walking round the square—' They stood together in the house, now silent save for the slow ticking of the clock, and she told of her arrival, the harsh laughter, the man and woman glimpsed in the fog. 'She said, "You've killed him." And he said, "You've finished with him as you wanted." Then they went on and I came here. I heard the child crying upstairs and went to her, settled her down again – and then I heard you call.'

Tom Collingwood had listened intently and now he asked, 'Would you know either of them again?'

'No.' Josie shook her head. 'The box he was carrying hid his face and her shawl covered hers. And in the fog and the darkness—'

He nodded impatient acceptance of that. 'Aye. But the woman sounds like Rhoda Wilks. She was the maid and lived in. I believe she's been acting dissatisfied for some time. Maria – James's wife – used to write to me and she mentioned Rhoda was not being satisfactory. And William was advertising so it sounds as if he might have been thinking of replacing her. But I must call the doctor.' He turned towards the door then halted and glanced up the stairs, and his gaze came down to Josie. 'There's Charlotte. I can't leave her alone in the house . . .' He hesitated, his eyes searching Josie's, and she met his stare. He went on, 'And you are applying for the post of caring for the child? You have references?'

Josie hesitated now. Apply for this post? She had only come here out of curiosity and a vague idea of laying a ghost. Shouldn't she disclose her true identity?

But Tom pressed her, suspicious again at this hesitation. 'Well, have you?'

'Yes.' Josie fumbled the letter from Elizabeth Urquhart out of her bag.

Tom read it and admitted, 'Very good.' Then he glanced at the date. 'But this was a year ago. You have nothing more recent than that? And you were in London. How do you come to be here?'

Josie explained how she had looked after Dorothy Miller and then sought work. Then: 'I obtained a position in London but shortly afterwards the household moved North, to just a few miles from here. And I left today without a reference.'

Tom folded the letter and handed it back. 'Dismissed? Why?'

'I broke a vase.'

His brows rose. 'Is that all?' But he knew it was possible; servants had been dismissed for less.

Josie returned his gaze defiantly. 'No. The son of the house laid hands on me and I . . . dealt with him.'

'I see.' Tom knew that happened, too. He looked away, embarrassed. Then they both turned as a motor car engine rumbled outside, brakes squeaked then the engine slowed to a steady tick-over. Josie saw the car through the open front door – a saloon, its coachwork and brass headlamps gleaming with polish. A chauffeur in uniform and peaked cap hurried out of the driving seat to open the rear door. A girl stepped out and ran up the steps.

'Thomas!' She cried his name as she entered the hall, opening her motoring coat of fur-lined wool to show her hourglass figure of curved hips, tiny waist and swelling bosom. 'I heard that your ship had docked.' She put her arms around his neck and kissed him, then pulled away and rubbed her cheek. 'Oh! You're all bristly!' and coyly, 'I should have remembered!' Then she became aware of Josie and asked, the smile suddenly brittle, 'Who is this?' It reminded Josie of Hubert Smurthwaite's greeting: 'Who the hell are you?' And the stare was similar, assessing her worth, grading her according to her dress.

Tom was smiling at the girl fondly. Now he explained, 'This is Mrs Miller. She's come to apply to be nurse to Charlotte. William advertised in the *Echo*.'

'I see.' The smile widened again and the girl dismissed Josie as just a servant, ignored her as she went on, 'Mother's busy making plans for the wedding and I came over to tell you because I have to go away tomorrow for a few days.'

Tom's admiring smile had faded. He began, 'Felicity, I have some bad—'

Josie decided she did not like the name either. Felicity was pulling off her gloves and a diamond winked from the third finger of her left hand as she went on, 'Is darling William about?'

Tom said, 'I'm afraid he's dead.' And as Felicity stared, face frozen, he explained how he and Josie had found the body. Felicity shuddered.

Tom went on, 'I was just going for the doctor, but someone will have to stay with Charlotte while I'm away, have to stay the night with her because I don't know what I may be called upon to do—'

'I couldn't possibly,' said Felicity quickly. 'My reputation – if I stayed in the house alone with you – and that horrible child is always difficult – and we are leaving early tomorrow morning for Scotland. Surely this . . . Mrs Miller?' She glanced interrogatively at Josie.

Who would not admit her deception and true identity in front of this girl and so replied, 'That's right, miss.'

Felicity went on, 'She can see to the child.' She glanced at the clock in the hall, then at the door of the dining room and shuddered again. 'I really must go now.' Tom followed her to the door but she paused then and smiled. 'It's very sad, but at least Langley's yard will be in good hands now. In fact, as James is dead, then it will all come to you.'

'Oh, no.' Tom was plainly startled by this. 'William has already given me more than I deserve.'

'But who else is there? Everybody says you are as good as another son to him.' Felicity kissed him again then ran down the steps to the motor car where the chauffeur held the door open for her. She ducked into the rear and the chauffeur slid into his seat. The car rolled away into the coiling fog, the light from its carbide lamps blurring then fading from sight.

Tom closed the door and turned back into the hall, frowning. Then he remembered the girl waiting patiently and apologised. 'I'm sorry. Can you stay and care for the child? What about your husband?'

'I'm a widow and quite alone, Captain Collingwood.' Josie had thought it odd that there had only been one maid in a house of this size. She would have expected at least a butler or housekeeper, a footman and two or more maids. But then she recalled the notices of foreclosure. Was the house mortgaged up to the hilt? And the absence of staff due to a lack of money? But that was by the way. What mattered now was that she was Charlotte's cousin and the child's only relative, for practical purposes. Her mother's family were on the other side of the world. It was her duty to care for Charlotte. At the same time . . .

Josie said, 'If I teach the child her lessons can I be treated as governess? In return I'm prepared to act also as housekeeper until you can make other arrangements.' That meant: until you know what staff the house can afford.

Tom appreciated that, was surprised at her appreciation and delicacy, taken aback by her request. There was an important point of protocol involved. A governess was usually the daughter of impoverished gentlefolk and as such treated as one of the family and sat at table with them. Josie was asking for a promotion already.

Tom said curtly, 'A month's trial at twenty pounds a year.'

'That will be satisfactory, Captain Collingwood. Thank you.' Josie turned to the stairs.

Tom halted her. 'Just a moment, Mrs Miller.' He coughed. 'There is the question of your reputation. After I have had the doctor and the police here I will seek lodgings.'

Josie looked over her shoulder at him. 'Your fiancée did not see any impropriety in my staying the night.'

'Miss Blakemore meant no slight on you.' He was angry now. 'I'll thank you not to presume to criticise.' Josie met his eyes but held her tongue and he went on, 'Have you eaten?'

'No,' she admitted.

'Then you must have some supper. You'll find something in the kitchen.' He showed her the way, along the hall and past the stairs leading upward. They passed a side passage on the left but she could not see where it led. Then came a sitting room with a large, round central table just visible in the gloom, and close-set chairs and armchairs crowding the floor space. Josie found later that it looked out on a small walled garden. Finally, at the end of a dark passage, they came to the kitchen door.

Josie entered once more the room she had remembered from childhood. Little had changed. A rack for drying clothes hung from the ceiling alongside the gas lamp which Tom lit with a match. The big black range, its fire banked up for the night, still emitted heat but needed cleaning. The sink held a stack of dirty pans and dishes. In the centre of the floor stood a big table. Josie considered that its wooden surface should have been scrubbed white, but it was not. There was a smell of burnt food. Josie recalled that Tom had said Rhoda was 'acting dissatisfied'.

In the corner was the door that opened on to the stairs leading down into the cellar. Its darkness had always frightened her; she had wondered what horrors that black hole hid.

Tom yanked open cupboard doors. 'There you are. Just help yourself. I'll go for the doctor.' He paused in the doorway, still puzzled by this girl who had come out of the night, who had a proud lift to her head and talked to him as to an equal. 'You'll be all right on your own?'

'Of course.' Josie's reply was cool and he shrugged and left. She heard the tramp of his boots along the hall and then the slam of the front door. She listened to the ensuing silence, alone in the house save for the sleeping child and the old man who would never wake. Then she shook herself, opened a window to clear the air and found the wherewithal for a pot of tea. As she sipped a cup she carried out an inventory of the kitchen, eyes skating past the door to the cellar, mentally listing what she needed in the way of provisions and what had to be done. At the end of it she wryly told herself that she would have her hands full here – and Tom Collingwood did not realise what she had taken on. That triggered a thought, and she busied herself in the kitchen until she heard the front door open again and voices in the hall.

Josie checked that a pan was simmering on the stove as it should, then walked through to the hall. Tom Collingwood stood there, and he glanced her way when he heard the light tap of her heels. The door to the dining room was open and the deep murmur of voices came from inside. Tom said, 'The doctor and a police sergeant are in there.'

Josie looked up at him and saw now that his eyes were red and shadowed. She asked, 'Have you had a difficult voyage, Captain Collingwood?'

He grimaced. 'We plugged up the east coast last night and all day and there was a lot of fog. I stayed on the bridge all through until we berthed in the river here a couple of hours ago.'

Josie nodded. 'You're tired.'

He shrugged. 'I've gone forty-eight hours and more on the bridge afore now. Last night and today were nothing much. But I'll sleep – when I can get down to it.'

They were silent, listening to the rumbling conversation in the next room. Then it stopped and a moment later a man came out into the hall. He looked to be forty years old and was tall, though still three or four inches shorter than Tom, with a barrel body on thick legs, all encased in blue serge. He wore three chevrons on his sleeve and carried his helmet under his arm. He said, 'There's no sign of foul play, sir.'

Tom introduced him: 'This is Sergeant Normanby. Sergeant, this is the lady I told you about, the . . . the child's governess.'

Josie noted his acceptance of the title. The sergeant's round, red face was mildly surprised as he looked at Josie. She smiled at him. 'Aren't I as you expected, Sergeant?'

'Er – yes. Well, no—' Normanby cleared his throat, embarrassed. 'That is, I more or less thought you would be an older lady.'

Because of Tom's description? Had Normanby got an impression of a greying widow of good family come down in the world? Josie shot a glance at Tom but she only looked puzzled. She decided he had probably given that impression of her by accident; he was not a drawing-room diplomat. She smiled at Normanby again. 'I'll take that as a compliment. Thank you.'

He grinned back at her, relieved, but now Tom intervened brusquely, first addressing Josie: 'The doctor is in the dining room, examining . . . the body. I've told the sergeant all I know.' And now he turned to Normanby. 'Would you like to hear Mrs Miller's account?'

Normanby unbuttoned his breast pocket and took out a notebook and pencil. 'If you could give me a few details, ma'am. You are Mrs Josephine Miller . . .'

Josie said, 'That's right. But come through to the kitchen. We'll be more comfortable there.'

She led the way, settled the sergeant at the kitchen table with a cup of tea and told her story. Tom did not follow them. Part way through the sergeant's slow questioning there came the sounds of more boots treading in the hall and low voices. Josie rose to her feet but Normanby said quietly, 'That'll be the men from the morgue, ma'am.' Josie sat down and they went on.

When Normanby closed his notebook, his questioning finished, Josie went with him to the hall. There they met Tom Collingwood, coming out of a door opposite the dining room. Josie glimpsed behind him a desk set under a window and concluded that the room was an office.

Tom said, 'The doctor has gone.'

Normanby asked, 'And the body, sir?' He glanced at the closed door to the dining room. When Tom nodded the sergeant took his helmet from under his arm. 'Then I think I'll be on my way, too.'

Tom demanded, 'What about the man who was here tonight? And Rhoda Wilks?'

The sergeant nodded. 'We'll be having a word with Rhoda – and him. You mentioned Packer drew up those notices of foreclosure so he'll be able to point out our man. Mind you, sir, there's no evidence that they've committed any crime – unless the coroner finds something.'

Tom said harshly, 'Whoever gave William those notices murdered him as sure as if they'd shot him.'

Normanby pursed his lips. 'I must advise you not to repeat that, sir. It can't be proved and so is slanderous.'

'I don't give a damn,' said Tom flatly. 'That's the truth and you know it as well as I do.'

Normanby did not answer that but said, 'Goodnight, sir – ma'am.' He put on his helmet as he walked down the steps and set off round the square.

Tom stared after him, broodingly, but Josie stepped past him and shut the front door, turned and started back towards the kitchen. She called over her shoulder as she went, 'Come and have supper, Captain.'

He questioned, surprised, 'Supper?'

'Cold beef, boiled potatoes and cabbage. It's not much but at least you'll have something inside you.'

He joined her in the kitchen, sat at the scrubbed table and ate hungrily. Josie kept him company but only picked at her food. The events of the day had taken away her appetite. They spoke little during the meal, but afterwards, as they sat over cups of tea, Josie said softly, 'You were fond of him.'

Tom nodded. He hesitated, but then, mellowed by the food and relaxing in the warmth of the kitchen, he answered, 'He took me in off the street, an orphan, when I was eight years old. He brought me up, had me educated, found me an apprenticeship when I wanted to go to sea. Whenever I needed help he was there.'

He was silent, staring down into his mug. Josie sat quiet. Then he shrugged, as if trying to shake off the mood. 'I'm sorry. You have had troubles of your own. Have you been widowed long?'

'A year. My husband was in the navy. He was drowned. And I had a fall and lost the child I was carrying.' She would be as honest as she could to make up for the lie she was acting out. She wondered how Tom would take this admission; miscarriage was not usually talked about, certainly not between a governess and her male employer.

He said uncomfortably, 'I'm sorry. I shouldn't have asked.'

'I understand. You were only extending your sympathy. I didn't want to shock you with an indelicate subject but I thought you should know the full story. But if you will excuse me now—' Josie had had enough of questioning and pretending. 'I must see to these dishes.'

'And I must look through more of William's papers.' Tom was frowning now. 'I must try to find out how serious the situation is.'

So Josie washed up the crockery, pots and pans, glanced around the kitchen to see that all was as she wanted it – for tonight at least; there was work to be done on the morrow – and turned off the gas to leave it in darkness but for the glow from the banked-up fire.

In the hall she tapped at the door of the office, then opened it and put her head around it. Tom sat at the desk under the window and was half turned towards her now. Josie said, 'You mustn't think of leaving to seek a bed tonight. I saw a bedroom adjoining that of the child. I will make that mine and if the door does not lock I will find some way to secure it. Then both our reputations will remain intact.'

Tom glared at her, outraged. 'That will not be necessary!'

Josie grinned at him. 'I was joking with you, Captain Collingwood. I think we both need cheering.' Tom's glare faded. He was not sure whether to allow this . . . impertinence, if that's what it was. But Josie went on, 'Sleep in your own room. I will be perfectly safe with Charlotte.'

Tom was about to argue but looked at the clock on the mantelpiece and saw that it was past two in the morning. He answered stiffly, 'Very well. Thank you.'

'Goodnight, Captain Collingwood.'

'Goodnight, Mrs Miller.' He watched the door close, then turned back to his papers, but not to read. He thought that there was something not quite right with Mrs Miller. Her looks? The straight way she talked back? Her smile? He did not know, it was just some instinct . . . Then he told himself that was nonsense. He was lucky this young woman had turned up to take care of Charlotte – and the house – so he did not have to worry about them. He decided to put the thought from him and concentrated on his papers. But still, with a part of his mind, he wondered about Mrs Miller . . .

Josie was in bed in the room next to Charlotte's. She had found the bed unmade, drawers pulled out and empty, a carpet kicked up and not replaced – all signs of a hurried departure and a lackadaisical occupant. This had been Rhoda's room. Josie tidied it, found clean sheets in a cupboard on the landing and remade the bed. She had looked in on the child and found her sleeping peacefully. The door between the two rooms was open and now Josie lay awake, watching the shadows on the walls cast by the faint glow from the nursery fire. The house was silent except for the creaks and groans of any old house.

She knew Tom Collingwood suspected her of not being all she seemed. She had seen his doubts and she was an impostor. If she confessed to him now that she was Josie Langley he would think that she had heard of James's death and come seeking a fortune, like a vulture. So she would have to keep up the pretence for the time being. She had a duty here – and she would not abandon it to this Felicity.

Josie became conscious of a new sound in the night, a quiet tread on the stairs. Then the soft *creak! creak!* approached along the passage, passed her door and went on, faded into silence. She found she was holding her breath, remembered her words . . . Fine words! She had not locked her door. That did not matter. She was safe here.

Josie closed her eyes and, almost at once, she slept.

An hour later she started up in bed, trembling. She had thought to lay the ghost that had haunted her for twenty years but now there was another. A man walked in mist that hid his face but she could still hear his cruel laughter and she knew he was coming for her.

12

'Who are you?' The child had woken early, of course, as they do. She stood up in the cot in her long nightdress, her dark hair hanging loose and with the rag doll dangling from one hand. She looked at Josie out of big eyes and asked again, 'Who are you?'

Josie smiled at her. 'I'm Mrs Miller. I've come to look after you.'

After this was digested: 'Where's Rhoda?'

Josie explained, 'Rhoda has gone away.'

'Is she coming back?'

Josie doubted it. 'I don't think so.' The child's mouth drooped. She was ready to cry and, to get away from Rhoda, Josie asked, 'What's your name?'

'Charlotte Langley,' the child replied. 'I'm four.' She lifted the doll: 'And this is Amelia.'

'She's lovely.' Josie climbed out of bed and pulled her coat about her. From this upstairs window she could see out across the square to the tall cranes of the shipyards ranked along the riverbank. Rain was driving in from the sea and making runnels on the windows. Josie shivered and knelt to stir up the nursery fire while Charlotte introduced her to the toys in the room, the doll's house, the pram, the rocking horse: 'His name is Matin Bell. Granddad said Matin Bell won the Northumberland Plate and he backed it.' She was still not far from tears.

Granddad. Josie sat back on her heels, the events of the night before flooding back – the dead man seated at the table, the harsh laughter in the darkness, Tom Collingwood standing at the foot of the stairs looking up at her ... She rose to her feet, mentally shaking herself, and replaced the guard around the fire.

Charlotte said, 'Can I go down and see Granddad now?'

Josie had known she would have to deal with this before long but was still unprepared. 'Your grandfather has gone away,' she said lamely.

'Like Rhoda?'

'No.' And forced into a corner: 'He died. I'm sorry, Charlotte.' She expected a bland response but Charlotte burst into tears. Josie was quick to lift her out of the cot, cuddle and comfort her, and surprised, because the child was obviously fond of old William Langley.

Through her sobs Charlotte said, 'He won't come back. Mam and Dad died and they didn't come back. Uncle Tom went away and promised to come back but he didn't.'

Josie bit her lip. Charlotte's world was disintegrating around her. It was no wonder she was fearful and insecure. Josie queried, 'Uncle Tom?' Could it be—? 'Do you mean Captain Collingwood?'

'Yes!' wailed Charlotte. 'He went away on a ship.'

Josie hugged her and kissed her wet cheeks. She knew Charlotte was going to need a lot of this. 'Well, he came home last night and you'll see him later.' She set about drying the child's eyes. Charlotte needed someone and clung to her because Josie was there. 'Time for your bath.' And Josie headed for the bathroom with Charlotte in her arms.

A half-hour later they descended the stairs together. Josie saw that there was another sitting room behind the office. This room looked out on another walled garden at the side of the house. She was uneasily aware of the task facing her in 'keeping' this house. There was the ground floor, with the office and a sitting room on one side, the dining room and another sitting room on the other. On the floor above were four bedrooms and a bathroom, with attic rooms above them on yet another floor. She would have her work cut out.

Josie saw that the door to the office was ajar, and as they reached the hall Tom Collingwood emerged. He was freshly clean shaven now, dressed for the street and business in a tweed lounge suit with a double-breasted reefer jacket, starched collar and a tie. Charlotte shrieked, 'Uncle Tom!' and threw herself at him. He caught her under the arms and swung her around, laughing. Josie looked on, surprised but smiling. This was a different Tom Collingwood.

Josie greeted him: 'Good morning, Captain Collingwood. You're early abroad.'

'Good morning, Mrs Miller.' He cradled Charlotte in his arms. 'I woke before it was light and went down to the ship. There were matters I had to attend to, orders to give. So I am finished with her now and can devote my time to affairs here.' This came easily as he bounced Charlotte, laughing, in his arms. But then he stumbled on uncomfortably, 'No one saw me leave but several were about in the square when I returned. I will find some lodgings for tonight.'

Josie thought, Still thinking of my reputation. Her lips twitched. Bless the man! 'I will serve your breakfast shortly, Captain Collingwood.'

He glanced at the clock in the hall. 'Thank you.' And he found a smile for her this morning. Or was that for Charlotte? she wondered. She looked back as she came to the kitchen door and saw him down on all fours, Charlotte seated on his back. Was this the austere Captain Collingwood with whom she had argued last night?

Josie served his breakfast in the dining room and he entered with Charlotte holding his hand. She appealed, 'Can I have toast with you, Uncle Tom?'

Josie said, 'I think it would be better if you had your breakfast with me in the kitchen, Charlotte. Your chair is in there.'

Charlotte wheedled, 'Please, Uncle Tom?'

Josie opened her mouth to be firm but Tom said, 'Well, you must behave. I'll fetch your chair.'

Josie's lips tightened at being overruled in this way and she knew the child had outmanoeuvred her, but she saw the delight on Charlotte's face and could not spoil her pleasure for the sake of making a disciplinary point. 'I'll bring your breakfast.'

Tom had seen Josie's anger at her orders being countermanded. Now he tried to make amends and, remembering Mrs Miller's status as governess, he said stiffly, 'Well, as there are just the three of us, there seems little sense in eating apart. Why don't you join us, Mrs Miller?'

Josie wondered, Was this an olive branch? 'Thank you.'

So they ate in the dining room, gloomy and lit by the gas chandelier because the curtains were drawn across the windows out of respect for the death in the house. Tom sat at the head of the table with Charlotte on his left, while Josie was on Charlotte's left, ready to render assistance when it was needed by the child. Conversation was mainly between Tom and Charlotte; he and Josie exchanged only a few polite words over the child's head.

His breakfast done, he pushed back his chair and rose from the table. 'I have a great deal to do today. I'll find some lunch in the town.'

'What time do you wish dinner, Captain?' And Josie added, 'I would not like Charlotte to be kept up too late.' She saw his brows come down momentarily at her mild warning.

Tom thought this girl was quick to lay down the law. He enquired curtly, 'Will seven be convenient for you?'

'It is not a matter of my convenience,' Josie replied evenly, refusing to be provoked. 'The child is fond of you and I thought you would wish to have her join you at dinner.'

Tom decided his judgment had been hasty. 'An excellent idea.' He kissed Charlotte. 'Good day, Mrs Miller.'

So Tom strode out into the rain and Josie was left with Charlotte. She cleared away the breakfast dishes then made the beds and began on a planned clean of the entire house, starting with the kitchen. Rhoda had not been 'satisfactory'. Wasn't that how Tom had said James's wife, Maria, had put it?

But first there was the outward face of the house. Josie searched in the kitchen and found a whitening stone, scrubbing brush and cloth. She filled a bucket with hot water and walked through to the front door. The steps leading up from the street were muddy where a succession of boots had trodden them the previous day. Josie washed the steps then whitened them with the stone, aware all the time that other women around the square were at their front doors and engaged in the same occupation. Inevitably, one called, 'Have you just come, pet?'

Josie stood and wrung out her cloth. 'I've been taken on to care for Charlotte and look after the house.'

Another chimed in: 'By, lass, you'll have your hands full there.'

Josie had already come to that conclusion and laughed. 'Yes, I will.'

A third voice questioned, 'You're from down South, aren't you?'

'Yes, I am.'

'Ah, well.' But then, charitably accepting that it was not Josie's fault: 'Now, hinny, if you want owt, or a bit o' crack, you just come round.'

That was echoed by a half-dozen voices: 'Aye!'

'Thank you,' said Josie, grateful for this gesture of kindness. Then she carried her bucket into the house to start there.

Charlotte trotted along after Josie, chattering or playing with her doll as Josie dusted, swept and scrubbed. There was an exciting – for Charlotte – interval when they took a cab to Monkwearmouth station and brought back Josie's portmanteau. Charlotte had to help unpack it, of course. Then afterwards the work went on.

But Josie was uneasy about the cellar. She worked around it until she had to admit that the kitchen was as clean as she could make it failing a complete decoration. So she finally faced the cellar. She opened the door and stared down into the darkness below. Charlotte said, 'That's the lamp.' She pointed to an oil lamp standing on a small shelf on the wall inside the cellar door. A box of matches lay beside the lamp.

Josie lit it and asked, 'Are you coming with me?' Charlotte shook her head firmly, nervously eyeing the black void. Josie said with forced cheer, 'There's nothing to harm you.' But she knew very well how the child felt. So she looked to see that the guard was around the kitchen fire, the door to the back yard was bolted and that leading to the front of the house was latched so Charlotte could not get through. Then she set her foot on the stone steps that led down.

There were twelve of them, running to form an 'L', down one wall to a landing then down another. When she stood at their foot she found that the cellar was some twelve feet square – and almost empty. There were some shelves on the wall by the foot of the steps, with bottles lying in racks or standing upright. There was room for the lamp and Josie set it down there for a while. She could see from marks in the dust that the lamp had stood there before, and more than once. In the middle of the floor a baulk of timber some six inches in diameter stood between floor and ceiling as a support for the floor above. Josie walked around it, not because there was anything to see but just to prove she was not afraid. The stone floor under her feet was thickly laid with dust.

Then Charlotte called tremulously from above, 'Mrs Miller?'

Josie seized on the excuse: 'Coming!' She paused just long enough to cast a glance over the bottles. She saw that some held beer and took one with her as she ran up the stairs, telling herself that she would clean out the cellar at a later date.

The rain had eased to a fine drizzle by the end of the morning, so after a light lunch Josie took Charlotte for a walk. First they went to the shops in Dundas Street and bought meat and vegetables, five pennies' worth of soap and a packet of soda. Then they turned back towards the river. For most of the time they meandered through streets that were strange to Josie, but now and again they would turn a corner and open up a vista that stirred a memory somewhere deep within her. At one of these Charlotte said, 'That's the yard.'

The big gates stood open but Josie could see the name: William Langley & Sons. Josie noted the use of the plural with surprise. So William had not changed the name of the yard when he turned his back on his elder son. Beneath the newer paint could still be discerned the older: Hector Langley & Son. Hector had been William's father, her great-grandfather. Josie peered in as they passed the gates. There were men working, but lackadaisically, as if filling in their time. No ship was being built on the stocks, nor lying at the quay to be fitted out. There was an atmosphere of gloom about the place, reflected in the sombre faces of the men. Josie remembered that they would have heard of William's death and must be wondering what that would mean to them.

The rain began to fall again and they hurried back to the house. As they approached, Josie looked up at its face. There were the windows of the office on one side of the door and of the dining room on the other, the curtains drawn across them. But beyond the latter there were more, the curtains also drawn, indicating a part of the house she had not known existed. Josie's curiosity was aroused. She hung up her coat behind the door in the kitchen, as a servant should, and set out to satisfy her curiosity.

'Where are we going, Mrs Miller?' asked Charlotte.

'Exploring,' replied Josie. She took Charlotte's hand and they walked down the side passage, between dining room and sitting room, that Josie had noted that first evening. At its end was a locked door, but the key was in the lock and she turned it. The door opened on to another hall. Two doors led to a dining-room and sitting room respectively. A third disclosed a small kitchen. A broad flight of stairs climbed to the upper floor. Josie and Charlotte climbed it, with the inevitable Amelia dragged at the end of Charlotte's arm. On the floor above there were two bedrooms and a bathroom. And on yet another floor, attic bedrooms for servants.

Josie wondered: Why? This was virtually another house built alongside the main one. All it lacked was a front door. The rooms were empty of any furniture except for the curtains at the windows and the floors were bare and echoed under their feet. But while there was dust there was no dirt, showing that the rooms had been cleaned before they were shut up.

Josie found another door on the upstairs landing but this one was locked with the key on the other side. When she returned to the main house she looked for that door and found it, turned the key and opened it on to the landing of the house they had just explored. Josie locked it again and left the key in the lock as she had found it.

Once again, Josie felt daunted. The main house was big enough but then there was this extra residence built on the side. How could she, alone, possibly care for all of it? She knew she could not and would need help, but also knew she could not ask for it because this house could not afford it. The notices of foreclosure and the single servant had pointed to that. Later, she wondered vaguely if the house itself could be put to some use.

Tom returned shortly before seven, striding long-legged round the square through the rain. He hung up his coat and sat down with Josie and Charlotte to a dinner of vegetable soup and a roast leg of lamb. As they neared the end of the meal, Charlotte said, 'We went exploring.'

'Oh?' Tom looked at Josie, suspicious again.

She explained, 'I saw the windows at the side when we came back from our walk today. I was curious so I took Charlotte to look. I hope you don't mind, Captain?'

'No,' said Tom, indifferent now. 'But you'll have found it a waste of time. There's nothing in there.'

'True, but it's strange. Why should another house be built on like that?'

'Hector Langley built it,' explained Tom. 'William's father. He built it for William and his wife when they married. Apparently William's wife wanted a place of her own. Then William was going to give it to David – his elder son – when he married, but I gather they had a hell of a row and David walked out. Then soon afterwards he was lost at sea with his wife and daughter. They were on their way to America and their ship went down.'

He was not looking at Josie and she gave thanks for that. She rose quickly from the table with her mind in a whirl. She muttered some excuse about 'bringing the pudding' and hurried out to the kitchen. She sat at the kitchen table until she felt able to return. She had thought William had known how her father had died, that he had known Josie and her mother were making a life for themselves but he had made no move to find them. Now she knew that was not the case and he had thought all of them dead. She recalled that her father had taken her and her mother off the ship just before she sailed. So presumably their names had not been struck from the passenger list and they were thought to have gone down with the ship. But what had happened to the letter her mother had written? She could only conclude it had been lost in the post. And there was another conclusion, that old William might not have been so heartless as she had believed.

Josie returned to the dining room with the dessert and Tom greeted her with: 'Charlotte tells me you passed the Langley yard.'

'Yes, she pointed it out to me.' Josie smiled. Then she added, 'They didn't appear to be building a ship.'

'They're not,' Tom said bitterly. 'The whole river is in depression. Langley's hasn't built a ship for a long time and doesn't have an order now. That's why William was borrowing money. He was trying to keep his men on when he didn't have work for them.' He stopped then. Josie waited for him to continue but he did not and she did not care to press him. It was a family matter and Mrs Miller was not family.

Reuben Garbutt had arrived at his home that morning after travelling through the night. He was accompanied by a shocked, jaded and bewildered Rhoda Wilks. She gaped at his substantial house, standing in its own spacious grounds in St John's Wood. As they got down from the cab, Rhoda whispered, 'Is this a hotel?'

'No. Don't be damned stupid.' Garbutt tossed two half-crowns to the cabbie and told the footman who came hurrying from the house, 'Get our bags.'

'Yes, Mr Garbutt, sir.'

In the hall they were greeted by the butler. 'It's good to see you home again, sir.' He held a silver salver with a few envelopes stacked neatly on it. 'This mail has been awaiting you, sir.'

Reuben picked up the envelopes and fanned through them as he walked on. 'Prepare a room for Miss Wilks. Let us know when it's ready. We'll be in the study.'

In the big, book-lined room he sat at his desk and began opening his mail while Rhoda stood in the middle of the floor. He glanced up at her and said impatiently, 'Sit down!'

As she sank slowly into a chair she said, 'That chap called you Mr Garbutt.'

He nodded without looking up from the letter he was reading. 'That's my name.'

There was silence for a time as Garbutt scanned letter after letter –

13

'Ashes to ashes, dust to dust . . .' They buried William Langley three days after his death. It was a day of bright sunshine, but the vicar's voice droned mournfully through the burial service. Josie Langley was in mourning today, her dress and coat of unrelieved black out of respect for her grandfather, though he was known to the world as her employer. She should have stood on the fringe of the crowd around the grave because to them she was just an employee, and an outsider come lately at that. The only ostensible members of family were Tom Collingwood and little Charlotte. But Josie was there to hold Charlotte.

There were many mourners, friends or business acquaintances of old William Langley, because he had been well respected. The men were in dark suits and black ties, top hats, bowlers or Homburgs in their hands. Their wives were all in black, skirts lifted decorously with one hand to keep them clear of the clay around the grave. The other hand steadied the high black hats pinned to their piled tresses.

And there was Felicity Blakemore, newly returned from Scotland and standing at Tom Collingwood's shoulder. She was in expensive black with a veil, and dabbing at her eyes with a scrap of handkerchief. Her father's big motor car waited outside the cemetery gates with her maid, who had accompanied her to put rubber galoshes on Felicity's shoes before she ventured into the grass and soil of the graveyard.

Josie was watching Tom Collingwood. He stood a head taller than the rest, bareheaded in a dark suit with a reefer jacket, his cap in his hand. She had sat beside him at the inquest, Charlotte on her knee. It had been held in the Albion Hotel in Dock Street on the afternoon following William's death. The coroner had delivered a verdict of death by natural causes – in fact, heart failure. Tom had been broodingly angry rather than grieving, stiff-backed, his black brows drawn down.

Josie had given Charlotte to Tom to hold on his knee while she gave her evidence, told how she found the body. When she reclaimed the child, Charlotte had whispered, 'Why is Uncle Tom so cross?'

Josie whispered back, 'He's unhappy because your grandfather is dead.'

'Oh.' Charlotte nodded, vaguely, the concept of death still strange to her. 'Like Mam and Dad?'

'Yes.'

'Are you going to die?' Now Charlotte was concerned.

Josie reassured her, 'No.'

Charlotte had been content with that but she was uneasy now, having seen the coffin lowered into the grave and knowing her grandfather was in it. Josie picked her up and held her close so the child could see the wheeling gulls blown in on the wind from the sea. That distracted her and she quietened again.

Josie wished she could comfort Tom Collingwood in some way. He was grieving now, his head down and tears in his eyes. Felicity was intent on her own seeming grief. But then the vicar's drone came to an end, the men put on their hats and the crowd began to drift away after murmuring their condolences to Tom. As it thinned, Josie saw Sergeant Normanby standing apart, and she eased away from Tom's side and went over to the policeman. 'Good afternoon, Sergeant.'

'Afternoon, ma'am.' Normanby put a thick finger to his helmet in salute. 'A fine day but a sad one.' He shook his head. 'So soon after—' He stopped.

Josie said, 'Would you like to see the horses, Charlotte?' The carriages that had brought the mourners stood outside the gates of the cemetery.

Charlotte, bored, answered quickly, 'Yes, please.'

Josie set her down. 'Just go as far as the gate. Not outside, mind. I'll be watching you.' And her gaze followed Charlotte as she trotted away, to halt by the gate and peer through the railings.

Josie turned to the sergeant. 'Captain Collingwood told me how Charlotte's parents died. I understand they were run down.'

Normanby scowled. 'It was some chap who was mad or drunk or both. They were walking down to the yard like they did every morning and this feller stole a lorry loaded with coal from outside a pub around the corner. He drove down the road, swerved off the kerb and smashed into them, crushed them against the wall. He got out and ran off. A few people saw him but not really close. Their descriptions varied. About all you could say for sure was that he was tall and well set up, with a moustache. We never found him.'

Josie said, 'Could it have been an accident?'

Normanby pursed his lips. 'The verdict of the inquest was manslaughter.'

Josie suggested, 'But surely, nobody would deliberately kill two innocent people like that. Why should they?'

'That's what I asked myself. Why? And I couldn't find a reason.' But Normanby did not sound convinced. He turned to go, lifting a hand again in salute.

Josie saw that Charlotte was edging towards the road and she started to move herself. 'Then you're sure it was deliberate?'

The sergeant paused. 'Well, he managed to start that lorry, drive it around a corner and then down the road without any trouble. So why should he turn off his course, summat like forty-five degrees, and run into them?' And he went on his way.

Josie stared after him for a moment then hurried to catch Charlotte and take her back to their carriage. She caught the child's arm at the gate. Just outside was the Blakemore car, huge and shining. The uniformed chauffeur stood some yards away, talking with a little knot of carriage drivers. Felicity's maid, a slim girl in a grey overcoat, stood by the car door. She waited, bored, for her mistress to return. Josie asked Charlotte, 'Would you like to see the motor car now?'

'Yes, please.'

So Josie let her wander along its length, peering at her distorted reflection in the gleaming brass headlamps. Josie smiled at the maid. 'I'm Josie Miller. I just started at the Langleys' a week back, looking after Charlotte here.'

The maid brightened at having someone to talk to. 'Susie Evans.'

Josie asked, 'What's her ladyship like?' And she jerked her head to indicate Felicity, now the centre of a group of wives, and grinned at Susie, 'all girls together'.

Susie grinned back. 'The job's all right and I can put up with her for the money. She's an only child and old Blakemore's got pots o' money, big house just outside the town and another one in London.' Then she grimaced. 'Here she comes now. I'll have to take her bloody galoshes off for her.'

Josie said sympathetically, 'Mucky job. Anyway, I expect I'll see you again.' She reached for Charlotte's hand.

As Charlotte reluctantly turned away from the car she saw Felicity coming out of the gates and said clearly, 'I don't want to ride with her.'

'Sssh!' Josie hushed her. 'Any more of that and—' She did not finish but Charlotte received the message and was silent.

Felicity smiled thinly at her and swept past. 'Susie! My shoes!' The chauffeur had come trotting up to open the rear door. Felicity seated herself inside and Susie knelt to pull off the muddy galoshes.

Josie and Charlotte were joined by Tom and they were driven back to the Langley house. Josie led the child inside while Tom sent the cab driver on his way. The curtains had been drawn across the windows since the night of William's death, but now Josie drew them back with a breath of relief to let in the sunlight. This cheered Charlotte, too, and she ran laughing up and down the hall and Josie pretended to chase her. After a minute Tom came in, leaving the front door open, and rapped, 'I would like a little more respect for the dead, please, Mrs Miller.'

Josie, flushed and laughing, halted in the game but gave him back: 'The funeral is over. Charlotte is only a child and she has mourned enough. Do you wish to see her with a permanently miserable face, Captain Collingwood?'

Tom looked at Charlotte, now peeping from behind Josie's skirts. She laughed up at him and he admitted, 'No, but—'

'Very well, then. Is that all?'

He took a breath. 'No, Mrs Miller, it is not all. While you are the child's nurse, I am her guardian because I'm the nearest she has to any family now, at least until I can get in touch with her mother's people in Argentina. Is that understood?'

Josie nodded gravely. 'It is. And while you are her guardian when you are here, I am her nurse for twenty-four hours a day and I will continue to carry out my duty as I see it. Is that understood?' They both stood very straight, he glaring down at her, she looking up at him defiantly.

Felicity's arrival broke the deadlock. She bustled into the hall, pulling off her gloves, and smiled at Tom. 'Here we are, darling. Arkenstall has just arrived.' Josie laid a warning hand on Charlotte's shoulder as Felicity went on, 'And we don't need that child. You – what's your name? Mrs Miller? Take her away, please.'

Ezra Arkenstall entered then, a middle-aged man with a pointed beard and stooped from sitting over a desk. He peered at Tom and Josie through wire-rimmed spectacles. Josie recognised the solicitor from a previous visit in the past week. He said, 'I am quite ready now.'

Tom turned his head to say, 'Yes. We will be there in just a moment.' Arkenstall opened the office door for Felicity and followed her in.

Charlotte sidled from under Josie's hand and gripped Tom's instead. She whispered pleadingly, mouth drooping, 'I want to stay with you, Uncle Tom.'

Tom looked down at her. 'I don't think you'll like a lot of legal talk.'

The corners of the mouth slipped further and a lip quivered. 'Please?'

Tom softened. 'All right, but you must be quiet.'

'I will.' Charlotte smiled sunnily and tugged at Josie's skirts with her free hand. 'Come on, Mrs Miller.' And before either could protest, 'I want Mrs Miller. I'll sit with her and be quiet.'

Josie made a mental note to deal with this behaviour in the future. But not now. She stood silent and Tom agreed, 'Oh, very well.' And to Josie, 'Arkenstall is waiting to read the will. Normally only family or those with an interest would be present but your presence will serve a purpose: you will see what my position is in law and that it is my right and responsibility to order how the child should be brought up.'

Josie had made her point and was prepared to settle for that. 'Thank you, Captain Collingwood.'

Tom began to caution her. 'You will understand that anything said in that room—'

Josie was quick to assure him, 'I will not repeat a word.'

'Thank you.' Then Tom added, muttering, 'Though I expect the state of affairs will soon be evident to everyone.'

Tom opened the door of the office and stood back. Josie took Charlotte's hand and sailed in. Arkenstall stood at the desk with its swivel chair. There was only one other chair, a leather armchair by the fireside, the grate of which was empty in this summer weather. Felicity was seated there, smiling graciously. The smile froze when she saw Charlotte and she snapped, 'What is that child doing here? Mrs Miller, I instructed you—'

'I want them here, Felicity,' Tom cut her off as he entered, carrying a chair from the hall. He set it down behind Josie, saying, 'Please be seated, Mrs Miller.'

'Thank you.' Josie sat down demurely and secured Charlotte on her knee.

Tom went on, 'Charlotte won't be any trouble and this will concern her as much as anyone. Mrs Miller will look after her and I have her word that she will not divulge anything she hears.' Felicity realised this was an explanation, not a justification, and not to be debated. The smile was switched on again.

Tom went to stand before the fireplace and addressed Arkenstall where he sat in the swivel chair: 'This is Mrs Miller, the governess engaged to care for Charlotte. I would like her to hear the terms of the will.'

Arkenstall raised his eyebrows but ducked his head in a little bow to Josie. 'Pleased to meet you, ma'am.' He picked up the will from the desk and read, 'This is the last will and testament of William Langley, shipbuilder—' He broke off to glance up at Tom. 'He went on to name his executors, James and yourself, but then he reverted to the wording of the previous will wherein he left the shipyard and this house to his eldest son, David, and the remainder of his estate to James. At the time I said that this was pointless as David and his entire family had perished. William replied that he was determined to have it that way. He said, "God forgive me, I tried to cut the boy out of my life. I will not disown him now." So that is how the will stands.'

He followed Tom's gaze as it strayed to Charlotte and Tom said, 'So Charlotte inherits all.'

'Not quite. There is just one other bequest—' Arkenstall read from the will again: 'To my protégé and staunch friend these last twenty years, Thomas Collingwood, I leave my yacht *Celia*. May she bring good fortune to him.'

Josie looked up to see Tom's lips working. He said huskily, 'He loved that cutter.' Then he cleared his throat. 'But having said that, the rest comes to Charlotte.'

Arkenstall nodded. 'That is correct, as she is the sole surviving relative.' Then he put the will aside and picked up another document. 'This is James's will. As you will recollect – you were at sea when it was read but I informed you by post of the relevant passages . . .' He paused, brows raised in enquiry, and Tom nodded. The lawyer went on, 'You will remember that James left everything to his widow and as she died intestate then it passed to his daughter. He also said – and this was possibly prompted by the untimely deaths of his brother and his family – that in the event of his daughter being orphaned then William and yourself would act as guardians and trustees.'

Tom nodded. 'I remember. God knows I never expected to act.'

'But you will, of course?' Arkenstall said this with confidence, obviously with faith in his man.

Tom confirmed it: 'I will. I gave my word and I will not break it. William taught me that.'

'Good.' Arkenstall smiled at the child. 'You will like having Captain Collingwood looking after you?'

Charlotte's gaze shifted from him to Tom and back again. She asked, 'And Mrs Miller?'

Arkenstall blinked at her and Tom said soothingly, 'Yes, Mrs Miller will be looking after you.'

Charlotte said, 'Good.'

Felicity was tight-lipped and complained to Tom: 'You will carry out the onerous duties and only Charlotte will benefit.'

He answered shortly, 'The duties are not onerous and it is right that Charlotte should inherit.'

Felicity sighed. 'Really, Tom, you're too generous. As a friend of twenty years you deserve better. The *Celia* is something, though I think it an expensive toy and you will not find me aboard a small craft of that kind.' She stood up, shaking out her skirts and pulling on her gloves.

Tom replied soothingly, 'Sailing is not a lady's pastime. But she is a lovely little craft.'

Felicity made for the door. 'Well, I have a luncheon appointment. Good day, Mr Arkenstall.'

Tom crossed to the door, opened it for her and followed her into the hall. Felicity's voice came clearly: 'You must instil some discipline into that child, Tom. See that . . . that Mrs Miller does it . . .' Her voice faded as she left the house and the engine of the car throbbed into life. Josie stayed in her seat, wondering if she should leave now. But it seemed that Arkenstall had not finished; he sat with his papers spread across the desk still, plainly waiting.

The car slid past the window and Tom came back into the office, took up his stand before the fireplace again. Arkenstall said, 'There is one final item—' He went back to William's will and detached a sealed envelope from it. 'This is addressed: "To my son, James, to be read after my death." I think it now comes to you.' He handed it to Tom.

Tom read it, silently, then passed a hand over his eyes. He looked at Arkenstall. 'He just said how much he regretted breaking with David, says he was wrong and realised too late. He finished: "Pray to God to forgive me."' He turned away to lean on the mantelpiece, his face in his hands.

Arkenstall shuffled his papers together and Josie stood up quickly and seized Charlotte's hand. She addressed Arkenstall and Tom equally with false brightness: 'If that is all you require of Charlotte and myself, sirs?'

Arkenstall answered, smiling, 'Why, yes, Mrs Miller. I think so.' Tom nodded, not turning.

Josie led Charlotte from the room and out to the kitchen. There she began preparing lunch while the little girl chattered around her legs and helped with the work, kneading the pastry for a pie and rolling it out with her fat little fists struggling with the rolling pin.

Josie was able to think with a part of her mind. The old man's letter left to his son had affected her, though not so deeply as it had Tom Collingwood. Her heart softened towards her grandfather, who had so bitterly regretted his treatment of her father and mother – and herself for that matter. She had come north to lay a ghost. The ghost had been laid but now – if he had lived she could have found it in her heart to pity him.

'Me! Me!' Charlotte demanded, and Josie gave her the fork so she could make the holes in the piecrust. It came to her then – though she admitted she should have realised it when the will was read – that she, as the daughter of David, the elder son, should inherit this house and the shipyard while Charlotte would have only the rest of the estate.

And if she disclosed her identity now?

Tom Collingwood would see her as an impostor and fortune-hunter who had somehow heard of James's death, though that fortune now consisted solely of this house.

A week later, on a morning when the wind blew in cold from off the river bringing a spit of rain, Josie walked home in a more cheerful mood. She was returning from the shops in Dundas Street, Charlotte trotting by her side. The little girl carried her own small basket with the rag doll, Amelia, cradled in her other arm. As they turned into the square, Josie saw the big house spread across the end of it. She also saw a number of her neighbours in white pinnies, shawls around their shoulders, gossiping at their doors despite the rain and the cold. Josie knew them all now. Ever since that first morning when they had called out a welcome to her.

They greeted her now: 'Hello, hinny!'

'Good morning,' Josie replied.

'"Mornin",' chimed in Charlotte.

One asked, 'How are you managing in that big house?'

Josie paused to answer, 'Just about coping, thank you.'

Another called, 'And how are you getting on wi' that Tom Collingwood?'

Before Josie could construct a careful answer to this yet another put in, 'I see he goes back to lodgings every night.'

He did. Josie tactfully answered so and let the previous question go. 'Yes, he does.'

Still another, mock solemn: 'It seems a shame wi' that big house and a dozen rooms in it. Surely he could fit in there.'

Josie's head kept turning, because there was still one more to call. 'I'd find room in the house for that big lad!' And now they all laughed. So did Josie but she hurried on, feeling the blood in her face. Then she heard them chorusing behind her: 'Hello, Captain Collingwood!'

And his deep reply: 'Good morning.'

He caught up with her at the foot of the steps leading up to the front door. 'Good morning. What were they laughing about?'

Josie told a white lie. 'I don't know. It must have been something I didn't catch.' She wondered if he would accept this.

He did, because he was preoccupied and said only, 'They won't be so cheerful later.' Josie saw that he was serious. As they passed through the doorway into the hall, he paused, considering her, then said, 'You'd better know. Everyone else will, soon. And as your employment as governess, nurse, housekeeper—' He smiled wryly over the multiplicity of titles – and duties. Then he continued, 'You would be justified in wondering what truth might lie behind the talk you will hear. So will you come in here for a few minutes, please?'

He dropped his cap on the small table in the hall, ushered Josie into the office and gestured to her to take the leather armchair Felicity had occupied at the reading of the will. He sat at the desk and took a thick sheaf of papers from an inside pocket. 'I've been busy this last week and the result is here.' He waved the papers, then tossed them on to the desk. 'It would take me most of the day to read all that's written there but it can be summed up very briefly: William had a large amount of insurance and that covered most of the outstanding debts. I've been able to clear them so I've managed to save the yard for Charlotte.'

They both glanced at the child, playing with her doll on the floor near Josie's feet, oblivious to the conversation. Josie had been listening carefully and over the past few days had been thinking and learning. She had decided she could not always pose as the servant answering in monosyllables. She had to speak her mind sometimes and risk his displeasure if it meant she might gain some respect. Now she questioned boldly, 'You said the insurance covered most of the debts. What covered the rest?'

Tom straightened in his chair and set hands on his knees to glare at her. 'That is none of your business, Mrs Miller.'

Josie went on as if she had not heard, 'I know you sold the *Celia*. People talk. Two gentlemen were strolling ahead of me just the day before yesterday, discussing the sale. It was bought by a Mr Billy Fredericks for—'

'That's enough!' Tom cut in, exasperated. 'Yes, the sale of the *Celia* helped.'

Josie remembered how he had received the news that he had inherited the cutter and knew he would not have let her go unless he had to. She ventured again, 'And your own capital?'

Tom opened his mouth to rebuke her again but then sighed and admitted, 'That's about the size of it. You may as well know that as well. Oh, you don't need to worry, I can find the money for your wages, but—'

'That was *not* my concern, Captain Collingwood!' Now Josie sat very straight and glared, outraged. 'I have not asked for money. My concern is for the child's welfare.' She would have worked for nothing. But then she remembered the part she was playing and amended: 'Of course, I am only an employee, not a member of the family, but I do care for Charlotte. And if my salary is . . . delayed or postponed, I will still carry out my duties.'

Tom ran his hands through his hair and growled, exasperated, 'I was only trying to reassure you, Mrs Miller. You understand, I know nothing of your personal circumstances, whether there is a child of your own, or some elderly relative, dependent on you and your earnings. That is not uncommon.'

Josie relaxed and bent her head in acknowledgment. 'Perhaps we may go on again. Have you more to tell me?'

'I said they would not be so cheerful later on.' Tom waved a hand at the window and looked out. Josie, too, could see through the lace curtains to the square outside. In passing she thought wryly that she had given those curtains a much-needed washing and ironing but, of course, Tom had not noticed. But she could see the life of the square and the women at their doors. Tom said, 'There isn't money to pay the men and no sign of an order. I'm closing the yard and laying off every man.'

Josie stared at him, appalled. 'Oh, T—' She corrected herself hastily: '—Captain Collingwood! That's awful!' From comments heard as she passed the women at their doors she knew that almost every woman in the square had a man working at Langley's, some of them with a husband and sons. 'Do they know?'

Tom shook his head. 'Not yet. I've sent for Harry Varley, the manager. I'll inform him of the situation first, then go down to the yard and tell the men. Harry's a married man with three small children. And there's all the rest.' He shook his head miserably.

Josie asked, 'Can't the banks help?'

'No.' Tom sighed. 'When he couldn't get an order to build a ship William kept the yard going on repair work and loans. But the repair work has dried up and we'll get no more loans without an order to build.' And now he held Josie's gaze, his dark eyes staring into her as he said, 'You ask some shrewd questions for—' He paused to choose his words, not wanting to patronise.

Josie thought, For a servant. And she forestalled him, 'I was fortunate enough to receive an education with the Urquharts.'

'Um.' Tom's answer was non-committal and he was still watching her. But then there came the *jangle-jangle!* heard faintly from the kitchen, caused by someone yanking on the front-door bell-pull. Tom rose from his chair. 'That will be Harry Varley now. Will you excuse us?' He opened the door and Josie led Charlotte out into the hall. There she gathered up her shopping basket and

Charlotte's and delayed long enough to see the man admitted by Tom.

Harry Varley was short and wiry, energetic. Josie learnt later that he had grown his beard to make him look older. It served now to hide any anxiety of expression, but that anxiety was in his voice when he said, 'You sent for me, Captain Collingwood.'

'Aye, Harry. Come on in.' And Tom set an arm round his shoulders and took him into the office.

Josie took the shopping along to the kitchen, hung up her coat and that of the little girl, then unpacked her purchases and put them away. Charlotte was absorbed in some game with Amelia, chattering away to the doll. Josie took advantage of this and sat down at the kitchen table to consider. The house was safe – so far. But the Langley yard was to close and God only knew if it would ever open again. That would take an order and money – a lot of it. Josie was the real heiress, not Charlotte, who was just a child. So Josie had inherited the responsibility that went with any estate. It was her duty to try to put the Langleys back on a sound footing. She could not hope to start up the yard but she could try to keep this house going. She was on a month's trial. How could she persuade Tom Collingwood to keep her on?

Josie chewed on the problem for some minutes but did not find a solution.

She need not have bothered.

She walked back to the hall again when she heard voices there. Harry Varley had lost all his energy and his shoulders slumped. Tom was picking up his cap and when he saw Josie he said sombrely, 'I'm just going down to the yard with Harry.'

Josie replied, 'I'll have lunch ready when you get back, Captain Collingwood.'

She had made a hotpot, having already found out that it was a favourite of his, but the effort was wasted. They sat down to lunch in the dining room, Tom at the head of the table with Charlotte between him and Josie. He ate abstractedly, his thoughts elsewhere. Josie knew he was upset by the closure of the yard and its effect on the employees. He finally pushed his plate away with the meal only half eaten and declined dessert. He rose from the table, saying, 'Sergeant Normanby left a message at the yard: he's coming to see us this afternoon. I'll be in the office.' He strode away across the hall.

Josie looked at her own picked-at plate and sighed. Charlotte said proudly, 'I ate all mine.'

Josie replied mechanically, 'Yes, you're a good girl.' She wondered what Normanby wanted with them.

Josie answered the knock on the front door with Charlotte trotting along at her heels. Normanby, helmet under his arm, apologised, 'Sorry to trouble you, ma'am.'

'Not at all, Sergeant. Come in, please.'

Tom appeared in the doorway of the office, repeated the invitation and included Josie: 'You, too, Mrs Miller. You were a witness.' He stood before the fireplace and nodded to Normanby to take the armchair. This time Josie sat in the swivel chair at the desk. The door of the office was open and she could see Charlotte playing in the hall. An open letter lay on the desk and the name 'Mrs Josephine Miller' leapt out at her, but she resisted the temptation to peep and tore her eyes away.

'I asked to see you, Captain, Mrs Miller, because we have now completed our enquiries,' Normanby said, apologetically. 'I could have told you one or two bits of news at the inquest or the funeral but I thought it would be better to do it at one go and somewhere like this.'

Tom nodded. 'Very well.'

Normanby took out his notebook. 'I talked to Packer, the solicitor. He informed me that the man who delivered the notices of foreclosure, and the man behind Shipbuilders' Finance Ltd, was a Reuben Garbutt.'

Tom interrupted, frowning, 'A local man?'

'No, sir,' replied Normanby, 'not now, but he was born around here. I remember his father, Elisha, that used to be manager at the Langley yard. Old Mr Langley dismissed him and the Garbutt family moved away. But that must be all of twenty years ago.'

Josie did not remember the name Garbutt, had been only four years old when she last heard it.

Tom was glaring at Normanby: 'Then this man Garbutt was acting out of spite!'

Normanby agreed equably, 'It could be. But he says it was only a matter of business.'

Tom asked, 'You've talked to him?'

'I have, sir.'

Normanby had sat in Reuben's office in the City of London, with its atmosphere of solid respectability, and asked, 'How was Mr William Langley when you left him that evening, sir?'

Garbutt shrugged. 'A bit down in the mouth. But what would you expect? I'd called in some loans and he was going to have trouble finding the money, but that's business.'

'He wasn't having a heart attack or a stroke?'

'I'm not a doctor but I wouldn't say he was having either of those. As I said, he was sitting at the table a bit fed up.'

'A witness reports seeing a man of your description leaving the house with a young woman believed to be a Miss Rhoda Wilks, employed as a housemaid and nurse by the late William Langley. This witness claims Rhoda said, "You've killed him." Were you that man and was that woman Rhoda Wilks?'

'I was and she was. You know how the world wags, Sergeant. Rhoda and I had an understanding. I'd agreed to take her away that night. She was excited – and hysterical when she saw old Langley looking so miserable. That's all.'

Normanby said, 'The witness reports you as saying, "Shut your mouth! You're finished with him and that's what you wanted."'

Garbutt nodded. 'Exactly. I told you, she wanted to get away and I'd promised to take her. I told her to shut up because I was annoyed. Langley had been insulting over what was a quite legitimate business matter.'

'Where can I find Miss Wilks?'

Garbutt shook his head, smiling, and lied: 'Sorry. I haven't seen her since that night. I paid her what I had promised and that was the end of it so far as I was concerned. I don't know where she is.'

Normanby asked one final question because Garbutt fitted the description of the man who had driven the coal lorry, though that description could have been applied to thousands of other men. The sergeant was unlucky in that Garbutt was yawning and rubbing his face in his hands so his expression could not be seen. For a second it might have given him away when the sergeant asked, 'Where were you on Tuesday, 8 September?' This was the day on which James Langley and his wife, Maria, had been killed.

Garbutt answered, 'I was here, in London. Why do you ask?'

'Just following up another enquiry I'm making, sir. Can anyone confirm your statement?'

'I was at home most of that day. You could ask my valet or my chauffeur.'

'Where will I find them, sir?'

Garbutt told him. And as the door closed behind him, Garbutt reached for the telephone and spoke to his valet.

Now Normanby looked up from his notebook at Tom and Josie. 'I spoke to them and they confirmed he had been about the house that day.'

Josie asked, 'Couldn't they be lying?'

'They could,' Normanby agreed, 'but we can't prove it. And really there is no evidence that this Garbutt was connected with the death of Mr and Mrs James Langley. Nor that he committed any crime in delivering those notices of foreclosure. That might be vindictive but it wasn't criminal.'

Tom demanded, 'So what now?'

Normanby put away his notebook and stood up. 'All we can do is to keep looking for further evidence relating to these deaths. But you'll appreciate, sir, as time goes by we're less an' less likely to find any.'

Tom said bitterly, 'It's a dirty, bloody business.'

Normanby agreed. 'Yes, sir.' Tom opened the front door for him and he trudged away round the square, clapping his helmet on his head.

Josie had come out into the hall but Tom stopped her there. 'A moment, please.' So she led the way into the office again, wondering if he was about to find fault with her again, bracing herself for the confrontation. But he stood by the desk, staring out of the window, brows down and lips tight. Finally he took a deep breath and shrugged as if to cast a weight from his shoulders. He turned towards Josie, saying, 'It still seems murder to me, but no doubt Normanby has the right of it and the law can't touch Garbutt. I must be content that I've foiled his plans to take the yard.'

Now he took the letter from the desk and asked, 'Are you prepared to serve here for the foreseeable future?'

Josie breathed a silent sigh of relief. 'Yes, Captain.'

Tom handed her the letter. He had foreseen this decision a week ago, knew he had to leave and someone had to see to the house and care for Charlotte. He still suspected that Mrs Miller was not quite what she seemed, but she had proved competent and fond of the child. Even more importantly, the same instinct that made him suspect Mrs Miller also, strangely, told him he could trust her. Now he said, 'That is a letter of authority, identifying you and authorising you to draw funds from the bank each week while I am away. I have written another letter to the bank confirming this arrangement. If you will be good enough to post it?' He handed the second letter to her, this one sealed and stamped.

Josie looked up at him, taken aback. 'You're going away?'

Tom was still angry, deep inside, at William's death and the manner of it. Also, he wanted to stay ashore and keep an eye on affairs but knew he could not. Out of frustration and anger he answered irritably, as if explaining the obvious, 'I must. I don't know what I can do about the yard in the long term but in the meanwhile Charlotte depends on me and there is this house to maintain. I've got a ship, the *Highgrange*, and she sails this evening.'

Josie noted his irascible tone but ignored it. 'So soon?'

'She's ready so we must sail.' Tom glanced at the clock on the mantelpiece. 'Do you think we could have a meal about half past five?'

Josie answered, 'Of course,' and cursed, because it gave her less than an hour. 'You've packed?'

'Not yet. I've cleared my clothes out of my lodgings, but all my sea-going kit is upstairs.' Tom waved a hand at the desk and the papers still lying on it. 'I have some loose ends to tie up, then I'll do it.'

Josie took the hint. 'I have work to do.' And she left him to it.

In the kitchen she worked rapidly but still maintained a running conversation with Charlotte at her side and 'helping'. Despite this help Josie cooked the meal in time. At five she heard the hooters that signalled the end of the working day in the shipyards. She stopped what she was doing and tiptoed along the hall with Charlotte, silencing the child with a finger to her lips. She passed the closed door of the office where Tom still worked and peered out of the narrow window by the front door. Usually she could hear the buzz of the men's chatter as they came home from work, hurrying past the square or entering it, but today they were silent.

Josie sighed and went back to the kitchen. She left the door to the hall open and so heard when Tom finished in the office and climbed the stairs to pack. He did this in short order, and she heard him when he descended again soon after. She peeped out and saw him drop his big kitbag in the hall. He was dressed in the old reefer jacket he had worn when she first saw him. So she whisked plates and dishes from the oven and on to a tray, then carried them through to the dining room where she had already set the table. As she passed Tom she said brightly, 'Dinner is served.'

She gave him broth – her stockpot was to thank for that – a grilled steak and sautéed potatoes and vegetables, with an apple pie for dessert. This time he ate steadily and with enjoyment through the courses and drank the bottle of beer Josie had opened for him. But he did not linger. His meal completed, he glanced at his watch and rose from the table. 'If you will excuse me.'

Josie went with him. She had eaten little but put that down to the cooking in haste having taken away her appetite. Tom stood in the hall with his cap in his hand. He said gravely, 'I leave Charlotte in your hands.'

Josie smiled down at her where she stood against her legs. 'I'll care for her. When do you sail?'

'Within the hour.' Tom looked around the hall as if to be sure he was handing it over in good order. 'Will you be all right on your own?'

Josie thought wryly that it was the first time he had given it thought. She replied, 'I think we will do very well, Captain.'

Tom crouched before Charlotte and kissed her. 'Be a good girl and I'll fetch you back a present.'

Charlotte giggled. 'A monkey?'

He tweaked her cheek. 'One monkey in the house is enough.' Then he straightened and they heard the murmuring engine then the squeak of brakes as the Blakemore car stopped outside. Josie saw it through the lace curtains at the narrow windows on each side of the front door. She thought that Felicity had known he was leaving, had come to take him to his ship. Well, she was his fiancée.

Josie heard herself say, 'Miss Blakemore is taking you to your ship?'

Tom was smiling at Felicity now and he answered absently, 'Yes. She is attending a dance this evening but she said she would see me off first.'

Josie continued, 'Are you to be married soon?'

'In just over a year from now, in October.'

Josie thought they would make a handsome couple. He remembered her now and turned. Josie smiled brightly, head back as he stood tall above her. Tom said, 'I don't know when I will be back. That depends on what cargoes the agents find for us. It may be weeks, months or a year or more. But I will write.' He swung his kitbag up on to his broad shoulder and set his cap on his head. 'Goodbye, Mrs Miller.'

'Goodbye, Captain Collingwood.'

Josie watched him stride away down the wide steps she had scrubbed and duck his head to enter the car where Felicity Blakemore waited for him. She wore a stole around her shoulders over an evening gown of white chiffon with a low neckline. The lace trim on it glinted silver, reflecting the light from the gas lamps. The door closed behind Tom, the car moved away and drove down the side of the square and out of sight.

Josie realised Charlotte was still shrilling, 'Bye, bye, Uncle Tom!' She led the child back to the kitchen and together they washed up the dinner things. Only then did she realise that Tom was leaving Charlotte with her for an indefinite period. Because he had been unable, or not had time, to find another nurse/governess/housekeeper? Or was it that he trusted her and believed she would not walk out at the end of the first month? Josie glanced down at Charlotte; there was no fear of that.

Briefly cheered by this, she dressed herself and Charlotte for the street, or rather the seafront, in warm coats, a bonnet for Charlotte and a shawl over her own hair.

They left the house, hurrying in the cold, and turned down towards the sea. Josie had not been this way before – or not since she had come North again. But she found her steps turning on a way she seemed to know by instinct – or had she travelled it as a child twenty years before?

They came to the old North Pier and walked out to its end. There the wind cut into them, driving a thin drizzle into their faces. They waited there for twenty minutes, in the darkness and with the sea washing cold and breaking white below them. Charlotte was cuddled inside Josie's coat, pulled round both of them for protection. At last they saw a ship. She was black with a single tall funnel and as she came out of the river between the piers Josie was able to make out her name on her bow: *Highgrange*.

She said, 'That's Captain Collingwood's ship.' They waved. There were men working on the deck of the ship as she slid past them but none returned their wave. In desperation Josie snatched the shawl from her head and waved that. A tall figure stalked out of the wheelhouse on to the wing of the bridge, took off his cap and flourished it.

Charlotte shrieked, 'That's Uncle Tom!'

Josie nodded. 'Yes.'

Then the ship was past, she could not see Tom any longer and the *Highgrange* ploughed on out to sea.

On their way home they passed Langley's yard, now silent and empty. Josie wondered for how long. She thought of Harry Varley, the manager, with a wife and three young children. Then there were all the others . . . And she could do little or nothing.

Josie filled a hot bath for Charlotte and afterwards tucked her up in bed. Then she went downstairs to the office and sat at the desk. She remembered Tom Collingwood sitting there, then shook herself out of her introspection and wrote to Geoffrey Urquhart, her former employer; the Urquharts might have returned from the Continent now and she knew he was grateful for her saving his grandchildren, so she would ask him a favour. When the letter was done she left it on the small table in the hall, with Tom's letter to the bank, to post the following day. She looked in on the kitchen to bank up the fire for the night. On the way out she saw that the door to the cellar was an inch or two ajar. She stopped to close it and fasten it with its catch. She told herself she was being silly but the cellar had frightened her as a child and old fears die hard.

Josie paused in the hall and the tall clock ticked slowly. She had found the body of old William Langley behind the closed door on her right. Tom had gone from the office, was at sea now, and she and Charlotte were alone in this big, empty house. He had said, 'Will you be all right on your own?' And she had replied, 'I think we will do very well.' Now she wondered if she would.

Josie lay awake in bed for a long time, with only the red glow from the nursery fire for company. She wondered what the morrow would hold for her. He had said he could be gone for weeks, months or a year. Dear God!

14

October 1908

Josie had come to the back door to look out at the night and breathe the night air. She had spent the day washing and ironing, was about to go to bed and stood in the doorway, savouring the quiet after the noise of the day. She thought that the hours of toil confirmed that the house was too big for any woman to keep up on her own, and maybe that was why Rhoda had given up trying. Also, there were jobs that needed to be done that were better left to a man, like mending the latch on the back gate – she could see it standing ajar now – and the shutter hanging askew on an upstairs window. Then there was the broken pane that someone, possibly Rhoda, had plugged with a piece of wood and some rag.

Josie thought she heard a noise in one corner of the yard and cocked her head, listening. The washhouse stood in that corner of the yard, and a faint glow showed beneath its door. It came from the dying embers of the fire under the boiler inside. Josie had laboured in there with poss-stick and mangle. She sighed, remembering, then held her breath. And she heard, very faintly, the sobbing. She hesitated, but then armed herself with a poker from the kitchen, shoved open the washhouse door and challenged: 'Who's there?'

The sobbing had stopped. Josie could just make out in the gloom that someone sat on the floor, curled up against the boiler. Josie called, 'Come on out!' The figure moved, rose to its feet. As it approached the door, Josie cautiously retreated before it, until it stepped into the rectangle of light falling out of the kitchen door. Then she saw it was a girl, and she halted and lowered the poker. She demanded, 'What were you doing?'

'I was going to sleep there.' The girl's reply was scarcely above a whisper. She kept her head cast down, the shawl pulled tight around her as if it would armour her against the world. Now Josie could see that she was young, respectably if shabbily dressed; she could see a neat patch in the sleeve of the girl's coat but it looked passably clean.

Josie put two and two together and asked, 'Why have you left home?'

'That's none of your business.' The girl's head came up and she started to turn away. 'I haven't done you any harm and I won't bother you again.'

Josie stopped her. 'Come inside for a bit, get warm and have a cup of tea.' An idea was taking shape in her mind but it was early yet. Wait and see . . . 'Come on,' she urged, and reached out to take the girl's arm. For a moment there was resistance, but the girl's eyes were on the open door, its light and promise of warmth beckoning her. She yielded and allowed herself to be led in.

Josie sat her down by the fire, gave her a cup of tea and a sandwich of cold roast beef, then said, 'I'm Mrs Miller, Josie Miller. And you?'

The girl swallowed. 'Annie Yates.' She was about twenty, blonde, blue-eyed and frightened.

'From?' Josie prompted.

But Annie wasn't giving that away too soon. 'I'm not going back!'

'I'm not going to send you back, but I might be able to help. Was there some trouble?'

It took a long time and some gentle coaxing, but Josie finally heard the whole story, of love, betrayal and fear of brutality. Eddie, the man she had loved so much and so recklessly, had deserted her. When Annie told him about the child he had signed on aboard a tramp steamer bound for Australia and he would not come home. The child was due in April but her own father would find out long before that. She could not, would not, suffer another beating at his hands.

Annie worked as a kitchen-maid in a businessman's house but lived at home, a terraced house in South Shields. She had waited until her mother had gone to the communal washhouse then left her work, hurried home and packed all she had in a pillowcase. She had set out to find work and a place to live where her father would not find her. But after a few days her money had run out and she faced a night on the streets without shelter or supper. Then she saw the gate of the yard standing ajar.

Annie finished, 'So I went into your washhouse to sleep.'

'You wouldn't be warm in there for long. That fire was nearly out.'

Annie said simply, 'I had nowhere else to go.'

Nor had she now. But there was some colour in her cheeks since she had eaten and warmed through. Josie considered her, wondering if she could take the risk of involving this girl, this 'fallen woman', in her plans. But then she told herself, Use your common sense. You can't turn her away. She said, 'You were a kitchen-maid. So can you cook and clean?'

Annie replied, 'Oh, aye,' in a tone that meant 'Of course'. She added bitterly, 'But have you ever walked the streets looking for a job?'

Josie had and she winced at the memory. But then she grinned at Annie. 'I'll give you a job. Seven-and-six a week and live in. Start now.'

Annie burst into tears.

Next morning, Josie called, 'Come on, Annie! Time to fit you out!' She and Annie, with Charlotte between them, walked down Strand Street and crossed the Wear by the ferry. Then they climbed the long hill of High Street East to the big shops, where Josie bought some clothes and aprons for Annie because she had pathetically little in the pillowcase holding her belongings.

At one point they passed the Palace Hotel and Josie returned home thoughtful.

'Eeh! Isn't it grand!' That afternoon Annie stared round-eyed, brush in one hand, duster in the other, when Josie unlocked the doors to the other wing that Hector Langley had built for William.

'It will be when we've cleaned it,' replied Josie cheerfully. She and Annie dusted, swept, washed and polished. They took down the curtains, washed them and found them falling to pieces. So they crossed the river again, bought material and made new curtains for the newly washed windows. Before the week was out they were a happily working team. Charlotte grew wet, dusty and healthily tired. At the end of each day she wallowed in a hot bath and slept the night through.

Josie did not. When the new wing was clean as a new pin she wondered what she was to do with it. In the first blaze of enthusiasm – the idea sparked by sight of the Palace – she had thought to open a small hotel. Now she saw that was impossible. The house might be clean but it needed a lot of work – and money – to make it into a hotel. Again, it was situated in a working-class neighbourhood of poor streets, grimy from the nearby shipyards. The idea was abandoned.

Josie stared into the darkness and wondered if she had wasted her time. Had she been stupidly, unreasonably optimistic to think that she, just a servant after all, could help to restore the Langley fortunes?

She finally slept uneasily and woke in fear with the giant standing black in the doorway and laughing at her.

But a new day brought Dougie Bickerstaffe. He knocked at the back door of the kitchen on a cold, windy morning. Josie opened the door and confronted the expanse of blue-jerseyed chest and the wide grin above it. The young man was in his mid-twenties, stocky and broad. He wore a tarpaulin jacket open over the jersey and carried a kitbag on his shoulder. He touched a finger to his cap and asked, ''Scuse me, missus, but can you point the way to the Seamen's Mission, please?'

Josie covertly inspected him and found him clean if somewhat hard worn. She asked, 'Are you looking for a bed?'

'That's right,' and he grinned frankly. 'Lost me money on the horses, y'see. Paid off yesterday after three months at sea and broke today. So it's a bed for tonight and another ship tomorrow if I'm lucky.'

In the last weeks Josie had learned about ships paying off their crews at the end of a voyage. And this sailor wanted a bed . . . The phrase stirred a memory: 'Everybody's got to sleep somewhere.' Josie wondered who had said that, then remembered it had been Albert Harvey. When he left the Urquhart house to start his first little hotel he had said he would make a living because 'Everybody has to sleep somewhere, soldier, sailor, tinker, tailor'. Josie's thoughts raced on, then a cough brought her back to the present and she realised she was staring vacantly at the puzzled sailor.

Josie apologised. 'I'm sorry. I just remembered something.' And she thought, Living in the Mission and on what it provided while he waited for a ship. She asked, 'What about your shipmates?'

'They'll lend me a bob or two,' he said comfortably. 'I'll look 'em up later, soon as I've left my kit at the Mission. What way is it?' He waited expectantly.

Josie persevered, 'I meant, have your shipmates got somewhere to stay? Lodgings?'

'Not yet. They're still living aboard but they'll be looking for somewhere today, same as I am. They'll be told to sling their hooks and come ashore.'

Josie stepped back and opened the door wide. 'We're just about to have a cup of tea. Won't you join us, Mr . . . ?'

'Dougie Bickerstaffe. And thank ye, ma'am, I will.' He entered willingly, glad to be out of the wind for a while, but awkward, as if not used to houses, certainly not a house of this size. He sat by the fire and Charlotte rested her arms on his knee and questioned him about his life at sea. He told her some tall stories while Josie and Annie busied themselves about the kitchen. This did not get in the way of him drinking the mug of tea Josie gave him, and he ate the thick sandwich of cold beef that came with it – then sniffed appreciatively at the smell from the oven.

Josie let him eat and relax, but when he had finished she sat down opposite him and got down to business. 'I'm opening a boarding house here . . .' Some fifteen minutes later Dougie went on his way. He left his kitbag in a corner of the kitchen and promised, still sniffing the aroma from the oven, to be back by noon. He also promised to bring some of his shipmates before the day was out.

He returned in time to eat a good lunch and his mates turned up an hour later. There were eight of them in jerseys and canvas trousers and each humped his big kitbag. They were wary and smelt of salt water and tar, paint and coal smoke. Meanwhile Josie had hastily crossed the bridge into the town and found a ship's chandler. There she bought blankets, ten mattresses stuffed with horsehair and bunk beds to lay them on. Dougie helped to get them off the cart that brought them and set them up in the bedrooms of the house next door. Josie turned the room at the back of the house into a dining room and common room, with two trestle tables and a dozen chairs from a second-hand shop. She fed her new guests in there that night.

'Well, that's one day over.' Josie sank down into a chair before the kitchen fire and grinned across at Annie. She had set out her rules after her nine guests had eaten: 'I lock the door at eleven. If you aren't in by then – or you turn up the worse for drink – you sleep outside.' They had all nodded solemnly. Now they were all abed.

But Annie said darkly, 'All right so far. But we'll have to wait and see. There's bound to be trouble.'

Josie asked, 'Has Dougie or any of them pestered you?'

'No!' Annie shook her head.

'Then – what sort of trouble?'

'Drink,' Annie replied. 'Eddie used to say: "Drink is the curse o' sailormen."'

Josie thought the departed Eddie had little right to make moral judgments, but she had a nasty feeling that Annie might be right. Still, she refused to be depressed. 'We'll have to deal with that when . . . *if* it happens.' And she went to bed content. She had already done her sums and was sure she would make some money out of this venture. Not enough to reopen the yard, that was an impossible dream, but probably enough to keep Annie, part of the help Josie needed, Charlotte and herself.

She had some good news of the Langley shipyard the next day, chancing to meet Harry Varley, the former manager, as she walked up to the Dundas Street shops with Charlotte. He was no longer the slumped, defeated man she had seen when he heard the news of the closure of the yard. Now he strode along briskly, his head up, and greeted her with a smile. ''Morning, Mrs Miller!'

'Good morning, Mr Varley. How are you?'

'Fine!' He halted and told her exuberantly, 'I've got another position. I still can't believe it. Just a few days ago I had a letter – right out o' the blue – from a chap called Geoffrey Urquhart, saying he might have a post that would suit me and would I go up to Glasgow to see him. I went like a shot and got the job! O' course, I'm not manager, just an assistant, and neither me nor the wife are keen on leaving Sunderland, but it's a good job and we're on top o' the world again.'

Josie smiled at him. 'I'm pleased to hear it.' She went on her way, thankful that her letter to Geoffrey Urquhart, asking if he could find work for Harry Varley, had borne fruit. She looked down at Charlotte skipping by her side. 'Isn't it a lovely day?'

That night was different. Archie Ruddock, one of Josie's boarders, banged on the kitchen door close on eleven. When Annie opened it to him he shoved it wide, throwing her back against the wall, and staggered in. He was a big man, normally placid and none too bright, with a deep laugh that came easily. Now he was tangle-haired and wild-eyed, unsteady on his feet. The smell of rum hung around him. He had been in a fight and there was blood on his hands and his face.

Josie was sitting by the fire but now she stood up. 'You're drunk.'

'I'm not drunk!' Ruddock shouted back at her. 'Jusht had a drink or two! Don't tell me I'm drunk, woman!' Annie, frightened, shrank back against the wall with her hands to her face as he started across the kitchen. Josie, trembling inside but trying to keep her mouth steady, stepped into his path. Ruddock pulled up short, hovering over her unsteadily. 'Gerrout o' my way!'

Josie had faced men like this when she had worked as a barmaid and held her ground despite his breath in her face. She met his gaze determinedly, spoke clearly and somehow without a tremor: 'I don't know if you've ever seen the inside of a prison before but you will if you lay a finger on me.'

Ruddock squinted at her and repeated foolishly, 'Prison?'

'That's right, prison! Now, there's the door—' Josie pointed and Ruddock half turned to look where she indicated. She seized the opportunity and his arm and helped him around, urged him towards the door. 'Out you go and come back when you're sober.' She kept him shambling forward until he was outside, then she shut the door behind him and shot the bolt.

Annie came out of the corner where she had sheltered and asked, 'Are you all right?'

Josie stood with her back to the door and tried to still the shaking of her hands. She said worriedly, 'I wonder if *he* will be all right.'

Dougie Bickerstaffe answered that. He tapped at the door leading from the kitchen into the hall and said, 'Thought I heard a rumpus, missus. Has summat been happening?'

Josie told him, with highly coloured interjections from Annie. Dougie listened and at the end shook his head. He said respectfully, 'Naw, you don't need to worry your head about Archie, missus. He's used to hard lying and he'll come back like the lost sheep. But I'll sleep down here in one o' these chairs and let him in when he knocks.'

Josie said, 'I'll wait up for him, too.' She was still worried.

Josie and Dougie sat by the fire and he did most of the talking. Josie led him into it, glad to be able to sit quietly herself. He rambled on about the countries he had visited and a life at sea. It seemed to Josie like a succession of short stays in ports that were all the same with long intervals spent uncomfortably at sea. Yet Dougie appeared to delight in it.

But then, after a long silence when he had run out of stories, and sat gazing into the fire, he said, 'I miss Iris.' And he explained, 'That's my young lady, Iris Taylor. I met her in London, a place called Wapping. But I can't go down South to live. Y'see, her father and stepmother, they've got no use for me, won't have me in the house. If I married Iris and we lived down there they'd be after us – Iris and me – all the time.' He sighed. 'If we lived up here we'd be out o' their road, but Iris is scared o' leaving home and coming all the way up North. The truth is, she doesn't trust me.' Then he admitted, 'And from what I know o' some sailors, I don't blame her.'

'Are they a well-to-do family?' Josie asked, thinking that this might be some middle-class couple reluctant to bestow their daughter on a common sailorman.

'No fear,' Dougie said scornfully. 'Her stepmother takes nearly all o' Iris's wages. That's why they don't want her marrying anybody, never mind a sailor. Iris works in a greengrocer's shop. That's how I met her. I stopped to look at what was in the shop because I was brought up in that trade. My folk were hawkers and I'll probably go back to it when I'm done with the sea.'

But then Archie tapped at the window of the kitchen, an hour after he had left, and they let him in, a colder, more sober man. Josie sat him in a chair by the fire, then fetched a bowl of water and a cloth and cleaned his face. Interrogated by Dougie, Archie recalled that somebody had punched him on the nose and he had replied in kind. Josie sent him off to bed, humble and cleaner.

The next morning Archie came to see her in the kitchen with the others crowding behind him. 'I've come to say I'm sorry, missus. About last night, I mean. It won't happen again.'

'Very well.' Josie eyed him severely. 'You know my rules and you've got to stick to them.'

'Aye, missus,' Archie replied, and the others joined in.

Later Dougie Bickerstaffe confided to Josie, 'I heard how you dressed him down when you threw him out. I was on my way down here. You got hold of him proper and stood no nonsense. I told 'em all: the missus'll have you in a cell quick as you like if you cross her.'

Josie thought that this was not what she had said or meant, but decided that if it had made the right impression she would let it be.

But she had not had the last of her problems with drink.

It was just two weeks later, as she trudged home, that Josie heard the slurred and discordant singing: 'The signal was made – For the Grand Fleet to an-chor . . .' She had been to the market in the east end on the south side of the river and returned to Monkwearmouth by the ferry. Charlotte had been left in Annie's care, so Josie had no worries on her account. But the day had been long, it was dark, raining and there was a cold wind coming in off the sea. Her shopping basket was heavy and she wanted to be home, toasting herself before a warm fire.

Josie had become increasingly aware that she still needed more help. Annie was willing and did a full day's work but there were all manner of jobs that the two of them did not have time for. There was the loose shutter, washing out the back yard regularly, and tending the two walled gardens outside the sitting rooms.

'. . . for the Grand Fleet to mo-or.' The singer tried to hold a note, wavering. Josie shifted the basket from one arm to the other. Food for the eleven adults in the house – nine of them hungry sailors – made for a heavy burden. She wished, yearningly, hopelessly, for someone to relieve her of the load.

The singing went on, a woman's wailing, hoarse and erratic. Josie had missed the middle of the chorus that had descended into a mumble, but now the words came stronger and clear again, if wavering still: '. . . On a bright sandy bot-tom, From Ushant to Scilly is—' But then the singing was cut short with a yell and a splash. Josie stopped in her tracks, for a moment uncertain. Had the singing come from behind her or ahead? She decided it had been ahead of her and now started to run – but carefully. The gaslights were some distance apart on this stretch of the riverbank and she was running in darkness. She could make out the edge of the quay but the tide was high so that the surface of the river lay only five or six feet lower than the quay. It would be easy, in that treacherous gloom, to wander off into the black water.

She was listening for a cry for help but heard none. Then a flicker of movement caught her eye, a flash of phosphorescence close under the quay and just a few yards ahead. Josie halted when she came abreast of it and made out something just below the surface which thrashed wildly at the water above it. An arm? She realised she still carried the basket, set it down and shrieked, 'Help! *Help!*' She did not receive an answer and knelt on the edge of the quay, searching for the body she had seen. For a moment there was nothing, then it appeared again, a hand and arm and then a head. It coughed and gurgled then sank again. And now it had drifted on the current another two or three yards downstream.

Josie jumped to her feet and tried to anticipate the drift by running along the bank before she knelt again. She could swim but had not done so for years, nor had she ever tried to save someone from drowning. She knew she could not dive in to make a rescue, but between the massive vertical piles of the quay there were equally massive timber baulks stretching horizontally. One lay a yard below her with the river lapping on to it, coating it with a thin film of water. Josie let herself down on to it, watching where she put her hands and feet, but also for the body. She shouted again, '*Help!*' Still there was no answer – but there came the body.

It had not drifted as far as she had expected. She reached out for it but it was still behind her – and further out. Josie shuffled desperately, precariously back along the timber as the hand and then the head appeared, coughing and gasping. She banged her knee on something painfully hard, then her hand was on it as she moved over it and she found it was a steel dog, like a staple, hammered into the timber for some reason. Mooring? But she did not care why it was there. She locked her fingers around its reassuring solidity and leaned out, far out, to seize the hand as it sank below the surface once more.

Josie hauled in and the body came easily. It bumped against the timber by her side and now the head lifted above the surface again. Josie saw long hair straggling wetly, but the face turned up to her was blank, the eyes closed and Josie knew she had to get the woman out of the river. She tried to lift her but could not. Holding her alongside was easy enough with the river supporting her, but lifting her out was another matter. Nor could she leave her to go for help. The pair of them were prisoners here, and Josie realised that as the tide went out and the level of the river fell, so the weight of the woman would increase. She would have to let her go.

Then she heard an irregular tread on the quay. She called, 'Help! I've got a drowning woman here!' The tread quickened, though still with a faltering rhythm, and a man appeared out of the night, trotting. He carried a pack slung over one shoulder, but now he shed this. He climbed down on to the timber to face Josie then reached out and grabbed the woman's other arm. Josie said breathlessly, 'If we lift her together!'

He replied, 'Aye. One, two, *three!*' He was strong. The woman came out of the river like a cork from a bottle, the man getting his other hand under her legs as she came out and hoisting her up and on to the quay. Then he lowered a hand to help Josie up off the timber to join him. As she caught her breath, he turned the woman face down, linked his hands around her middle and lifted. The woman retched and vomited water, coughed and gasped.

The man growled at her, 'Now, Kitty, how're ye feelin'?'

She coughed again, spat and moaned, 'Give ower. Are ye trying to murder me?'

The man turned her and set her so she sat with her back against his leg. He looked at Josie. 'We'll have to get her home.'

Kitty mumbled, 'I'm not goin' back there. To hell with him.'

Josie whispered, 'You know who she is? Where she lives?' She was warm from her exertions but the woman was sitting in the cold wind in soaking-wet clothes.

'Aye. It's auld Kitty Duggan.' He glanced down at her. 'I don't know where she lives, but it sounds as if she won't go there, anyway.'

Kitty was old but she had sharp ears. 'I've told ye: I'm not goin' back there. He's a bad bugger.' Her teeth chattered and now she wrapped her arms around herself, shivering.

The man muttered, 'She'll have pneumonia if she stays out here.'

Josie pulled off her coat and wrapped it around the old woman. She looked over Kitty's head to ask the man, 'I don't live far away. Will you help me get her there – Mr . . . ?'

'Dan Elkington. Aye, I'll give you a lift with her.' He turned and hoisted the pack he had laid down and slung it on to his shoulder again. Josie retrieved her basket and they lifted Kitty between them, her arms around their shoulders. With her legs under her she could stand, though unsteadily, and they half carried her back to the Langley house. The front door was nearer the river so Josie used her key to let them in and they took Kitty through the hall to the kitchen. Annie was working at the table, kneading dough for bread with Charlotte by her side.

'Glory be to God!' Annie gaped at them in shocked surprise. 'What's happened?'

Josie explained: 'This is Kitty Duggan. She fell in the river.' She lowered Kitty into a chair by the fire. The old woman looked to be in her seventies, with no flesh on her bones, a leathery skin and pale blue eyes that watered now. Her hair was grey and tangled, her hands when she held them out to the fire were blue with cold and on arms thin as sticks. Josie took the cold hands, chafed them and asked Annie, 'Will you run upstairs and get a nightdress out of my drawer and bring it down with my dressing gown?'

Annie dusted flour from her hands and hurried off. Dan Elkington cleared his throat and said, 'Well, missus, if you're all right now, I'll get away.'

Josie had not looked at him closely before. Now she did – and saw his eyes slide to the pans on the hob. He was in his thirties, not tall nor broad in the shoulder but deep-chested and, despite his limp because of one leg slightly bent, he stood ramrod straight. His clothes were old but neatly patched and he was clean shaven with a wide moustache. Josie said quickly, 'Thank you very much, Mr Elkington. But we'll be eating supper shortly. Will you stay and have a bite? Please,' she urged, 'I couldn't have managed without you.'

'Well, that's good o' you, missus, if you're sure you can spare it . . .'

'I'm sure.' Josie crouched in front of Kitty Duggan as Annie returned. 'Kitty, I've got some things for you to put on while we dry your clothes.'

Kitty snapped, 'I'm all right as I am.'

Josie reasoned with her, 'You'll catch a chill if you don't get those wet clothes off.'

'Bugger that.' Kitty sniffed. 'All I need is a drink.'

'Brandy?' Josie asked.

'Aye.' Kitty's answer came quickly. 'That'll do fine.'

'When you've changed – in there,' and Josie pointed to the scullery. She was not going to pour brandy down on to an empty stomach – and she had witnessed the emptying of Kitty's.

The old woman grumbled but yielded, and returned from the scullery wrapped in Josie's nightdress and dressing gown. 'Where's that brandy?'

'When we've had our supper,' Josie told her, and ignored the muttered curses that ensued. The table was set and the meal served while Annie carried broth, cold meat and bread through to the seamen boarders. Josie gestured to Dan Elkington where he sat discreetly in a corner, 'Bring your chair up, Mr Elkington.' And she brought Kitty to the table. Both rescuer and rescued ate hungrily. Josie thought one must be as empty as the other, but while Dan was silent, Kitty was ready to talk.

'I'm not goin' back there,' she declared again, as she passed up her plate for more broth.

Josie questioned, 'Home?'

'Home!' Kitty snorted. 'No home there. One room in Hedworth

Street I had, damp and full o' mice. But the landlord wants me out to do it up and put his woman friend in. He's made my life a misery for months now. So tonight I went out for a drink or two.' She looked up from her plate and found Josie's eye on her. She said defiantly, 'Well, I had a few gins to finish off after the stout. I shouldn't ha' gone near the river because the light's very bad there. But I wasn't going back to that room. I'd sooner go to the workhouse.' This time she caught Dan Elkington's eye. She stared at him for a moment, then said blandly, 'What's your place like?'

Dan hesitated, then realised they were all watching him. 'Very nice.'

Kitty grinned at him. 'Now tell the truth. You're carrying a pack wi' everything you've got. It's a dosshouse or sleeping under a cart for you.' She looked round at them. 'He's too proud to admit it.'

'I'll be off now.' Dan shoved back his chair.

'No, canny lad.' This time it was Kitty who reached out to hold him. 'There's no shame in being down on your luck. Mine's been out these ten years, since my man was lost at sea.'

Dan subsided into his seat again and Josie said softly, 'I'm sorry.' She could sympathise with Kitty, remembered her own grief when Bob Miller was drowned. That seemed now to have happened in another life.

Kitty waved a hand impatiently. 'It was a merciful release for him. He'd been a sick man for years. He owned the ship he was in and I wanted him to sell up and come ashore but he wouldn't have it. He kept on because he wanted to leave me wi' plenty o' money but I'd ha' been content to have *him*. Then those last years he did some very bad business. When the ship went down her insurance just covered his debts.' She still held Dan with one hand on his sleeve and now she shook him gently. 'This is the one you want to worry about. I've had my time but he's got a lot o' years yet.'

Dan said, 'I'll be all right.' He returned their stares, proudly.

Kitty said, 'Show 'em your medals.'

'Medals?' Josie looked from one to the other.

'Aye,' said Kitty. 'He was a soljer. Look at how he carries hissel.'

Josie saw from Dan's face that this was so. He knew she saw it and said, 'I served sixteen years in the Durhams, signed on when I was twenty. Then I stopped one in India, on the Frontier, that left me with this gammy leg. They turned me out after that. They gave me a pension but that doesn't go far and there's not much work for a feller wi' only one good leg. I'd ha' changed my name and signed on again, like many another man has done, but they wouldn't take me wi' the leg, o' course.' He detached Kitty's hand from his sleeve and stood up. 'Thank you for the supper, missus, but I'll get away now.'

He left the table and picked up his pack. Josie had sat pensive but now she said, 'Can you paint?'

Dan paused and repeated, 'Paint?'

'Paint a door or a window.'

'Aye.'

'Climb a ladder, sweep a yard – carry a sack of groceries?'

''Course I can. I—'

'I'll give you a job here. Live in. Ten shillings a week and your keep. What about it?' She was careful to speak briskly as between equals, without patronising or any suggestion of charity. She knew he would recoil from either.

Even so, he looked at her sharply, searching for signs of them. But then he slowly relaxed and at last he grinned. 'That'll do me fine.'

'Come on and I'll find you a room.' She turned, saw Charlotte asleep in an armchair and laughed. Then she took Kitty's arm: 'I think you'll be another one the better for a night's sleep.' She helped the old woman up from her chair, but then Kitty put away her hands. 'I can manage.' She and Dan followed Josie, who led the way with Charlotte in her arms.

There were still attic rooms to spare at the top of the house and Dan was settled in one, Kitty in another. Annie came running up the stairs with a hot shelf from the oven to shove into the old woman's bed. With Kitty tucked in, Josie sat on the edge of the bed, cradling the sleeping Charlotte. She said, 'I could do with another woman to help me here. You see, this is a lodging—'

Kitty broke in, 'I know. I heard about you taking in that lass and them sailors. Folks talk.'

Josie explained, 'It's a big house—'

Kitty cut her off again: 'I know that an' all, knew this house afore you were born, lassie. Knew Will Langley and I cried when I heard he'd died. After my man was lost, if Will found me when I'd had a drop too much, he'd always see me home.' She wiped at her eyes. 'And I know that Tom Collingwood, knew him from when he was just a bairn and Will took him in.'

Josie didn't like the sound of the 'drop too much'. It suggested tonight's drunken escapade had not been the first, as Kitty had suggested. But could she send the old woman away, or to the workhouse? She had been a friend of old William, that seemed like the truth. Josie said, 'What I'm getting at is that I could give you a job and a room here, just as I have Dan.'

Kitty peered up at her. 'You would?' And when Josie nodded the tears rolled down the old woman's cheeks. She turned away abruptly to hide her face. 'I owe you something for what you did tonight, so I'll help you out. Now get away and let me sleep.'

'Goodnight.' Josie grinned and left her.

She was startled next morning to see Kitty descending the stairs, albeit stiffly and with a hand to her brow. Josie folded the letter she had just finished reading and was still smiling. 'Good morning. How are you?'

Kitty grumbled, 'Me head aches. It must ha' been the way you and that soljer manhandled me.'

Josie thought the true cause might lie in something Kitty had drunk, but only said, 'Come and have breakfast.'

The old woman followed her to the kitchen. As they passed the side passage leading to the house next door, Kitty said, 'What will Tom Collingwood think about you turning this place into a lodgin' house? Some of them has a very queer reputation and he worshipped old Will. *And* you've got Will's granddaughter here.'

Josie knew what Kitty meant by 'reputation'; there were lodging houses which were little more than brothels. She replied, with relief because of the assurance of Tom's letter in her hand, but also, surprising herself, with more than a tinge of regret: 'Captain Collingwood is not here.'

Kitty said ominously, 'He will be – one day.'

15

November 1908

'Have you gone mad, woman?' Tom Collingwood stood in the hall, a towering, black-browed, wrathful figure. His kitbag lay at his sea-booted feet, his cap was gripped tight in one big hand.

Josie had just come out of the kitchen into the passage leading to the hall. She stared at him, trying to collect her wits, and gave thanks that she wore a clean, white blouse and long, dark skirt, and had stripped off her apron before leaving the kitchen. Only three days had passed since she had told Kitty confidently, 'Captain Collingwood isn't here.' He was now, come like a sudden storm.

She said, 'I had a letter from you, written in Spain.'

Tom answered deliberately, 'I posted it the day before I learned we had a homeward-bound cargo.'

'I see. I wasn't expecting you.'

'I wasn't expecting to find *this*!' Tom pointed along the hall to the side passage leading to the boarders' quarters. That was their only entrance to the house next door. 'I saw three or four men duck into there just a second or two ago. This . . . lady' – he gestured with his cap towards Annie, pressed back against the wall, blue eyes wide and hands to her face – 'who admitted me, tells me they are sailors lodging here.'

Josie swallowed but walked on into the hall to confront him. 'That is correct.'

Annie sidled along the wall, seeking to hide behind Josie. Tom's gaze switched to her again and he started, 'And—'

Josie grasped the nettle. 'This is Annie. She had to leave home because she was in trouble, but she is a good girl really and a great help to me.' Tom stared at her, incredulous. Then Josie heard the kitchen door open behind her and she turned her head and saw Kitty Duggan. Josie sought to introduce her: 'And this is—'

Tom broke in: 'Kitty Duggan. Yes, I know all about Kitty. Do I understand that she is also a member of this household now?'

'She is, and—' But Josie stopped as Tom swung away, found his kitbag at his feet and kicked it aside to slide across the floor, which had been polished by Josie on her knees, and slam into the wall. He yanked open the door of the office, gestured with his cap and said in a low voice that rumbled deep in his chest like distant thunder, 'Perhaps we can discuss this in private.'

Josie plucked up the front of her skirt with one hand and walked past him into the office with her head held high. From the corner of her eye she glimpsed Annie scuttling away down the passage to the kitchen. She expected Tom to slam the door but he did not. She turned in front of the fire in time to see him shut it firmly but quietly. He pointed to the chair at the fireside, wordlessly, and Josie took it. Then he stood before the desk, half the room between them. Josie had to tilt back her head to look up at him. His frame filled the window, blocking out the light. She could have wept.

He asked, 'Well?'

Josie faced him across that desert and echoed, 'Well?'

'I take it you have an explanation for the presence of these people?'

'I have.' Josie was miserable but hid it and replied coolly, 'You wish to hear it – without interruption?'

'I do.'

'Very well. This is a big house, an expensive house to run—'

Tom broke in, pointing a finger. 'I left you an authority to draw funds.'

Josie snapped, 'You also said you would not interrupt. Yes, you left funds and they were ample to keep myself and the child and for that I thank you. But I repeat, this is a big house, and it takes a great deal of work just to keep it clean. But you may also have noticed that the exterior needs painting. Doubtless if Mr Langley and his son had lived the matter would have been taken in hand, but as it is the work still needs to be done. That takes money. So I took in Annie and Kitty to help me with the work, the seamen because what they pay me for lodgings will more than cover the cost of keeping this house in a fit condition and show some profit besides. I also took in a man who had been a soldier to help with the heavy work about the place. There is your explanation.'

Tom scowled down at her. 'Why this pregnant girl? There are plenty of honest women who would work here.'

'She *is* an honest woman!' Josie glared at him. 'But she was betrayed by a scoundrel. And when I took her in it was because we were both lonely and frightened. You will remember there was just the child and myself in this house.'

Tom was silent a moment, then said, 'I see. And Kitty? What about her? Are you aware she staggers home, drunk, from some public house every night?'

'I helped to pull her out of the river when she fell in one dark night. She was homeless, would not go back to the room she had and I could not put her out on the street. Could you?'

Tom took a turn across the room and back, long, fast strides, brooding. He stopped and addressed Josie again: 'The sailors; I have been one myself and I know that mostly they are more sinned against than sinning, but they are rough-and-ready men in a rough-and-ready profession. They are not innocents. They have their faults, drink for instance—'

Now Josie butted in: 'And bad language. I do not permit it in my hearing. The drinking I do not allow at all. A drunken man will not cross the threshold and I established that rule at the beginning.'

Tom blinked at her. 'You did? How?'

'I suggest you ask one of them. Dougie Bickerstaffe will give you a true account, though I admit he is prejudiced in my favour.'

Tom prowled across the room and back again like a caged tiger. 'You seem to have an answer for everything, but I am not happy with this state of affairs. William Langley left this house and the child in my care. He also left his reputation and I think I have failed him in all three.' He stopped to glower out of the window. 'He would turn in his grave if he saw how this house – his house – was being used.'

Josie said, 'I don't think he would.'

Tom glanced over his shoulder. 'You did not know him.'

Josie had thought she had known her grandfather but in recent weeks she had changed her mind. She replied, 'I have come to know him by reputation. I know he often helped Kitty home. I know he took you in—' She stopped there, and quickly apologised. 'I'm sorry. That wasn't fair.'

Tom had spun around on his heel to face her, angry. But then he nodded. 'Yes, it was. He was a hard man with high standards but he would help anybody in need – if he thought they deserved it. He let the thieves and the lazy go to hell.' He was still for long seconds while he stared down at Josie. Finally he said slowly, and as if surprised by the discovery, 'I think – possibly – he would approve of what you did.'

Josie let out a silent sigh of relief and smiled at him. 'Thank you.' She rose to go and then remembered. 'I have been using the desk while you were away. You will find a small account book in there. It shows a record of my dealings and you will see I used little of the money you left me and made a profit.'

Tom turned to the desk, found the book and opened it. He scanned the figures inside then looked across at Josie and said, grudgingly impressed, 'You've done very well.'

Josie smiled again, basking in his meagre approval, and said eagerly, 'The money is in an account I opened at the bank.' She had also opened another to save what she could from her small wage. 'It may help towards reopening the yard.' And when he stared at her, dumbfounded, she went on, 'That is your objective, isn't it?'

He laughed bitterly. 'My dream, more like. Your profit' – and he waved the book – 'and my pay, if we saved them for a year they wouldn't be enough to open the yard for a single day.' He saw her mouth droop and said quickly, 'But I meant what I said, you have managed remarkably.' He put the book back in the desk, hesitated a moment then said, 'I suggest we let this matter rest while we think it over.'

'Very well,' Josie agreed, though she decided she would not be going back on what she had done. So there would be another row at some time in the future. She looked at him across the space between and said, 'If you will excuse me?'

'Of course.' Tom reached the door in two of his long strides and held it open, looking down on her, stiffly formal, as when he had ushered her in. Josie left the room as she had entered it, straight in the back and head held high – but her heart no longer in her mouth.

She paused a second in the doorway to look up at him. 'And you will see I am now adequately chaperoned, Captain Collingwood, so there will be no need for you to seek lodgings; you can occupy your own room.' Then she swept on, having had the last word.

In the kitchen, peering out along the passage through the half-open door, Annie whispered, 'Did they have a row?'

Kitty Duggan, standing at her side, sniffed. 'Aye. You can see that by the look o' them. And this time they fought a draw so there'll be another tussle or two.' Then they backed into the kitchen and busied themselves there as Josie approached. Tom climbed the stairs, kitbag on his shoulder, heading for his room.

Josie looked around the kitchen brightly. 'Is everything all right?'

Annie answered quickly, 'Oh, aye.' And Kitty nodded, glancing sidewise as she stood at the sink peeling potatoes.

Josie saw that Charlotte was playing happily with her doll, Amelia, and snatched her coat from its hook behind the door. 'Then I'll walk up to the shops for a few things.' And she was gone, out of the back door and pulling on her coat.

Annie said, 'She's happy enough, then. It can't have been much of a row.'

Kitty said grimly, 'She's not and I think it was. She's gone for a good cry, I reckon.'

She was only partly right. Josie fought back the tears of misery and rage, misery because of Tom's attack on her, rage because he had made her miserable. Rage may have won because the tears did not come. Instead she vowed to go on doing what she thought was right, and fight every inch of the way if she had to.

Tom unpacked his kitbag, quickly and methodically. Anger still simmered, but seamanlike he tried to take a commonsense view. He had not so much lost an argument as been given an explanation. And this Mrs Miller had only been right, it seemed, so far. He sat down on his bed and pulled off a sea boot. It was difficult to argue with her, but a pretty face did not mean she was invariably right. He had taken her on originally because she was there and her reference was good, but he could give her notice now. He shifted uneasily and told himself that finding a replacement would not be easy. And Charlotte was fond of Mrs Miller.

He pulled off the second boot and decided it would be better to extend Mrs Miller's engagement and keep an eye on her. But if he wanted to do that he would have to leave the sea. He stopped there. Give up the sea? He could not imagine that. It had been his life for seventeen years. Take a shore job? If he did he would still not make enough money to open the yard again, would probably earn less than he did commanding a ship. He wanted to go to sea *and* keep Mrs Miller. He swore out of frustration and hurled the boot across the room to bang against the door.

The knock on the door came like an echo. He crossed to it on stockinged feet, yanked it open and barked, 'Yes?'

Kitty Duggan stood there with a large mug of tea in one hand. 'I thought you'd be ready for this.'

'Thank you, Mrs Duggan.' Tom reached out to take the tea.

'You should remember me.' Kitty craned her neck to peer up at him. 'You've seen me off and on since I skelped your arse twenty years ago for puttin' a football through my window.'

Tom's ill temper faded. 'I recall running a few errands for you.' And afterwards there had been slices of cake, glasses of home-made ginger beer.

Kitty nodded, then turned it into a jerk of the head, gesturing at the stairs behind her. 'She's a good sort, that Mrs Miller. You won't find anybody with a word to say against her.' And when Tom guardedly said nothing, she went on, 'You'll have to find out for yourself. But one thing I'll tell you: I've been off the drink since I came here to live. I just have the odd bottle o' stout by the fire last thing, that's all.'

Tom said politely, 'Oh?'

The little woman eyed him. 'I know what you're thinking, but it's true. I used to go on the bottle because I was so bloody miserable and on my own. I've got company here and I'm happier.'

Tom said sincerely, 'I'm glad.'

Kitty reached up to pat his cheek. 'I always thought you'd turn out a fine young feller and a credit to the auld man.' Then, as she turned away, she glanced down at Tom's feet in their socks with a toe poking through. 'You always had holes in your stockings then an' all. Let me have them later on and I'll darn them.'

Tom drank the tea standing at his window and looking out over the square. A distant tugboat hooted on the river, reminding him of the sea. He decided he would have to give it up, a bitter decision – but he would think about it some more for a day or two.

So they entered on an uneasy truce. Tom and Josie ate their meals in the dining room, waited on by Annie or Kitty. Charlotte ate lunch and tea with them but went to bed before dinner. Tom would have spoilt her but Josie would not allow it. 'No, thank you, Captain Collingwood,' she ruled, as he tried surreptitiously to slide a slice of cake on to Charlotte's plate as Josie poured tea. 'Charlotte! Eat some bread and butter first – cake later.' And because it was Mrs Miller, Charlotte obeyed.

Tom was out of the house for most of each day, investigating what opportunities there were for work ashore – and calling on Felicity at the Blakemore mansion in the country. Josie ran the Langley house and her staff of Annie, Kitty and Dan, while teaching Charlotte as well. At the end of a week Tom announced his decision that evening at dinner. They sat at the long table, Tom at its head, Josie an arm's length away with Charlotte between, allowed to stay up because it was Saturday. As Kitty left the room after serving the main course, pulling the door to behind her, Tom said, 'I've decided to take a shore job for a while.'

Josie smiled, but it quickly faded. 'May I ask why, Captain?'

Tom met her gaze. 'I think it would be better if I spent more time at home. My responsibilities lie here.'

Josie thought, Because he does not trust me; because of what he found when he returned from his last voyage. But she was aware of the child by her side and said only, 'I see.'

He saw that she did and guessed that she was hurt and angry. He was not happy about it but thought he saw his duty clearly, and there was the child to remind him of it. 'I must do what I think is right.'

Josie agreed. 'Of course.' It was his sense of honour again. He had given his word to old William Langley that he would care for Charlotte and he would keep it, no matter what happened. As he had given his word to marry Felicity Blakemore next October.

They went on with the meal in silence and ate little. Kitty, on the other side of the door with her ear clapped against the panel, listened to the silence then tiptoed away. But she went only as far as the foot of the stairs and sat there thinking. She stopped Annie later as the girl picked up the tray carrying the dessert. 'I'll do that,' she said firmly, and took the tray from her.

In the dining room she found Tom and Josie sitting stiff and wordless over the half-eaten meal while Charlotte talked to Amelia, the doll propped on another chair. Kitty cleared the previous course and served the dessert. Then she asked primly, 'Can I say a few words, ma'am – Captain?'

Josie looked up at her from wiping Charlotte's mouth, then across at Tom. He said, curious, 'I should think so. What is it?'

Kitty bobbed her head in thanks. 'When my man was lost it got about that he'd done some bad business and not left me much.' Kitty sniffed indignantly. 'I let them think that because he always used to say, "Never flash your money in a bar." By that he meant that if you shout about how much money you've got somebody will try to get it off you. So I kept quiet about what I had left. It was enough to buy me an annuity that would keep me in comfort. But then there was the *Macbeth*.'

'*Macbeth*?' Tom frowned, searching his memory. 'Wasn't she—'

'Aye,' Kitty nodded. 'She was his first ship. Kitty Macbeth was my maiden name. She was old and he'd left her laid up in the Tyne for a year while he sailed the new ship. But I used to sail with him in the *Macbeth*. Good days they were . . .' Her voice trailed away and she was silent a moment, remembering, then shook her head impatiently. 'Anyway, there she lay, and there she lies still. Over the years nearly all my annuity has gone to pay her charges. I couldn't bother to use her and I couldn't bear to part with her.'

Tom said gruffly, 'I can understand that.'

Josie reached out to squeeze the old woman's hand, and said softly, 'Thank you for telling us.'

Kitty blinked. 'I haven't finished yet. Y'see, I've been thinking that I've been a daft ould woman. Instead o' me keeping up the ship all these years, she should ha' been keeping me. So I was wondering' – and now she looked at Tom – 'would you like to go into partnership? I put up the ship and you skipper her? O' course, she's only good for the coastal trade, but properly handled she should make a profit.'

Tom thought that might be the case. And the voyages would be short and he would be home for a day or two every week or so.

He would not have to give up the sea.

He said slowly, 'I thought I'd try for a berth in the coastal trade but there are skippers queuing up for that kind of work.'

'You'll do it, then?' Kitty urged.

Tom nodded decisively. 'That I will!'

Kitty clapped her hands with glee. 'We'll all profit.'

Tom questioned, 'All?'

Kitty corrected herself quickly. 'I mean the partners.'

'I'm not too sure about the profit,' said Tom drily, staring off into the distance, calculating. 'We've got to make her fit for sea because I'm not sailing a coffin ship and that will cost money, though I can find it; the banks will lend it to me for that. Then we'll have to find a crew, cargoes—'

Josie saw the change in him, from stubborn determination to eager optimism. She realised this was because he would still be going to sea. But not for long. He would not sail away for months or years. She turned quickly, a smile spreading, and caught a self-satisfied smirk on Kitty's face, but it vanished before Josie's stare.

Josie said, 'That sounds like a good idea. Thank you, Kitty.'

Tom got up from the table. 'It's too late to look at the *Macbeth* tonight but I'll go through to the Tyne tomorrow. Now, we'll need a name to trade under. How about the Langley Shipping Company? Because I'm doing this for Charlotte and William.'

Kitty shrugged. 'That's fine wi' me. Now all I want—'

But Tom was going on: 'Tonight I'll draft the terms of our partnership and when we've both agreed on it I'll get a lawyer to write it up legally.'

Kitty protested, 'There's no need for that. Your word's good enough for me.'

But Tom would not have that. 'I knew your husband and I know he would want your rights protected properly. So we'll have a legal agreement.'

Kitty gave in: 'If that's what you want. There's only two things I ask.' She was looking at Josie now.

Josie asked, 'What are they?'

'That we go on just as before, me in the kitchen working for you. Y'see,' Kitty put in quickly as Josie opened her mouth to protest, 'I'm happy like that, so I don't want to change.'

Josie looked up at Tom because this was his house as Charlotte's guardian. He nodded and Josie said, 'All right, Kitty. Now, you said you wanted two things; what was the other?'

'I want you to be a partner as well, because you got me out o' the river *and* you've given me a new life here.'

Josie, after a moment's dumbfounded silence, exclaimed, 'Oh, no! You don't owe me anything. I'm only too grateful for your help with the house.'

Tom first looked startled, then thoughtful. This woman as a business partner? A . . . governess? Housekeeper? He could see no point in it, but the ship belonged to Kitty Duggan and if she insisted . . .

And now Kitty said firmly, 'That's what I want. If the pair of you don't agree to that, I'll agree to nothing and the old *Macbeth* can rot at her moorings.' And she started for the door.

Josie stopped her: 'Wait! Please!' She did not want this for herself, but she wanted it for Tom. 'Very well. Thank you. I'm very grateful, but I warn you, I know little of ships or shipping.'

'You'll learn, I reckon.' Kitty looked at Tom. 'Well?'

He said, 'You mean Mrs Miller will be a—' He stumbled over his words, then went on: 'Will not be taking an active part.' He had almost said 'sleeping partner'. Josie knew it and coloured, turned her back to them and fussed over lifting Charlotte down from her chair.

Kitty knew it, too, and grinned at him. 'If you like. But you might want both of us to take an active part afore we're finished.' She paused at the door a moment longer to say – ominously again – 'You've not seen the old *Macbeth* yet.'

16

'My God!' said Tom under his breath. 'She's filthy!' The three partners of the Langley Shipping Company had come to inspect their vessel and stood on the quayside in Newcastle.

Josie heard him, looked quickly at Kitty Duggan, but the old woman had not caught the hushed comment, was gazing proudly out at the ship where she lay at her moorings in the Tyne. Josie looked up at Tom and said brightly, 'She looks very nice.'

But Kitty heard that and snorted. 'No, she doesn't! She's thick wi' muck and rust!'

The *Macbeth* was also small. Josie could not believe that this ship would actually venture to sea. She had only one hold. Forward of this was the little forecastle where the crew would live. Aft in the stern was a superstructure that housed the saloon where the master and the mate ate, two tiny cabins – and the galley. On top was the bridge and wheelhouse. Now Kitty went on, 'But we might as well get out there and have a good look at her while we're all here.'

Josie had announced at breakfast, flushed and excited at the novelty, 'I got up early and packed a lunch for the three of us and did most of the work for the men's meals. Annie can manage the rest and look after Charlotte.'

Tom stared at her, surprised. 'You're coming?'

'Well, I am a . . . a partner.' Josie was careful to keep her eyes on her plate. 'So I think it's my duty to go and see the ship. One must always discharge one's responsibilities.' She looked at him now.

Tom realised she was paraphrasing his own words and his eyes glinted dangerously. But then he admitted, 'I agree.'

Now Tom hailed a boatman plying for hire and he rowed them out to the *Macbeth*. A Jacob's ladder hung down her rusty side. It was not a long ladder because the little ship's deck was not far above water. Tom climbed it first then waited on the deck above them. Josie had not expected this. She needed both hands to climb the ladder. Before she started she could feel the wind driving upriver and flapping her long skirts about her ankles. Then Kitty addressed the boatman: 'You keep your eyes inboard!'

'Oh, aye, missus.' And he dutifully studied his boots as Josie mounted the short ladder. At the top she had the obstacle of the bulwark to surmount, but Tom seized her under the arms and lifted her over, set her down on the deck.

'Thank you.' Josie, flustered but laughing, shook her skirts to straighten them. She saw, ruefully, that already just one passage up the few feet of the ship's side had left its marks of dirt and rust.

Tom helped Kitty over the side then hauled up the picnic basket on a line, and the boatman sheered off. Tom said, 'I'll rig an accommodation ladder as soon as I can.' And he made a note in the notebook he had brought for the purpose.

It was the first note of many. Josie and Kitty went with him as he toured the ship. He refused to allow them to descend into the engine-room and went down alone. He emerged some time later smeared with dirt and coal dust and shaking his head. 'The sooner I get an engineer to look at those engines, the better.' But they went with him to examine the cabins in the superstructure, the damp, dark, dingy and odorous forecastle where the crew would live, and the galley where the food would be cooked. Josie made her own – mental – list of notes and shuddered at the galley.

They paused at midday and lunched from the basket in the little saloon. Then they carried on, and only when the light was failing in the gathering dusk did Tom hail another boat to take them ashore. In the train, busy with his thoughts, he said, 'I'll come through again tomorrow, get an engineer aboard and start work on her.'

Josie said, 'So will I.'

Tom was startled out of his preoccupation. 'Why?'

'Because there's plenty to do.' Then Josie amended: 'Plenty that I can do, I mean.'

Tom's brows lifted in doubt. 'You?'

Josie affirmed determinedly, 'Yes.'

Kitty added, 'And me.'

'There's the saloon.' Josie ticked off points on slim fingers. 'And the cabins, the galley—' She wrinkled her nose in disgust, then went on: 'The . . . the fo'c'sle—'

'The *fo'c'sle*!' Tom shook his head. 'The crew look after that, as far as anyone does.'

Kitty sniffed. 'Aye, I've heard that. But I believe they take it as they find it, leave it as they finish with it and do damn all to it in between.'

Josie said, 'And I want to work my share of the partnership. These are all jobs that need to be done, you'll not deny that.'

Tom could not. He looked from one to the other then grinned and went back to his planning as he stared out of the window. So did Josie. While Kitty watched them, content to let them get on with it. And when at last they were home and Kitty and Josie were at work in the kitchen, Josie asked, 'Will you tell me something about ships?'

Kitty had been expecting the question and answered, 'I'll tell you what I can.'

'Well, how do you get a crew and cargoes?'

Kitty said, 'You could go to the shipping office in Tatham Street for a crew but you could do as well or mebbe better right here.'

So Josie asked Dougie Bickerstaffe. She and the young seaman stood in the kitchen on the morning after their first visit to the *Macbeth* and Dougie said, 'Aye, you can count on me.' Then he scratched at the curls cut short and close to his skull. 'I dunno how many o' the others, though. One's already signed on in another ship and some won't sail anything but deep-sea, long voyages, and they won't have owt to do wi' running up and down the coast.'

Josie asked, 'Then will you sound them out? And I suppose we'll need an engineer.'

Dougie nodded. 'You'll want an engineer and a couple of stokers but we don't have none o' them in here.'

'What about the man who came in the day before yesterday,' Josie suggested. 'Simmie?'

'Not him, neither,' and Dougie explained. 'See, he's a sailorman, same as us. Now engine-room fellers, they're different. We get on together, like, but they've got their ways and we have ours.'

Josie told herself that she was learning, and shifted her ground. 'Will you ask if any of them will sail with us? And whether they know an engineer?'

'And stokers,' said Dougie. 'Right y'are, ma'am.'

He returned to the kitchen in minutes with three other men treading on his heels. 'Here y'are, ma'am. These are willing. And I've asked about the engine-room and got some names.'

Josie smiled at them all. 'Good.' She whipped off her apron and hung it up. Then said, remembering what Kitty had told her: 'Now, I hope you all have clean conduct sheets?' They all nodded, albeit uneasily, and Josie picked on the new man, Simmie, because he was the one she knew least. 'Why did you leave your last ship?'

Simmie was short, squat and bullet-headed. 'We was running coal up the coast to Aberdeen or thereabouts but the owner gave it up, paid all of us off and sent the ship to the breakers because she wanted a lot o' money spent on her.'

Josie was satisfied. 'Now, Captain Collingwood will want to see you.' Kitty had been definite on that, saying, 'He'll want to pick his crew. You can feed them to him but he'll decide whether he ships them.'

So now Josie tap-tapped along the passage and hall with the sailors clumping behind her. She knocked on the door of the office then opened it and announced, 'There are some seamen here who would like to sign on, Captain Collingwood.'

Tom stood up from his desk, at first frowning but then thoughtful as she ushered the men in and he sized them up – and they took their measure of him. He glanced at Josie and said, 'Thank you, Mrs Miller.' Josie shut the door and left them to it.

She returned to the kitchen, donned her apron again and worked happily alongside Annie and Kitty.

Another packed lunch had to be prepared, and meals made ready for the house this day, so Annie would be left with Charlotte and just enough work to manage while Josie and Kitty were aboard the *Macbeth*. There was one minor emergency when Kitty announced, 'We've used the last of the flour and that shop down Dame Dorothy Street has shut down so one of us will have to go up to Dundas Street.' That was ten minutes further to walk.

Josie was familiar with the little shop that had been at the corner of Dame Dorothy Street. She asked, 'Why did it close?'

Kitty shrugged. 'Not enough stock – and as soon as he made any money he spent it on drink.'

Josie said, 'I'll go up to Dundas Street.' And forgot about the empty shop – for the time being.

Later, when she had returned from her errand, she heard the shuffle of booted feet in the hall. She hurried out of the kitchen, wiping her hands on her apron, and met Dougie Bickerstaffe and the men in the passage. Josie asked, 'Well?'

Dougie grinned at her. 'He turned us over good and proper but signed us on at the end.'

'Oh, good!' Josie clapped her hands.

The three of them – Tom, Josie and Kitty – and the crew, worked on the *Macbeth* all that week. Tom found an engineer and stokers and they toiled down below. Then a Lloyds Agent surveyed the ship and issued a Certificate of Seaworthiness. That cost ten pounds. On the Thursday Tom announced, weary but proud, 'She's ready for sea, but—' He stopped.

Josie questioned, 'But?'

'We haven't a cargo yet, and so long as we're without one, we're losing money.'

Josie was up early, as usual, the following morning. In spite of the hard work and long hours, she was happy. She sang as she worked, but her thoughts were still with the ship and the lack of a cargo. Then she stopped in the act of rolling out pastry for a pie, seizing on the thought that had slipped into her mind. She sought out Simmie and found the squat seaman in the common room. He had just finished eating his breakfast with the rest of the boarders and was sipping at a mug of tea. He moved to stand up when Josie approached him but she put her hand on his shoulder. 'No, don't get up. I just want to ask a few questions. You said the owner of your last ship had given up on the job?'

'Aye.'

'What was it?'

Simmie told her and minutes later Josie pulled on her coat in the kitchen. As Dan Elkington carried in a bucket of coal for the kitchen stove she handed him a slip of paper on which she had written an address. 'Do you know where those offices are?'

Dan read the address. 'Aye. If you cross over the bridge into the town—'

'Will you show me, please?'

A half-hour later Josie stood before the front door of an office. A polished brass plate was mounted on the wall by the door: Owen Packer, Solicitor. Below it was another that read: Coal Carriers Ltd. Josie passed through the front door into a hall with a smell of dust, carbolic and stale air. To her left was an open door leading to a room in which a big-bosomed young woman sat at a desk, pecking at a typewriter. She stopped and glanced at Josie as she knocked on the open door. 'Aye?'

Josie marked her down for lack of courtesy and said, 'I would like to talk to someone in Coal Carriers Ltd.'

'Ah! That's Mr Packer. He's Coal Carriers.' The girl had a fringe of curls and her hair was swept up at the back. She poked at it with fat fingers and got up from her chair. 'I'll see if he's in.' Josie knew that meant. 'I'll ask if he'll see you'. She waited as the girl crossed to another door and paused there to tease the curls, smooth the skirt over her hips and put on a smile. Finally she opened the door.

Josie called clearly, 'I want to discuss a profitable business enterprise.'

The girl started and stumbled, glared over her shoulder at Josie, then passed through the door, the false smile reappearing as a simper. The door closed behind her but she emerged again almost at once, shot a cold stare at Josie and held the door open. 'He'll see you.'

Josie walked past her, head high, and sniffed at the strong smell of cheap perfume. The door banged shut behind her. Packer, thin and cadaverous, got up from his desk and came round it to greet her. His smirk showed yellow teeth, and as he held out his hand to Josie his eyes ran over her. She halted and stretched out her arm so she touched his hand only with the tips of her gloved fingers, held him at a distance.

'Good morning,' said Packer. 'Please sit down, Miss—'

'Mrs Miller.' Josie perched on the chair, stiff-backed, and peeled off her gloves to show the ring on her finger.

Packer seated himself with pencil poised over notepad. 'And what was this business opportunity? You wish me to carry out some legal work?'

'No, I've come to you in your capacity as representing Coal Carriers Ltd.'

Packer's smile widened. 'I am Coal Carriers Ltd.'

Josie took a breath. 'I am here to make enquiries on behalf of the Langley Shipping Company.'

Packer, taken by surprise, blinked rapidly. 'I don't know it.'

'It has only recently been formed.'

'I see. And your position in this company?'

'I am a partner.'

Packer probed, 'And the other partners?'

'Captain Thomas Collingwood is the principal partner.'

Packer nodded, making notes now. 'I know of Captain Collingwood.'

'And Mrs Kitty Duggan.'

Packer wrote it down. 'And why "Langley"?'

'We are trading from the Langley house.'

'I see. And the nature of the business?' But Packer had already decided to be involved. He wanted to know all he could about the Langleys because Garbutt would pay for the information.

When he finally escorted Josie to the front door and returned to his office, he sat at his desk, smirking still. Reuben Garbutt would be pleased. Packer had to go to London on business soon and he would report to Garbutt then. And the transaction he had just agreed would be profitable – for him, if not for the Langley Shipping Company.

Josie returned to the Langley house in a horse-drawn cab. She got down at the front door and once in the hall she knocked on the door of the office and entered at Tom's call, still unbuttoning her coat. As Tom rose from his seat at his desk Josie said breathlessly, 'I've got a cargo, Captain Collingwood!'

Tom blinked at her, incredulous, but Josie explained and he listened, then examined the figures Packer had supplied and Josie had noted down. She waited nervously, but he looked up and said, 'I've heard of Packer, and not all good, but this seems straight, if a bit unusual. He supplies the coal, we deliver it just south of Aberdeen and collect payment, pay him the cost of the coal and the rest is our profit.' He tapped the paper with the figures. 'That selling price will give us a handsome profit. Better for him, of course. We do all the work while he sits back and takes his cut.'

Josie said, hopefully and eagerly, 'But you agree it's an opportunity?'

Tom frowned but nodded. 'Aye. I'm just wondering where the catch is.'

'I can't see any.' And Josie ventured, 'Maybe there isn't a catch. And it is a cargo. The ship would not be lying idle and losing money. There would be *some* profit.'

'True enough.' Tom had to admit it, though he was wary of this strange woman who was intruding in a man's world. 'But we need to see this contract.'

'I have it here.' Josie produced it from her bag. 'I've read it. You could look it over in the cab – it's waiting outside. Then you could sign it in Packer's office. He wants us to load tomorrow and sail that night.' She hesitated then and asked uncertainly, 'Can we?'

Tom saw her doubt and grinned. 'Aye, we can.' Her enthusiasm was infectious and he was ready to go to sea. 'I'll do it.' He took the contract and started for the door.

Josie watched the cab wheel away down one arm of the U-shaped carriage drive – as the Blakemore motor car drove up the other. It halted at the foot of the steps and the chauffeur got down and opened the rear door for Felicity Blakemore. Josie swung the front door wide for her as Felicity mounted the steps with her maid, Susie, at her heels.

'Ah! Mrs Miller. Tell Captain Collingwood I'm here.' And as she swayed past into the hall, 'Then bring some tea and give Susie something in the kitchen and send a cup out to Jarvis.'

'I'm afraid the captain has just left on business, miss,' replied Josie, realising Felicity could not have seen Tom on the other arm of the drive because of the trees and shrubs of the garden between them.

Felicity frowned. 'I *told* him I would call some time today.' She sighed. 'Well, I'll wait.' And she walked on into the sitting room.

Susie pulled a face and Josie grinned at her and led her through to the kitchen where she introduced her to the others. 'This is Susie Evans, Miss Blakemore's maid.'

Kitty took a loaded tray in to Felicity, muttering as she set out, 'Hope it poisons the stuck-up . . .' The door closing behind her cut off the last words. Then Annie carried a mug out to Jarvis, the chauffeur.

Finally all four sat down around the kitchen table and Annie asked, 'What's she like to work for?'

Susie shrugged and nodded at Josie. 'Like I told you the other day, the money's good. And she likes to get about a bit: Paris, London, Biarritz, South o' France. And I go with her.' Josie nodded understanding; she had been to all of those places with the Urquharts. Susie was going on, 'I could tell some stories – but I won't.' She giggled. 'And then I get to wear some lovely clothes when she's not there. Her and me are about the same size and I've got the pick of her wardrobe. You should see me when I go out, it would make your eyes pop out.'

Kitty stood up and said reluctantly, 'I'd better go and see if she wants anything. It's only good manners.'

But Josie, wary of Kitty's plain speaking under provocation, said quickly, 'I'll go.'

Tom had returned. Josie heard the bass rumble of his voice as she walked along the passage and into the hall. The sitting-room door was open and now Felicity emerged, saying, 'I'm sure you know best, darling, but I think this Langley Shipping Company is a waste of your time and talents. You would do better to take command of a big, ocean-going ship that's part of a fleet.'

Josie silently admitted that this was true.

Tom replied patiently, 'I've already explained: this way I can spend more time ashore attending to affairs here.'

Felicity sighed. 'And you're sailing tomorrow. Very well. At least I can pass the time while you are away planning my trousseau.' She paused at the front door, waiting for Tom to open it for her, and saw Josie approaching. 'Where is that girl Susie? Send her out immediately.'

'Yes, miss,' Josie answered, and called the maid out of the kitchen. Susie came hurrying and scuttled down the steps to climb into the car after her mistress.

As the car turned out of the drive and was lost to sight, Josie asked, 'Is everything all right, Captain Collingwood?'

Tom nodded. 'There's only one thing – we still need a cook. None of the hands have any experience of that and I'd rather they didn't learn at the expense of my stomach.'

'Is that all?' Josie laughed, full of confidence now. 'Kitty will do it, of course.' She watched Tom stride into his office, smiling at his broad back. Then she sauntered along the passage to the kitchen, singing.

'No!' Kitty shook her head decisively. 'I'm a partner. I didn't sign on as cook.'

Josie explained, 'But we haven't got a cook. Captain Collingwood wants one and he sails tomorrow night.'

Kitty shrugged. 'I can't help that. I'm not going to sea.'

Josie reasoned, 'But you used to sail with your husband.'

Kitty agreed: 'Aye, when we were first married. But I was as sick as a dog every time. I had to give it up and come ashore.'

Josie looked around the kitchen desperately. 'I wonder if Annie—'

But Kitty shook her head. 'You can't ask that lass. She's being sick in the mornings now anyway.' And as Josie stared at her in dismay, 'You do it.'

'*Me!*' Josie squeaked.

'Why not?' And Kitty pointed out: 'You've been cooking for sailormen this past month or more and had no complaints.'

'But I've never been to sea.'

'It's about your turn, then.' And Kitty presented the closing argument: 'There's nobody else so you'll have to do it.'

So Josie packed a suitcase and was aboard the *Macbeth* when she slipped her moorings and tugs towed her upstream. Felicity Blakemore stood on the quay in a tailored costume of white and a silk blouse, waving a gloved hand. The seamen and stevedores gaped at her, awed. But she was back in her motor car and on her way home when the tugs manoeuvred the *Macbeth* up to the coal staithes. There the little ship loaded coal in her bunkers to feed her fires, and in her hold as cargo. The coal poured out of the railway wagons and thundered down the chute to cascade into the hold. The *Macbeth* was enveloped in a cloud of coal dust. Josie, in her cramped little galley below the bridge, was unprepared for it. She had not shut the hatches and scuttles that let in the sea air and light so she and the galley were dusted black.

As night fell the *Macbeth* steamed out of the Tyne, her old engines ticking over steadily. Tom Collingwood was on his bridge, happy at going to sea, but wondering again about the girl below. He still felt there was more to Mrs Miller than she pretended. The way she had intruded into the affairs of the house – and of this ship – was not only unladylike but unwomanly. Yet she was – womanly. Sometimes he was silent in her presence because he was tongue-tied. And he was glad of her competence now, was sure she would cope effortlessly.

In the galley, Josie wiped away the tears that cut pale scars through the grime, smearing it. She supposed Tom was on his bridge and dreaming of the radiant Felicity. She started work again.

17

Josie worked into the night in the galley by the light from a swinging oil lamp. It smelt strongly and now she was glad of the open scuttles and the draught of cold salt air that came from the *Macbeth*'s jogging seven knots. First she washed her hands and face, then she cleaned the galley. Tom, on the bridge with Dougie Bickerstaffe at the wheel, saw her stagger from the galley to tip a bucket of dirty water over the side. Then she let the bucket down on a rope to fill it again – Kitty had told her about that, to Josie's shock. She tottered back to the galley with it, weaving as the deck rocked under her. When the galley was clean she fastened the door on the inside, closed the dead-lights over the scuttles and, thus secure from interested eyes, she stripped to the skin and bathed in the bucket.

It was close to midnight when she climbed the short ladder to the bridge, with her skirts flapping about her legs. She handed a precariously balanced mug of tea to Tom, now at the wheel. 'Thank you.' He held the spokes negligently with one hand, the tea in the other, and sipped at it. He had discarded his jacket and rolled up the sleeves of his sweater because the little wheelhouse was right in front of the single funnel and warmed by it.

The deck of the little coaster was empty and Josie said, 'You're all alone, I see.'

'Don't need anyone else.' Then Tom explained, 'Bucko will be up at midnight to take the watch.' Bucko Daniels was the mate, thirty years old and sixteen of them spent at sea. Short and wiry, he was known as a hard man who would stand for no nonsense. Tom went on, 'Dougie Bickerstaffe can take the wheel so long as Bucko or me are up here to keep an eye on things. I've seen Dougie steer and he's all right. I'll put some of the others on when I've seen them steer a course.'

Josie looked around the wheelhouse and saw the brass-mouthed voice-pipes by the wheel. 'What are those for?'

'One to speak to the engine-room – if I have to. Most of the time I use the telegraph.' It stood by the wheel. Different segments of its circular head were marked 'Half ahead', 'Slow astern', and so on. 'You set the handle to the order you want to give and another in the engine-room copies it. The other voice-pipe is to my cabin.'

Josie knew where his cabin was – next to hers. It had been a wild rush to pack, catch the train to the Tyne and lay in galley stores for the voyage. She had not given the matter thought before but now she realised she was the only woman aboard, and single and unchaperoned. She remembered that Tom had been stiffly concerned for her reputation when they first met, but he seemed to have forgotten about it now. She said nothing.

Tom passed her the empty mug. 'So you've settled in all right.' He peered ahead, twirled the spokes of the wheel, then steadied on course again. 'And had a rest? I don't blame you.'

A rest? Josie stood open-mouthed a moment then laughed softly. Tom glanced at her. 'Have I said something funny?'

She could not tell him she had laboured until she was weary. 'Nothing. I'm just happy.' That was true. And he was close and they were alone in the wheelhouse, with just the glow from the compass binnacle leaving them clothed in shadows.

Josie said, 'Goodnight.'

Tired though she was, she lay awake until she heard the rumble of his voice above, greeting Bucko Daniels. Then she slept peacefully.

Their destination was not, in fact, Aberdeen, but a fishing village some miles away. Tom steered the *Macbeth* into the little harbour in the late afternoon. Josie stood at the door of the galley, looking out at the little drifters and cobles lying at buoys or at anchor, the scatter of whitewashed cottages and the solitary public house with its weathered sign: the Fishermen's Rest. Since the early morning Josie had cooked breakfast and lunch and was now preparing dinner. To her surprise and relief she had not been seasick, and she was humming softly now as she wiped her hands on her apron.

Tom laid his ship neatly alongside the quay and men standing there, fishermen by their jerseys and sea boots, seized the lines the *Macbeth*'s crew threw to them and made her fast. The steady, muffled *thump, thump*! ceased beneath Josie's feet as Tom worked the handles of the telegraph, signalling 'Finished with engines'. In the silence the crying of the gulls seemed suddenly loud as they swooped and soared around the ship.

Tom came down the short ladder from the bridge to the deck, frowning, eyes searching. Josie asked, 'Is something wrong?'

He muttered, puzzled, 'I can't see any coal yard. We've got to unload somewhere.' The hands had turned to and run a gangway ashore. Tom walked down its slight slope – the tide was at the full and the *Macbeth*'s deck rode a foot or so higher than the quay. He talked with the fishermen, then strode back up the gangway, tight-lipped.

He growled savagely, 'I wondered if there was a catch in this business and now I've found it. They've been expecting us for the past week. The only ship that comes in here is the one bringing the coal. They say there's no yard to unload it in. Now we're here people will come in from miles around with their carts. We rig a derrick and use that to fill up the carts on the quay.'

Josie said blankly, 'Oh! Surely that isn't usual?'

Tom exploded. 'You're damned right it isn't! But that's how it's done here. Some of them will be along today, some tomorrow, then the day after and the day after *that* – until we've discharged our cargo. Meanwhile we – and the ship – lie here losing money because it has always been done that way.' Tom indicated the men on the quay with a jerk of his head. 'So as far as they are concerned, it always will be.'

Josie wailed, 'But Simmie didn't say—'

'He didn't know. He's a seaman and not concerned with profitability. That's the owners' worry.' Then Tom muttered, 'I might as well see to the rigging of that derrick.' He strode forward, calling the hands. Josie went back to her galley and her work, but no longer singing. Their brave little enterprise was going disastrously wrong.

Some barrows and carts arrived from nearby cottages that evening. The crew of the *Macbeth* filled sacks with the coal from the hold and hoisted it ashore to the carts and barrows using the derrick, powered by a clattering steam winch. There was little dust from the coal under these conditions and Josie, wiser now, kept doors and scuttles closed and the dust out of her galley.

The next morning, with breakfast cleared away, she changed into a good dress and ventured ashore. Strolling among the cottages, she exchanged smiles and greetings with the aproned women at their doors. The wife of the publican, a grey-haired woman in her forties, was sweeping the path at the front of the Fishermen's Rest. The public house lay only feet from the edge of the quay, the ship and the coal. She paused in her task to chat. 'I saw you at the door o' the galley.'

'Yes, I do the cooking,' Josie answered.

'Och, aye.' The woman's gaze drifted to Josie's hands – she was carrying her gloves and bag – and noted the gold band on her finger. 'That saves a bit o' money.' Josie realised the woman had assumed she was the wife of the ship's captain. She did not – dared not – disillusion her, lest she was labelled a loose woman.

The woman set her broom aside. 'Come away in and have a cup o' tea.' She led the way down a path along the side of the pub and flanking a field of potatoes. They passed a man who came out of the back door of the pub, carrying a garden fork. He was short, broad, bearded and nodded to Josie, 'Guid morning.' And then to the woman, 'I'm away for some tatties, Lizzie.' He plodded on. As Josie followed Lizzie in at the back door she glanced over her shoulder and saw him starting to dig in the potato field.

The back room of the Fishermen's Rest was kitchen, sitting and dining room in one. A bright coal fire set the brass fire-irons in the hearth to glinting. A big table sat in the middle of the room with straight-backed chairs around it. There were two armchairs before the fire and a crockery-laden dresser against one wall. A basin full of eggs stood on the dresser and a side of bacon hung from a beam. When Lizzie poured the tea, she added milk from a brimming jug.

Josie exclaimed, 'Fresh milk!' On the *Macbeth* she had to use condensed milk from a tin.

Lizzie smiled. 'Aye. Milk, butter, bacon, eggs, cabbages, leeks, neeps – all that sort o' thing we get from the farmers around about. And cheap! The puir divils have a long road to get to market and a puir price at the end of it.'

There was a pause, and Josie was conscious of the quiet; there was only the soft ticking of a clock on the mantelpiece and the distant voices of the men on the quay. She said, 'This must be a peaceful place to live.'

'It is that.' But Lizzie's face was gloomy. 'Too quiet by far.' And she explained, 'We're not wanting to make a fortune. We ran a pub in Glesca for twenty year and there was money enough – aye, and work enough. We took this place to ease off a bit but the only trade is what you see here' – she waved her hand at the cottages around them – 'and now and again a farmer coming in. We're barely making a living and Davy's got too much time on his hands. Y'understand,' she said proudly, 'we're no' short of a quid or two, but he'd be better off making a bit o' money than spending it drinking his own stock.' Then she smiled conspiratorially at Josie. 'But that's my Davy for you. What about your man? Do you keep him busy?'

Josie evaded the question: 'There's always something to do aboard a ship.' And made her excuses: 'That reminds me that I have to get back.' And she went on her way.

Lizzie's good wishes followed her. 'Come again, lassie.'

More carts appeared that day but slowly and at irregular intervals, coming in from the farms in the hinterland. They were pulled by shaggy, plodding horses, their drivers sitting balanced on the shafts. Late in the afternoon, Josie stood in the stern of the ship, watching the derrick at work.

The wind coming from behind her blew the coal dust away from her. The steam winch hammered, reeling in the wire cable on the derrick. It lifted the net, loaded with sacks of coal, out of the ship's hold. The jib of the derrick travelled through ninety degrees as one of the hands hauled on a line, swinging the net with its load of coal over the side to hang above the cart on the quay. Then the wire ran out slowly and the load settled in the bottom of the cart.

But darkness came early that time of the year and the wind had a bite to it. Josie shivered and went back to her galley and preparing the evening meal. Later that evening, the meal and the dishes cleared away, she retired to her cabin. There she undressed, climbed into her bunk and settled down to read by the light of an oil lamp. But she worried about the loss being made on this voyage. It could wreck the Langley Shipping Company at the outset. She could hear Tom moving in the cabin next door. And there was something gnawing at the back of her mind, demanding her attention . . .

She sat up in her bunk with a jerk, hands to her head, pushing at her hair which hung loose and shining. She was very still for some seconds as the thoughts raced – the coal rumbling down the chute when the *Macbeth* had loaded it, Lizzie saying the farmers had a long way to market and a poor price when they got there – then they tumbled into place. She swung out of the bunk and shed her nightdress, shivering in the cold until she had pulled on her clothes. When she tapped at Tom's door he bellowed, 'Come in!'

Josie opened the door and Tom lifted his head out of the basin, but not too far, still stooping under the deckhead. Water dripped from his face and neck and he reached for a towel. He was stripped to the waist. Josie met his startled stare for a second then looked away. 'I'm sorry. I didn't know. You said to come in—'

Tom said, 'I thought you were one of the hands.'

'I just wanted to see you.' Then Josie realised what she had said. 'I mean, I wanted to talk to you. About an idea. About this place.' She stumbled to a halt, embarrassed.

Tom scrubbed at his face with the towel. 'Well, not in here.'

'No, of course not.' Josie backed out.

'In the saloon.' That was where they ate their meals. The crew took theirs in the forecastle. 'I'll be there in a couple of minutes.'

Josie waited for him in the little saloon with its scarred old table which she had got to shine again with polish and elbow grease, the leather settees down each side. At first she upbraided herself for blundering into such an embarrassing situation. Then she shifted the blame. Why should Tom Collingwood assume it was a member of the crew knocking at his door? He knew she was aboard. But then she admitted her guilt again: why would he expect a lady to knock at his cabin door after nightfall? No lady would. Josie buried her face in her hands.

She had to lower them again when Tom, fully dressed now, entered the little saloon, seeming to fill it. The light from the lamp did not show her colouring and they avoided each other's eyes. The dead-lights of the saloon were open so anyone could see them talking innocently. Tom sat down opposite Josie, only the width of the narrow table between them. His long legs brushed hers as he slid in and along the seat. They both sat back and Tom questioned, 'You've had an idea about this place? What do you mean?'

Josie told him and in her eagerness the words spilled out of her. Tom was sceptical and looking for faults at first but then he became infected by her enthusiasm. At the end he said, 'It depends on whether they'll *want* to do it, but it sounds as though they will. It's worth a try.' They smiled at each other and it was then they realised they were both leaning forward on the table. Josie sat back, then Tom.

Josie urged, 'Shall we?'

Tom pulled out his pocket-watch, snapped open the case with his thumb and glanced at the face. 'There's time.'

Josie fetched her coat and hat from her cabin, then they spent some minutes on the quayside where Tom paced distances and made rapid mental calculations. Satisfied, he nodded, 'The derrick will reach. It'll work.' They went on to the Fishermen's Rest and Tom entered while Josie waited outside as a woman must.

The bar was low-ceilinged so Tom had to stoop. There were a dozen fishermen standing at the bar, jerseyed and sea-booted, some sucking on pipes, all with glasses of whisky before them. Davy, the bearded publican, stood watchful behind the bar, and Tom asked him, 'Can we have a talk?' He was aware that conversation had stopped and all the drinkers had become listeners. He went on, 'Somewhere private? I have a lady with me, waiting outside.'

'Aye. Tak' the leddy round the side. We can talk in there.' Davy indicated the room behind him with a jerk of his thumb. Tom saw through the open door that it was the kitchen. Davy called, 'Lizzie!' And when his wife came bustling out of the kitchen into the bar: 'See to the men here while I chat wi' the captain.'

'Aye, Davy.' Lizzie took his place.

Tom rejoined Josie and led the way down the whitewashed side of the pub, at first treading cautiously in the pitch dark; there was not a streetlight in the village. Josie followed his tall figure, equally careful. But then the kitchen door opened ahead of them, framing the publican, and light spilled out to show them the way. The three of them were soon seated around the scrubbed table in the warmth of the kitchen, the men with tots of whisky, Josie a glass of sherry.

Tom lifted his glass, toasting, then drank and nodded at the fire, pulsing red with heat. 'Where would we be without coal?'

'Aye,' Davy agreed, curious as to the reason for this visit but prepared to wait to find out. His gaze drifted to Josie again and again while Tom talked, because he was also curious as to the reason for her presence, this smiling girl with hair that glinted coppery in the light. Tom started, 'It's coal I've come to see you about.' He was aware that Lizzie, in the bar but strategically sited close to the door of the kitchen, was listening to every word. At the end Tom produced paper and pencil, wrote down figures then tapped them with the pencil. 'At those prices we'll all make money and everybody will gain.'

Davy savoured a sip of whisky a moment, then swallowed. 'Aye.' Then thoughtfully, 'Ye say we'd be needing a chute?'

Lizzie poked her head in from the bar: 'Ecky Gow will build that.'

And to Tom, explaining, 'He's a carpenter and does all that kind o' work around here. Ye can see him the morn.' Then her gaze switched to her husband. 'It sounds like a grand bit o' business to me.'

Davy eyed her. 'You look after the trade, woman. And let's be having another one in here.'

So there was more whisky – and the bargain was struck.

Davy bade them 'Goodnight', echoed by his wife. Then he shut the kitchen door and the sudden darkness left Tom and Josie blind. Josie stood still, then Tom's hand, rough and callused, wrapped itself around hers. His voice came above her head: 'This way.' She followed where he led her, but when almost to the road she stumbled. He caught her before she could fall headlong, his free hand clamping itself around her waist. He held her a moment and she could feel the coarse wool cloth of his reefer jacket against her face, smell the salt and coal smoke on it. Then he set her on her feet again and they were out on the road; their eyes were growing used to the gloom and there was the amber glow of the oil lamp lighting the *Macbeth*'s gangway.

They did not speak until they were aboard and had stopped at the door of Josie's cabin. She said, 'I think that was a successful evening, Captain.'

'Yes.' Tom still stood, a bare foot away.

Josie said quickly, 'Goodnight, Captain Collingwood,' and backed into her cabin.

As she closed the door: 'Goodnight, Mrs Miller.'

Josie stood with her back to the door, head turned, breathing shallowly. Finally she heard him walk away, sea boots heavy on the deck. As she undressed by the light of the oil lamp and then lay in her bunk she heard him moving in the next cabin. He had called her Mrs Miller. If she had truly been just Mrs Miller she could have . . . But she was not.

Josie was still awake long after all was silent.

With the help of Tom and the crew it took Ecky Gow, sandy-haired and with a stub of pencil behind his ear, just two days to construct a rough chute. He built it of timber and it led from the quay to the corner of Davy's potato field beside the Fishermen's Rest. During the third day they discharged all of the *Macbeth*'s coal using a huge iron bucket. The derrick swung it, filled with coal, out of the hold and across the quay. Then the bucket was tipped so the coal it held dropped into the chute and rumbled down into the corner of the field.

When the hold was empty it was hosed out. Then on that third day, Davy having passed the word around, a few farmers arrived on the quay with loaded carts. They held cabbages and swedes, bacon, butter, eggs and cheese. The farmers were cautious but Tom met them on the quay and, primed by Josie, offered them prices for their goods and deals were struck. Tom told them what he had promised Davy: 'We'll be here every week, and after we've unloaded the coal we'll make you a decent offer for whatever you bring in.'

One said drily, 'There'll be a sight more of us next time. A lot o' fellers waited to see if what we'd heard was true.'

Later Tom asked Josie, 'How do you know we'll make a profit at these prices?'

Josie waved at the stacks of greens and groceries, the sacks of potatoes bought from Davy. 'I know what all these things will fetch in Monkwearmouth.'

'How do you remember?'

Josie replied, a touch grimly, 'If you have to pay for them, you soon learn how much they cost.'

They sailed in the evening, Tom with Davy's money in his pocket in gold sovereigns. The publican had bought the *Macbeth*'s cargo of coal to sell on, as he surely would, at a profit, and he was now the accredited agent of the Langley Shipping Company. Henceforth the *Macbeth* would land her coal as soon as she berthed, load the farmers' produce and sail again without delay. As the little ship ran south, Tom poked his head in at the door of the galley to say jubilantly, 'There'll be no time wasted there any more; a quick turnround every trip!'

It could not have come too quickly for Josie. She was eager to be ashore for good. The *Macbeth* was too small for the two of them. Yet when Kitty Duggan came aboard and said, 'I've found a cook for your next passage,' Josie felt disappointed. And Kitty watched her with sharp little eyes.

Then Josie, remembering, asked, 'Has that shop on the corner of Dame Dorothy Street and Barrington Street been taken?'

Kitty shook her head. 'Nor likely to be, either.'

'Yes, it will.' And when Kitty stared, Josie said, 'I've got enough to stock it aboard the *Macbeth*.'

Dougie Bickerstaffe asked hopefully, 'Has there been a letter for me, Mrs Duggan, please?'

Kitty replied, 'No, lad. I'm sorry.' Then, after he had trudged away, shoulders slumped, she said, 'He's still mooning over that lass in London, hoping she'll write to him, but she's told him it's no good.'

Josie remembered very well. The girl worked in a shop . . .

They had berthed this time in the Wear, not far from the Langley house. Kitty had come out in a boat, the boatman tugging at the oars, as the *Macbeth* was still being made fast to her buoy. Felicity Blakemore, however, waited on the quay for Tom to go ashore and then complained, 'It's such a shabby, *little* ship; absolutely awful!' And pouted when he laughed. Josie evaded her and went home with Kitty.

She realised then that she now thought of this house as home, and told herself it was not. She was a hireling here, a servant like Annie or Dan. But that was hard to remember when Charlotte came running to leap into her arms, and when neighbours in the square stood at their doors to call, 'Home again, bonny lass!' Annie scurried to make tea for her while the others – even the boarders – gathered round, smiling.

Later she went to Tom in his office, where he sat at his desk still in reefer jacket and sea boots. Josie had heard Felicity ensure Tom's attendance at the Blakemore house for dinner that evening before picking her way disdainfully off the quay. Now Josie sat in the armchair again, with the width of the room between her and Tom, and said, 'I need some money, Captain Collingwood, to rent a shop in Dame Dorothy Street. We need it to sell the goods we brought back today.' Josie explained her plans and finished, 'The business will be owned by the Langley Shipping Company and profits will be shared equally as before.' A surprised and impressed Tom agreed.

She went on, 'And I would like to have an advance on my wages, please, five pounds, if that is possible. I have to go to London because there is some family business I must attend to.' This was only a small deceit, to cover her if her scheme failed.

Tom suspected that deceit there was, but he said slowly, 'I see no reason why you should not have that amount. You have earned your share of the profit on this voyage, and there certainly will be a profit.'

Josie stood up and hurried on, wanting the interview over, 'I won't be away long and I'm sure Charlotte will do well with Annie and Kitty for a few more days.'

'Of course.' Tom was on his feet, looking down at her, and her eyes fell before his. Josie could feel the blood rising to heat her face, knew she was a poor liar and turned away quickly. Then he called as she sought to escape, 'Mrs Miller!'

'Yes?' Josie halted in the doorway but did not turn to face him.

Tom said stiffly, 'Thank you for all you've done.'

'I'm glad to have been of service,' Josie replied in kind. 'Thank you, Captain Collingwood.'

Tom went to Packer's office and told the solicitor, 'From now on we'll find the coal ourselves. We'll do the work and take any profit. And if you're thinking of shipping coal there yourself in competition, mark this: I have an agreement with the farmers and people living around there to buy what they produce if they take coal from the Langley Shipping Company. I doubt if you'll tempt them back to you.'

So did the fuming Packer. But he was already plotting his revenge.

Josie paid a month's rent on the shop in Dame Dorothy Street – little more than a pound – while Kitty, Annie and Dan Elkington promised to stock it with the goods shipped in the *Macbeth*. Josie took the train south to London the following day.

Tom Collingwood wondered at the 'family business', was sure she had not spoken all the truth and was once more suspicious. He also wondered if she would return.

Josie wondered if she should, but knew she would.

And on a later train, just two hours behind Josie, travelled Owen Packer, on his way to report to Reuben Garbutt.

18

Packer found Garbutt at his London home, the mansion in St John's Wood. The solicitor's taxicab crunched up the gravel of the drive, to halt at the porticoed front door as Garbutt descended from another. He was surprised to see Packer but welcomed him. 'Come in! I wasn't expecting you.'

Packer explained, fawning apologetically as they passed through the hall on the way to Garbutt's study, 'I wrote to you saying I had something to report and as I had business—'

'I suppose it's waiting for me' – Garbutt waved the neat pile of letters the butler handed him – 'among this lot.' He tossed the pile on to his desk. 'I've been away. France. What'll you drink?' He was in a good mood. He had gone to Calais to visit a bank where he held a safe-deposit box. In the privacy of the vault he had opened his box, taken from an inner pocket of his jacket several highly valuable items of jewellery and added them to those already stored in the box. Garbutt had other boxes in other countries.

Now, with he and Packer settled in armchairs before the fire, glasses of whisky to hand, Garbutt asked, 'So what do you have to tell me?'

Packer recounted how a Mrs Miller had come to him and that she was a partner: '—in the Langley Shipping Company.'

'What!' Garbutt sat up, glaring. 'Langley!'

Packer nodded, little eyes gleaming, sure now of his reward. 'There are two other partners: Captain Thomas Collingwood and Mrs Kitty Duggan. I decided I should make some enquiries.' He reminded Garbutt how Mrs Miller had been the first to find the body of William Langley: '—and she was the one who gave evidence of a man and woman leaving the house. I told you about that.' And when Garbutt nodded: 'She was only supposed to be the child's nurse, but—' He went on to describe how Josie had taken in Annie and Kitty and started a lodging house, the fitting out of the *Macbeth* and her first voyage. He put in quickly, 'I thought I should give them the business as it might help me to get closer to them, if need be.' He did not mention his fury when Tom told him the Langley Shipping Company would do no more business with him.

Garbutt nodded approval of Packer's actions then sat brooding, fists clenched, knuckles white. He summed up: 'This woman seems to be into everything. Giving evidence against me, keeping the house going, now a partner in this company. Why her? Collingwood was the boy the old man brought up and the Duggan woman owned the ship, so those two I can understand. But why this Mrs Miller?' He stood up, drained his glass and stalked over to the decanter. 'Watch them. I want to know what they're up to – and especially *her*. They can't be hoping to start up the yard again; they'd never find the money to do it. But whatever it is, I want to know.'

Packer knew he was dismissed, set down his glass and got up. Garbutt said, 'You did right to tell me. Here—' He dug a hand in his pocket, pulled out a roll of banknotes and slapped them in Packer's hand.

'Thank you.' Packer backed to the door. He thought of pointing out to Garbutt that a true gentleman did not carry cash except to tip, charging everything to an account. He decided against it. Garbutt would not pay for the information; far worse, he might feel slighted and Packer would not risk that. He promised, 'I'll keep in touch.'

Garbutt was left staring into the fire and wondering. Who was this Mrs Miller? Why was she meddling? She was no more than a servant! He had thought he had finished the Langleys but the house and the shipyard still belonged to the brat. Surely in time the name of Langley would wither and fade away into obscurity. But if it did not, or if this woman continued her meddling, he would have to . . . deal with them.

When she arrived in London, Josie found cheap lodgings in a house near the station. The next morning, a cold, clear day, she set out on an open-topped omnibus headed for Wapping. She dressed for the weather in a long 'Russian' coat with a decorated hem and a belt emphasising her slim waist. It had been a gift from one of the Urquhart daughters, altered to fit her by Josie herself and cherished for years.

Josie had been given an address by Dougie Bickerstaffe, but when she got down from the bus she had to ask her way several times before she eventually reached the right street and the right door. It was in a long row of narrow little terraced houses, the living-room doors opening directly on to the street. Lace curtains covered the windows and Josie could just make out the dark green spread of an aspidistra within.

She knocked at the door and while she waited looked round and smiled at the dozen or so ragged and grubby children who had gathered, curious, behind her. The street swarmed with others at their games.

The door was opened by a stout woman with a full, sensuous mouth and little eyes that stared coldly at Josie – and then suspiciously when she took in the coat that had cost the Urquhart girl all of thirty-five shillings. There were men in the street bringing up families on twenty shillings a week.

Josie asked, 'Does Iris Taylor live here?'

The woman challenged: 'What if she does?'

Josie smiled, 'I'd like to talk to her.'

'What about?'

Josie kept the smile in place with an effort. 'I just want to talk.'

'She's not here.' The door slammed in Josie's face.

She wondered, What now? She started back along the street, the children trailing behind her. Then one pigtailed girl said, 'She's in the shop.'

Josie halted. 'Where is that?'

They showed her. It stood on the corner of the next street, its window filled with stacked vegetables, fruit in banked pyramids or boxes outside on the pavement. A tubby man in his forties hustled about between the shop and the nether regions and a woman, seemingly his wife, sat at a cash desk in a corner. A girl wearing a long sackcloth apron was serving the customers queueing at the counter.

Iris Taylor was slight, light-footed and her smile was genuine. Dougie Bickerstaffe had said she was nineteen but Josie thought she looked younger than that. Josie took her place in the queue, asked for a bag of apples when it was her turn and said softly when the girl was close, 'Iris Taylor?' And when the girl stared in surprise but nodded, Josie said, 'I know a friend of yours, Dougie Bickerstaffe. Can I talk to you? When do you get off?'

For answer, Iris turned to the man. 'Can I nip out for a few minutes, Joe?'

''Course you can. You go on, gal, but not all day, mind.'

'Ta, Joe.'

They talked on the pavement a few yards away. Josie explained how Dougie lodged at the Langley house and sailed in the *Macbeth*, then said: 'He talks about you all the time. He wants you to go up North. He said it would be no good for the pair of you down here.'

Iris said bitterly, her smile gone, 'He's right there. Hilda wouldn't give us no peace. Wherever we went around here, she'd find us.'

Josie asked, 'Hilda? Your stepmother?'

Iris nodded. 'She comes up here and gets my wages off Joe. I never lay my hands on a penny except what she gives me and that's precious little. I do all the work around the house and her and Dad go out boozing. Anytime I stick up for myself I get a bloody good hiding off the pair o' them.'

Josie, appalled, asked, 'Why don't you walk out?'

'I daren't. I've got nothing saved and nowhere to go. Nobody to go to, either. Hilda told me, "You go to the police," she says, "and I'll tell 'em you fell down the stairs. It'd be your word against ours and I'll settle wi' you afterwards."'

Josie started, 'Suppose I—'

But Iris hadn't done. 'I'm only telling you this because you'll be off as soon as we've finished. I wouldn't dare tell anybody around here in case it got back to Hilda.'

Josie tried again: 'Dougie—'

'I know what Dougie wants.' Iris's smile returned briefly, fondly. 'I can read him like a book, I think. But – there's never been anybody else, you know? And I'm frightened to trust him. Sailors – I'd see him for a day or two, or maybe a week or just a few hours, then he'd be off to sea again.'

Iris paused and Josie finally got in: 'You needn't be frightened. I'll give you the fare to come up North, find you lodgings and a job.'

'What?' Iris stared in disbelief.

Josie repeated what she had said and they talked for a few minutes more. Then Iris said, 'Oh, Lor'! I'd better get back.'

Josie fished in her bag and pressed coppers and silver into the girl's hand. 'That will pay your fare to King's Cross station and you'll find me there. I'm catching the ten o'clock train tomorrow morning.'

Iris looked dazed but the smile was back for good now. 'All right. Ta. Tomorrow.' Then she ran back to the shop.

Josie was at the station before ten the next day and Iris arrived there only minutes later, nervous but excited. She wore a shabby coat and dress and carried a handbag but had no luggage at all. 'I couldn't get nothing out o' the house except a few little bits me mum left me and they're in me bag.' So they went shopping – hurriedly – and when they boarded the train the guard was blowing his whistle, but Iris carried a suitcase of her own filled with clothes. Josie was eager and happy.

They arrived at the Langley house in the dusk of a bitterly cold day. As their cab slowed to turn into the square, Josie saw another already at the front door. She called quickly, 'Stop, cabbie!'

He reined in the horse. 'What is it, missus?'

Tom Collingwood stood on the steps of the house in conversation with two gentlemen, marked out by their top hats. They were obviously on the point of leaving but Josie decided it might not be tactful to break in on their farewells. She called, 'Turn around!'

So she and Iris got down at the back door of the house and walked into the kitchen. Annie and Kitty had their backs to the door, singing as they worked, and its opening went unnoticed. Little Charlotte stood by Annie's legs, her chubby hand wrapped in Annie's skirts. Josie remembered that she herself had stood just so in this kitchen twenty years ago. Then she saw the child's face change.

Josie looked up and her heart lurched as she saw the giant in the doorway, cut black against the light behind him. Then she realised it was Tom Collingwood, come from the front of the house, and her heart missed another beat.

He crossed the kitchen to her in a second, long-striding, to grasp her arm. 'What's wrong?' he demanded, and stooped to peer into her face. 'For a moment you looked as if you'd seen a ghost.'

'It's nothing,' Josie answered breathlessly. Thinking quickly, she made the excuse, 'I think it was coming into the warm kitchen from the cold outside.' And to distract him and give her a breathing space: 'This is Iris Taylor. She's going to run our shop in Dame Dorothy Street.'

Tom grinned at Iris. 'Welcome.' And to Josie, 'So this was your "family business".'

'Yes.' Josie felt a blush rising under Tom's stare. But then Charlotte was pulling at her while Annie and Kitty were both talking at once, taking coats, putting on the kettle. Tom retreated to the door and Josie was aware of him there, no longer a threat from her past. She was laughing happily. He nodded, smiling, and strode away along the hall. It was good to be home again.

Later that evening, just the two of them sat at supper at the long table in the dining room. Prompted by Josie, Tom talked business throughout the meal, telling how he was about to make another voyage in the *Macbeth* to deliver coal to Davy at the Fishermen's Rest. 'All goes well there.' Tom had also found another cargo to carry down to Hull. 'And I've arranged for more.' He went into details yet again. Josie listened, smiling.

But at the end of the meal he said, 'That shop you rented before you went to London is doing a roaring trade.'

Josie replied happily, 'Yes. And now we have Iris to run it, instead of Annie and Kitty having to fit it in with their other work. They've been marvellous.'

Tom's gaze was fixed on her face. 'So have you.'

'I'm glad you approve of my efforts.' Josie's eyes fell before his.

Tom saw her embarrassment, wondered at it but changed the subject. 'I had visitors earlier this evening.'

Josie hurried to his assistance. 'Yes, I saw them as they left, so I told my cabbie to take us round to the kitchen entrance. I thought it would be better if we did not disturb you.'

'We'd done talking, but I appreciate your consideration.' Then Tom said ruefully, 'They'd come to offer me a plum command, a ship bound for the Far East. It would be quite a big step up.'

Josie smiled, pleased for him. 'That's wonderful!'

Tom shook his head. 'I turned it down. I feel my duty lies closer to home. Besides, I already have a command in the *Macbeth*. She needs a captain.'

Josie stared at him, open-mouthed. Then: 'But that is a wonderful opportunity! It is a great compliment to your ability that they should seek you out and offer this command to you! You must take it!'

'I can't. I—'

Josie cut in on his protests. 'Did they come to you because there is a great shortage of captains?'

Tom grinned wryly. 'No. There are plenty of good men with master's tickets looking for a berth.'

'Then engage one for the *Macbeth*.'

'There are still matters here that I—'

'Would you expect to run this household and care for Charlotte while I was here?'

'No, of course not, but the business—'

Josie, flushed with excitement now and with that proud lift to her head, pressed him. 'You approved of my efforts in business matters so far. Trust me. Please. I know you want this ship and that you are sacrificing your career because you believe that is your duty – but it isn't necessary.' And now Josie begged him, 'Trust me. I will never fail you, or Charlotte, or this house. Believe me.'

Tom saw that the girl was on the verge of tears but it did not influence his answer. 'I believe you.'

He accepted the command the next day and found another captain for the *Macbeth*. Felicity Blakemore called and was delighted at the news: 'I'm glad you've taken my advice and given up that dirty little tramp.'

Tom protested, 'She's not dirty!'

Felicity did not listen. 'When you return we must fix a day for the wedding . . .' She sat in the armchair in the office – Josie's chair – and chatted of her plans while Josie brought tea. 'And we are invited to a dance at the Pendletons' this evening.'

Tom did not return from the dance until long after midnight. Josie, lying wakeful, heard the clattering hooves of his cab and the jingle of the harness, his tread as he passed her door. Hours later she stood at the front door in the dawn as he climbed into another cab, this one headed for the station, to catch an early train bound for London. Annie and Kitty stood beside her and Charlotte danced on the steps with excitement. Felicity was not present because of the dance the previous night.

Dan Elkington and Dougie Bickerstaffe swung Tom's big sea chest up on to the roof of the cab. He had said, 'A lot more to carry, dress uniforms to dine with the passengers, tropical kit . . .'

Tom lifted Charlotte high in the air then kissed her. He smiled at them all as the cab pulled away and they all waved and called their 'goodbyes'. Except Josie, who only tried to smile.

He would be gone for half a year.

19

December 1908

'Good morning, everyone.' Josie had slept poorly for several nights after Tom's departure but had striven to exhibit a forced brightness. She smiled around the kitchen now as she entered with Charlotte by her side. Kitty and Annie replied in chorus as they started the work of the day.

Josie joined them, trying to keep up her end in the singing and the chatter. 'How are you, Annie?' She covertly eyed the girl.

'I'm fine, ma'am.'

Josie nodded, satisfied. She had – gently but firmly – relieved Annie of any heavy work because of the child she was expecting. That work had simply been transferred to Dan Elkington and he had taken on the added burden cheerfully. That reminded Josie: 'Dan!' she called him as he entered the kitchen by the back door. 'I'll need you down at the quay later on, then at the shop.'

'Right y'are, ma'am.'

'I'll tell you when.' Iris Taylor had taken over at the shop and this day they were expecting another delivery of produce from the *Macbeth*.

'There's the postman.' Josie heard the *clack*! of the letterbox. She swept the kitchen with one swift glance and saw that all was now ready to serve the breakfast to her boarders. 'I'll leave you to finish off. Charlotte! Mind you do as you are told.'

'Yes, Mrs Miller,' Charlotte replied as she fed a crust of bread to Amelia, her doll.

Josie picked up the letters from where they lay inside the front door, carried them into the office and flicked through them quickly. There was one addressed to her in Tom Collingwood's neat hand. She dropped the others on the desk and opened that one. The two sheets inside began: 'Dear Mrs Miller . . .' They were businesslike, almost curt, describing his doings since he had left, his ship and her crew. Josie smiled and shook her head. 'Bless the man.' They closed: 'We sail within the hour. I trust you and all there are well.' There was that word. He trusted her. And he had found time to write to her when he was on the point of sailing and must have been very busy. Josie slid the letter inside her dress to read again later.

The other letters were also businesslike. Josie kept the accounts and handled the affairs of the *Macbeth* and the lodging house. She banked any income and paid out wages and other expenditures. This besides bringing up Charlotte and running the house. Josie worked at the desk for half an hour, replying to letters when necessary, entering items in her accounts. As she put away her books she glanced at the clock on the mantelpiece and nodded with satisfaction. There would be plenty of time to visit the Langley shipyard on her way back from the bank. 'Charlotte!'

Soon afterwards she was walking briskly out of the square with Charlotte skipping by her side, both of them wrapped in warm winter coats against the cold wind. Josie knew it would be colder still by the river. At the bank in Bridge Street she drew out the money she needed and put it in the capacious bag she carried for the purpose. Then she and Charlotte went on to the Langley yard.

As they approached the yard, Charlotte asked, 'What are those men doing?' A horse and cart stood outside one of the end houses in a long terrace. Two men in overalls were lifting a wardrobe on to the cart which was already loaded with cheap, old furniture. A third man in a suit shiny with age was inside the house, fixing a crudely lettered sign to the window: 'To Let.'

Josie said, 'The people who live there are moving.' She thought it was a pity she had not seen the house some weeks earlier. It would easily convert into a shop and was much larger than the premises Iris Taylor worked in. But would it be too large? Josie decided to think about it and walked on.

The big gates of the yard were shut, as they had been for months, but a door at the side opened on a passage that led past the timekeeper's office and the watchman's little hutch and so into the yard. The watchman, old Sammy Allnutt, came out to greet her, touching his cap with a thick, broken-nailed finger. 'Aye, aye, Mrs Miller.'

'Good morning, Sammy.' Josie did not remember him from twenty years ago but she had been visiting the yard for some weeks now.

She found it depressing – the melancholy aura of abandonment and desolation, the grass and weeds growing up between the rusting sheets of steel, the stacks of timber turning green with age. But something always drew her back again. She wondered if it was the Langley blood in her.

Sammy limped around the yard with Josie and Charlotte, glad of 'a bit of crack'. Talking to Josie relieved the boredom of his long, solitary hours. He told her of old times as old men do, of when he was young and the yard was busy. He had a wealth of stories about the Langleys, William in particular, and Josie encouraged him to tell them. She was hungry for anything she could learn about these relatives of hers.

Now Sammy was saying, 'Aye, he was a good man, auld Billy Langley, a man's man. Fair, straight as a die. Mind, he could be hard when he thought it was needed.' Josie knew that, remembered the day he had turned away her father. Sammy went on, 'He had his ideas of what was right or wrong and he'd stick to them come hell or high water. Like when he caught Garbutt takin' the money out o' his pocket.'

'Who?' Josie questioned.

'Elisha Garbutt,' said Sammy. Josie frowned. The name struck a chord of memory but was elusive; she could not make a connection. And Sammy was going on, 'He was manager here all o' twenty years ago and the auld man had been good to him. When Billy Langley found Garbutt had robbed him – for years, mind – he sacked him on the spot. Billy came down into the yard to find him and told him in front o' the men. "Get out," he said. "You can go to hell on the road you've made. You'll not work again on this river." And Garbutt never did. He upped sticks and moved, him and all his family. I heard they went to Liverpool. Anyway, nobody saw them round here again.'

Josie shivered and Sammy squinted at her, his eyes narrowed against the wind. 'Feelin' the cold?'

'No.' But Josie could not tell him why she shivered. She corrected herself quickly. 'Yes, a bit. But I'd better be getting away.' She turned back towards the gate.

Sammy went with her. 'Come and warm yoursel' at my fire for a minute.' And as Josie held out her hands to the blaze in his little cabin, with its single armchair and small table, he said, 'But I've known Billy Langley send a parcel o' grub along when he found out one of his men was off sick. He did lots o' things like that. And he took that lad in,

Tom Collingwood. A fine, big feller he's turned out, a ship's captain and a rare good 'un, but when Billy took him in he was roamin' the streets with his belly empty and his trouser's arse hangin' out. And he wasn't a lad that would get any pity or ask for it, either. He'd look you right in the eye as if to say: "I'm as good as you." Aye.' Sammy nodded. 'They were two of a kind.'

Josie called as she left the yard, 'Goodbye. I might look in tomorrow, but I'll be in on Friday, anyway, with your wages.'

One day she would go there and regret it.

Josie waited on the quayside as the *Macbeth* came upriver and was nudged in against the quay by a bustling tugboat. When she was tied up and the gangway run out, Josie went aboard with Charlotte. 'Hello, Captain Fearon. Did you have a good voyage?'

'Aye. Weather wasn't over-good but you expect that at this time of year.' Fearon was in his fifties, tubby, grey, stolid and competent. He had been a master for nearly thirty years and had wanted a berth that gave him more time at home in the years running up to retirement. He had said when he applied for the job, 'Captain of the *Macbeth* will suit me down to the ground.'

Now he stood by as Josie paid the crew their wages and then counted out the captain's money. As he scooped up the sovereigns, Josie said, 'I've got a cargo for you, sailing tomorrow night for Harwich. It's all in there.' And she handed him an envelope with the papers.

Fearon looked them over, nodding, then mentioned as an aside, 'The supplies you ordered, they're all below. When d'you want them up?'

Josie glanced at her watch then out of the scuttle, and she saw that Dan Elkington was on the quay on time, with the hired horse and cart as she had requested. She smiled at Fearon. 'Now, please.'

So the derrick whisked the sacks and crates of produce out of the hold. Dan and Dougie Bickerstaffe loaded the eggs and butter, cabbages and potatoes, on to the cart. Josie and Charlotte climbed up on the seat beside Dan while Dougie jumped up on the tail of the cart, where he rode with legs swinging in time to his whistling.

Iris Taylor was waiting at the shop, ready in her sackcloth apron, and arranged her stock as Dan and Dougie unloaded it. Dougie was inclined to linger by Iris, murmuring in her ear while she laughed. Josie accepted this philosophically. The pair of them were still much more productive than Iris on her own. Josie heard Dougie say, 'I'm off over the water as soon as I'm finished here.' That meant he was going to cross the bridge over the river into the town. 'I want a new pair o' sea boots.'

Iris asked, 'Can't you buy them over here?'

Dougie shook his curly head. 'There's nobody this side of the water that sells anything like that.'

Josie had been on the point of leaving but now she waited until the job was done and Dan had returned the horse and cart to their owner. Then, as she walked home with Dan, she asked, 'Do you mind if we go a bit out of our way?' And when he shrugged cheerful acceptance she led him towards the Langley yard. As they came to the empty house she had seen earlier, she asked, 'Do you think you could run a shop, Dan? A chandler's? Selling sea boots, oilskins and suchlike to sailors?'

It was settled before they reached the Langley house. Again the business would be owned by the Langley Shipping Company, Josie having a one-third share. She was well pleased.

Dinner was waiting, to be eaten in the middle of the day and in the warm kitchen, now that Captain Collingwood, master of the house, was away. Josie told Charlotte, 'Lessons for you this afternoon.' But that did not frighten Charlotte and she ate on happily.

And afterwards Josie would go to her room and read Tom's letter again.

Reuben Garbutt sat at his desk in his study. He saw that the letter was addressed in Packer's own writing – the solicitor would not let his secretary know of this business. Packer had paid an unemployed clerk to follow Josie and report her movements. Garbutt read the account of Mrs Miller's activities, her visits to the bank, the *Macbeth*, the shop – the yard? Garbutt read that again. She had visited the yard, not regularly but frequently. Why? What could be there to interest her, a children's nurse?

But she was also a partner in the Langley Shipping Company which was keeping the name of Langley alive. Was she also attempting, somehow, to breathe life into the Langley yard again? Garbutt swore. If she was he would stop it – stop her. He would go and—

There was a tap at the door of his study, then it opened and the butler entered. He carried a woman's coat and hat in one hand and announced, 'Miss Wilks, sir.'

Garbutt glowered at the interruption. He recalled hearing the wheels of a cab crunching on the gravel of the drive and realised it had brought Rhoda. She had a flat of her own now, paid for by Garbutt, and no longer lived in St John's Wood. She wore a silk dress embroidered with lace which had cost him four pounds. She smiled timidly at him. 'Hello.'

He snapped, 'What do you want?' The woman was a nuisance. He had installed her in a fine flat, bought her expensive clothes and gave her an extravagant allowance to pay her maid and her cook and live in style. What more did she—

Rhoda complained, 'I haven't seen you for days. You're always off on business somewhere.' But she wondered about that business. And once he had lusted after her body every night, but now—

Garbutt crossed to the fire and threw the letter into the flames. 'I have to go away now. Up North.'

'Can't I come with you?' Rhoda was becoming desperate. The promised marriage had not transpired. He had told her brutally, 'Forget it. I'm not the marrying kind, but I'll see you right.' And he had provided for her, amply, Rhoda admitted, but how long would it continue? She remembered how she had once pleased him and rubbed against him. 'Take me with you. Please.'

Garbutt had nothing but contempt for her intelligence but knew that she was devoted to him. She would do anything for him and that could be useful. Now . . . He reached out for her.

When he stepped down from the taxicab at King's Cross station, Rhoda was already there, a porter beside her with her suitcase. She knew better than to keep Garbutt waiting. She had tried to hide the bruise on her cheek with powder and rouge but it showed through. Garbutt saw the work of his hands but said nothing. Rhoda made the excuse for him, told herself that he had been drinking. She saw that he had shaved off his moustache, opened her mouth to comment but then thought better of it.

In the first-class carriage he barely spoke to her throughout the journey. At Newcastle they booked into a small hotel as husband and wife. Next morning, as he shaved, Garbutt looked at the face of a stranger, now that he was without the moustache he had worn since reaching manhood. He had removed it because Packer had told him that witnesses had seen and described the driver of the lorry that killed James Langley and his wife. Garbutt did not want to risk one of those witnesses identifying him now, unlikely though it might be.

By mid-morning they had taken the local train to Monkwearmouth and were down by the river. Garbutt hired a boat there and flipped an extra half-crown to its owner. 'I'll pull it myself.' And to Rhoda, 'Get in.'

She wanted to say 'I don't want to go', because she was terrified of boats and the water, had never ventured out on to the river before. But she dared not deny him and swallowed her protests, climbed nervously into the rocking boat.

Out in the stream, Rhoda asked unhappily, 'Where are we going?'

The winter wind blew cold up the river from the sea and the little boat pitched as Garbutt tugged at the oars. 'We're just going for a row.'

'How far?'

'Until I've seen what I want to see. Today, tomorrow or whenever. Now shut up.'

They had caught the tide at high water. When they were opposite the Langley yard Garbutt paddled gently, just a few strokes now and then to hold the boat on station, keeping it from drifting. He had brought a pocket telescope with him and now extended it, set it to one eye and searched the yard. There was the slip where the ships were built and to one side was the quay where they were fitted out after their launching. There were rusting steel plates, stacks of timber, and one tall tower of it, made of huge baulks a foot in diameter and with a ladder propped against it. He saw no one, but knew there would be a watchman.

Garbutt pulled on the oars, beginning his slow patrol back and forth in front of the Langley yard. He saw Rhoda shiver and ignored her. She would have to put up with it. If she waited all day or all week.

'Hello, Sammy.' Josie, with Charlotte by her side, passed the time-keeper's office and looked in on the watchman in his hutch. 'How are you?'

'Canny, Mrs Miller, canny.' Sammy stood a kettle on the stove and a teapot beside it to warm. 'I'm just making a cup o' tea. Will you have one?'

'If there's one in the pot when we get back. We're just going for a look round.'

'Righto.'

Josie passed on into the yard and strolled slowly down a wide, cobbled track towards the river, stopping frequently to examine things she had not noticed before, making a mental note to ask Sammy about them. Charlotte talked to Amelia, the doll clutched in her arms, as she toddled alongside.

Out on the river, Garbutt snatched up the telescope again and set it to his eye. There was still no watchman to be seen – no doubt he was staying in the warmth of his cuddy – but there was a woman, looking just as Packer had described her. It had to be Mrs Miller. And with her? That would be the Langley brat, Charlotte. All just as Packer had said. They were walking a wide, cobbled track leading past the timber tower and down to the river.

Garbutt dropped the telescope and seized the oars. With swift, powerful strokes, he drove the boat in to slide against the quayside near the slip. He jumped out holding the painter – with the tide at the full the boat rode only a couple of feet below the quay. He paused only to loop the painter round a bollard and toss the end down to Rhoda. 'Hold on!'

She squeaked, 'No! Don't leave me here!'

But he was already running. He crouched low so the heaps of timber and piles of steel plates hid him. He was sure that if Mrs Miller continued on that cobbled path she would pass close under the tall tower of timber. He came to the ladder propped against it, still out of sight of the woman. He was breathing heavily but climbed quickly; he must not be too late. At the top he wriggled on to the top of the tower, keeping flat on his belly. Its surface was green with moss, damp and slimy. When he raised his head he saw the woman steadily approaching and only about thirty yards away, the brat at her side. They would pass right under him.

Garbutt squirmed towards a baulk that lay nearest where they would pass. It formed part of the floor on the top of the tower and, like the others, this timber was eight feet long and a foot square. It lay a foot from the edge of the tower. Could he move it? There was a gap between it and the next baulk which admitted his hands. He got up on to his knees, though still keeping low, and curled his fingers under the timber. He lifted and it moved an inch or two. He tried again, gained another inch, but it was awkward lifting while kneeling and too slow. They would be past and gone!

He rose to his feet. The woman was only yards away. If she looked up . . . But she and the child had their heads bent over a rag doll. Garbutt stooped once more to get his hands under the timber and now it lifted smoothly—

'*No!*' The scream was piercing. Garbutt's head turned as he started and his foot skidded on the greasy surface. The timber toppled but one end went first so that it bounced from the side of the tower, turning end over end – and over the heads of the woman and child.

Now Garbutt saw Rhoda, her hands framing her horrified face, standing between him and the quayside. She had been mortally afraid, left in the boat, and had scrambled out then followed him slowly, wondering what he intended. Until she saw him about to launch the lethal timber.

Garbutt knew only that it was she who had screamed.

'Hey!' At the shout his head twisted the other way and he saw the watchman coming down the yard from his office.

'Damn you!' Garbutt cursed Rhoda, glanced down and saw the woman below, clasping the child to her and staring up at him. Then he turned, scrambled down the ladder, dropping the last few feet, and ran for the boat. As he passed Rhoda he struck her a backhanded blow that sent her sprawling. Then he came to the quayside and saw that Rhoda had used the painter to haul herself out of the boat but had not made it fast. It had drifted away and was already a dozen yards out in the river.

Garbutt spun around and ran back up the yard. He passed Rhoda, lying with a hand to her bloody mouth, without a glance. The Miller woman, with the child hidden behind her, shrank away from him but he had no time for her now. The watchman barred his way but Sammy's running days had ended long ago. Garbutt swerved around him, avoiding Sammy's clutching hands, saw him gaping then heard him yell, 'Here! I know you, you bastard!'

Garbutt ran on, through the passage past the timekeeper's office and so into the street. He ran until he reached the next corner, the bellows of the watchman receding behind him, not caring who saw him or what they thought. But once around the corner he slowed to a fast-striding walk so as not to draw attention to himself. A few minutes later he was just in time to catch the ferry across the river.

In Langley's yard, Sammy returned from his hopeless pursuit. He went wheezing and gasping to where Josie still stood by the tower with her arms around Charlotte. He asked, 'Are you and the bairn all right?'

Josie's heart went on pounding and her face was pale but she answered, 'Yes.'

'By, lass, you were lucky.'

'I was.' Josie stared at the baulk of timber only a yard away. It had gouged a hole for itself in the weed-grown, hard-packed earth. What would it have done to the tender flesh of herself and the child?

Sammy said, 'That wasn't an accident. He got up there and threw it off to try to kill the pair o' you.' Then, as Josie nodded, he went on, 'And I know who it was. It's twenty years since I saw him, when he was a lad of fifteen or sixteen, but I wouldn't forget him.' When Garbutt had shaved to avoid the possibility of recognition he had made it easy for Sammy, who recalled him as a youth before he grew the moustache. Sammy said, 'He was a bad little bugger then. That was Elisha Garbutt's lad, Reuben. I told you the other day how auld Billy Langley sacked Elisha Garbutt.'

Josie remembered that – and a lot more. Sergeant Normanby had questioned Reuben Garbutt in London following the death of William Langley. He had said that Garbutt matched the description of the man who murdered James Langley and his wife, Maria, but he had an alibi, men who had sworn he was in London at the time. What was that alibi worth now? Tom had said Garbutt had effectively killed William Langley, had done it out of spite. Then today there was the attack on Charlotte.

Josie could only come to one conclusion: Garbutt was attempting to destroy the Langley family. She shuddered and held Charlotte a little tighter. But Garbutt had failed; Josie and the child were alive and she knew who had saved them. Her gaze shifted from the timber to the woman who had screamed, 'No!' Josie had seen how that scream had distracted Garbutt so that he slipped and the timber fell askew. And she had seen the mad glare of hatred in his eyes as he stared down at her.

The woman was now sitting up in the dirt, careless of her skirts jerked up around her knees, her hands wiping at her bleeding lips with a stained handkerchief. Josie pushed Charlotte towards the watchman. 'Stay with Mr Allnutt a minute, there's a good girl.' She did not want the child to see the woman's battered face. Josie went to her, kneeling before her so she could peer at the sallow, blood-smeared face with its broken mouth. She did not know the woman, but searching back in her memory deduced: 'You are Rhoda Wilks.' And when Rhoda nodded: 'You were with him.' No nod this time. The dark eyes slid away, avoiding hers, but Josie stretched out a hand to turn the head and eyes back to her again. 'You were with him at the house when old Mr Langley died. And he was driving the lorry that ran down young Mr Langley and his wife. You came here with him to kill little Charlotte and—'

'No!' The word was wrung from Rhoda Wilks again, but this time it was not a shriek but a moan.

'*Yes!*' Josie insisted, shaking Rhoda in her shock and anger. 'I saw him, Sammy saw him – you did!'

'I didn't know.' Rhoda was shivering now. Josie had released her but she still shook. 'I was with him but I didn't know what he was going to do. He never said and I didn't dare ask him. He said that time before wi' the lorry was an accident and I believed him because I couldn't believe he would . . . But just now, when I saw him up there, and you wi' that little bairn I used to look after, I couldn't let him. No.' The tears had come to run down from her eyes as her head shook. 'No. No. No . . . !'

Josie helped her to her feet and led her, stumbling, to the watchman's hutch, sat her by the stove. She wiped Rhoda's bruised face passably clean, put the kettle on the stove and made a fresh pot of tea. Josie let Sammy bring Charlotte in then and she hugged the child. 'Now you play in the corner with Amelia for a bit.' Then to Sammy, doubtfully, 'Can you write?' She doubted it because few of his generation were literate.

But he answered proudly, 'Aye. Me father paid for me to learn at the church school.'

At Josie's request he fetched a pen, ink and paper from the timekeeper's office. Then Josie had Rhoda tell her story before she could change her mind and Sammy set it down, slowly and with some strange spellings, but clearly enough. Josie would not have entrusted the task to Rhoda. Josie presumed Rhoda could read and write as compulsory education started around the time she was born, but her hand still shook. She needed little prompting, however, and she even included the fact that she had witnessed the murder of James and Maria Langley. She seemed relieved, at the end, to have lifted a weight from her conscience.

Josie asked her then, 'Can you read?' When Rhoda nodded, Josie handed her the statement. Rhoda read it slowly and signed it, shakily but legibly, where Josie indicated. Sammy and Josie signed and dated it as witnesses. Ten minutes later Sammy was able to hail a passing policeman and he took Rhoda and her statement away. Sammy was left comforting Josie, now sick and shivering from reaction, with hot tea. 'And I put a drop o' something in it.'

Garbutt entered Packer's office by way of the back yard. His face was streaked with sweat despite the coldness of the day. Packer stared at him when he burst into the room, at his dishevelled dress and clean-shaven face, but he hastened to do Garbutt's bidding when he demanded hoarsely, 'Get that damned woman out of here!'

Packer scurried out to his secretary and told her, 'You can finish for the day.' And, inventing a pretext, 'I've had a bet on a horse come up.' He gave her a half-crown. 'Go and celebrate and I'll see you tomorrow.'

She leaned against him as she stood. 'Can't we celebrate together?'

'Tomorrow.' He helped her into her coat and held the door open, bolted it as soon as she had gone. He returned to his office and asked fearfully, 'What's wrong?'

Garbutt knew the reason for that fear and snapped bitterly, 'You don't need to worry. You won't be involved – unless they take me. I went after the Miller woman today and that stupid cow, Rhoda, let me down.' He recounted briefly what had happened at the yard and went on: 'Rhoda might have the sense to keep her mouth shut, though I doubt it, but the watchman saw everything: old Sammy Allnutt. I remember him – *and he remembers me*! They've got my name, description, witnesses, so you've got to get me out of the country quick – for your sake as well as mine.'

Packer smuggled Garbutt back to his house in a cab after darkness fell. The solicitor lived alone. His housekeeper came in daily but she had left him a meal and gone before the two men arrived. Packer went out again that evening. He had criminal contacts and Garbutt had money. The arrangements took time and Garbutt had to hide in Packer's attic each day while the housekeeper cleaned and cooked. But before a week was out he was on a ship bound for Antwerp.

* * *

Josie had returned to the Langley house in fear and clutching Charlotte by the hand, reluctant to let the child out of her sight. Sergeant Normanby came to see her that evening to take a statement from her. He agreed with her conclusion that it seemed Garbutt was waging a vendetta against the Langley family. But then he assured her, 'I reckon Garbutt has run for his life.'

A week later he returned. 'We've been to Garbutt's house outside o' London. We thought we'd find all manner of evidence there to incriminate him but the place was clean as a whistle. Not that it matters because it's a certainty he'll hang when we get him. We talked to his staff – and they talked to us. None of them had criminal records – till now – but they admitted he paid them a hefty bribe to alibi him and they'll go down for perjury.'

Then Normanby added, 'One thing in particular they told us, though, was that Garbutt went across the Channel frequently, for a few days or a week. So it sounds like he had a hiding place waiting for him over there. It's a certainty he's over there now and he'll never come back unless we fetch him.'

Josie slept peacefully that night for the first time in a week, mistakenly relieved and secure.

Garbutt had drawn on his funds in France and gone to ground. But his hatred of the Langley family had now widened and he was vowing vengeance on the Miller woman.

20

May 1909

'I wish I understood the stars, Captain.' Adelaide Freebody said it plaintively, but only so Tom Collingwood could hear. There were some ninety diners in the saloon of the *Dorothy Snow* in mid-Atlantic, seated at two long tables spread with thick white damask cloths. Adelaide sat on Tom's left with her parents on hers, both of them engrossed in conversation with other passengers or ship's officers. She was tall and shapely with a deal of bosom on display. Now she went on huskily, 'I stand in the back of the ship every night after dinner and try to work out which is which but I just get mixed up. There sure are a lot of them.'

Tom was sympathetic: 'There are. So I usually navigate by the sun.' He had been captain of the *Dorothy Snow* for over five months now and he had grown used to passengers. It helped that he was briefed by the ship's purser, so he knew that Adelaide was heiress to a fortune, made by her father out of property in New York. Tom's ship had recently sailed from there, bound for Southampton.

There was a lull in the conversation at his end of the table as Adelaide thought about his answer. A man in his fifties, two places away on Tom's right, leaned forward to say, 'I understand this ship will be paying off when she gets to London, Captain.'

Tom replied, 'That's so, Mr Harvey. She is to undergo a major refit and after that she will be back on the transatlantic run.' The purser had told him: 'Albert Harvey is a big nob in hotels. He has three or four in England and now another two in the States. He makes the crossing two or three times a year on business.'

Now Harvey confirmed, 'Then I will certainly be using her. She suits me down to the ground.'

Tom nodded in acknowledgment. 'Thank you.'

Irene Carr

Harvey went on, 'So you will have some time with your family?'

'Yes, I will. I'm looking forward to it.'

Harvey queried, 'Children?'

'A little girl: Charlotte. She's four years old.' He sensed Adelaide's declining interest and grinned to himself. This tactic usually saved him from unwanted advances. But the grin faded when he wondered how things were in the Langley house. Letters occasionally caught up with him. Written by Mrs Miller, they were polite and cheerful, assuring him that all was well, but he wondered if she was keeping her troubles to herself?

He would be glad to be home. It was almost guiltily that he remembered Felicity Blakemore, but of course, he loved her and he was pledged to marry her.

'Aye, I knew Kitty Duggan years back when her man owned the ship he captained.' Sammy Allnutt stumped along beside Josie as she strolled around the Langley yard. She had taken to visiting it again after a period when she went in fear of Garbutt returning to attack Charlotte again. Gradually that fear had receded, helped by Sergeant Normanby's certainty that Garbutt had fled the country. Something drew her back to the yard. Her grandfather, father and uncle had all worked here. And legally it was hers and not Charlotte's, for what that was worth. Which now and for the foreseeable future was nothing. But she liked to browse in the yard and listen to Sammy's 'crack', his reminiscing about old times in the yard and in Monkwearmouth.

He went on, 'Why, I've lived here all my life except for those few years when I was at sea. And most o' that time I worked here in Langley's yard. I knew all the fellers that worked here. And I know what most o' them are doing now. A lot are still looking for a job but some o' them are working in other yards on this river. A few got jobs on the Tyne. One feller, that was Varley, the manager, he's up on the Clyde now.'

Josie knew that, having been instrumental in arranging the job for Harry Varley, but she kept quiet, watched over Charlotte as she played in the deserted yard, and listened to Sammy. He went on, detailing where the former members of staff were now, and Josie committed it all to memory, then recited it again to herself as she walked back to the Langley house. Until Charlotte squealed excitedly, 'Race you the last bit!' Josie glanced around to satisfy herself there were no male witnesses, hitched up her skirts and ran.

They arrived at the house, laughing, as Annie wheeled her perambulator up to the kitchen door. Josie asked, 'Is he asleep?' She peeped in to see Annie's baby wide-eyed and awake.

Annie grimaced good-humouredly. 'Not him, but so long as he sleeps through the night now, I won't complain.'

Josie grinned. 'No fear.' Because she had helped, walking the floor in the night when little Andrew could not get his wind up.

Kitty, making bread, left the dough she was kneading to wipe her hands on her pinny. She came to lift him out of the pram and Charlotte wanted to hold him. Kitty cooed, 'Nothing wrong wi' him.'

Josie said drily, 'Except being spoilt.'

Kitty ignored that. 'Dan says the chandler's is going well.'

'Yes, it is.'

Dan Elkington had jumped at the chance to run it. He and Josie had stocked it with oilskins, sea boots and stockings, jerseys and caps – they had made it an Aladdin's cave of seafaring wear. Dan kept a lot of his stock on the upper floor where he lived, but as he said, 'I only sleep here.' He had a bed and a gas ring to heat water and was content with them. He still came to the Langley house for meals and did odd jobs there.

'You've got your fingers into everything,' said Kitty, but she was smiling, pleased rather than censorious. Then she went on, lowering her voice, 'But sometimes you miss what's going on under your nose.' And when Josie stared, Kitty explained, with a nod towards Annie who was making a cup of tea and was out of earshot, 'Her and Dan, they've got an understanding.'

Josie had not noticed the signs. True, Dan came around for his meals and was to be found in the kitchen with Annie all evening and every evening. She asked, 'How long—?'

Kitty chuckled. 'Weeks ago, I spotted them.'

Josie smiled now, watching Annie. 'I'm glad.'

'Don't get too pleased,' warned Kitty. 'They'll probably give you plenty o' trouble afore they're wed. That's a long way off at the moment.'

'Why?' Josie asked.

'How should I know?' Kitty replied indignantly. 'I don't go poking my nose into other people's affairs. I just happen to have overheard one or two things, like he wants to get wed now and she wants a place of her own first. But it's none o' my business. I think young folks are best left to sort themselves out, like I had to.' She shot a sidewise glance at Josie. 'Though there's some better at it than others.'

This left Josie smiling to herself, puzzled, but then she shrugged off the remark. She would take Kitty's advice – for the present – and leave the young lovers to fend for themselves, but if Annie or Dan needed help . . .

As they sat down to tea, Josie told herself she had much to be thankful for. The *Macbeth* was proving profitable and so were the boarding house and the shop run by Iris. Its previous owner had failed because he kept too small a choice of goods and drank his takings. Iris, bright and cheerful and selling the produce brought by the *Macbeth*, was busy all day long.

Josie retired to the office in the evening to write up her accounts. Then she put on her coat and walked down to the river because the *Macbeth* was due to berth. She watched the little ship come plodding in between the piers, smoke curling from her funnel, then walked back to the Langley house. It was in darkness now. She went once more into the office. Some weeks ago she had found a drawer of the desk filled with photograph albums, with posed portraits of the Langleys, starting with William's parents and carrying on through to Charlotte. There were several of Josie herself, as a baby and as a small child, in her mother's arms or on her knee. Her mother sat very straight in a chair, her dress carefully arranged. David Langley stood behind her, one hand on her shoulder, the other gripping the lapel of his jacket. Everyone in the photographs stared solemnly at the camera. The most recent of Charlotte appeared to have been taken a year ago. Josie frowned; that would have to be remedied.

One album held photographs of every ship built in the Langley yard, with details of their tonnage. She leafed through it as she had done so often before, absorbed in the sepia-toned pictures, and finally retired to bed when her eyes kept closing. She fell asleep wishing: If only it was possible to open the yard again for Charlotte.

The next day Josie boarded the *Macbeth* to be greeted by Bucko Daniels, the mate, with the news: 'They've taken the skipper to the infirmary.' Ben Fearon had broken his leg when the *Macbeth* was just twenty-four hours from Sunderland. 'He just started to climb down the ladder from the bridge but she rolled and he missed his grip on the handrail. He came down like a sack o' bricks.'

Josie paid the crew then took a tram to the infirmary to comfort Ben Fearon, but all the time she was worrying over the problem now presented. She had contracted to take on another cargo in the *Macbeth* the next day, but where would she find another skipper in that time?

When she walked into the kitchen of the Langley house Kitty Duggan challenged her: 'What are you so down in the mouth for? I thought you'd be dancing. I would ha' been at your age.'

Josie looked at her blankly. 'What are you talking about?'

Kitty jerked her head towards the door leading to the hall and the front of the house. 'He's back.'

'T . . . Captain Collingwood?'

Kitty said drily, 'Aye, the big lad.'

Josie said primly, 'That is good news. I'll go and see him.'

'Aye.' Kitty's voice followed her as she remembered to walk sedately down the passage. 'See if he's brought you back a parrot!'

His kitbag and suitcases were in the hall and the door to the office was open. Josie paused in the doorway. Tom sat in his swivel chair at the desk but Charlotte was on his knee and in full flow: '. . . and Annie's baby used to cry a lot but he's all right now. Annie lets me hold him sometimes. She says she doesn't know where she would have been now if it hadn't have been for Mrs Miller, in her grave very likely, but Kitty said she shouldn't say that in front of me though it's prob'ly true and Mrs Miller seems all right to me but Kitty says she'll be the better for you—'

Josie cut her short: 'Really, Charlotte, you must let Captain Collingwood catch his breath.' Then she scooped up the child from Tom's knee and fussed over her so she did not have to meet his gaze. 'Did you have a good voyage? Can we look forward to having you at home for a while?'

He was standing over her now, the height and breadth of him cutting out the light. 'I'll be here for some time. The ship has gone into the dockyard for a few weeks for refit. I don't know whether they'll want me when she's ready for sea again.'

'I'm sure they will!' Josie looked up at him confidently. 'I'm sure you've done very well.'

'Thank you.' He grinned. 'Is that your opinion as a shipowner?'

And now she remembered her earlier problem – and made the connection. But . . . She said doubtfully, 'Ben Fearon has fallen and broken his leg, so we don't have a captain for the *Macbeth* and there's a cargo waiting for her tomorrow. I don't suppose . . .' She left the sentence hanging.

Tom Collingwood stared at her in pretended outrage. 'What? I come home after six months and you want me to sail again tomorrow?' Then he laughed. 'Don't worry. I'm only too glad to sail the *Macbeth*. It just shows how busy you've been, organising cargoes for her. And then there are the shops and this place.'

Charlotte said, 'I told you about them, Uncle Tom, didn't I? And what Kitty said—'

Josie said firmly, 'That's enough, Charlotte.' She made a mental note to be careful how she acted and talked in front of Charlotte in future. And to have a word with Kitty and Annie. Now she understood Kitty's remark about 'young folks sorting themselves out'. She looked up at Tom. 'Thank you.' Then she whisked Charlotte away in a flurry of confusion.

Josie cornered Kitty alone later that evening and challenged her: 'I think you've been linking my name with that of Captain Collingwood.'

Kitty answered, 'There's an old saying: Don't believe what you hear, only believe what you see. I know what I've seen.'

'That's only what you *think* you've seen. It's not true, Kitty. Captain Collingwood is engaged to be married and there is nothing between us. If talk like yours gets about I will have to leave. My position here is that I am employed to care for the child and look after the house. I cannot maintain that position if you spread such rumours. So no more. Please?'

Kitty sighed and shook her head. 'I wouldn't do anything to hurt you, lass. I'll keep my thoughts to myself, but I can't stop thinking them.'

Josie went on her way, unhappy. She joined Tom in the office, at his request, to bring him up to date with the affairs of the *Macbeth* and the house. But she sat in the armchair while he was seated at the desk, the width of the room between them – as Josie wanted. First she told him how Garbutt had tried to murder her and little Charlotte, and her conclusion, shared by Sergeant Normanby, that Garbutt was waging a vendetta against the Langleys.

Tom stared at her aghast. 'And you weren't harmed, either of you?'

Josie smiled wanly. 'No, just badly frightened.' She went on quickly, 'And there's no cause for concern now. Garbutt has fled the country to escape hanging.'

Tom said softly, 'I'm relieved you weren't hurt.'

Josie hurried on, 'Now, as to the *Macbeth* and other business . . .' She went through it quickly, remembering what she had said to Kitty regarding 'my position here', then bade Tom goodnight. But from the door, as she slipped out, she had to turn her head to say, 'I'm glad you're home, Captain Collingwood.'

Inevitably, Felicity Blakemore called, this time accompanied by her mother. She was a matronly woman, alternately coy with Tom and gushing. Kitty took tea to them in the sitting room, but Josie was passing through the hall as they were leaving. Tom escorted them to the gleaming car where Jarvis, the chauffeur, held the rear door open for them. Mrs Blakemore clutched Tom's arm and beamed at him. '. . . so we've determined on an October wedding. We must hope for a fine day.'

Then Felicity chimed in, 'I won't see you sail tomorrow because Mother and I are off to the shops in Newcastle, but don't forget the ball on the twentieth of this month. I'm so looking forward to it.'

Tom answered her, 'I will be back on the nineteenth. Don't worry.' He watched the car drive away. Josie thought, An October wedding. She hurried away before he could turn around and see her, ask her what was wrong.

Tom went down to the ship the next day to see her cargo loaded and ensure that she was ready for sea. He returned at noon, striding along the hall and passage to put his head around the kitchen door. He saw Josie cooking in there with Annie and Kitty and said, 'I'm glad to see you are in practice.'

Josie smiled. 'How is the ship?'

'The *ship* is fine.'

Josie detected his emphasis and paused in her stirring. Charlotte seized the opportunity to poke a finger into the basin of raw cake and lick it. Josie asked, 'Then is something wrong?'

Tom shrugged. 'Nothing too serious, just the cook is out of action.'

Josie protested, 'The cook? He was all right yesterday when I paid him.'

'No doubt. But it seems he's been spending it in the pubs ever since.

He won't be fit for sea for days, certainly not this voyage.' Then he eyed Josie. 'I don't suppose—'

Josie remembered she had used those words when suggesting he captain the *Macbeth* for this next voyage. Guessing what would come next she said, 'No.' Then, as he nodded firmly, she wailed again, 'No!'

Tom said, mock serious, 'If it's good enough for me, then it's good enough for you. I'll enter you in the ship's papers as cook.'

So when the *Macbeth* sailed that evening Josie was in her galley. She thought she could still hear the mocking laughter of Kitty Duggan and didn't care; she was happy.

They had delivered their cargo and were homeward bound when a grave Tom Collingwood said, 'We're in for some bad weather.'

21

'Oh my God!' Josie put a hand to her mouth.

'Now you can see where it's coming from!' Tom Collingwood shoved his head out of the wheelhouse to shout down to Josie. She stood at the door of the galley of the *Macbeth* as the little old ship plodded southward and stared with dread across the lumpy North Sea to the eastern horizon. The clouds hung low and black there, fat-bellied with the rain inside them. The wind, cold in her face, came out of the north-east and was bringing those clouds down on her and the *Macbeth*. They heralded an early dusk and a night of storm.

'If we were close to a port I'd run for shelter,' Tom called down to her. 'But we aren't, so we'll just have to ride it out. You'd better make everything fast in the galley.'

Josie replied, 'I've done that. What isn't wedged securely is tied down. I thought that, when the storm came, anything not fastened would be thrown about.'

Tom blinked, taken aback that his order had been anticipated. Then he complimented her. 'Well done. Now I want you to get into your cabin, fasten the dead-light over the scuttle and lock the door. I don't want you thrown about, either.'

Josie did not want to do that, hated the idea of being shut in the airless cabin, unable to see what was going on about her. But she could see that Tom was preoccupied with the preparations for the coming storm. The crew had already secured everything above and below deck and were now setting up lifelines so that they could cross the open deck in the storm if necessary. So Josie did not argue but retired to her cabin, locked the door and took one last look out of the scuttle, then screwed the dead-light over it. She sat on the bunk as the deck rose and fell with an increasingly savage rhythm; the oil lamp swung and the shadows danced on the bulkheads. She prayed she would not be sick. The cabin was like a tomb.

Josie had a clock above her bunk so she was able to measure the passage of time. It was in the early hours of the morning, when it seemed the storm had battered and tossed the little ship for ever, that she decided she could stand no more. The cabin creaked and groaned around her, rose like a lift and dropped with stomach-churning speed, lurched over on one side then on to the other. Josie was bruised and numbed, physically and mentally. She was not sick but she was mortally afraid. She went to the door, gingerly unlocked it and turned the handle.

Crash! The door was flung back against her and would have thrown her across the cabin if she had not clung to it. The wind howled in through the doorway, stripped the cloth from the little table and strove to tear Josie from her hold. She in turn tried to close the door, bracing her legs and thrusting against it with all her strength. As she did so she was able to take in the scene outside and gained a horrified impression of a wave like a black glass wall marching past the ship. The wind whipped spray from its crest to fly like lace. Some of it smashed into Josie's face, stinging. Then that wave had gone and she could see further, out over a dark sea of mountains and valleys under a sky that hung low and leaden with never a star to be seen. Then the *Macbeth*'s bow soared upwards again as she lifted to another towering wave. Briefly the wind eased and Josie, by exerting all her strength, was able to shut the door and turn the key in the lock. She was still afraid of being locked in the cabin but even more frightened by what lay outside.

She waited in the rolling, bucketing cabin, hanging on to the bunk with hooked fingers all through that long night. Until there came a banging at the door and Tom's voice came to her above the roar of the breaking seas, the howl of the wind: 'Mrs Miller! Open up!'

Once more Josie staggered to the door and unlocked it. Prepared now, she kept her weight behind it – but that did no good. This time there was not only the wind to contend with, fearsome though that was. Now as she turned the handle the *Macbeth* suddenly heeled over on her side. Josie fell back, fought to hold on to the door, but as it opened so Tom, also taken by surprise by the sudden heeling, was hurled forward. He fell over the cabin's coaming and on to her. Together they blundered across the cabin as if in some mad dance and ended on the bunk.

Josie gasped for the breath that the weight of his body had forced out of her. His face, black-stubbled and wet with salt spray, was only an inch above hers. For a second they stared into each other's eyes, then Tom shoved himself up, grabbed Josie's hand and pulled her after him. He made for the door, moving from handhold to handhold. And as he went he shouted, 'You can't stay in here any longer! I think she's going!'

They were walking uphill, the deck under their feet at a steep angle, the door hanging down towards them. Josie could see past Tom's broad shoulders to the outside world and now she saw there was a greyness to the darkness, the day was coming. Tom passed through the doorway out on to the deck and hauled Josie after him. Now she could see that the *Macbeth* lay over on her side, her starboard rail level with Josie's eyes, the rail to port immersed in the sea that washed over the deck.

Tom released her hand then threw his arm around her, wrapping it about her slim waist and squeezing the breath out of her again. Together they climbed the short ladder to the wheelhouse and Josie glimpsed the crew huddled in its lee, trying to find some shelter from the storm. The door to the wheelhouse had been smashed by the sea and hung crookedly from its hinges. Inside they found Dougie Bickerstaffe at the helm. The wheel spun in his hands as he turned the spokes, but uselessly. He bawled, 'Her steering's gone!' And then he left the wheel and went to where the mate, Bucko Daniels, lay in the corner of the wheelhouse.

Josie pulled away from Tom and staggered past Dougie to kneel by the unconscious figure of the mate. She heard Dougie telling Tom, 'Bucko was keeping her head to the seas but then this big one came along and she sheered off. I think that must ha' been when the steering went. She swung broadside to this sea and it laid her over.'

Tom shouted to him, 'Fetch them up out of the engine-room and get the boat away! We'll have to abandon her!'

Meanwhile Josie was examining the mate as well as she could in the gloom. She found he was breathing, then, cautiously lifting his head, she felt at the back of it the stickiness of blood and a lump.

'How is he?' Tom was stooping over her.

'He has a lump on the back of his head but he's breathing.'

'Thank God for that.' Then Tom went on, 'She's been making water for two hours or more. She was gradually going down. I thought she might go in a hurry and that's why I brought you up here. And that's why the men were under the wheelhouse; they didn't want to be in the fo'c'sle if she sank.'

Josie answered with sincerity, 'I was glad to be out of that cabin.' Then: 'Have you any bandages that I can use to bind up his head, to stop the bleeding and keep the dirt out?'

Tom shook his head. 'No. Only in my cabin.'

Josie said quickly, 'Don't go down there.'

'Not likely. Just a minute. I think we've got some cotton waste and twine in here.' Tom straightened and went searching at the back of the wheelhouse. He was less than a yard away in that cramped little place but his back was turned to Josie and she decided she could do better for the mate than cotton waste and twine. She hoisted up her skirts and tore a long strip, four inches wide, from the hem of her petticoat. She was pulling down her skirts as Tom turned back to her. He held out a handful of cotton waste but said nothing when he saw the makeshift bandage.

Josie took the waste. 'I'll see to him.'

Tom answered, 'You haven't got long. As soon as we've lowered the boat, we're leaving.'

Josie nodded, trying to stifle her fear, to hide from it by finding work for her hands. She bound up the mate's wound, using the waste between folds of the linen as an extra pad. As she knotted the dressing in place Tom took her arm. She rose to her feet as he lifted her. He said, 'Put this on. It'll keep the worst of the wet off.'

Josie saw he held out an oilskin coat but she shook her head. 'Wrap it round Bucko. He'll need it more than me.' Her dress was soaked, anyway.

Tom seemed about to argue but then said, 'Let's have him out of here. We're going now.'

Dougie Bickerstaffe and two other men lifted the mate on the oilskin coat and carried him out to the deck. Tom hustled Josie out after them. He shouted at her, 'Hold on!' and pushed her up against a stanchion. Josie gripped it, eyes narrowed against the wind that tore at her again now they were out of the shelter of the wheelhouse, meagre though that had been. The deck sloped away from her to the rail. The boat had been lowered into the sea there, with two of the seamen in it at bow and stern trying to hold it in position with lines, two more gripping oars and attempting to stave it off from smashing against the *Macbeth*'s rusty side. But one second it was level with the rail, the next it had plummeted to twenty feet below, then it was close to the ship's side and the next second was yards away.

Josie waited, swallowing her fear. She could not bear to watch the wild tossing of the boat and raised her head to look out over the mountainous seas. For a moment there was a break in the solid, banked clouds overhead and a lightening of the sky in the distance. Josie thought she saw something, like a black brush stroke on the leaden horizon. Might it have been a ship? She was not sure. Then the gap in the clouds closed again, the far-off horizon was blotted out – and Tom Collingwood bawled at her, 'In you go!'

The loose dead weight of Bucko Daniels had been swung out into the boat, laid in its sternsheets, and now Tom turned to Josie. He lifted her in his arms and stood with one booted foot braced on the rail, the other on the canted deck. Despite not wanting to look, Josie twisted her face from where it was hidden in his chest. She saw the boat far below her and a hideous drop into sea churned into foam as it boiled between the boat and the ship's side. Then it soared up to meet her, the men on the lines hauling in furiously to keep it close to the steel wall. It hung there for a fraction of a second and Tom passed her over the rail into the stern of the boat. Josie stumbled and fell, but into the bottom of the craft. She was aware that it was falling again, could see Tom's head above the rail where he was watching to see she was safe, saw him soaring away from her. She lifted a hand and waved and the head disappeared.

'Up you come out o' that!' The seaman manning the line in the stern of the boat reached down to lift Josie. She was well aware that the bottom of the boat was inches deep in water that washed from end to end and swirled around her. She rose willingly as he dragged at her arm and pushed herself up to sit in the sternsheets beside Bucko Daniels. She peered down into his face, saw his eyes still closed, and could not tell whether he breathed or not. She wrapped her arms around him.

'She's capsizing!' The seamen in the boat yelled in chorus and fear. Josie looked up and saw that the *Macbeth* had listed further still and that her deck was almost vertical. Dougie Bickerstaffe and the rest of the crew were seated on the thwarts in the waist of the boat and now only Tom Collingwood hung on to the deck above. Then, as she watched, the boat made its swift ascent once more. This time it did not rise quite so high, was not so close to the ship's side, and Tom stood poised, seeming to hesitate.

The men shouted, '*Come on, Skipper!*'

Josie was infected by the fearful chorus and shrieked, '*Jump, Tom!*' This time he waved a hand, to show he heard. Josie realised he was judging the best time. Then, as the boat started to fall, it also surged closer to the ship's side. Tom saw his chance, stepped out from the rail and dropped down into the boat. He stumbled and fell between Josie and the men seated on the thwarts, but then he was up and sliding on to the seat at her side.

'Shove off!' At his bellow the men in bow and stern cast off the lines holding the boat to the ship and the men gripping the oars used them to push it clear of the *Macbeth*. Then the oars went into the rowlocks, the rowers bent to them and hauled. As the little craft moved out of the lee made by the *Macbeth*, its motion increased.

'It's easing!' Tom shouted in Josie's ear. 'And it's getting light!' Josie wanted to believe him, and the darkness was turning to grey now, though there would be no hint of a sun rising this day. But to her mind the boat rode no better. The big seas rose in front of it like mountains of green glass, each one to be climbed to the crest. Then they would hang, poised on the crest, looking down into the dark valley below, and slide bow first into it.

Tom fumbled beneath his seat in the sternsheets and hauled out a folded tarpaulin. He shook out its stiff folds and wrapped it around Josie and the inert Bucko Daniels. Josie said, 'I thought I saw a ship – just before I came down into the boat.'

'Where?' Tom demanded. And as Josie pointed, he muttered, 'There's nothing to be seen now. Maybe when it's lighter—'

'She's going!'

'Aye, she's going!' The men at the oars spoke, looking over Josie's head as they bent and pulled. She and Tom turned as one and saw the *Macbeth* roll completely over. Above the noise of the storm she heard a rumbling across the sea and one of the stokers said, 'That's her engines working loose and dropping out of her. She'll flood now.' On the heels of his words the bow of the *Macbeth* sank from sight and her stern lifted so they could see her single screw. Then she slid down and was gone in a hiss of steam.

There was silence in the boat and then Tom said harshly, 'Watch your stroke, you men at the oars. You're like a lot o' bum-boat men. The rest of you start bailing.'

Josie realised they were adrift in an open boat and any rescue would depend on a passing ship seeing them, just a dot on this wild ocean. And they had lost the *Macbeth*.

22

The light grew until it was full day, when it showed an empty sea. Tom muttered, 'I can't see any sign of that ship you thought you sighted.'

Josie protested, 'I only thought it was a ship. I thought I saw . . . something . . .' Her voice trailed away. It was difficult now to recall just what she had seen.

He looked around the green waste that now rolled in long, slow swells. The boat still rose and fell ten to twenty feet, but slowly, and it rode easily now as it took the seas on the bow. 'I think we can steer towards where you saw it, anyway.' He glanced down at the boat's compass and eased over the tiller. The bow swung to the new heading and the motion increased as the seas broke against the side now, but Tom held the course and little water was shipped.

Bucko Daniels was conscious now, sitting in the sternsheets on one side of Tom while Josie sat on the other. Josie thought he looked like some Sikh in his turban of white bandage. He had shrugged off the tarpaulin, refusing to wear it, and Josie sat with it wrapped stiffly around her. Despite its protection, she could feel her skirts clinging damply to her legs.

The men pulled steadily at the oars. They were working in two shifts, one rowing while the others rested. For a while on the new heading they were cheerful and joking, encouraged by the thought that they were steering towards possible help and not just to keep the boat's head to the sea to stay afloat. But as time went by and there was no sighting they grew quiet. Finally Tom sighed, 'I think we would have seen her smoke by now if she was there.'

'Maybe I was mistaken,' said Josie in a small voice. 'But I was sure I saw something.'

Tom explained, 'It's possible you did see a ship but she was more than likely steaming away from us and moving a sight faster than we are.'

Josie shivered, from the chill dampness of her clothes and also from apprehension. She wondered how long they could survive in the North Sea in this weather. But, casting her mind back to when she had been standing by the wheelhouse, she was still sure. She persisted stubbornly, 'I did see something, a long, low shape in the distance.'

Tom nodded acceptance. 'We'll hold this course.' And they did as the morning wore on and Josie sank gradually into a stupor of cold and misery.

Until Tom stiffened in his seat beside her and a second later stood, holding the tiller against his leg, balancing as the boat rolled and pitched. He squinted against the wind, waiting as the boat rose on a wave, then he grinned and called down to the others, 'There's a ship!' That brought a cheer and heads turned, but Tom said, 'You won't see it from down there. Just wait a while.' He was silent a moment, then added slowly, 'She doesn't seem to be making any smoke.' He glanced down at Josie. 'That's why we couldn't see any. It's strange, though.'

He sank down on his seat again and now Josie sat up straight, peering ahead eagerly, looking for a first sight of this ship. Then she realised that Tom was watching her, and she was suddenly conscious of how she must look, wrapped in the tarpaulin and with her hair blown on the wind. She fixed her gaze on the sea ahead and blamed the wind for bringing the colour to her cheeks.

'There it is!' And Josie added, 'That's what I saw.' It was no more than a black smudge, a blip on the horizon, but that was how it had appeared the previous night.

A half-hour later Tom said, 'It baffles me why she's still here. There is some smoke' – and there was just a wisp of it from the single tall funnel – 'but she isn't moving. There's no bow wave, no wash at her stern. Her screw isn't turning.'

When they were close enough to read the ship's name on her bow – *Northern Queen* – he cupped his hands around his mouth to bellow, '*Ahoy!*' Then again and again, '*Ahoy!*' But there was no answer. The ship lay still and silent in the water. He said, 'I think she's derelict. Her boats have gone and you can see the falls hanging from the davits where they lowered them.' Josie saw the 'falls', the ropes by which the boats had been lowered. Now they hung from the davits that stuck out from the ship's side like gibbets, so that the ropes dangled some feet out from the black and rusty wall.

'She's low in the water,' Tom muttered. As the boat rose on a wave the deck of the ship was only a few feet above them. Then the ship lifted and the boat fell, the gap opened. As it rose again Tom called, 'Lay hold of one o' those lines!'

Josie grabbed at the rope that swung by her side. Then, as the boat fell once more, dropping away from under her, she was yanked out of her seat and her nest in the tarpaulin. She clung to the rope and, looking down with horrified eyes, saw the boat filled with gaping men and the sea washing below her. She climbed. Reacting instinctively, remembering the far-off days in the woods of Geoffrey Urquhart's country house with little Bob Miller, she twined her legs around the rope and shinned up it. At the top she desperately transferred her hold from the rope to the davit and slid down that to the deck. Only then did she seem to draw breath, and only then did she realise what she had done. She found with relief that her skirts had clung to her legs and not ridden above her knees, thus retaining her modesty.

'Mrs Miller!' Tom's voice. Then the rope shook and a moment later his head appeared, eyes searching for her. He saw her with relief, swung across the davit and dropped to the deck beside her. 'You're not hurt?' he questioned. Then, when she shook her head, he went on, 'Why did you do that?' And grinning now, 'I couldn't believe my eyes. You were like an acrobat in a circus.'

'You said to grab a rope.' Josie had been frightened and embarrassed and now was becoming angry. 'Did you know that would happen?'

'Yes, but—'

'How dare you!' And Josie slapped his face.

It was not much of a slap because she had had little practice. Tom was not hurt, merely startled. As she swung her hand again, he caught it. 'I knew that would happen as would any of the men in that boat, but I didn't mean it to happen to you. I intended one of them to catch hold of the line and then pay it out, or haul in, to hold us alongside.'

'Oh.' Josie saw that it had been no more than a misunderstanding. She winced. 'Please.'

He let go of her wrist and she rubbed at the weals his fingers had left. He said stiffly, 'I'm sorry. I didn't mean to hurt you.'

Josie managed a smile. 'And I'm sorry I lost my temper.'

'You must be tired.'

'Aren't we all?' Josie saw that her hand had left its mark on his face. She reached up to stroke it gently with the tips of her fingers, as she might have comforted Charlotte. Then she remembered this was Tom Collingwood and dropped her hand.

He said, 'I'd better get the men aboard.' He turned away and swung the davits inboard so that the ropes hung close against the ship's side. The men climbed up and soon all of them were gathered on the deck of the *Northern Queen*. They were weary and empty-bellied, shivered in their wet clothing. Tom addressed them, his voice harsh and demanding: 'You'll get warm by working and you might stay alive that way. We'll not hoist our boat in until we find out if this ship is sinking or not. She seems to have been deserted. We'd better find out why and what we can do with her. I want to know if she's holed or making water some way and whether she can be steered, whether we can raise steam . . .'

He had no orders for Josie. When the group scattered she set out on her own exploration and found the galley where she expected it to be, in the superstructure amidships and alongside the saloon where the captain and his officers would eat. The galley stove was still alight – just – and she added more coal, pulled out the damper and soon it was roaring with life. Meanwhile she washed, found a comb in a little pocket in her dress and examined the contents of the cupboards. Soon she was able to step outside the galley again, looking for Tom Collingwood. She didn't see him but caught Dougie Bickerstaffe as he hurried by. 'Dougie! Do you know where Captain Collingwood is?'

'Up forrard. I saw him a minute ago.'

'Will you tell him I have some tea and sandwiches for everyone, please.'

'Oh, aye, ma'am.' Dougie trotted away.

In a few minutes he returned with all the others, including Tom, and they gathered in or around the galley. They wolfed sandwiches and gulped the hot tea, each mug coloured and sweetened by a spoonful of condensed milk. Josie stood slender and comparatively trim among the ruffian crew. All were wearing old clothes for working at sea and were blear-eyed from tiredness, unwashed, unshaven and filthy. The black gang from the engine-room were particularly so, coated with coal dust and oil. They all smelt of sweat, salt and smoke.

Tom summed up the results of their investigations, talking as he ate, staccato and urgent: 'Her steering's intact. She's taken a lot of water aboard but I can't tell how fast she's making it. I think most of the trouble lies in the number one hold forrad. The seas battered through the hatch covers and it's full. I think her captain and crew thought she was going to sink – that would be easy to believe with the weather we had last night – and so they took to the boats. I pray that they are safe but I doubt it. The chances in an open boat with these seas are not good.

'Now, Joe Kelly' – and he glanced at the little engineer in his boiler suit – 'tells me the fires are still burning and he can raise enough steam in an hour or two to give us steerage way.' A shivering Joe nodded agreement and Tom said, 'One more thing. I've had a look at the barometer and what it told me matches with what I see out there.' He pointed over the weather rail. Josie and the others looked out in that direction and saw the black storm clouds massing again on the horizon. Tom said grimly, 'The bad weather hasn't finished with us yet. I want you to bear that in mind.'

He paused to give them a second or two to think about what he had said, then went on, 'We have a choice. We can stay aboard her, fight to keep her afloat and risk her sinking under us, but I don't think she will. Or we can get back into the boat and hope for a rescue.'

He swallowed the last of his tea and passed the empty mug to Josie. Their hands touched briefly and their eyes met.

'I don't want to get into the boat again,' Josie said primly. Then, as they stared at her: 'And then there's the way I have to get out. I'd rather stay here.' There was silence for a second and then hoarse guffaws.

Tom grinned, realised he had been forgiven and looked around. 'Is that how you all feel?'

He got a rumbling chorus of 'Aye!'

Tom started again to drive the weary men on. He gave his orders: 'We want steam, Joe, as soon as you can. And the pumps working, the donkey-engine to hoist in the boat. We need timber for the hatch on number one hold, hammers, nails and canvas . . .'

Josie went back to the galley. She did not need to be told what to do. During the next two hours the boat was hoisted in, the pumps started to suck some of the water out of the *Northern Queen* and the broken hatch covers forward were repaired. Josie worked in the galley, cautiously because the rolling of the ship – which had never ceased – gradually worsened. She was wary of being scalded by some pan hurled from

217

the stove despite the 'fiddles' around it, designed to prevent just that. Every few minutes her gaze was drawn to the scuttle that gave her a view of the distant skyline and the approaching storm.

She finished with the stove just in time. And just in time she felt the first tremor through the gratings under her feet, heard the rumbling, regular, *thump*, *thump*! of the engines turning over. She ran outside on to the deck, looked up and saw Tom in the wheelhouse on the bridge. The *Northern Queen* was under way. And the storm was upon them again. Josie saw the black shadow of the first squall sweeping over the sea towards her, then it was on her with a cold wind that snatched at her skirts and hurled a spatter of rain into her face.

Josie waved at Tom up on the bridge and saw him lift a hand from the wheel to reply, then she ran back to the galley. She had cooked a pie made from corned beef, and a jam tart. She served the meal in the saloon that was next to the galley and the men ate in shifts as they could be spared from their work. Tom came last, leaving Bucko Daniels at the wheel. Josie staggered in from the galley, bearing the hot plate held in a cloth and balancing against the roll and pitch of the ship. As she set his meal before him, Tom stared. 'I thought it would be sandwiches again.'

'Tomorrow it may be,' Josie replied darkly. 'I can't use the stove in this weather.' But she did. Over the next six hours she twice boiled water to make hot drinks for the men, steadying the kettle on the stove with one hand swathed in a cloth, while holding on to the solidly fixed galley table with the other. The sea pounded the ship. She had closed the dead-lights over the scuttles so she could not see out, but she could hear the smash of the seas against them and against the door of the galley.

The storm growled away as the day died. Josie slowly realised that the ship was not rolling so badly, she was steadier. The howling of the wind had dropped to a whisper. Her legs trembled but it was not from continual bracing to keep her balance but from tiredness. She was in a daze of weariness when she ventured out on to the deck and found the sea still rising and falling in long slow humps and valleys but not whipped into mountainous waves by the wind.

She fetched yet another mug of tea and climbed to the bridge. Tom Collingwood, standing tall and rock steady at the wheel, turned to blink red-eyed at her. Josie said, 'I've brought you a drink.'

'Thank you.' He let go of the wheel with one hand to gulp at the tea.

Josie asked, 'Are we going to stay afloat?'

'Aye.' Tom nodded and grinned at her.

'You're tired.' She knew how she felt.

'Aye, but I could go for another twenty-four hours. I won't need to, though. Bucko will be up in another half-hour. Then I'll sleep for a bit.' He drained the mug and handed it back to her. 'You do the same, Mrs Miller. You've earned it. Find a cabin and get some sleep.'

Josie was too tired to argue, did not want to. She turned away, but as she reached the head of the ladder leading down to the deck he called after her, 'You've been a first-class hand, Mrs Miller.' Josie laughed. First-class hand, indeed!

She found a cabin with its bunk neatly made up. Suits of clothes hung behind a curtain in one corner and a small chest of drawers held clean shirts and socks. The cabin looked as if it waited for its owner to return. Then Josie realised that the owner had probably drowned. She borrowed a robe that hung behind the door but would not touch the other clothes. She washed herself and her clothes in a bowl she found in the galley, behind its locked door, and hung the clothes above the stove to dry. Then she handed Bucko Daniels a mug of tea as he went up to the bridge and told him, 'Call me when you come off watch, please.' Because she had no clock, let alone an alarm.

'Righto, Mrs Miller.'

In the cabin she bolted the door and took off the robe, shivering as she remembered its owner. She crawled into the bunk naked, curled up small because of the cold at first, but the heat of her body soon dispelled that and exhaustion brought sleep rushing down on her.

Her last thought was: First-class hand. She fell asleep smiling.

'Mrs Miller! *Mrs Miller!* You asked me to call you!' Bucko's voice came hoarsely through the cabin door.

'Yes, I'm awake!' Josie lied. She had been jerked from sleep by his hammering at the door and now it took a huge effort to get up from the bunk. How long had she slept? Four hours, the length of the mate's watch on the bridge. It felt more like four minutes. Yawning, she pulled on the robe and her shoes. In the galley she washed and dressed in the clothes that had baked dry over the stove. They looked as she had expected them to look but in the absence of an iron she grimaced and carried on.

She prepared a meal and set it to cook then made two mugs of tea and carried them up to the bridge. As she handed a mug to Tom Collingwood she said, 'It seems calmer.' The sea was smooth and the *Northern Queen* was rising and falling gently as her blunt bow butted into the waves.

'This swell is fading away.' Tom sipped at the tea. 'I've had men checking the level of the water in her every hour and we're gaining; the pumps are sucking more out of her than is coming in. We're making seven knots and we'll be home and dry tomorrow.'

Feet thumped on the ladder and Dougie Bickerstaffe appeared on the bridge. ''Scuse me, Skipper, Mrs Miller, but the chaps are asking if we're putting in to Blyth or the Tyne?'

Tom chuckled. 'To hell with that. We're putting in to neither and taking her home.'

'Aw! That's champion!' Dougie dropped down the ladder to report the good news, and Josie followed. She went back to her task of feeding the men and making unending jugs of tea all through the day. Then she slept again, soundly, and woke in the night still ready to sleep but puzzled at what had awakened her. Then she heard boots clumping on the bridge ladder and realised the watch was changing. She got up and dressed, went to the galley and made tea, then took the two mugs to the bridge.

The wheelhouse was dark save for the glow from the compass binnacle which lit Tom's face dimly. It hung, eyes gleaming in shadows, over the wheel which he gripped with one hand while reaching for the mug with the other. He smiled at Josie. 'You'll be glad to get ashore.'

'I will.' She was definite about it and they both laughed. Then, scanning his face, realising that the shadows around his eyes were not all due to the light, she said, 'There's a chair just here.' It stood to one side of the wheel and was about four feet high, with a cushion on the seat and a step that would serve as a footrest.

'Captain's chair,' explained Tom. 'He could sit in that and look out over the screen.'

'Well, could I steer? Then you could sit in that chair for a rest.'

He glanced at her, startled by the suggestion. 'Steer? You?'

'Why not? Does it need a lot of strength?'

'No,' he admitted, 'not when the sea is like this.'

'Or skill?'

'Not when—' He broke off from repeating himself. Instead he looked across from the compass card, studying her for some seconds. Then: 'What if I say no?'

'I'll go back to bed.'

He grinned. 'All right. Come here.' He set her behind the wheel with her hands on the spokes. Josie was nervous at first but then interested as he taught her, standing close behind her, his hands on hers, swallowing them. And after a time he stepped back and said, mildly surprised, 'You seem to have got the idea.' Josie had shown that she had got it some time ago. He climbed on to the chair and settled down to watching over her. He said little and once or twice he dozed for a minute or two to jerk awake and sit up straight, blinking. He would rub at his jaw and the black stubble that now bristled thick there rasped under his hand.

They were together on the bridge when the sun came up. He took the wheel from her then and steered for the mouth of the River Wear and Sunderland. He said, 'You know what this will mean to us?'

'Yes.' And she told him.

He nodded. 'Charlotte is going to be all right.'

Josie reached up to pull his head down. She kissed him, not caring about the stubble, then ran back to her galley. The men, and Tom among them, would want breakfast. She went at it singing.

Tugs nudged the *Northern Queen* alongside the quay and Tom Collingwood rang down 'Finished with engines' on the engine-room telegraph. The ship lay still and he climbed down from the bridge, his weariness forgotten in the exhilaration of bringing her in – and knowing his mind and heart now. He knew what he wanted and who he wanted. Then he saw the sunlight glinting on the big Blakemore motor car standing on the quay. His lips tightened and he looked for Felicity but did not see her. He recognised her maid, Susie, standing by the car, and now Jarvis, the chauffeur, was coming up the gangway Bucko Daniels and the hands had just rigged. He looked for Tom and handed him an envelope. 'From Miss Felicity, sir.'

Tom ripped open the envelope and read the note: Felicity had been distraught when he had not returned to take her to the ball. The ball? He remembered he had said he would be back in time to take her – and he was forty-eight hours too late. He muttered, 'The damn ship sank!'

He read on: fortunately a friend of her father's had escorted her. He had invited her family to his villa in Biarritz and she was going with them. 'Everyone goes to Biarritz about this time.' They would all be returning to London in a month or so.

Tom crumpled the note and crammed it into his pocket. He could not write to her to tell her he could not, in all honesty, go on with the marriage. In the code of the time, a gentleman did not do that. He had to speak to her and her father. And until he did so he could not court Josie Miller, a girl in his service and in his house. That would seem like the seduction attempted by her former employer. He had to wait and keep his mouth shut.

Josie had seen the note delivered, saw him scowling now and guessed Felicity was the cause. She was not singing as she made her way down the gangway. Kitty Duggan was hurrying along the quay towards her but still some way off. Josie stopped to greet Susie: 'What are you doing here?'

'I came wi' Jarvis to get out o' the way,' Susie answered cheerfully. She was very smart in an expensive tailor-made motoring costume that showed her ankles. Josie thought it would be one of Felicity's. Susie explained, 'Everybody's packing stuff to take out to France. I've done my whack and I wasn't going to slave away doing theirs.'

Josie queried, 'France?'

'That's right. We're off to that Major St Clair's villa in Biarritz. The family went yesterday and me and a few more are going tomorrow.' Susie grinned. 'Your boss won't half cop it when she gets back. She was bloody furious when he didn't turn up to take her to the "do" the night afore last. The major took her. I haven't seen him but they say he's an officer in the French Army. While she was there she signed up another two bridesmaids. That makes six so far.'

Now Jarvis returned and Susie skipped into the car, crying, 'Ta-ra!'

Josie walked on as the car pulled away, thinking, Six bridesmaids. Then Kitty was hugging her and demanding, 'What's the matter with you?'

Josie answered, 'Nothing, I'm fine.'

Kitty disagreed. 'You look as miserable as sin!'

Josie forced a smile. 'I'm just tired.'

She was facing bitter reality. They were no longer at sea in a world of their own. She could not go on with this *affaire*. Sooner or later Tom would find out her true identity and conclude that this impersonation meant she was up to no good. And he was to be married to Felicity Blakemore in just a few months from now.

Josie could see only one way out.

23

June 1909

'I will now call this meeting of the Langley Shipping Company to order.' Tom Collingwood's tone was jocular but he had an unusual air of uncertainty about him. He stood in his office in the Langley house, his back to the empty fireplace; now they were moving into summer the fire was not needed on a fine day like this. In the square outside the children were playing barefoot. Josie sat upright in the swivel chair at the desk but was turned to face him. Kitty Duggan poised equally straight on the edge of the armchair. The morning sunshine winked on the brasswork of the fender around the fire.

'It's been a week now,' Tom went on, 'since we brought the *Northern Queen* into this river, the first fuss has died down and we're now able to see our way more clearly.' He grinned. 'That means I've been to the bank and the manager, pending the salvage settlement and the insurance from the *Macbeth*, will let us have enough money to open the yard.' He explained, 'The insurance on the *Macbeth* will go a long way towards building a replacement. We can expect the court will award half of the value of the *Northern Queen* and her cargo. The owners of the salving vessel, the *Macbeth* or the *Macbeth*'s boat, will take up to three-fourths of that. The balance will go to the crew.'

Kitty Duggan chuckled. 'Dougie Bickerstaffe will be a happy lad.'

Tom agreed, grinning. 'Aye. And the rest of the lads. I just hope they don't booze it away.'

Josie said, 'I don't think Dougie will.'

He had come to her a few days before and said gloomily, 'I told Iris about the money I'll be gettin' but she still won't have me.'

Josie had replied, 'I'll have a word with her and see if I can help.'

Dougie had brightened. 'That's good o' you, Mrs Miller.'

And Josie had warned, 'I only *might* be able to help. I can't change her feelings for you.' But Dougie had gone away more hopeful.

Now Tom continued more seriously, 'But what I've said about opening the yard and building a successor to the *Macbeth*, that's what I propose, but it occurs to me that either or both of you ladies might prefer to take your share and leave the partnership.'

Now they saw the reason for his uncertainty. 'For my part,' said Josie, 'I prefer to open the yard and build the ship.'

Kitty agreed. 'Hear! Hear! There's ower many men standing idle. You can see them at their doors in this square.' That was a fact and Josie nodded. Kitty summed up, 'So we can give them some work and make the yard a going concern for Charlotte.'

Tom laughed, relieved, the uncertainty gone. 'Then I declare the meeting closed.'

Kitty rose and made for the door but Josie paused to say, 'It seems to have been some time since a photograph was taken of Charlotte.' She explained about the albums she had found. 'If you have no objection, I propose to take her to a photographer.'

'Not at all,' Tom agreed. Josie turned to the door then, but he called, 'Mrs Miller, I have some letters to write but then I need to go down to the yard and get some idea of what needs to be done. I believe you've been there several times. Would you like to go with me?'

Josie would, but she said, 'No, thank you, Captain Collingwood. I'm afraid I have a great deal to do today. If you will excuse me?'

'Of course.' Tom watched her leave, his smile fading.

Out in the hall, Kitty challenged, 'What have you got to do today?'

'I have to go and see how Iris is getting on and then take Charlotte to the photographer.' This was true, though both errands could have waited, but Josie had decided she had made enough trouble for herself and would not become more deeply involved with Tom Collingwood. She bustled about, brushing Charlotte's hair and dressing her in her best, then pulling on her own coat, putting on her wide-brimmed hat. As she passed through the hall with Charlotte, she turned aside into the house next door and put her head in at the door of the men's common and dining room. Dougie Bickerstaffe sat by the fire in a new blue suit, a high stiff collar and a silk tie – ready, as Josie had asked him to be. Now she called, 'Give me ten minutes' start.'

Dougie jumped to his feet. 'Oh! Aye, righto, ma'am!'

Josie walked round to the shop in Dame Dorothy Street, holding

Charlotte by the hand and answering her unending stream of questions. The shop had the name above it: Langley and Co. There was a window either side of the door and in one was fruit and vegetables, in the other bacon, butter, cheese and eggs. Two or three women were in there, long skirts sweeping the sawdust on the floor and baskets over their arms, gossiping as they waited to be served by Iris Taylor.

Iris called cheerfully, 'Hello, Mrs Miller. I'll be with you in a minute.'

And, quick to serve, she was as good as her word. As the shop emptied, she turned to Josie. 'We've got a minute or two, now.'

Josie released Charlotte's hand. 'Why don't you pile up the potatoes for Iris like she showed you once before?' Charlotte went willingly. It was a familiar game: stacking the potatoes into pyramids.

Josie turned to Iris: 'You're doing well.' She had been looking at the books for the shop only the night before. 'Captain Collingwood has contracted for a ship to take the place of the *Macbeth* for the next few months and she'll be bringing your stuff down as before. There'll be a delay of a day or two before the next delivery but you'll just have to buy locally to bridge that gap. It will mean less profit but that can't be helped. Is that all right?'

'That's fine.' Iris nodded with the confidence of competence.

Josie asked, 'What about Dougie?'

'What about him?' But Iris was blushing.

'Has he been around to see you since we got back?'

'He has. He says he'll be coming into some money from bringing that ship in. He wants me to marry him.'

'And you can't make up your mind?'

Iris laughed ruefully. 'I made up my mind long ago. I'd marry him tomorrow but like I said before, a sailorman, he'd be here today and gone tomorrow for weeks or months. That hasn't changed. Money and sailors are soon parted. When he gets this cash it'll run through his fingers and he'll be as broke as ever.'

Josie smiled and suggested, 'You'd better look for some young chap that's careful with his money, then.'

'No!' Iris was definite about this, angry at the suggestion. 'There's never been anybody like Dougie, and there won't be anybody else.'

Josie shook her head. 'You're in a fix, then.'

Iris smiled lopsidedly. 'I might marry him anyway. Not for the money, 'cause I won't see it. Just because I won't be able to say no to him no longer.'

'You could have a contract.'

Iris blinked, taken aback. 'A contract? What d'you mean?'

'An agreement. You'd be equal partners in a business and Dougie would put in his money as his share. You'd agree to take so much each out of the business. That way he wouldn't be able to throw the money away and when he was ready to give up the sea he could work in the business.'

Charlotte said, 'Can we go and see the ducks?'

Josie answered, 'Later. We want some things from the shops first.'

Iris said, 'You mean, go to a solicitor?'

'No.' Josie shook her head. 'Just write it out on a sheet of paper and you both sign it.'

Iris said doubtfully, 'Would that be legal?'

'Dougie would think so.' They smiled at each other, conspirators.

Then Iris asked, 'But what business? And you said equal partners. I couldn't put up nothing 'cept what I've saved since I came up North.'

'I'm talking of my one-third share of this business. As a going concern, free of debt, with the rent paid for this quarter. I'm giving it to you.'

Charlotte asked, peering up at Josie, 'What sort of things do you want at the shops?'

Josie countered, 'What sort of things would you like?'

Iris had her hands to her cheeks, framing her face, her mouth a round O. Then she whispered, '*Give it to me*? You're pulling my leg.' And as Josie shook her head: 'Why?'

'Never mind why. Let's just say I don't want the bother of it any longer. There are two conditions, mind.' Josie looked at her watch.

Iris said wryly, 'There's always a catch. What conditions?'

'That you keep this to yourself. This is just between you and me.' Then she continued quickly, her eyes on the door and before Iris could ask further questions: 'And when Dougie walks in through that door you've got to kiss him.'

'*What?*'

'Agreed?' And as Iris still stared, blushing again, Josie pressed, 'Agreed?'

'Yes,' Iris nodded. 'But—'

Charlotte asked, 'I want some sweets. Can we go now?'

'Yes.' Josie took her hand as Dougie Bickerstaffe took off his cap and entered the shop. Iris looked from him to Josie, who nodded and said, 'Contract, remember.'

As she led Charlotte from the shop, Iris put her arms around Dougie's neck and kissed him.

Josie thought she had taken a step towards the end of her journey and it gave her no pleasure.

'No, I don't want to!' Charlotte proved difficult at the photographer's studio. She was wary of the equipment and suspicious of the photographer's smirking attempts to placate her. 'I want to go to see the ducks.'

Josie said patiently, 'I said we'd go later and we will, but not if you don't behave.'

Charlotte pouted sulkily. 'I don't like that thing.' She pointed at the camera.

'It won't hurt you.' Josie crouched on her heels to come eye to eye. 'I'll tell you what: I'll ask the gentleman to take a photograph of the two of us together, then one of you on your own.' She met Charlotte's gaze, full of distrust, and was hard put to it not to laugh. To hide it she urged, 'Now, come on.'

So Josie sat very straight on her chair as her mother had done in the photographs in the album, with Charlotte standing solemnly by her knee. The photograph was taken and then, while Josie chattered brightly, another of Charlotte alone. Josie gave a sigh of mixed relief and triumph.

The Langley household was now on a normal footing and Tom, Josie and Charlotte ate their meals together in the dining room.

'Somebody's writing to you from France.' Kitty laid the bundle of post beside Tom's plate as they sat at breakfast, two days after Josie's talk with Iris.

Tom ripped open the top envelope that Kitty had indicated and Josie thought, From Felicity? Kitty asked, 'From your feeansee?'

Josie said, 'Kitty!'

Tom snapped, 'Yes, it is!' He scanned it, frowning, then said stiffly, 'The weather is glorious out there.' That was the only information of note in two scrawled sheets of gossip. He concentrated on opening the other letters. But he was in good humour those days, though often abstracted because he was deeply involved in negotiations with the bank and in starting up the Langley yard again. Minutes later he looked up with a smile, 'I wrote to Harry Varley – he's working in a yard on the Clyde – and he's willing to come back to us as manager. That's good news.'

Kitty had bustled in with more toast, just in time to hear this remark, and she put in, 'Aye, that's good news. I don't know if mine is.' When they looked at her she went on, 'Iris is in the kitchen and she's got an engagement ring on her finger. It came from that Dougie Bickerstaffe. I hope she knows what she's doing. I know what these sailors are like.'

'Thank you.' Tom addressed her back, grinning, as Kitty marched out. Then he laid down the letter. 'I've got to find a lot more of the staff. I've taken on twenty of the old hands, with a foreman, to start cleaning up the yard ready for work.' Josie knew this. She had been to the yard when he was not there and had seen the men at work. He went on, 'But it won't be so easy finding the old staff. There was Dobson, the chief draughtsman, and Williams, his second. I wrote to both of them but they've moved and left no address.'

Josie asked Charlotte, 'How do you get so sticky?' And wiped the child's face clean of marmalade as she told Tom, 'Dobson is working for Gray's yard at Hartlepool and Williams is with Ropner's at Stockton.' She turned back from Charlotte and found Tom staring at her. She explained, 'Sammy Allnutt, the watchman at the yard, can tell you where they've all gone.'

Tom laughed. 'Well, I'm damned. You continue to surprise me, Mrs Miller. I'll go down and see him. Would you care to come along?'

'Thank you, but no, Captain Collingwood.' She searched for an excuse. 'It's time Charlotte caught up with her lessons.'

Charlotte protested, 'I don't want to do lessons. Yesterday you said we could go to the yard and see Sammy today. I like Sammy.'

Josie automatically corrected her, 'Mr Allnutt.' She kept her head in the face of this betrayal. 'I'm sorry, but I wasn't thinking at the time. You must keep up with your lessons. That is most important.' And to Tom, in an aside and not meeting his eye, 'She has fallen behind in recent weeks because of my absence.'

Tom said curtly, 'As you wish.' He left the table and stalked out. He strode down to the Langley yard in a black mood. He was sure

Josie was avoiding him and could guess why: he was engaged to be married to Felicity Blakemore. This morning's letter had been a sharp reminder of that. He swore.

Back in the Langley house, Charlotte asked, 'Is Uncle Tom cross?'

Josie lied miserably, 'No, not at all. Now finish your breakfast.'

Afterwards they went to the kitchen and admired Iris's engagement ring. Annie asked, 'What changed your mind at the end? 'Cause you'd turned him down half a dozen times.'

Iris laughed shyly and glanced at Josie. 'We came to an agreement. I can't tell you no more than that.'

Kitty asked, 'Is he giving up the sea?'

Iris shook her head. 'He says he could afford to but he doesn't want to. He says Captain Collingwood is hoping to get a ship soon and has promised him a berth. He's keen to go 'cause he thinks the world o' the captain.' Now she was staring at Josie, who looked away. She had not known Tom was about to get a ship. But did it matter?

Afterwards, when they were alone in the kitchen save for Charlotte playing with her dolls in one corner, Kitty said, 'Now there's only the other lovebirds to worry about.'

'What? I'm sorry,' Josie apologised, 'I wasn't listening.'

'I said,' repeated Kitty, 'that there's still the other courting couple: Annie and Dan. He's mooning around here every minute he can spare from that chandler's, and she's watching out o' the window for him when he isn't here.'

'Yes, I know.' And Josie had given the affair some thought.

'I wish they'd make their bloody minds up,' Kitty grumbled.

'Kitty!' And with a glance at the door leading to the house, 'How can I ask the men to control their language in here if you—'

'Well . . .' Kitty's complaint subsided into muttering. Then she said: 'But we sorted ourselves out quicker in my time. We knew what we wanted. Seems to me some young women today can't see opportunity when it's under their noses every day.' The door slammed behind her.

Josie smiled ruefully, knowing the target of the last remark and thinking that Kitty meant well.

Then she shook herself out of her abstraction and told herself, No time like the present. She called to Charlotte, 'Time we went for a walk. Upsadaisy!' And she lifted her to her feet. She found Annie in the back yard, pegging out some washing. Annie's baby was in his perambulator in a corner. Josie said, 'Put your coat on, Annie, and we'll get some fresh air.'

'Aye, all right. As long as we're back in time to get the dinner ready. Dan will be round and he has to get back to the chandler's afterwards.'

'Don't worry,' Josie told her. 'We'll see to the dinner in good time.'

They strolled gently, taking their time from Charlotte's toddling pace. Josie asked, 'When are you and Dan going to get engaged?'

Annie said unhappily, 'Not for months or years. Dan doesn't want to get engaged; he wants to be married and I can't see that happening. I want somewhere decent to live to bring up my bairn.'

'Can't you find anywhere?'

'Dan says there's no need and we can live over the chandler's. That might be all right for him, that only wants a bed and a gas ring to make a cup o' tea, but it's not a home. That flat above is just full o' boots, oilskins and all kinds o' kit for sailors. And I sometimes wonder if he's settled. He says he is, but he was a soldier and if he hadn't been wounded he would still be a soldier. I wonder if he's just a roamer and he'll throw up the job here and move on some day.' She stopped, then said: 'Why, there it is.'

Annie had not noticed that they had wound their way through the streets to the chandler's. It stood on a corner near the Langley yard. As they approached, Annie's eyes were fixed on the door, but Dan did not appear. Josie pushed the door open and the bell jangled above it, announcing the entry of a customer. It was not needed on this occasion because Dan Elkington was behind the counter serving two sailors who were looking at oilskins and long, woollen stockings for sea boots. The boy who assisted Dan set aside the broom he was using to sweep the floor and asked, 'Can I get you anything, Mrs Miller?'

'No, thank you,' replied Josie. 'I'll just have a word with Mr Elkington in a minute.' And when the two sailors had tramped out she asked, 'Will you come outside a minute or two, Dan?' It was easier than sending the boy on some errand.

Dan smiled at Annie. 'Why, hello!' He stooped over the pram. 'Is he asleep?'

'Aye, and you leave him like that,' ordered Annie. 'You can give him his dinner later on but let him alone now.'

As Dan straightened, content with this, Josie asked Annie, 'If

Dan took all of his stock out of the flat could you make it fit to live in?'

Annie, taken by surprise, said, 'I don't know. Well, I suppose so—'

'Would you help?' Josie put the question to Dan.

'Aye, I would, but—'

'You could put the stock in a shed in the yard at the back of the shop.'

Dan asked, puzzled, 'What shed?'

'You could buy one. The bank statements show there's plenty of cash in the shop's account. And the books are showing a handsome profit.'

Dan thought he understood now. 'You mean you'll lend us the money out o' what the shop's making?'

'No, I don't mean that.' And as they both stared at her, Josie explained, 'I'm turning the shop over to you, Mr and Mrs Dan Elkington, if you want it.'

'Want it?' Dan asked incredulously.

'And want each other,' Josie reminded him.

'I've made no secret of what I want,' said Dan straightly. 'With or without the shop.' And he was talking to Annie now. 'But we could make a good life for ourselves here.'

Josie questioned, 'And no yearning to wander?'

'I'm a bit older than Dougie Bickerstaffe,' said Dan drily. 'He still wants to go to sea wi' Captain Collingwood, but I've done my wandering.'

This was an unwelcome reminder that Tom might get another ship, but Josie tried to put it out of her mind. She said, 'There's one condition, that you keep this to yourselves for a while. I'll tell you when you can talk about it. That will' – and she invented – 'save me some embarrassment. Now, can I have your promise, both of you?'

'I'll keep my mouth shut,' said Dan.

Annie nodded, bewildered, then went on, 'But I don't want to leave you, don't want to let you down, after you've been so good to me, ever since that first night you found me.'

Josie laid this worry to rest. 'I'd be grateful if you would still work at the house, coming in daily and bringing the baby with you.' She put her arm around the girl. 'So now all you want is a ring.'

Annie nodded, and Dan said, 'I've got one. Had it for weeks, only waiting for you to say the word.' But Annie could not speak, just reached out to hold his hand.

Josie said, 'You'd better take Annie in and make her a cup of tea on that gas ring of yours. And you can make a start on planning what to do with the flat.'

Dan helped Annie lift the pram into the shop and Josie left them. As she strolled past Langley's yard with the dawdling Charlotte she paused to glance in through the open gates at the men of the maintenance gang at work.

Charlotte demanded, 'Can we go and see Sammy?'

'Mr Allnutt,' Josie corrected again, patiently, then went on, 'Not today. Another time.' Tom Collingwood was in the yard. She walked on.

She had taken another step.

Josie collected the photographs that afternoon. That of Charlotte on her own was as good as Josie had expected but no more than that, a solemn little girl nervous of the camera. In the other she held a hand on Josie's knee for support and courage, while Josie herself . . . She blinked at the picture of the young woman that stared back at her, a smile almost suppressed on her lips but crinkling the corners of her eyes. She had the look of her mother but also of the Langleys, that straight nose and proud lift of the head, the carriage of the body. And there was an aura of life, a bloom on this girl.

Josie showed the photograph of Charlotte to Tom Collingwood that evening as they sat at dinner. He grinned his approval at the child, allowed to stay down because of the photograph. 'Very nice, Charlotte.'

She beamed at him and said, 'Can we see the other one, Mrs Miller?'

Tom looked at Josie. 'The other one?'

She explained, 'Charlotte would only be photographed if I had one taken with her.' She left it there but Tom held out his hand. Josie gave him the photograph and he looked at in silence, then turned it over to read the photographer's name and address on the back before handing it over. 'It's a very good likeness.'

Josie busied herself with putting the photographs away.

* * *

It was on a Saturday morning a week later that Tom Collingwood burst out of the office in the Langley house and strode along the passage to the kitchen. Josie, Annie and Kitty swung around as he entered, waving a letter in one hand. He said jubilantly, 'I've got the command! They've confirmed me as master of the *Dorothy Snow*! She'll be sailing out of the Port of London to New York, a regular run. So I'll be home for a few days every month.'

Josie clapped her hands. 'Congratulations! It's no more than you deserve. I'm so glad for you.'

'Thank you.' His eyes had never left her, but now—

'When d'you go?' asked Kitty.

'Not for a week or two yet. I'll probably be here for the opening of the yard, but the board want me to go down to London to look her over' – and he glanced at the letter – 'on Monday. So I'll have to travel down tomorrow.'

So on the Sunday morning Josie stood in the hall with Charlotte as the cab swayed around the square, pulled by its trotting horse. Tom appeared in tweeds, an overnight bag in one hand, his cap in the other. Josie expected the parting to be brief but Charlotte cried, 'Can I go to the station?'

'Of course you can.' Tom jammed his cap on his head and scooped her up. 'But you've got to behave properly.' He grinned at Josie. 'Come on, Mrs Miller. I don't want to miss this train.'

So Josie, biting her lip, had to run for her coat and Charlotte's, then sit in the cab opposite Tom while he carried Charlotte on his knee. The horse ambled over the bridge across the River Wear, crowded with shipping. They caught a brief glimpse of Langley's yard and Tom said, 'The yard officially opens tomorrow.' A maintenance squad had been working there for two weeks to prepare it for opening. He went on, 'What about a party next Saturday – in the yard – to celebrate?'

Josie agreed. 'That sounds like a good idea.' And thought, Celebrate?

Tom set the child down only when they were on the platform of Sunderland station. His train was due, which Josie thought was a blessing. Charlotte prattled happily but Josie and Tom stood in silence. Then his train pulled in with a hiss of steam. Tom climbed into a first-class carriage, tossed his cap and bag on to the rack and leaned out of the window. He said, 'Well, goodbye. It won't be for long. I expect to be back the day after tomorrow.' And: 'Give me a kiss.'

This last was said to Charlotte as the guard waved his flag. Josie lifted her and Charlotte put up her face to be kissed. Tom said, 'Take care, Mrs Miller.'

They looked at each other across the gap, he smiling and sure, she forcing a smile and miserably certain of what she had to do. Then Josie said, 'I will.'

The train pulled out and Tom disappeared. Josie and Charlotte made for the exit and as they climbed the stairs Charlotte said clearly, 'I did behave properly, didn't I?'

'Yes,' replied Josie, 'we all behaved properly.'

There was a report of the salvaging of the *Northern Queen* in *The Times*. It mentioned Captain Thomas Collingwood and First Officer Cuthbert Daniels – this amused a number of sailors and enraged Bucko. The report also described the cook of the lost *Macbeth*: Mrs Miller.

Reuben Garbutt read the report sitting in the apartment he rented in Paris. He read it again and again, so that when he finally crumpled the paper into a ball and hurled it into the fire he could almost recite the report word for word. He could also guess what it might mean, that now there would be the money to reopen the Langley shipyard.

Mrs Miller. Again. She had foiled him and sent him running for his life. But now the hunt for him would have died down. Now she would no longer be on her guard.

Now he could destroy her.

When he got down from the train in Rotterdam he looked for a ship sailing to England, but not the cross-Channel packet. Down by the harbour he entered a bar and asked the shifty-eyed man cleaning glasses with a cloth, 'Do you speak English?' When the man didn't answer, Garbutt spread a banknote on the bar.

It was whisked up. 'I speak English, *ja.*'

Garbutt said, 'I want to talk to a skipper sailing for England who isn't too particular about the law. Understand?' He held up another note.

The bartender thought for a moment that he might haggle or cheat this man, but then he caught the mad glare in Garbutt's eyes and changed his mind. 'I know a man.'

Garbutt boarded the ship he wanted when darkness had fallen. It sailed at midnight.

24

'I like her. She's a lovely ship and the work on her has been handsomely done.' Tom Collingwood had looked over the *Dorothy Snow* privately from masthead to keel, and then in a more sedate tour of her in company with his board of directors. Now he gave his verdict: 'It will be a privilege to command her.' He smiled around at them, standing almost a head taller than any of the frock-coated and top-hatted directors. He was similarly dressed but only for this formal occasion, while this was their normal dress for the working day. He stood out like an eagle among peacocks.

The chairman patted his shoulder. 'We're glad to have got you. We'd made our decision before we heard about your remarkable salving of the *Northern Queen*. That only confirmed it. Now, let's have some champagne to celebrate.'

So they fêted him in the dining saloon with its long tables gleaming with polish, the glasses sparkling in the sunlight that streamed through the scuttles. They congratulated him and drank his health. And one asked, 'And what about this lady who was with you throughout? A hard case, eh?'

'No.' Tom set down his glass carefully. 'No, she isn't. She is a lady in every sense of the word. Brave, competent, loyal. I will not hear a word said against her.' He turned away. 'Now, gentlemen, if you will excuse me, I have some urgent private business to attend to.' And he left them. He told himself that it was not good policy to walk out on one's employers, but nor was it likely to cement the relationship if he dumped one of them over the side into the Thames.

The ship from Rotterdam berthed in the Wear that afternoon. Her boat took Garbutt and a half-dozen sailors ashore that evening and he made his way to Packer's office. He entered by the back door as before, but this time carrying a cheap, cardboard suitcase. The cadaverous solicitor started up from his chair and demanded, 'Who the hell are you? What d'you mean by sneaking in here—' but he stopped then. For a moment he had not recognised Garbutt, who had grown his moustache again and also a beard. But now he whispered, 'Good God! What are you doing here? The police are still looking for you on a murder charge!'

'Get rid of that slut outside,' Garbutt told him. He saw a tray on a side table holding a decanter of whisky and glasses, and helped himself.

Packer snapped, fear lending him courage, 'She went long ago. I'm working late; it's nearly seven.' He again upbraided Garbutt: 'That disguise might work on people who have nothing but a police sketch to go on, but it won't fool anyone who knows you – like that Miller woman, for instance. Have you gone mad?'

But then Garbutt turned on him and he fell silent before his glare. Garbutt said, 'That's why I'm here. I'm going to settle with her and the Langleys, once and for all. I want you to put me up for a day or two. And I need somebody to keep me informed of that woman's doings, someone boarding in that house.'

Packer did not want to put Garbutt up, wanted no more to do with him, but was afraid to refuse. He agreed, reluctantly. 'Just once more. I'll take you there tonight, in a cab.'

Garbutt had noted his reluctance. He said, 'Never mind. I'll find some lodgings.' Then he pressed, 'And the man? Who did you have following her?'

Packer shook his head. 'He was just a clerk. No, if you want somebody in the house then the best man will be Barty Kavanagh. I've had him do odd jobs for me where I needed some chap that would keep his mouth shut. He's a sailor sometimes, and the rest of the time looks for easy money. You'll find him in the Fleece or the Shipwright's Arms. He's a big feller, tattooed, red-faced, always smiling. He looks like your honest Jack Tar but he isn't.'

Garbutt asked, 'Where are these places?'

Packer started, 'Down by the river—'

But Garbutt cut in, 'Forget about that. Show me.'

'Isn't that taking a risk?' Packer asked worriedly.

Garbutt said, 'It will be dark soon and I'm not likely to meet the Miller woman there.' Packer nodded nervously; that was true.

'We'll go out the back way.' Garbutt pointed at his suitcase. 'And I'll leave that here for the time being.'

Packer led the way down to the river. He pointed out the two pubs and, standing in the darkness outside the Fleece, he said, 'That's Kavanagh, at the end of the bar.'

Garbutt nodded. There was no mistaking who Packer meant – a grinning, open-faced, burly man of thirty or so. Garbutt looked around him now, remembering this place from his youth. He had first learned to steal and worse, much worse, around here. He said, 'I think I know where I can find some lodgings. Come along here.' He headed along a deserted quay, the river flowing black and oily on the left, warehouses towering on the right, casting black shadows that swallowed the two men.

Barty Kavanagh lowered his pint glass and licked his lips, then found a bearded stranger at his side. Barty smiled at him and said jovially, 'Aye, aye, man!'

The stranger said, 'Do you want to make some money?'

'Why – aye,' replied Barty. 'What's the job?'

'Come over here.' Garbutt led the way to a quiet corner. When they were seated on the wooden bench he said, 'Do you know the Langley house?'

'Aye, on the other side of the river. There's fellers boards there, sailors like me, atween ships.'

'The woman who runs it, Mrs Miller. I want to know where she goes and when every day. And I want to know what's going on in the house, the comings and goings. Can you do it?'

Barty asked suspiciously, 'What's your game?'

'I'm working for a solicitor. He's acting for Mr Miller who wants a watch kept on his wife. She claims she's a widow but she isn't.' Garbutt spoke the truth when he thought he was lying to suit his tale.

'Ah! Well, then—' Now Barty was satisfied. 'How much?'

'A pound a day and every day when you report to me.'

'I'm your man.' Barty did not need to think about it. There were plenty of men bringing up families on a pound a week or less. 'Now, let's see—' He thought for a minute and Garbutt waited. Then Barty said, 'It'll be best if I board there. So I'll go over there in the morning and see if I can get in.' He glanced sidewise at Garbutt. 'Mind, that'll cost me money.'

Garbutt slid a hand into an inside pocket and brought out a sovereign, surreptitiously in a closed fist. He transferred it into Barty's eager palm and dug his hand into his jacket again. He said, 'Be here tomorrow night at this time.' He rose, then turned and bent over Barty, his back to the room, so hiding his next move. Garbutt said, 'Don't cheat me.' Barty stared at the knife only inches from his throat. Its blade was long, wickedly sharp and pointed. Then it had disappeared inside Garbutt's jacket and he was shouldering his way out of the bar. Barty let out a shuddering breath. He had thought that he was going to make some easy money but he would have to be careful, very careful.

Garbutt returned to Packer's office and entered, as before, by the back yard. He drank some of the whisky as he searched the office, but took care to leave everything tidy; he did not want to arouse the suspicions of Packer's secretary. He found nothing relating to him, but some cash in a locked box in a drawer. He forced the lock with ease and pocketed the money. The only other thing he took, and that with just a vague idea that it might be useful, was a length of thin chain and a padlock, such as might be used to chain a briefcase to a man's wrist.

He left with his suitcase, crossed the river by the ferry to Monkwearmouth and found lodgings in Dock Street, only minutes from the Langley house. He ate the supper of bread and cheese that his landlady set out for him then went to bed and slept peacefully.

Packer's body, his pockets weighted with stones, lay under a jetty, unlikely to be found for weeks or months.

Kitty had said that morning, 'A party? What does he want a party for?'

'To celebrate the opening of the yard,' answered Josie.

'Well, I'm not stopping out till all hours.'

'You'll have to stay there for a reasonable time as representing the owners of the ship they'll be building,' Josie pointed out. 'It would be a discourtesy if you left too soon.'

They were working in the kitchen of the Langley house with Annie, already baking for the party. Now Kitty cackled, and admitted, 'There was a time I'd ha' stayed all night. I must be getting old.'

'Never,' chorused Josie and Annie, and they all laughed. Then the front doorbell rang.

'I'll go.' Josie wiped her hands, took off her apron and hurried along the passage, wondering who it might be. As she opened the door she realised there was a cab outside. Then she recognised the man on the steps, in frock-coat and with top hat in hand, as the manager of the bank with whom she and Tom had been dealing these past weeks. He looked surprised to see her, and Josie realised he had been expecting a maid to open the door.

But he recovered and smiled. 'Ah, Mrs Miller. I came to see a member of the Langley Shipping Company. I have an invitation for all of you, to dine at my house this Thursday. It's to celebrate the reopening of the Langley yard and also for you to meet some people who are eager to meet you – businessmen hoping to do business with you. Can we look forward to seeing you?'

Celebrate. There was that word again. Josie replied, 'Captain Collingwood is away at present but I think I can answer for him, and, of course, I will be delighted. I'll consult Mrs Duggan and let you know her decision as soon as I can.'

'Excellent! Until Thursday, then.' He smiled, put on his top hat and the cab took him away around the square.

Josie closed the door slowly. This was Tuesday. That left plenty of time to prepare for the dinner. She had to go, of course, told herself she could not let Tom go alone as the sole representative of the Langley Shipping Company.

She returned to the kitchen and told Kitty, 'We've been invited to dinner with the bank manager on Thursday – you, Captain Collingwood and myself.'

'Not me,' Kitty replied flatly. 'I never was one for them fancy dinners and nowadays I don't eat much anyway.'

'Then I'll write and tell him that you're otherwise engaged.'

'Ha!' Kitty snorted.

Annie giggled. 'With a bottle o' stout.' Because that was the extent of Kitty's drinking now, a glass of stout sipped before the fire in the evening.

'That's more like it,' agreed Kitty.

The mention of stout reminded Josie of something else she had to do. She opened the door to the cellar and lit the oil lamp on the shelf just inside the door with the box of matches that lay there. She descended the steps, with a slight shiver at the dank chillness, and stood the lamp on the shelf at the bottom in its usual place. Its light left shadows in the corner of the empty, stone-floored cellar.

The six-inch-thick timber support standing in the middle of the floor cast another black bar of shadow, but shadows and cellar did not frighten Josie – with Annie and Kitty chattering just above her head. She found a bottle of beer for Tom's dinner that evening, dusted it off and retraced her steps.

Later, in the office, Josie wrote the note confirming Tom's and her acceptance of the dinner invitation, and made Kitty's excuses. Then she sat on at the desk, nibbling at the pen, in frowning thought. What should she wear? She had two frocks that might serve as evening wear. And she did not want to dress up too much to go out with Tom, did not want to invite more trouble. The dark grey would have to do. But she hoped he would like her in it, just the same.

Tom Collingwood returned that evening in time to drink the beer poured for him and to eat dinner with Josie. It was then that he broke the news: 'We're sailing on Friday night.'

Josie's appetite left her. 'So soon?'

'I'm afraid so.'

Josie smiled brightly. 'Well, we must make sure all your kit is ready in time.' Then: 'This means you'll miss the party at the yard on Saturday – and it was your idea.'

Tom pulled a face. 'I'm sorry. I would have liked to have been there.'

They were silent for a moment while Josie took in the news and its implications, pushed the food about her plate. Then Tom said softly, 'You've been a great help here, Mrs Miller. I will miss you while I'm away.'

'Thank you.' And Josie escaped from the room as soon as the meal was finished, to take refuge in the kitchen. Then, when her heart had stopped thumping, she decided that the grey dress would no longer do. No.

The next day Josie left Charlotte in the care of Annie and Kitty and took a tram across the bridge into the town. First she called in at the bank and drew all the money from an account she had opened when she first came to Sunderland. The savings from her small wage had been considerably augmented by her share of the profits from the boarding house and the Langley Shipping Company. Then she made for the shops with her full purse. She spent recklessly, dressed herself from the skin out. A hansom cab was needed because of the number of her packages. She was proud to be going out to dinner with Tom Collingwood and wanted him to remember her with pride.

Josie took care to return to the Langley house in the late afternoon, when she knew Tom would be down at the yard, checking on progress. She left her packages in her room and went to the kitchen. Taking off her hat and unbuttoning her coat, she asked, 'Is everything all right?'

'No bother,' Kitty assured her. 'But there's a feller come looking for lodgings, a sailorman called Barty Kavanagh, and he's waiting for a ship. He's in next door. I said he'd have to wait till you came back but he looks a decent enough lad to me.'

Josie found him in the boarders' common room and immediately agreed with Kitty's evaluation of this cheerful, patently honest sailor. She smiled. 'I hear you want to board with us. Did Kitty tell you the terms and the rules?' And she reeled them off, finishing: '— no drinking in here and you don't come home drunk. Can you keep to them?'

'Oh, aye, ma'am.'

'Then I hope you'll be comfortable here.'

'Thank you, ma'am.'

Satisfied, Josie went on her way. She spent a happy hour laying out her purchases on her bed, determinedly not looking too far ahead, pleased and excited. She would make the most of this.

That Wednesday evening she spent a long time in her room, writing a short letter. Then on Thursday morning she handed it to Dougie Bickerstaffe as he ate breakfast. He was to take a train to London that morning to join the *Dorothy Snow* with the rest of her crew. Only Tom Collingwood, her captain, would join on the Friday. Josie said, 'Will you give this to him on Saturday? And keep this a secret between us? Please.'

'Aye, Mrs Miller. Don't you worry.'

Now she was ready.

'My dear! You look charming!' The banker's wife was at once admiring, startled and envious, emotions shared by the other women at her dinner party. They were well aware that the men were staring at this Mrs Miller. Granted, she was a partner in the Langley Shipping Company, but only weeks ago she had been no more than a nurse and governess.

'Thank you.' Josie was well aware of how they were scrutinising her evening gown of sky-blue silk, simple and sheer, which was cut very low over her breasts and moulded itself to her body. 'You're very kind.'

Tom stood by her side, tall and handsome in his dinner jacket, face dark above the starched white shirt. He smiled but was wryly bemused. He had always believed there were hidden depths to this girl and now he was seeing another side to her. But he was proud.

They talked, laughed, ate, drank and were toasted: 'Ladies and gentlemen, I give you the health of Mrs Miller and Captain Thomas Collingwood of the Langley Shipping Company and the Langley Shipbuilding Company. Long life and success to them.' And a cab took them home at midnight.

When it set off they were laughing, happy and relaxed, but as the horse trotted on they fell silent and an electricity crackled between them. They got down from the cab outside the house and Josie drew her stole about her and shivered, tried to joke: 'Someone walking over my grave.' And knew she had failed. The narrow windows by the front door threw out long fingers of light. Annie and Kitty, long abed, had left the gaslights on in the hall. Tom's suitcases were there, his kit ready for his departure the next day.

He said, his voice a low rumble, 'I don't want this evening to end so soon.'

Josie knew he was tempted, as she was, but also believed she had gone too far already, in an *affaire* that should never have started, was doomed from the outset. And it was all her own fault. Now she lied again. 'I'm sorry. I'm tired.'

And she was close to him and he didn't care that she was his servant living in his house or what anyone thought. He reached up to turn out the gaslight in the hall and they climbed the stairs. At the door to her room she turned to him. 'Goodnight, Captain Collingwood.'

He stretched an arm over her to set it against the wall. He leaned over her and said deeply, 'Tom.'

'Goodnight, Tom.' She breathed it, lips parted and eyes bright as he loomed above her. Then he bent his head to kiss her gently, but she held him off, her hands against his chest, fighting her instinct again. 'No! Please!' Because she would not seduce this man. He was to be married; another letter from Felicity had arrived only that morning. If Josie took him to her bed now it would be little short of adultery. She would not spoil what they had.

'Goodnight.' And she closed the door on him.

Tom turned away. He thought he knew why she had resisted: because he was not a free man. But the waiting was becoming intolerable.

Josie heard his firm tread recede along the passage. She stood in the darkness of her room, her back against the door and tears on her face. She whispered, 'Goodbye, my love.'

25

Josie slept little and heard Tom go down in the early morning. He was leaving her.

In the kitchen Tom whistled softly as he made a pot of coffee and drank two cups of it. He breakfasted on cold meat and bread, sitting at the scrubbed table. When he walked through to the hall he found the post lying on the mat by the front door. He picked it up and dropped it on the small table, but then saw the letter from France. He took it into his office, frowning, and ripped it open.

Felicity's scrawl was jagged with rage and hate. She had read the report in *The Times* of the salving of the *Northern Queen*. 'Now I know why you sailed on that dirty little ship! Because of *Mrs Miller!*' This was heavily underlined. 'The harlot you called a cook. That is what you were up to behind my back when you were engaged to *me*! Everyone will be sniggering at me! But I won't set you free. I'll take you through the courts for breach of promise! I'll ruin you and that trollop!'

Tom read it with rapidly mounting anger. Then he became aware of the horse standing outside the window, the cab waiting at the door. He thrust the letter into a drawer of the desk and hurried out. He told himself he must try to put this poison out of his mind. What needed to be done had to be done coolly. But it would be hard to keep his temper now.

In the house behind him, Josie wiped her eyes. She heard movement again, this time on the far side of the door to the nursery, and knew that Charlotte would be calling her soon. Josie slid out of the bed, bathed and dressed listlessly. She had to put on a show again but it would be for just this one more day.

'Mrs Miller!' Charlotte called.

'Coming!' Josie replied, and went to her.

Charlotte greeted her excitedly, jumping up and down on her bed

– she had been promoted out of her cot some months ago. 'This is the day of the party!'

Josie smiled. 'No, it isn't. That's tomorrow.' Charlotte pouted in disappointment but giggled when Josie tickled her.

In the kitchen they talked of the party and planned for it as they cooked breakfast for the seamen boarders. Kitty said, 'I'll be coming home at ten o'clock. I'll be ready for me bed by then.'

Josie warned, 'I don't think you should leave before because Captain Collingwood won't be there and I must bring Charlotte home at eight – or soon after.'

Charlotte, sharp of hearing, demanded, 'Is that early?'

'No, it's late,' Josie assured her, straight-faced, as Annie grinned.

Kitty told Annie, 'I'll bring your little 'un home, if you like. That'll give you and Dan a chance to enjoy yourselves.'

'That's good of you, Kitty,' said Annie. 'Thank you.'

Josie chanced to look around and found one of the seamen boarders standing at the door from the hall. He held his empty mug in his hand and grinned at her. 'Any chance of a drop more tea, ma'am?'

'Why, yes.' Josie remembered his name now: Barty Kavanagh. 'Let me have your mug.' She gave him his tea and he went away.

Dan rose from his seat at the table, his breakfast finished. 'I'm looking forward to this do. It's a long time since I did any dancing.' He planted a kiss on Annie's cheek and she squeaked and blushed. Then Dan looked at Josie and asked, 'Is it all right if I wash down the yard now? Then I'll get along to the chandler's.'

'Yes, fine,' replied Josie.

Dan got out the long hosepipe, connected one end to the tap over the kitchen sink and ran the other end out to the back yard. Soon the splash of water from the hose, and the scrubbing of the bass broom in Dan's hands, made a rhythmic background to the chatter in the kitchen.

In the evening, Josie went into the office to make up her books as she did every day. She found it hard to concentrate and worked slowly, with long periods spent staring wearily ahead of her. When she found she needed more ink for her pen she searched for another bottle. In the second drawer she came on a letter written in a jagged scrawl. A name leapt out at her, heavily underlined: '*Mrs Miller!*' The letter was brief, barely a note; she took in its contents at a glance before thinking, I was not meant to read this. But she had read it, and felt sick.

Josie closed the drawer. This only confirmed her decision. She would not be the cause of Tom Collingwood being maligned in court. The crew of the *Macbeth* would testify that he and Josie had not misbehaved, but she would not be there. If she went to court her identity would be disclosed. How credible would her testimony be when she had practised a deception for almost a year? Tom, and others, would think she had posed as 'Mrs Miller' to worm her way into the house, pursuing some dark scheme of her own.

No. What she felt for Tom – and he for her? But she knew there was no question mark there – what they shared, she would not have that soiled.

Josie laid her head on her hands and wept.

That evening, Barty Kavanagh met Reuben Garbutt in the little pub down by the ferry. They talked in low tones and Barty said, 'There's not much to tell you. I don't know if any o' them are going anywhere today.' Then as Garbutt glared, Barty pleaded, 'Give us a chance. I can't hang about that kitchen all day. They would wonder what I was up to.'

Garbutt growled, 'Then what do you know?'

'Just that tomorrow night, they're all going to this party – but we've known that for days, they've been talking of nowt else. The only difference now is that she's bringing the bairn home early, at eight o'clock, and the old woman is coming back a coupla hours after. She's bringing the babby o' that Annie so the lass can stop on till the finish, like all the rest.'

'What do you mean, "all the rest"? Everyone in the house, boarders as well?' Garbutt's glare was fixed now.

'Aye,' Barty answered. 'Everybody has been invited and not just them in the house. All them living in the square are going. Well, what d'ye expect? Free grub and beer, a band and dancing, o' course they'll be there. I will.'

Garbutt was silent. He had hoped at best to be able to catch Mrs Miller walking alone one night, but this! He smiled and Barty did not like it, remembered the knife and said uneasily, 'Look, I told you, I can't hang about—'

'Never mind.' Garbutt cut him off and passed him a sovereign. 'You've done your best. Meet me here tomorrow, same time.' He left the pub and Barty tucked the sovereign away, but wondered if he should return the next day. The money was good but this bearded stranger was scaring him.

Garbutt did not intend to return. He expected to finish his business the following night.

When Tom boarded the *Dorothy Snow* where she lay in the Pool of London, he found the ship's agent waiting for him, and apologetic: 'I'm afraid a large item of your cargo has been delayed; it won't be ready for another two days. I've notified the passengers due to board this evening, by telegram, that they will be boarding two days hence.'

'Very good.' Tom nodded and told his steward, 'See my kit gets stowed in my cabin. I'm going ashore for an hour or so. I have some business to attend to.' He strode off, grim-faced.

The steward, who knew him, muttered, 'I wouldn't like to be the business he's going to deal with!'

Tom took a cab to the Blakemore town house in Mayfair. A butler answered the door and informed him, 'The family do not return until late this evening, sir. Might I suggest you call again tomorrow?' Then he flinched under Tom's glower.

'I see.' Tom wanted this settled but now his ship was not sailing for another two days. He conceded grudgingly, 'Very well. Please tell Mr Blakemore, *and* Miss Felicity, that I will call on them at ten tomorrow morning.'

The butler was quick to agree. 'Certainly, Captain Collingwood.'

So Tom returned to the ship and unpacked his kit. He had a sleeping cabin with bathroom and a separate day cabin. The latter was spacious, designed so that he could entertain a few chosen passengers in there. It held a large desk gleaming with polish and several comfortable leather armchairs. The desk was empty save for a blotter. Tom took from his case the framed photograph of Josie and Charlotte and stood it on the desk. He had obtained this privily from the photographer the day after Josie had shown him the original. Then he sat down in the swivel chair behind the desk and looked at the photograph until his steward called that his dinner was served.

He returned to the Blakemore house at five minutes to ten the next morning. He wore his best uniform, brushed and pressed by his steward, the buttons and gold braid gleaming. He had come to tell Felicity that he would not marry her and she could sue and be damned. He had made his decision – or had it thrust upon him –

when he and Josie had steered the *Northern Queen* into the River Wear and the port of Sunderland.

The butler took his cap as he entered. 'I'm sorry, sir, but Miss Felicity is not here. However, Mr Blakemore is waiting to see you in the drawing room.' Tom thought, She's keeping out of my way. But he followed the butler.

The drawing room was over-furnished with small tables and ornaments, as if the room and its contents were there to display Mr Blakemore's wealth. He stood at the window, a florid, portly man in checked tweeds with a thick gold watch chain looped across his paunch. 'Ah! Captain Collingwood. Be seated, please.' His tone was hushed, his manner mournful, yet Tom felt the man was acting.

But no matter. This business could wait no longer and Tom would start now. 'I've come to—'

'To see Felicity, of course.' Blakemore coughed, embarrassed. 'She told me about the letter she had written, but only after she had posted it. I can assure you, sir, I would have stopped it if I could.' Tom believed him. Blakemore would not want the family name blazoned in the newspapers. Now Blakemore went on, 'And I'm afraid my daughter isn't here. I must tell you – it has come as a terrible shock – that Felicity has run off with Major St Clair. We were staying at his place in Biarritz but we – Mrs Blakemore and I – we suspected nothing. Nothing! Then yesterday we woke to find them gone and just a note saying they were to be married in Paris. My wife is prostrate, of course. She was making plans for the wedding in October.'

Tom stared at him, incredulous, for a moment, then he asked drily, 'Has he money?'

Blakemore shrugged as if that did not matter, but admitted: 'He's very wealthy as it happens. His uncle, the Vicomte, died barely a month ago and left him a fortune. And the title, of course.' He could not keep the satisfaction out of his voice as he said this last.

Tom grinned to himself, but said thoughtfully, 'I still don't see why she eloped. Why not come back to London for a spring wedding?' Because that was much more Felicity's style. Blakemore shook his head and Tom thought again that the man was acting – and uneasy.

The butler handed Tom his cap and let him out. As he strode away he almost collided with a girl who stepped out of an alley leading to the rear of the house. 'I beg your pardon.' Tom put one hand to his cap in salute and steadied the girl with the other as she staggered.

''S all right.' She smiled at Tom. 'I was watching for you. Ventris – that's the butler – he said you were calling this morning and I saw you come in. Captain Collingwood, isn't it?' And when he nodded, she went on, 'I saw you up in Sunderland a few times. I'm Susie Evans. I was on the quay when you brought that ship in what was sinking. I was Miss Felicity's maid.' Tom remembered her, and the last time he had seen her, with the Blakemore car while the chauffeur was delivering Felicity's note. But Susie was going on, with a jerk of her head towards the house, 'Did they tell you about her running off?'

Tom nodded. 'Yes.' He now realised the girl had been drinking. Some of her words were slurred and there had been that initial unsteadiness.

She said solemnly, 'I'm sorry for you, sir.'

Tom grinned at her. 'I'm not.'

'Oh?' Susie brightened. 'That's good. 'Cause I came to give you a tip, see.'

Tom recalled something said earlier. 'You say you "were" her maid?'

Susie pulled a face. 'She sacked me a week back. Just happened to catch me wearing one of her outfits. Wouldn't care, but the bloody dress won't fit her in a month or two, anyway. I came back yesterday with old Blakemore and his missus.' Now she giggled. 'They were putting it on that they were all upset over her running off with that Major St Clair as he called himself. But what I wanted to tell you, because I like that Josie Miller and you, was why she run off with him. You're well off out o' that. I could tell you some tales.' She winked at Tom. 'Anyway, I heard the three o' them talking, Blakemore and his missus and Miss Felicity—'

Susie stopped then, to peer about, making sure she was not overheard. But there was only a scissor grinder with his wheel some ten yards away, sparks flying as he sharpened a knife. Reassured, Susie lowered her voice and said, 'This was a month back. Her ma was saying she had to get rid of it and Felicity was bawling her eyes out wi' fright. That's why she eloped. She's expecting and she can't wait till next October to be married, never mind next spring. But the major was courting her heavy so – I reckon – she told him old Blakemore wouldn't have him for a son-in-law but she would run off with him. An' they did.'

Tom took a breath, then said, 'Well, it seems Felicity has fallen on her feet.' He could be magnanimous now. 'But what about you?'

'Oh, I can get another job easy.' Susie flapped a hand impatiently, then used it to grab Tom as she staggered again, off balance. 'Whoops! I had a drop of old Blakemore's sherry this morning, just to wish them all luck. Fallen on her feet? More like on her arse.' Susie laughed outright this time, then, shaking Tom's arm, she told him, 'Afore I got this "place" I worked for an old girl called Smurthwaite. Only stopped there a week 'cause I heard her son was coming home and the girls there told me how he mauled 'em. But I saw Hubert afore I left and that's him: Major St Clair as he calls himself now. I would ha' told them if they'd treated me proper, but they didn't.'

Tom blinked at her, taking this in. Susie sniffed. 'Serves 'em right, I say. And that Hubert, I'll lay he thinks Blakemore will buy him off, but he's got another think coming. The old feller loves his money and he won't part with it. Hubert will finish up in a jail in France or Italy.'

Susie would be proved right. Major St Clair had only leased the villa in Biarritz with its staff for the summer and the owner's agents were seeking him for the unpaid rent. Inside a month he would be torn from the arms of his wailing young bride. Before the year was out Major St Clair, alias Commander Sackville RN, who had defrauded a Frenchwoman, alias Hubert Smurthwaite, would hear the cell door of a French prison slam behind him.

Tom had never heard of Hubert Smurthwaite. He disengaged his arm from Susie's grip and pressed a sovereign into her hand. 'That will help tide you over.'

Susie called after him, 'Gawd bless you, Captain, you and that Josie!'

'Thank you!' Tom returned to his ship, whistling happily, and sat down at his desk to smile at the photograph of Josie. Then he started to write to her.

At noon, the steward tapped at the door of Tom's cabin and entered to announce, 'A gentleman has just come aboard, sir, a Mr Albert Harvey.' He laid Harvey's card on the desk and added hastily, 'He's not boarding until tomorrow, but as he was close by he thought he would like to renew your acquaintance, sir.'

'I remember Mr Harvey.' Tom nodded. 'Show him in and bring us some sherry, please. He can have lunch with me.'

'Captain Collingwood!' Harvey greeted him warmly, hand outstretched. And as Tom shook it: 'Delighted you have been appointed to command her. I'm proud to say that I wrote to the directors months ago, after I came over with you the last time, saying how much you had impressed me. A lot of the other chaps who make regular crossings did the same.'

Tom grinned. 'Thank you. I'm grateful.'

They chatted as they sipped the sherries poured by the steward, and afterwards as they ate lunch in the saloon. They returned to Tom's day cabin for coffee and Harvey glanced around, taking in the space and comfort. Then he leaned forward to look more closely at the photograph on Tom's desk. 'You know Josie?' he asked, mildly surprised.

Tom said, 'Mrs Miller?'

Harvey blinked. 'I didn't know she was married.'

'Widowed,' Tom explained.

'Oh dear,' and Harvey shook his head sadly. 'I haven't seen her for six or seven years. That was when I went to her mother's funeral. She was Josie Langley then.'

Tom stared disbelievingly, then said, 'The child in the photograph is my ward, Charlotte Langley.'

Harvey asked innocently, 'Any relation?' Then added, before Tom could answer, 'I've known Josie since she was about that age.' He peered at Charlotte, then said with a bashful grin, 'I tell you, I proposed to Josie's mother but she wouldn't have me.' Then he told Tom the history of Josie Langley as told to him by her mother. How she and David Langley had meant to sail for America but had to bring the ailing Josie ashore at the last moment, then David's sudden death and her letter to old William Langley informing him of this.

Tom exclaimed, 'But he received no letter! He went to his grave believing David and his family were lost with that emigrant ship!'

'Good God!' Harvey sucked in a breath. Then he went on, telling how Josie had grown up in the Urquhart house and service. Tom listened intently, at the same time trying to sort out his jumbled thoughts.

Harvey had barely finished when Tom's steward put his head around the door to say, apologetically, 'Sorry to interrupt, sir, but Seaman Bickerstaffe would like to see you; says it's urgent.'

Tom answered absently, 'Yes, I'll see him.'

Dougie Bickerstaffe edged into the cabin cautiously, cap in hand, unused to this splendour. He laid the letter on the desk. 'Sorry, sir. Mrs Miller said I was to give this to you today but I've just remembered.'

The letter was no more than a single sheet and began simply: 'My Dear'. It went on to tell how Josie had used the name 'Mrs Miller' because of fear of her grandfather, and had stayed on to care for Charlotte. How she had put off telling the truth because she was afraid she would be thought guilty of trying to take Charlotte's inheritance. And finished, 'I can no longer maintain a pretence I should never have begun. I send you this letter because I cannot tell you the truth and face your doubt and distrust. You have all my love and I wish you well. Goodbye, Josie Langley.'

Tom looked at his watch then ran from the cabin, leaving Albert Harvey and Dougie Bickerstaffe staring.

Josie was at the party that evening from its beginning, of course. It was held in a big shed in the Langley yard, and with the other women she laid out the food she had helped prepare. She organised the children's games and later led off the dancing, to a fiddle and piano, with Dan Elkington. Kitty muttered, 'Pity that Tom Collingwood isn't here.' Josie managed to smile. Kitty was enjoying herself, and had obviously changed her mind about deserting the party early. If challenged she would doubtless claim that she had to 'show the flag' as a partner in the Langley Shipping Company, but she would stay until ten, no doubt of that. And equally she would return to the Langley house then, because she had promised Annie. She was rocking the baby's pram now.

Josie finally left at twenty minutes past eight, after a long succession of farewells that almost reduced her to tears, but she had to put a brave face on it and held them back. She walked back to the Langley house, leading a reluctant but yawning Charlotte by the hand. The last hours of forced gaiety had exhausted Josie, but she still had to chatter brightly to jolly the child along. She told herself she had done some good with Charlotte. When Josie had first met her she had been grief-racked and insecure after losing her parents, her grandfather, even Rhoda, who had been a substitute for them, albeit a poor one. Now she was happy and confident after a year of loving. Josie would miss Charlotte and the child would miss her, but Charlotte was fond of Annie, Kitty and Tom. In time she would get over Josie's leaving. But Josie?

Darkness had swept in from the sea and when they entered the square it was deserted under the few gaslights, one set at each corner. It was quiet, the riveting hammers in the shipyards stilled. The tall cranes loomed unmoving, cut in black silhouette like gallows in the night. The house stretched across the back of the square, dark and silent. As she led the sleepy Charlotte around the square there was not a soul to be seen, not a sound from any of the houses; everyone had gone to the party.

Josie had no need to plan any longer because it was all done. Her suitcase was packed and waiting in the hall. She had been the last to leave the house to go to the party and had brought the case down then. She had ordered a cab for ten o'clock. When Kitty returned Charlotte would be asleep and Josie would leave her in the old woman's care. She would tell Kitty that she had to go away on family business. It was the excuse she had used before, but it would have to do. She was too tired to invent another. Kitty would suspect it was only an excuse but that didn't matter because Josie would be gone. She had posed as Mrs Miller, acting out a lie, day in and day out, for almost a year now. She could go on no longer. And she had come here and found the man she loved, but too late.

There was a train leaving Monkwearmouth at 10.38 p.m. and Josie would be on it. She could afford an emigrant's passage to America and would try to make a fresh start there. Tom Collingwood would be at sea by now and would have read her letter. He would know that she had deceived him from the beginning. Probably he would tear up the letter and forget Mrs Miller.

She used her key to open the front door and passed through with Charlotte clinging to her hand in the darkness. As Josie groped for the matches on the side table she thought that the darkness was somehow not total, that there might be some light from the square outside filtering in through the front door which still stood ajar. She scraped the match and held its flame to the gas mantle above her and in that instant realised that a faint radiance came from the direction of the kitchen. Then the gas lit with a soft *plop!* The front door slammed shut behind her, a hand clamped over her mouth and a knife was laid across her throat.

'Keep still and keep quiet!' The voice came in her ear, his breath stirring the soft auburn hair on her neck. Josie could not keep still, her body shuddering from his touch and that of the knife. Out of the corner of her eye, looking down, she could see Charlotte, frightened and beginning to cry, her hand still gripped by Josie. Then the knife was whipped from her throat and laid against Charlotte's back. The voice said, 'Hold on to her and do as I say, for her sake.'

Josie knew it was not just a voice, knew who it was, who it had to be: Reuben Garbutt, who had tried to murder her before. But he was supposed to be in hiding on the Continent, not in this country, this house, with his hands on her body. She quailed and then Garbutt said, 'In the kitchen.' He urged her forward and she obeyed on shaking legs, leading Charlotte along by the hand. The child did not attempt to run, only clung more fiercely to Josie's hand in her terror.

Josie pushed open the kitchen door with her free hand and the faint radiance she had seen was explained: the door to the cellar was open and a weak light came from down there. It had shown as no more than a slit under the closed kitchen door. Something else was also explained: a pane of one of the sash windows was broken, the window unclipped and shoved open. That was how Garbutt had got in. And in the light from the cellar she could see that the hose Dan Elkington used to wash down the back yard was fitted to the tap on the kitchen sink. It led across the floor and disappeared down the cellar steps.

Now Garbutt turned her towards the cellar. 'Down there.' Josie instinctively revolted for a moment, tried to halt, but then she saw a twitch of the knife set the blade to winking in the light from the cellar. Garbutt had said, 'Do as I say, for her sake.' Josie gave in, passed through the door and started down the steps to the cellar. As she went she found the hose lying beside her faltering feet, and sometimes it slid dank and cold against her ankle like a snake. She heard Garbutt close the door behind them.

Before she reached the foot of the stairs she found the water. The light came from the oil lamp that had been brought down from the top of the stairs and stood on a shelf at eye level. It reflected from the water that lay across the floor of the cellar. There was no sound of it running because the end of the hose lay below its surface. Josie stepped down into it, her skirts lifting as it rose above her knees. Charlotte whimpered and Garbutt hesitated, for a moment uncertain what to do about her. Then he said, 'Let go of her. Tell her to sit down here. Don't bother shouting because nobody will hear you down here.' He switched the knife to Josie's throat and took his hand from her mouth.

Tongue thick in her mouth, she said, 'Sit there, Charlotte, please, there's a good girl.' Charlotte obeyed, unhappily, and sat on the steps above the water with tears in her eyes.

Now Garbutt thrust Josie into the middle of the cellar, both of them wading, until they stood by the central timber pillar. He said, 'Put your arms round it.' Josie, under the threat of the blade that pricked her flesh, had to do as he said and stood with her face to the pillar, arms outstretched before her on either side of it. Garbutt fumbled in his pocket with his free hand.

Josie whispered, 'Please, why are you doing this? I've done nothing to harm you.'

'The Langleys have and you've taken their side, tried to help them up when I'd put them down.' Garbutt yanked a length of thin chain from his pocket and began to knot it around Josie's wrists. 'The Langleys murdered my father or as good as, when old Billy Langley sacked him and he had to leave this town. That's what killed him. So I swore they'd pay for it. I ran down James.' He heard Josie's gasp of horror and laughed madly. 'Aye! And his wife – I caught them together. Then I bankrupted the firm and that finished the old man.' He yanked on the chain, ensuring it was tight. It bit into Josie's flesh and she cried out. Now her wrists were lashed together and he pulled a padlock from his pocket.

Josie pleaded, 'But I didn't know anything of this – how your father died – I had nothing to do with it.'

'He drowned, that's what the doctor said,' Garbutt snarled, and slipped the padlock's hasp through the links of the chain. He inserted the key and turned it, retrieved it and tested what was now a rough but efficient pair of handcuffs. 'He died o' pneumonia and the doctor said he drowned with the fluid on his lungs.' He released the lock and chain but leaned one hand on the baulk of timber as he shoved his face close to hers and shouted, 'And that's how you're going to go!'

Tom Collingwood caught the 2.20 p.m. train out of King's Cross – just. He ran from the ticket office as the guard's whistle shrilled and sprinted past the gaping ticket collector as the train pulled away. He stretched out one long arm to seize the handle by the guard's open door and leapt for the step. He caught it with a toe and hauled himself into the guard's van, to be told sternly, 'You ain't supposed to do that' – then, with a glance at the four gold rings on Tom's sleeve – 'Captain.'

At Newcastle, Tom changed to the local train to Sunderland. He jumped down from it before it stopped at Monkwearmouth station. He ran through to the street and stood between the massive columns at the entrance, head turning, searching, but there wasn't a cab to be seen. He had deduced that if Josie had told Dougie Bickerstaffe to give her letter to him on Saturday it was because she thought he would be at sea and unable to prevent her leaving. So she would still be in Monkwearmouth, and as she would want to leave quietly, without fuss, it would not be before the party.

He gave up the hunt for a cab and started to run across Bridge Street. It was then that he saw the cab turning out of Barclay Street to head towards the town.

He yelled, '*Cabbie!*' The driver sat up on his box with a jerk, woken from a reverie. Then he saw Tom running towards him and reined in the horse. Tom jumped in. He was certain where he would find Josie and ordered, 'Take me to Langley's yard! Quick as you can!'

Garbutt shouted, 'And that's how you're going to go!' He had released Josie's chain-bound wrists and reached forward with his left hand – the right held the knife – and locked his fingers in her hair. He dragged her closer to the timber pillar that stood between them and her head cracked against it. For a second the cellar rocked around her, then was still again. Josie could see the madness in Garbutt's eyes, only inches away. And she could see Charlotte sitting on the steps, petrified. Josie knew she had to save her. In desperation and fear she jabbed her thumbs into Garbutt's eyes.

He screamed with pain and shock, recoiled and let go of her hair to clap his hands to his eyes. Then, sobbing with pain and rage, he flailed around with his left hand until he found the pillar. With that as a guide he lashed out with the knife, underhanded at waist level. His target was Josie, drawn back to the full length of her arms on the other side of the pillar. She twisted aside, away from the thrust, but pain flickered along her side. Josie knew that, tethered as she was to the timber pillar, it could only be seconds before the knife found its mark again. And again.

Garbutt pulled back the knife and lifted both his hands to wipe at the tears of pain that ran down from his eyes. Josie, acting instinctively, used the trick Garbutt had used on her. Perhaps subconsciously trying to stun him by striking his head against the pillar, she lunged forward, grabbed his hair in her hooked fingers and threw herself backwards again. Garbutt was caught unprepared and off balance. He was yanked forward and his hands started to come down as he stumbled. The knife was between him and the pillar. As he was slammed against the pillar, the blade sank into the side of his neck.

Garbutt screamed again. The knife fell as he used both hands to tear at Josie's, prising her fingers from their grip on his hair. Now he was in agony, sobbing and wailing. Once free he stepped back and fumbled his way, nearly blind, along the wall to the steps. He climbed them on all fours, one hand groping ahead to test the way, the other on the wall at his side. He passed the shrinking Charlotte, without seeing her or caring, and at the head of the steps he stood and opened the door, then passed through and out of sight. Josie heard his boots shuffle erratically across the kitchen, along the passage and the hall, then there was silence. He had left a thick red trail on the steps.

Josie was leaning against the timber, weeping, exhausted and faint from shock. Then she slowly became aware of Charlotte again. The child still sat on the steps, crying. Josie knew she had to get her out of this. As she began trying to fight her way free from the chain that held her, she tried to steady her voice and called, 'Charlotte! Charlotte, there's a good girl. Go on out of the house and find someone, tell them I'm here.' When Charlotte did not answer Josie repeated her instruction, but still the little girl cried.

Until she lifted her head and wailed, 'I want to stay with you!'

Josie pleaded, cajoled, begged and then in desperation shouted, but this only set Charlotte to weeping more than ever. 'It's dark there and the man will get me.' She had sat, face crumpled with horror, as Garbutt had fumbled his way past her, brushing against her, leaving his red stain on her dress. And she had seen him go into the kitchen. 'I'm not going! I *can't*!'

And all the time Josie fought to break free, twisting her slender hands, trying to slip them out of the chain, but they were not slender enough.

Then the lamp flickered, and again. Josie peered at it and saw the reason. The water had risen until it lapped at the flame. She had been aware of it creeping up her body, felt its slow, chill, inexorable progress. Now it was up to her chin and she was already standing on her toes. Then the lamp flickered once more and went out. Pitch darkness descended on the cellar.

Josie tried to climb up the timber as she had once climbed trees, and the rope dangling down the side of the *Northern Queen*, but her waterlogged skirts were wrapped around her legs and foiled her attempts. There was no sound in the cellar but her own rapid, shallow breathing, soon to be cut short, and the whimpering of the frightened child on the steps.

Then Josie heard the tramp of boots returning in the passage above. Charlotte stopped whimpering and Josie could picture the child holding her breath. As was Josie. Somehow Garbutt had bound up his wound and come back to exact some final revenge for it. There was the scrape of a match in the kitchen above and light filled the rectangle of the doorway at the top of the steps. A figure appeared, towering huge and black against the light behind it, and Josie regressed twenty years. Shock, fear and nervous exhaustion took their toll. She was four years old again and there was the giant, growing, becoming more monstrous with every beat of her heart. And as her senses left her . . .

26

'*Josie!*' Tom Collingwood shouted it.

Tom. Josie silently mouthed his name.

He had been headed for the Langley yard when he realised that if Josie had left the party she might also leave the house before he got to it from the yard. He had bawled at the cabbie, 'Take me to the Langley house!'

Now he clattered down the steps but slowed as he came to the water, realising that if he jumped into it the resulting wave would wash over Josie's head. He let himself down into it and waded slowly and cautiously across to where her face was turned up, her head back, straining to keep her mouth and nose above the surface. Despite his care, water still slopped into her face, setting her coughing and gasping. Tom lifted her, vital inches that raised her mouth clear of the water. Then he seized the chain that bound her wrists but saw at once that it was not some cord that he could snap – or cut. He held Josie up with one hand and with the other reached down into the water to his pocket. He pulled out his sailor's clasp knife and opened the blade with his teeth. Then he raised it with his arm at full stretch and with an overhand blow sank it deep into the timber high above Josie's head.

'Put your hands over!' Tom ordered, and lifted Josie bodily. She obeyed, clumsily eager but her hands shaking. Tom held her with one arm around her and hooked her wrists over the knife so she hung from it by the chain. Now her head was well clear of the surface. She swung like some carcase from a hook, her face rubbing against the timber, but she could breathe and the strain was taken from her neck and her legs from standing on tiptoe.

'I'll be quick!' Tom waded away to the steps. As he climbed them he scooped up the child who sat there and carried her with him. In the kitchen he set Charlotte down in a chair, crossed to the sink in two long strides and turned off the tap. Then he went to a cupboard and raked through the miscellany of tools he knew were kept in a box there. With a hammer and chisel he plunged into the cellar again. He smashed the padlock with his second blow then dropped the hammer and chisel. When he pulled off the padlock and loosened the chain, Josie began to slide down again, but he was quick to catch her before she went under. He lifted her in his arms and carried her up the steps and out of the kitchen.

Josie clung to him and cried, 'Don't leave me!'

It was long past midnight when Josie faced Tom outside her door. She wore a dressing gown, her wet clothes discarded. She had told her story and Tom his. The others had come home and all were abed, Charlotte sleeping peacefully after drinking hot milk with a powder administered by a doctor. He had dressed the slight wound on Josie's side. It did not bother her now.

Sergeant Normanby had come and gone after reporting, 'We've found Garbutt in Church Street. I suppose he was making for the hospital in Roker Avenue, thinking they could save him. But if he'd survived he would have hung.'

The house was silent save for the slow ticking of the clock downstairs in the dark hall. There was only one gas jet hissing on the landing, leaving it a place of shadows. Tom said, 'When we brought in the *Northern Queen*, I knew then how I felt about you. But I couldn't court you when I was still engaged to Felicity.' He had told Josie of Felicity's elopement. 'And if you had been a fortune-hunter you could have claimed your inheritance at any time. And you wouldn't have run away – or tried to – as you did.'

He stood tall and broad above her, blotting out what light there was from the single jet. He reached out for her and Josie whispered again, 'Don't leave me!'

'Never!'